[illegible]

BLOOD MOON

Dreena Whiteley

ISBN: 978-1-7384286-2-5

Dedicated to my nephew Adam John Boness
22 April 1971 – 18 May 2023

1

Eamon observed Josephine from a short distance behind as they made their way off the plane, through the terminal to the arrivals hall at Miami Airport. He noticed heads turning to admire the sultry Latina whose curvy figure appeared to hold them spellbound. She donned chic sunglasses and strode with a confident air.

He had enjoyed her company throughout the long flight from Paris. He found her brutal honesty refreshing. He did not judge her, nor did he envy her single life without children or a soul mate. She had always sold herself to the highest bidder. Her lover was a married man, and a powerful one – the Miami mafia boss Don Ricardo Barossa.

Josephine had revealed to Eamon that she often travelled to 'visit' other clients. She said that Ricardo Barossa had given her free rein, stating that he had no problem with her 'seeing' other men. His only stipulation was that it not be on his doorstep. Josephine had also disclosed to Eamon on the long flight that she knew that Ricardo Barossa did not love her but only thought of her as a mere possession – something else that he owned. She went on to say there was no jealousy on his part, however, he always wanted to know the intimate details of what she did when she was not with him.

Eamon had only given Josephine snippets about his life with Marcia and their four children, and the club that they owned. They had said their goodbyes as the flight landed. Josephine had pressed Eamon to keep in touch, giving him her card and instructing him not to be a stranger. He had no intention of keeping in touch, but, out of politeness, he took her card, intending to dispose of it later on. Although he could not deny that he found Josephine very attractive, his desire was only for the one woman who held his heart, Marcia.

Walking not far behind Josephine was the man Eamon had taken note of earlier before the plane had begun its descent. He had got up from his seat to use the toilet when he made eye contact with a man in an aisle seat two rows behind, whose steel-grey eyes were trained on Eamon. From that fleeting connection, Eamon's senses went on high alert, triggering alarm bells. The nerve endings in his solar plexus jumped with warnings of danger. He was not usually paranoid, but his finely attuned antennae were what kept him outside of the prison bars and not behind them.

Eamon observed the man, slowing his pace to ensure he stayed behind him. When the man stopped to answer a call, Eamon, without hesitation moved forward alongside him. Pretending to be speaking to someone on his phone, Eamon discreetly snapped a picture of the man's profile.

Eamon exited the terminal to a cacophony of noise from the various modes of transport. He couldn't live with that kind of pandemonium all the time. He valued the tranquillity of his home in Altea Hills in Spain. Marcia and his children were his haven.

Suddenly, among the hustle and bustle, he spotted Joey, Alphonso's man.

Joey was standing alongside a Lincoln limousine. He raised his hand, gaining Eamon's attention. The big man stood with the passenger door open, sunglasses donned, suited and booted. *He certainly looks the part of a gangster's bodyguard*, Eamon mused, smiling warmly at the man whom he had the greatest respect for. Joey was old school and had been loyal throughout his service to the old man. Joey smiled thinly as he took Eamon's cases and put them in the boot.

"How is the old man coping since Marcella's passing?" Eamon asked, clipping the seatbelt in. "When he rang me, it sounded as if he was trying to put on a brave face. Nonetheless, Joey, his bravado does not fool me!"

Joey exhaled, shaking his head, his tone heavy with sorrow. "Alphonso is devastated! Marcella will be sorely missed. I am struggling to cope with Alphonso's pain that is etched on his face. Marcella was his rock, as most good women are to their men." The big man threw in, "She was the one that kept the family together."

Eamon nodded. Joey concentrated on his driving, expertly manoeuvring the car into the queue of rush hour traffic, edging between two vehicles. A yellow cab blasted its horn behind them. "Such angry people! No manners, shaking ya fist!" Joey spoke towards the rear-view mirror, waggling his head, raising his hand in apology at the irate driver who responded with another blast of the horn.

"Alphonso has moved into his other condo that he had purchased after Carlo was killed. Marcella could not stand seeing the constant reminder of her boy's old bedroom. Even though Carlo had lived in his condo, his former bedroom remained untouched. Alphonso had the place locked up. He has moved lock stock and barrel to the security of the island of Aqua, and the all-important waterfront views that the old man loves. It appears that the nearness of the Atlantic view brings him a kind of inner peace. Marcella loved the ocean. It was the Atlantic that brought Marcella and Alphonso's family to America from Sicily."

Eamon nodded. He knew the story that Alphonso had told him. His parents and uncles were among the 100,000 that came in on the ships from Sicily and other parts of Italy to America.

Joey continued, "Although the condo is near to where Alphonso and Marcella previously lived, Marcella seemed less despondent after they had moved. However, nothing could have prevented her death," he said sadly.

Joey changed the subject to the Midnight Club, the name that Alphonso had come up with for his watering hole in down town Miami, near to Little Havana. He spoke of how Alphonso had a few old Cuban associates who had family who owned restaurants in the area, who had invited Alphonso to dine there. Although the old man had no great desire to eat Cuban food, he knew that the camaraderie would prevent any trouble between the Italians and Cubans. Joey said how he had taken Alphonso there on a couple of occasions. Joey filled Eamon in on the renovations to the club that were near completion. He went into detail about the no-expense-spared furnishings.

The apartment above the Midnight Club, he said, was furnished to the same high standard as Alphonso's luxury home. He mentioned that Alphonso had his heart set on persuading Eamon to bring his wife and family to Dade County. Eamon was deep in thought on the 28-mile journey from Miami Airport to Dade County about how to not upset the old man. Alphonso did him a massive favour by preventing the informer from giving evidence against Franco Gennaro junior and his men. It was a weight off Eamon's shoulders. A long prison sentence had been avoided due to Alphonso's intervention. Furthermore, now that the 'canary' had been dealt with, Franco Gennaro's feathers were no longer ruffled, due to Marcia's instigation, albeit. Unwittingly. Alphonso had informed him that Marcia's name had been mentioned by the New York don. The debt of honour that Eamon owed Alphonso required repayment. He knew that he had no choice but to return the favour.

Eamon was taken aback by how much Alphonso had aged since he had last seen him. Joey had pre-warned him that Marcella's passing had taken its toll practically overnight. Both men smiled warmly in greeting as Joey held the door open for Eamon to enter the expansive lounge. Eamon strode towards the seated man, reverently kissing the back of his proffered hand. Eamon momentarily saw a flickering light, that spark, the fire behind the once powerful man's eyes that Eamon recognised from his first meeting with Alphonso.

"Take a seat son," Alphonso indicated towards the matching leather recliner opposite the one that he was lounging in. He adjusted his position as he sat facing Eamon. "How was ya flight?"

Eamon shrugged. He thought about the man who he had sensed had an interest in him as he left the plane. Then he remembered the woman who had been seated next to him on the flight. After all, she was Ricardo Barossa's mistress. Unsure how to respond at that moment, Eamon decided that he would discuss it later, at a more appropriate time with Alphonso. "So, so!" he smiled, unbuttoning his suit jacket.

The old man appraised him. "Family life certainly suits ya!" he paused for a couple of seconds. "Streamlined!" he complemented. Pursing his lips, and giving a sharp nod, he said,

"Ya weight loss has taken a few years off ya. Marcia been on to ya?" Grinning, he continued, "However, your black hair has taken a hammering, nevertheless the silver-fox look gives ya an edge. As does the chin hair," he teased, referring to Eamon's goatee. "Your woman appears to be a good influence on ya. As was my Marcella!"

Standing by the drinks cabinet, Joey interceded, "Would you like your usual, boss?"

"Yes, please, Joey. Make that two!" Alphonso stated.

Eamon stopped Joey. "Could ye make mine a mineral water and lime, if there is any?"

Joey nodded, leaving them to talk while he made the drinks.

Alphonso laughed, his mood becoming lighter. "What gives with ya? If my memory serves me right, ye could normally put a few under ya belt."

"I had my quota on the flight over," Eamon explained.

The old man nodded as they took their glasses from Joey. Eamon recognised the Baccarat Louxor crystal tumbler that Alphonso used at home along with the Eagle Rare 10-year-old bourbon whisky, that the old Italian favoured. Rolling the mouthful around his palette, Alphonso returned the chair to its reclining position. "Marcia appears to have straightened you up all the way round. Are ya content with your lot?" His hazel green eyes narrowed, demanding an honest answer.

"To be sure, Al!" Eamon smiled. "My wife is up behind me, ensuring that I do not deviate from my healthy regime. Nevertheless, I must admit that I do feel the benefit of eating healthier and drinking less. I've been swimming daily. I have a heavy schedule at home, also, to be able to keep up with a young family I need my stamina!" He exhaled and said, "There are times when my eldest boy has given me a few headaches. That can make me feel weary. 'Tis not that I cannot handle it, but I do have to keep on top of the situation wit him, It appears that the boy is jealous of his siblings. His younger brother has borne the brunt. However, that's when I stepped in!" Eamon smiled thinly.

Alphonso continued his probing. "There has been no interest outside of the marital bed?" He crooked an eyebrow. Then Alphonso confessed, "I had my share of women in my younger days. Not that I am proud of it!" Taking a small sip of the golden liquid, Alphonso waited for Eamon to answer.

Eamon did not normally speak candidly to anyone about his private life. However, he knew that Alphonso was speaking man to man, and he knew that whatever was said between them would go no further. Eamon smiled, shaking his head. "No, Al!" He paused for a few seconds. Appeasing the old boy's curiosity, he added, "Marcia ticks all of my boxes!"

Alphonso grinned widely. "Commendable! Looking back on my marriage, I did Marcella wrong," he spoke wistfully. "It is the best way to play it straight with ya woman!" he advised. Then smirking, he said, "Especially when ya woman gives ya everything ya need." His eyes twinkled. "There are not many men that are that fortunate."

Eamon nodded.

Alphonso continued. "I was in my prime when I came to power. Good looks, money, top of my game. Attracts the women to ya, like bees to honey. There was one time that I required my private doctor to treat me for a sexually transmitted disease." Alphonso disclosed. "Ya tend to forget at the time when ye stray, the downside of playing away. Ya tend to get distracted by a shapely broad who gives ya the come-on! I could not go near Marcella until I was given the all-clear!" he said. "It makes a liar out of ya! Down the line, it can bring regrets!"

Eamon's thoughts strayed to the attractive woman on the flight over who had revealed her life to him. But he had no interest in extramarital bed-hopping. Marcia was the love of his life. She had given him four children. Although three out of the four babies had come with drama – the anguish had nearly destroyed him. However, his resolve to keep Marcia by his side prevailed. Eamon considered himself a lucky man, although he realised that he could not get overly comfortable. He knew his past indiscretions could come back to haunt him at any time. There would always be the 'canary', the person who gave up his name to the Law to save themselves and shorten their long prison sentence. He sipped his lime and water, listening to the old man unburdening his sins of the past.

Alphonso brought up the subject of Marcia and Joyce Grant. Speaking candidly, he said, "Although your woman had caused ripples in New York with the Gennaro family, thankfully everything is now sorted out. But…" he spoke with warning, "one cannot get too comfortable. Believe me, son, Franco Gennaro senior has a long memory. However, from what I hear, the old man is gratified that his boy Franco and the men that were locked up with him have been released from prison." Alphonso chuckled. "With the stool pigeon out of the way, the prosecution had no witness!" He took another slow draw from his glass. "Let's hope that ya wife is more careful in the future! My Marcella and my youngest girl Chiara were believers in all that mystical stuff too. They watched these paranormal television shows all the time. It's not that I don't think there's something to it. Back in the day, I would stand my ground and do battle with anyone," he stated. "The living don't frighten me as much as the dead!" he said, giving a soft laugh. "All that spooky stuff unnerves me!"

Eamon nodded. " 'Tis my viewpoint too, Al!" he declared.

"Nevertheless, I take my hat off to ya wife. By the sound of things, Marcia has a gift. What with delving into all this..." Alphonso momentarily struggled for the right words. "...voodoo and the likes."

Eamon chuckled.

"Got to hand it to her, the gal has transformed ya for the better!" Alphonso appraised. Joey appeared on cue to refill Alphonso's glass as he drained it.

"How are ya baby girls?" Alphonso asked, smiling fondly. "Marcella would have liked to have seen your children. We would have had a houseful if she had not eventually had Carlo. He came after the three girls."

Eamon smiled and said, "The twin girls are grand! Growing up into wee women. Although they are just toddlers, they have already sussed out how to play me wit their tears, to get what they want. They are so very different in ways and looks to my boys, who are dark-haired wit olive skin, whereby Aine and Aisling are red-heads, wit pale skin. Two green-eyed beauties!" He threw in. "The girls have inherited my granny's genes copper hair and emerald-green eyes. Even though they are young, ye can see their strong characters forming. More so, wit Aisling." Eamon laughed, recalling his grandmother. "My granny used te scare my brother and me witless when we were boys, with tales of witches and banshees. She always warned us to be wary of beautiful women who would lure us into their web of destruction!"

Both men laughed.

"My three gals were the same with me. Twisted me around their fingers as youngsters. The three became a little wayward in their late teens. What with night clubbing, boys etc. Although I had rules they were always trying to cross the line. But I could never come down as hard on them as I did with Carlo. Not that it did much good, with the way he turned out. His mother had his back, though!" He threw in. "That's the way it is with mothers and their sons." Alphonso paused a moment, then continued speaking, "I appreciate ya coming all this way, son!" He smiled warmly at Eamon.

"My pleasure, Al." Eamon returned his smile, meaning every word. "Marcella was dear to me. I am in debt to ye for stepping in and dealing wit what could have been a difficult situation that I was facing!"

Alphonso waved Eamon's statement away. "Once the funeral is out of the way, there's something I want to show ya. There's a building I have purchased in downtown Miami within a stone's throw from Little Havana. However, I have spoken to an old acquaintance that has a lot of sway with his Cuban associates, to put it out there that I do not want any trouble with my new venture. The Cubans can be territorial, even though what I have in mind won't interfere with any of their businesses. The building was previously owned by an old pal of mine who had hit hard times – gambling debts. I figured I'd help him out of a sticky situation as the debtor's men were knocking at his door. But I saw an opportunity." Alphonso's face lit up. "I have decided that I need something to distract me. To keep me going until my maker calls my number. I require ya expertise!"

Eamon nodded.

Alphonso enthused, "Furthermore, I intend to open a nightclub, a watering hole where the men can bring their women. I plan on including an eatery, singers, jazz, blues, that sort of thing. I have a couple of highly rated vocalists in mind whose agent owes me a favour!" The old man paused briefly. "Eamon, ya previously said that ya have good men beside ya!"

Eamon nodded slowly, feeling uneasy at the thought of where this conversation was heading. "They are men that I trust, Al. Proven men!" Eamon knew might be walking into a situation that he would not be able to back out of.

"These men are standing in for ya back in Spain?" Alphonso queried.

Eamon had the feeling that he was about to step through a trapdoor.

"One hundred per cent, Al!"

"That sits well with me, son since I will need ya by my side here for a while until I find someone trustworthy enough to step in and manage the club. It should not take up too much of ya time," Alphonso said. "I would say at a guess, no more than three months." He added, "If we don't hit any hurdles, that is. Bring the wife and ya kids out here for a holiday. Ya never, know, your woman might take to it. The designers' shops would be a draw, as they were with Marcella and the girls!"

Eamon's heart sank. He retained his composure, but he struggled to muster up enthusiasm. He smiled warmly. He could not let Alphonso down, and he knew he had to repay the favour he had done for him. Alphonso had put his neck on the line for him by contacting his associate who knew someone in the prison system where Joyce Grant's son-in-law Matt was being held as the prosecution state witness against Franco Gennaro's son and his men. Alphonso had had the 'rat' wiped out, absolving Eamon from the trouble that would have followed if Franco Gennaro's son had been found guilty.

Alphonso placed his glass on the small table near his chair and clasped his hands together. "I am not a man to pry into ya business affairs, son. However, I am aware that ya were previously Jimmy Grant's right-hand man – the fall guy. Grant had sent ya to Miami seven or eight years back to deal with the big narcotic consignment with my boy Carlo, and it all ran smoothly." His rheumy, intense gaze held Eamon's. "Furthermore, Jimmy Grant's death would have set ya up financially," Alphonso said with a hint of a wry smile. "At a guess, knowing from the experience of dealing with Jimmy Grant, he would have been secretive about the shipment. He trusted ya. Much to ya advantage when he was wiped out. Leaving only three men that knew about the vast amount of money that was made." Alphonso smiled knowingly. "Fortunately for ya, ya secret died with two of them! Jimmy Grant and my boy Carlo. Leaving only you and me with the knowledge that ya was left a wealthy man!". He grinned. "Albeit, unclean money…"

Eamon sipped his mineral water without replying or taking his eyes from the shrewd old man. He knew Alphonso wouldn't expect a response. Both men knew that it was true.

Alphonso continued. I paid the required taxes and any dues that would make me a legal American citizen." He chuckled. "I have lived my life under the guise of being a restaurant owner. It has been a long journey from the time when Marcella and I opened our first eatery. It was the first step that aided me with my side-line." He chortled.

Eamon smiled knowingly.

"Ya don't need me to tell ya that laundering money isn't easy. More so today than in the old days." Eamon nodded in agreement.

"I can help ya, son, if ya require any assistance with investing ya unclean money." He pressed on without Eamon replying. "Art and precious stones are the way forward. It's a great way to go to turn dirty money clean." Alphonso left his proposition hanging in the air.

Eamon nodded twice in acknowledgement. Again, reluctant to add anything to the one-sided directive.

Alphonso then called for Joey, informing Eamon that it was way past his bedtime. "Think about it, son," Alphonso said as he bid Eamon good night.

Eamon came from the shower into the bedroom. Joey had unpacked his case earlier and hung up his suits and shirts in the large wardrobe. The sheer opulence of the room did nothing to lighten his mood. The furnishings in the room were French renaissance style. Two crystal chandeliers hung elegantly at either end of the high ceiling. Eamon guessed that they were Baccarat. He knew that Alphonso marked the French company as his favourite for luxury crystal. Eamon also remembered that Marcella had previously told him that Alphonso had presented her with two bespoke Baccarat chandeliers for their bedroom after she had given birth to their only son, Carlo. Marcella, at the time, had told Eamon that she was not interested in frippery but found the crystal somehow magical.

He glanced at his nakedness in the ceiling-high mirrors as he wrapped a towel around his waist, making a mental note to have mirrors installed in his bedroom at home. He smiled to himself, knowing that Marcia would enjoy observing their lovemaking, as much as he would. Picking up his phone from the bedside cabinet, he moved towards the floor-to-ceiling window, next to which was an overstuffed armchair facing Biscayne Bay. Although Eamon enjoyed the Miami metropolitan area, he had no wish to live there. Slumping into the soft leather armchair, he exhaled, suddenly feeling weary. He checked the time, knowing that Spain was six hours ahead of Miami. It would be just after 6 am in Altea Hills. He paused, undecided as to whether or not to phone Marcia.

He was not angry at Marcia for her indiscretion when she gave information to Joyce Grant during a tarot reading about her son-in-law's narcotic dealings with the Gennaro family. She had been unaware of the consequences. Furthermore, Eamon had closed the door on it. Alphonso had saved the day. Now that the time had come for Eamon to return the favour, he realised that both he and Marcia would have to pay the price. The Atlantic Ocean would separate them for three months, maybe more. Eamon did not want to uproot his children. The boys were settled at school. He felt of late that they were safe because they were close at hand. Niall and Quinn were driven to school and collected by him or Marcia. On rare occasions he had phoned the principal, giving his permission for Jane to pick them up.

Before Alphonso dropped the bombshell earlier, Eamon had planned to watch the home video of him and Marcia making love. He had purposely brought the SIM card that he had taken from his safe at home. However, his lustful thoughts had dissipated. For the moment, Eamon could not separate the longing that he felt for Marcia from the thought of what lay ahead of them both. He sent Marcia a text message.

2

Marcia came out through the terrace doors, flanked by her two Belgian shepherds, wrapping the towelling dressing gown around her in the early morning air. She hadn't slept well due to her concern about her two small sons. Sitting at the large garden table, she looked to the heavens, the glowing orb of the moon stared back at her. The night of Eamon's departure to Miami, Marcia observed the blood moon in the earth's shadow. She recalled how years earlier there had been a blood moon – the night when she had received the awful news that her son Reuben had been arrested at Heathrow Airport trying to smuggle narcotics into the UK.

Marcia sensed that it could be a sign of friction to come. She inhaled, putting the harrowing feelings to the back of her mind. Marcia heard her mobile phone ping and she smiled upon seeing Eamon's text message. She replied that she missed and loved him and longed for his return. Although she desperately missed him, she was grateful that he had texted and said that he would call her the following evening after Marcella's funeral. She wanted to speak with him regarding the situation with Niall and Quinn, which had been weighing on her mind, but she wanted to wait for the right moment.

There had been times when Marcia had chastised Niall for his misdemeanours and for being rude to her. However, this time Niall had taken things too far. The situation had become serious – frightening even. Nevertheless, she felt that the time was not right to burden Eamon, with him being in Miami for Marcella Gabrette's funeral. With a heavy heart, she recalled the conversation that she had had with Quinn the previous night. She had gone in to kiss the boys goodnight. She saw Quinn's head turned away from her into the pillow, wiping away a tear. Marcia assumed that Quinn was upset that his father had gone to Miami. She sat with him, drawing him into her chest, explaining that his father would return shortly. Quinn, sobbing, gradually revealed the reason for his night terrors. Horrified, Marcia lay with him on his bed, cradling the small, frightened boy in her arms, until he eventually drifted asleep. She gently prised the tight grip of his small hand from her fingers and she went downstairs to make a phone call to Maureen O'Reilly.

Maureen tearfully confessed that she had withheld the incident from Marcia and Eamon after the last time the boys had been staying with them in Marbella. Maureen said that something had happened when she and Dom had taken the boys out on Dom's boat. Maureen emphasised that both boys had been wearing life jackets at the time. Dom had steered the boat out of the busy marina and was heading out to the deeper waters of the Benalmadena coast. There were plenty of fish that he was hoping would attract dolphins. Dom had planned to drop anchor, spend a couple of hours having a picnic and allow the two boys to observe the dolphins that frequented the area. Maureen went on to say that both boys had been excited. Dom had anchored the boat. Niall and Quinn were sitting with her on the portside, watching the sea for signs of a pod of dolphins. Maureen said that she went to get the boys a drink when halfway to the saloon, she happened to turn as she forgot what drink Quinn had asked for. She broke down, tearfully explaining that she had seen, to her horror, Niall push Quinn overboard. Sobbing, she said, "I screamed out to Dom, who jumped into action. We both moved like lightening, grabbing Quinn by the life jacket back to safety!"

Marcia gasped in horror. Maureen explained to her that Niall also cried to see Quinn sobbing. She said that Niall, through tears, had said that it had been a game, an accident and that he had not meant to push Quinn so hard. Maureen had been beside herself, throughout the confession, pleading with Marcia not to tell Eamon.

Although there had been no physical harm done, thanks to the actions of the couple, Marcia knew very well the mental anguish that Quinn was experiencing, and the effect his suffering was having on him. Marcia realised that the ageing couple, whose health was on the decline, were no longer able to cope with her two young sons. Quinn on his own would not cause them any trouble, but Niall was a different story.

Marcia, at times, struggled with Niall's strong will, making excuses to herself that he was troubled and psychologically disturbed. She concluded that she would need to have a frank discussion with Eamon regarding Niall's targeting of Quinn. Although Eamon was tolerant, understanding and sympathetic to Niall's problems with communicating and expressing himself, he would not tolerate any form of aggression towards his younger brother. So far, Niall had not shown any aggressive behaviour towards the twin baby girls. For the most part, he tended to avoid them. However, sometimes, while Eamon was playing, hugging and kissing Aisling and Aine, Marcia would notice Niall's look of loathing towards his baby sisters. Marcia had hoped that given time, Niall would change and become less jealous as he grew older, but Marcia had to admit to herself that Niall would not improve. He could cause harm to his siblings. Thinking of what could have been the dire consequences of Niall pushing Quinn over the side of the boat, she shook the image out of her mind's eye.

Marcia did not know which way to go with Niall. She knew that Eamon would question Quinn, and he would leave no stone unturned until he learned the truth from both boys. If it was deemed not an accident but a deliberate act to hurt Quinn, she dreaded to think what Eamon's reaction would be. She pondered, knowing that. Eamon would come down hard on Niall. The quandary plagued her. She had seen Niall being spiteful to his brother, she tried to figure out what his reasons might be to inflict unkindness on his brother. Marcia had tried to sweep it under the carpet and dismiss it as sibling rivalry, but she had come to realise that, as much as she and Eamon had tried to help Niall, she would one day face heartache with him, if there was no intervention. In the few hours of restless sleep that she had snatched the previous night, she had an old reoccurring dream that haunted her. She was running towards her son, screaming, as she vividly recalled her son's profile, knife in hand, dripping with blood. His face was obscure, so she was not able to see which son out of the two was the perpetrator. Her intuition pressed her to admit that the aggressor in the dream was Niall. She sat there thinking about her youngest son – Quinn who wore his heart on his sleeve, the gentlest of souls. He was a sensitive, caring, loving and affectionate boy. There was not a bad bone in his body. Her melancholy thoughts turned to her eldest son Reuben who was lost to her. There had been no word or knowledge of his whereabouts for so many years. Nevertheless, she persisted in sending out daily prayers to the unseen realm to watch over and protect him, as she did for all her family.

3

Alphonso had retired to his bedroom. The ordeal of Marcella's wake and funeral was now over. Many of Alphonso's friends and associates, past and present had flown in from all over to Miami to pay their respects. The day had mentally and physically taken its toll on Alphonso, however, Eamon knew that the old boy would be up and running the following day. Alphonso had said that the next day they would visit the building that he had purchased for his new venture.

Joey offered Eamon a large glass of Riserva Barolo, the Italian wine that Alphonso favoured, pressing him to take the whole bottle with him to his room. Eamon didn't take much persuading. After showering, he wrapped a towel around his waist and relaxed on the bed, taking a gulp of the wine. He had decided to wait for an hour to ring Marcia, to allow for the time difference. The tautness in his shoulders from the draining day began to evaporate. He took another large mouthful, which helped to put him in a more chilled-out place. Reaching for his wallet on the bedside table, he took out the phone SIM card and swapped the old one out of his phone. Sinking into the pillows, he held the phone up in front of him. He smiled, adjusting his position, glass in one hand, ready to view. He placed the glass on the bedside cabinet and watched the vision of Marcia astride him play out on the screen. His breathing became heavy, heat filled his groin and his shaft throbbed, aching, longing to hold his wife in his arms. Marcia's breasts filled the cupless, black silk bra, enhancing her dark, erect nipples. With her legs wide, she guided his primed penis through the opening of her ouvert panties. Eamon observed the synchronised movement of him inside of her, his hands placed firmly on either side of her buttocks. As she began to orgasm, Eamon, lying on the bed so far away from her now, across the Atlantic, joined her. Both climbing to the height of ecstasy, the screen depicting Marcia freefalling, him pumping, increasing the depth of pleasure, holding her fast in the last throes. Eamon switched off the phone and returned to the here and now, involuntary shuddering. He felt satiated in the only way he could without Marcia being there. "How the hell am I going to withstand another prolonged absence from her?" Eamon said aloud to the vast room. Refilling the glass, he took a large mouthful, closing his eyes and savouring the distinctive notes of tobacco and dried fruits playing across his palate.

Marcia sleepily answered his phone call. "Hey, sleepy-head. 'Tis not like ye. I thought that ye would be awake!" Pausing for a couple of seconds, he added with a hint of concern, "Is there anyting wrong?"

She evaded the question, and said, "I find it difficult to sleep without your arms holding me. Eamon, when are you returning? I miss you. The children ask for you."

He did not mention that Alphonso had asked him to stay in Miami for three months or more to help set up the nightclub. He would tell her once he returned to Spain. "There is going to be a day's delay. Alphonso wants to show me a building that he has purchased. He wants me to give him my opinion." He did not go into details.

"Have you missed me?" she asked, sounding more alert.

"To be sure. Ye don't need to ask. It goes without saying that I long for ye!"

"Did you take the video recording of us with you?"

Eamon gave a soft laugh. "To be sure. I enjoyed watching our last moments together earlier! The latest one of ye in the black silk underwear."

She giggled. "Did it fulfil your needs?"

"For the moment!" He gave another soft laugh, adding, "until I come home to ye. Then we can make up for the lost time! How are the children?"

She hesitated, before saying, "The girls have been swimming with me every day, they also both join me on the yoga mat, rolling their bums, giggling!"

Eamon took note of the change in her voice, sensing that something was bothering her. He would unearth whatever it was that was bothering her upon his return.

"Niall and Quinn?" Eamon asked. Marcia knew that Eamon was referring to Niall, as Quinn was always good.

Marcia was quick to respond, "Billy and Jane have been giving them both horse riding lessons. They return home tired after helping clean out the stables. Dan comes in to check on us twice a day." She laughed. "Aye feeds Dan his favourite Thai dishes, always pressing him to take some home for Cindy."

Eamon had checked in with Dan earlier, before speaking to Marcia. Dan, along with Billy, was always up early. Both men were on the ball. Their military training was etched into their psyche. Eamon told Marcia that he loved her and she said goodbye, saying she loved him and to stay safe.

He sat up on the bed thinking about Marcia. He realised that she would not be able to cope with Niall while he was away in Miami for three months or more. He knew that Niall looked up to Billy, and he knew that he could rely on Billy to step in with his son if needed. Jane and Billy, childless themselves, both had a real rapport with Niall and Quinn. Billy and Jane tried to instil in them a strong work ethic, insisting that the boys feed the horses and help clean out the stables after their riding lessons. But they made sure that Niall and Quinn had fun and enjoyed riding the horses. Billy and Jane loved them and both boys respected the couple.

The old Italian appeared to have perked up, now that his wife's funeral was out of the way. Joey drove Alphonso and Eamon to downtown Miami. "Here we are!" Alphonso beamed when the car turned into a side road near Collins Avenue and 16th Street. The building was on Washington Avenue, which had various restaurants and hangouts advertising night-time entertainment. Joey dropped them off and said he was going to pay his pal a visit who had a nearby burger stall. Eamon closed the doors to the building behind Alphonso who threw on the light switches, flooding the place with light.

Eamon's first impression was that the place would need a lot of money ploughed into it. He knew Alphonso wouldn't scrimp, and that he would do whatever it took to make a success of the place and to make his last mark. Eamon knew that this new venture was not about making money for Alphonso, it was to help him get through the days without Marcella. Alphonso owned a few restaurants already, however, he had help from his daughter Chiara who kept on top of the management of his empire. Eamon strolled to the centre of the space, giving the large area the once-over. There was a small stage at the far end, with a crescent-shaped bar to the right.

"What's ya thoughts, son?" Alphonso asked, sitting down on a chair that had seen better days.

Eamon nodded, smiling his approval, although he realised that the renovations could take longer than three months. In fact, in his estimation, it would take approximately six to get it to the luxury standard that was Alphonso's trademark. "'Tis grand!" he replied, showing enthusiasm. He owed Al that much for what he had done for him in the past. He stretched out his arms, sweeping the area. "The space is perfect for what ye have in mind, Al!"

Alphonso beamed and slapped his hand on his knee in self-congratulations. "I told ya! This watering hole will draw the men. I know them. Father and son will become members!" Alphonso enthused. "Take a look at the room at the back!" Alphonso directed him towards some double doors with glass portholes at the rear of the room.

Eamon did as he was bid. Upon entry, he could see that it was once a large kitchen. Eamon exhaled. This project was going to take much longer than he had previously thought. The dilapidated kitchen itself would require a massive overhaul. He came back to where the old man was seated.

Alphonso was grinning. "I know that there is no car parking area. However, the men that will frequent this club all have drivers, so parking won't be a problem," Alphonso declared.

Eamon pursed his lips, nodding, turning to walk towards another pair of doors.

"That's going to be the restaurant!" Alphonso called after him.

Eamon ran his hand a few times over his goatee beard, nodding. He thought that the room could be turned into a large seating area for the proposed eatery. In his mind's eye, he genuinely thought that the new venue appeared to have great potential. Eamon decided that he had no choice but to throw himself wholeheartedly into the old Italian's plans, even though the thought of being separated from his family weighed heavily upon him. There would have been a much larger price to pay if Alphonso had not intervened with the Franco Gennaro situation and had the 'canary' dispensed with. Without the old Italian's intervention, Gennaro's son could have been put behind bars for decades and Eamon and his family would have been in Gennaro's firing line.

Eamon knew that back in the day, Alphonso had been a powerful man, highly respected by many. Even though he had now stepped down from his throne, he continued to hold a great deal of sway. Eamon had seen it first-hand at the funeral – the reverence that had been shown to Alphonso by the congregation of powerful men in attendance as they paid tribute to Marcella Gabrette. Eamon thought about the grand entrance of the powerful Miami don, Ricardo Barossa with his lethal-looking henchmen flanking him at the hotel where Marcella Gabrette's wake was being held. Ricardo Barossa had reverently kissed the back of Alphonso's hand, paying homage. Nonetheless, Eamon noticed his smile did not reflect his dark-brown, shark-like eyes that spoke to him of malice. He looked up and directed Eamon an arctic glare. He sensed right away that the man disliked him on sight.

Alphonso had filled Eamon in on each man after they had paid their respects. Among them was Lucca Barossa, the younger brother of Ricardo, also handsome, as many Italian men were. He sensed that Lucca was approachable; his smile was genuine, unlike his brother Ricardo's. He had taken note of another man who had been at the wake who seemed familiar to him. He recognised him as the man on the plane who he had taken snapshots of in the airport arrivals area. He had been standing at the hotel bar with Ricardo Barossa.

Alphonso enlightened Eamon that the man was one of Ricardo Barossa's foot soldiers, Johnnie Guzzardi. "Believe me, that man is Barossa's eyes and ears. If he was on the plane tailing Barossa's woman, she would have no knowledge of it. Guzzardi would not be known to her." Alphonso said that Johnnie Guzzardi's father had been gunned down a few years back, due to opposing family issues. Eamon figured that Guzzardi must have been tailing Josephine. Eamon knew that he would have reported back to his boss that he had seen Eamon seated next to Ricardo's mistress on the plane. Eamon understood why the Miami boss had glared at him. However, Eamon had no interest in him or his woman. Nonetheless, he was certain that Ricardo Barossa did not see it that way.

4

Eamon heard the landing gear engage. The plane began its descent and then approached the runway. Just a few more miles to go, Eamon thought to himself. Glancing out of the window, he saw the Costa Blanca coastline, which he had called home for so long, looming. His life was now very different to when, as a young man, he first landed on Spanish soil. It had taken what seemed a lifetime to reach the place in his life where he was now, feeling content with his lot. He regarded himself to be very fortunate to have met the love of his life, Marcia, who had given him four children, when he had once thought that he was destined to be alone and childless.

He smiled to himself, musing back on how quickly she had become pregnant – twice within ten and a half months – two sons. One had not entered the world without drama. The second came without any problem, befitting each boy's personality. A vision of his feisty pair of copper-red-headed daughters rose before him. He was eager to see them all.

The plane touched down smoothly and taxied along the runway. Eamon took his mobile phone from his suit pocket. He felt the calling card that Josephine had given to him. Studying the gold lettering, name and cell phone number, he thought he would dispose of it later when he found a bin. He remembered the conversations that he had had with her on the flight, albeit, it had been more of a monologue on her part. Although the woman had not held the slightest interest for him romantically, he had found her lifestyle. He wondered if she ever considered what she would do when her beauty and figure faded. What then would she have to fall back on emotionally? He did not envy her future. He thought that loneliness awaited her, and desolation, having given up having children in return for wealth, as she had revealed to him. Untold riches could not replace a lover's or a child's embrace. He always knew that Marcia would be waiting for him, but who would wait for Josephine? She had entertained him with her candid stories of her numerous influential lovers. He had enjoyed her company. She was certainly a beautiful woman, there was no denying it. He had accepted her proffered calling card out of politeness, nothing more.

His thoughts turned to the man who he had felt was overly interested in him on the flight over to Miami, Johnnie Guzzardi, now that he had a name to the face. It was obvious to Eamon that Ricardo Barossa did not trust Josephine. Eamon's gut instinct told him that Ricardo had his man watch her every move. If Eamon had been in Ricardo Barossa's shoes, he would have used the same method to unearth any new faces on the scene, potential threat or otherwise. Not that type of situation of having an open relationship with a woman would appeal to him. He could not share his woman with another man. Marcia was his, he was hers. He wanted nothing more. His thoughts turned to Josephine again; he didn't think there was much hope of her ever escaping a man like Barossa unless he tired of her.

He was eager to take Marcia in his arms and to see his children. They had spoken briefly on the phone before he entered Miami Airport. He could hear one of the baby girls crying in the background. Aisling was teething, while Aine had recently cut her teeth. He made a mental note to call his brother Patrick in County Armagh, Ireland. Eamon sent Marcia a message to tell her that his flight had landed. He sent another to Dan who was picking him up from the airport. He stretched his long legs, thankful that he had no one in the seat beside him. The uninterrupted five-and-a-half-hours sleep had refreshed him.

Eamon exited the arrival hall on level 0 and crossed the street where the taxis were lined up. Spotting Dan's car at the rear of the rank, he hurried towards him. Dan raised his hand in greeting and jumped out of the idling car to take his luggage. Both men ignored the irate taxi driver in front who was hurling abuse, stating that it was illegal to park there. Eamon did not need to ask if anything was wrong, he could sense by Dan's face that the man had had no sleep. "Trouble?" Eamon quizzed, looking at Dan, who was making a quick exit from Alicante airport.

Concentrating on the traffic, Dan shook his head. "You could not fucking write it, boss!" Dan said, with a heavy cadence. "Scott Lord is in a bad way. He was set about in the club car park by a couple of gutless wankers that sneaked up on him after we closed for the night. The spineless pair thwacked him across the skull before I could come to his aid. The poor fucker did not have a chance." Dan sympathised with Scott Lord's plight. He put Eamon in the loop. "Scott and I were the last ones in the club; everybody else had gone home. Fortunately, I happened to glance at the security monitor screen that covers the parking area as well as the inside of the building. I zoomed in upon seeing two shadows by the rear wall next to mine and Scott's cars. The pair of cunts were skulking, hidden from his view. Before I realised what was happening, they raced towards him. I left the club as fast as I could to save him from being beaten. They jumped him from behind when he opened his car door. One of them had a baton, bringing it down on the back of his head before I could reach Scott. Forcing the baton from the attacker's grip, I simultaneously gave the pair a good kicking before any more damage could be done. I'm telling you, boss, they would have killed him if he had had to endure any further blows. I'm sure that was the intention!" Dan exclaimed reliving the nightmare of his pal's attack. "However, I made sure that I did some damage to the pair of bastards. The pair scarpered. They did not want any more of me. Furthermore, I was relieved because I knew that Scott was in trouble. I realised that he needed urgent medical treatment. He was unconscious so I carried him to my motor, laying him on the back seat, and drove straight to the hospital. The roads were empty, so I made it in double quick time." Dan exhaled.

Eamon, running his fingers through his hair, shook his head.

Dan continued, his voice choked with emotion, "He is in ICU fighting for his life."

Eamon shook his head again. "That bad! Poor bastard," he commiserated. "Take me to the hospital!" he directed. "What the fuck do ye tink has brought this about?" he asked. "Ye don't get two fellas waylaying someone in the early hours for no reason!"

Dan nodded in agreement.

"What age bracket were they?" Eamon asked.

Dan shrugged his shoulders, and said, "Youngsters in their twenties, maybe. We can go back over the camera tapes later, boss." Eamon nodded. "Where is Sandy?"

"I had phoned Cindy from the hospital to tell her what happened. She drove to reach Sandy at her villa before the

Guardia went to her home to inform her. The hospital contacted the Law. Two Guardia questioned me at length. Nonetheless, I said the usual, that no video cameras were covering the car park, only the inner building, and that I had no idea about the attackers' identity. Nevertheless, although I only had a fleeting glance of the pair of young cunts, their faces are imprinted on my brain!" Dan stated vehemently. "I will find them!" Then Dan's tone softened. "Cindy was with Sandy earlier at the hospital, giving her moral support, but Sandy insisted that she wanted to stay on her own with Scott and insisted on Cindy leaving. She is back at home now trying to get some sleep." Dan returned to the topic of the assault. "I have racked my brains as to the identity of Scott's assailants. From what I saw of the pair, I don't think that I have seen them in the club before. We can get Billy and the rest of the security team to look at the camera footage. Maybe one of the men had a run-in with the attackers at some point."

Eamon nodded in agreement. He knew that Marcia would be on the school run. He texted her to briefly explain the situation, without going into detail, stating that he was heading towards the hospital in Benidorm. He would inform her after he had been to see for himself how the situation was going with Scott Lord.

Eamon and Dan walked to the hospital reception area. Dan explained that he had brought Scott Lord into the hospital. The young woman at her station directed them to the waiting room. "I would like to speak wit a doctor about Mr Lord. Please tell Mrs Lord that we are here!" Eamon commanded. She nodded, picking up the telephone.

Sandy came into the room where Eamon and Dan were waiting. Both men stood up. Eamon stepped forward, putting his arm around the heavily pregnant woman's shoulders. She appeared to have aged ten years, with tears streaking her face. Eamon pulled her towards him as she sobbed into his chest. "I don't want ye to concern yerself about bills or any money worries that ye may have to deal wit. Dan will deal wit Scott's wages and I will also foot the hospital bills. I want ye to take care of ye and yer lad. Scott would want that!"

The door opened; a white-coated doctor smiled thinly, introducing himself as Doctor Perez. He explained Scott's position to Sandy while the men listened. "The MRI scan shows that Mr Lord has a subdural hematoma, where the blood collects between the skull and the brain," he said with a heavy tone.

"Is it life-threatening?" Sandy asked, wringing her hands, eyes pleading that it was not.

The doctor looked sadly at her. "I am afraid, Mrs Lord, that it can be." He glanced at the two men, speaking to them all. "One must pray at times such as this that a miracle occurs." He continued, "However, I am not trying to give you false hope. The condition is very serious." Then he said warmly, glancing at her pregnant condition, "Your husband appears to have a lot to live for! The next forty-eight hours are crucial." He bade them farewell. Sandy took a tissue from her bag, wiping her tears.

"Scott needs me!" she looked at both men. "Thank you both for all that you have done and for your support." She looked at Eamon. "There is just one thing. My son Brady is young and…"

Eamon interjected, "Billy will take him under his wing. Don't worry!" Once they had left the hospital, Eamon asked Dan to drive to the Hawk Wind club. He wanted to see the footage of the attack on Scott Lord.

Dan zoomed in on the two men, Eamon winced when he observed Scott Lord being struck from behind with the baton. Eamon shook his head as he saw Scott slump to the floor.

Dan's powerful arms came into profile on the monitor. His hands simultaneously yanking and feet dropkicking the pair. Dan froze the frame.

"The pair of young gutless cunts are not familiar to me," Eamon spoke angrily. "I am going to ensure that they both pay. Show everyone on the security team their faces," he ordered. "Someone's mind could be jogged about some incident that occurred."

Dan nodded in agreement, as he shut down the computer. "I am only surmising that two drugged-up wankers were waiting in the shadows for the club to close to get payback for some perceived slight. Unfortunately, for Scott Lord, he was the first one to come out on his own."

"They are not going to get away wit this!" Eamon vowed. "Get the men on it. Someone must know them!"

Dan said that he would start the ball rolling that night.

Eamon let himself in the front door of his villa, leaving his luggage in the lounge. The two dogs wagged their tails in welcome as he entered. Walking across the marbled floor, towards the open double doors that led onto the terrace, he could see Marcia in profile sitting at the garden table wearing sunglasses, a large sunhat and a flowing Asian-style, multi-coloured, full-length dress. He smiled to himself, removing his jacket and placing it across the back of a dining room chair. As he stepped through the terrace doors, Marcia turned her head, beaming upon seeing him. she stood to greet him and then looked concerned. "How is Scott, Eamon?" Shaking her head in dismay, she said, "I could not believe that this has happened. What about Sandy?"

Eamon sat on a garden chair, pulling Marcia onto his lap. Her arms went around his neck. Eamon explained Scott's condition and what Dan said had occurred in the early hours that morning. He told her that he would see to it that Sandy had no financial worries.

"My heart goes out to her. She is due to have the baby shortly. I will go to see Sandy at the hospital later. She does not have any family in Spain to help her! I can't imagine how she feels. One moment the couple are planning their family together..." Marcia left it hanging in the air, aware that the lives the men led put them in a vulnerable position.

Eamon nodded slowly.

Marcia kissed him. He held on to her, kissing her slowly, deeply, taking in the light notes of rose and jasmine in her Roja Haute Luxe perfume that she favoured, as he did.

"Where are the children?" he breathed, nibbling her earlobe.

"Jane came to take the boys to her place. They're unaware that you were coming home today. The girls have been in the swimming pool, However, but Aye just fed them, so now they are both sleeping soundly with their bellies full. Aye has prepared some food for you.

"We could have two hours of privacy while the girls are asleep?" Marcia invited, letting her hand wander, caressing Eamon's forming erection.

"Give me five minutes while I shower! He replied, then added, "Leave the dress on!" he winked.

Minutes later Eamon stepped from the shower, drying himself. He knew that he had much to sort out. He knew he had to tell Marcia that he was going to have to return to Miami for a while until Alphonso's club was up and running, however, he had decided to put it on the back burner. He wanted to enjoy being with Marcia while they were both in the mood. He had longed for her while he was away.

He smiled, throwing the towel onto the stool at the dressing table, catching Marcia's glance in the mirror as she admired his rear view.

She lay on the bed admiring his physique as he came towards her. He never failed to take her breath away with his body, his prowess and his lovemaking, even though his hair was no longer raven-black but silver-grey. Marcia thought it only added to his handsome mature looks. She realised that he would still be a good catch for any female predator that tried to lure him. "How often did you watch the recordings of us making love?" she asked him as he knelt on the bed.

"Three in total!" he grinned, raising her dress above her waist. "Bare buttocks!" he caressed her firm cheeks, and his fingers began exploring. "Wet!" he said, smiling, holding her up while he sidled his head between her legs – his tongue slowly teasing, his finger aiding as he pleasured her.

Marcia cupped his face, bucking in ecstasy.

"Relax and enjoy the moment. Don't let it take ye!" Eamon coaxed.

Her breathing became rapid. "Eamon…" she breathed, as his rubbing facial hair, tongue and fingers drove her towards the point of no return.

Eamon eased. "I want ye to join me!" he said. They changed position at her suggestion. Kneeling before her, he watched her tongue move with loving tenderness, her mouth manoeuvring across his shaft, then withdrawing, each time taking him deeper. Her hands caressed his buttocks, then moved down, fingers lightly manipulating his scrotum. His hold on her shoulders tightened, gripping, fighting to release her hold on him, yet, allowing her to take him. At the last moment, he broke free. In one swift move, he removed her dress. His powerful thighs clamped hers and their bodies entwined, tongue seeking tongue, deepening the heat that rose between them, uniting and bursting with the pleasure they gave one another.

"I yearned to hold ye," Eamon whispered, kissing Marcia lightly, without withdrawing, feeling both their heartbeats. "I have missed ye so much."

"You had videos of us together to give you relief. Unlike me!" she said, playfully.

He nodded. "To be sure, watching you on screen pleasuring me is comforting when I can't be wit ye in real life!" he said smiling. "Nevertheless, there is a difference because I cannot hold ye. Without ye in my arms, 'tis nothing more than a release!" he declared, waggling his head. "Although, to watch us making love is something else – seeing us together as lovers in the privacy of the bedroom," he confessed, holding her dark-brown eyes with his. Eamon admitted, "I did not realise the beauty of the act before filming us in the privacy of our bedroom with the wall-to-wall mirrors catching every angle of the intimacy of our love making. 'Tis sensual. Something to behold!"

His resting penis began to rise again inside her. Marcia smiled and wrapped her arms around his neck, kissing him. Eamon responded, their soul kiss deepening their union. She tightened her pelvic muscles, clamping hard.

"Mmm… there is no comparison." he breathed, softly biting and kissing her neck. He moved down, his mouth engulfing her dark nibbles, their bodies synchronised with deliberate motion. His hand slid beneath her, cupping her buttock, locking them together. "Relax!" he said, when she gently but firmly bit into his shoulder, her fingers clamping. "Take it slowly, enjoy each movement" he instructed.

Marcia relinquished her hold, arms and head thrown back on the pillow. Her hands clenched with every deep movement within. Timing the moment, Eamon covered her, taking her higher. "I am going to join ye!" he breathed. Observing the gratification that he was giving her, he said, "Let it take ye!"

Holding her in his arms, he felt their heartbeats gradually returning to normal. "To observe ye being fulfilled. By me!" He threw in for good measure, smiling lovingly. "'Tis something that I have found incomparable!"

Marcia judged that he was speaking of his past experiences with other women, but she did not voice her thoughts.

Eamon continued, "When ye are young ye don't value sex. It's only a moment of enjoyment, then it's over. Until ye are fortunate enough to meet the right one, that is." Smiling, he pulled her closer. "Then everything changes from that moment on. The act becomes beautiful, meaningful," he added.

Marcia sensed a change in Eamon since his return from Miami. She had never known him to be so open and verbal in his emotional expression as he was at that moment. She pondered if there might be something occurring in his life that he was withholding from her.

The screen on the baby monitor on the side table squawked to life. The two girls, copper-red curls damp from slumber sat up in their cot beds. On cue, Aye opened the girl's bedroom door. Marcia and Eamon quickly dressed.

As Eamon opened the door, both girls clapped and squealed in unison, "Daddy!" Both wriggled excitedly, pulling away from Aye as Eamon approached them. Marcia smiled when Eamon picked one up in each arm. "Be Jesus, youse two are big girls. Dadda has missed youse!" He kissed under their necks, his facial hair tickling them causing the pair to squeal. Aisling chewed his earlobe and Aine snuggled into his neck, chubby arms holding him fast.

Eamon walked into the lounge, seating the twins in their highchairs, strapping each one in to prevent them from climbing out, as they were wanting at times.

Aye secured the lids on the babies' drinking cups and handed them to the girls. Both quickly smacked their palms together, placing their small fingers in a pyramid shape, heads bowed in gratitude, the Thai way, as Aye had shown them. Eamon smiled as Aye tied their bibs before they ate. "Kin Khao!" (Eat food!) Aisling said, banging her cup after draining it. "Nam!" she said, asking for more water, then pausing. "Kha!" she added, remembering afterwards to say thank you.

Marcia went outside to the terrace as Eamon went to get the food that Aye had prepared for them. The soft breeze blowing in from the bay kissed her skin and the sun shone down. She donned her sunglasses, feeling fortunate that Eamon was safely home from Miami. Her mobile phone rang as she sat down under the garden canopy on the terrace. Sandy Lord's number appeared on the screen. Her telephone number, as with all the girls who worked at the club, was logged into her phone, even though Sandy no longer worked at the Hawk Wind club.

Marcia answered and heard Sandy's voice. "Marcia, I am sorry to bother you, however, I feel as if my heart will break watching Scott looking so helpless in a coma." She sobbed quietly. Marcia heard the desperation in her voice. "I need you to tell me that Scott won't leave me!" Marcia could hear that Sandy was on the brink of breaking down. Her emotional plea filled her with an element of sadness.

Marcia exhaled before she began to speak. "Sandy, please listen to me." She directed firmly but kindly. "Scott will face a battle," she predicted, "however..." she paused for a second, "he will pull through and live to see his son being born." Continuing to reassure Sandy with her foresight regarding the couple's future together, Marcia added, "Also, you will not stop there." Marcia pressed on, trying to give Sandy the confidence to stand strong throughout the crisis. "There will be a daughter, and another two boys after your firstborn's first birthday." She tried to console Sandy. "Please don't cry," she said. "You and Scott will have a wonderful life together. It'll only be a short time before the tide turns in your favour." Marcia proclaimed with certainty.

Between sobs, Sandy profusely thanked Marcia.

"Would you like some company?" Marcia asked her. "I can sit with you at the hospital. I will ask Aye to prepare you something to eat. You will need to eat to keep up your strength. Also for the baby." Marcia advised.

Sandy replied, sounding slightly cheerier. "Marcia, I will be fine now that you have given me hope. Jane has phoned me to say that she and Billy are going to look after my son Brady. I will get something to eat from the hospital. I promise!"

After he had finished making some phone calls in his office, Eamon came out through the terrace doors carrying two plates on a tray. He placed the plates of fish salad on the table, along with a glass of wine for him and a fruit smoothie for Marcia. He sat down opposite her. Marcia viewed him sheepishly, knowing that he would not want her to intervene in the situation with Scott Lord by predicting the outcome of what could be a dire situation. "Sandy just called me. She is distraught," Marcia said. She was pleading with me to give her some reassurance that Scott would survive."

Eamon chewed slowly, looking at her, listening.

"Eamon it was heart-rending to hear her."

He stopped eating and held her gaze.

"I had to reassure her that Scott will pull through."

Eamon exhaled, and Marcia continued. "I know that you do not like me to get involved by offering predictions, Eamon, but this situation is different. There will not be any repercussions as there were with Joyce Grant. I relayed what I felt I should. I told her that soon the tide will turn in Scott's favour."

Eamon began eating again. He slowly nodded, without replying. Pointing his fork towards her dish, he directed her to eat. Marcia picked up her fork. "How did the boys behave while I was away?" he asked, taking a forkful of salad.

His question threw her and she struggled to reply, pushing the food around on her plate.

He swallowed, cocking an eyebrow at her, seeing her hesitation. Eamon spoke, "Billy telephoned to inform me that he was concerned when the boys last stayed overnight. He said Quinn would not go into the swimming pool. Even with his coaxing." Eamon ate another forkful, waiting for Marcia's reply.

"Quinn…" she paused for two seconds, "has become afraid of the water."

Eamon put down his cutlery. Picking up his wine glass, he took a long sip, leaning back in his chair. Marcia pushed the plate to one side and responded, "I telephoned Maureen to ask her if there had been any reason why Quinn would not go near the pool." Marcia went into detail about her conversation with Maureen.

Eamon paled, sucking air through his teeth, shaking his head. "Eat your food!" he directed, returning to finish his.

Marcia picked at hers.

Eamon did not speak again until he had finished eating, pushing the empty plate to one side. Running his fingers through his hair, he said with an exasperated air, "What the hell am I going to do wit the boy?"

Marcia knew that he was speaking more to himself.

He looked at her. "Marcia, I have tried everything wit the boy." His look darkened. "Niall has crossed the line this time. What the fuck is going on in the boy's mind to push his brother over the side of the boat? He could have killed him! Maureen and Dom should have told us right away! I think they are getting too old to cope wit Niall! It makes me wonder if my son has any empathy." Eamon had known men with psychiatric disorders who had been violent with their siblings, but Eamon kept this to himself.

Marcia turned away, unable to fight back the tears. He reached for her hand, stood up and moved round the table. He gently pulled her up, holding her close to his chest. He exhaled, lifting her chin with two fingers so that she would look at him. Both remained silent. Eamon brushed her lips with his. "Marcia I cannot allow this to continue. It is for Niall's sake, before anything happens that I won't be able to help him. How can we trust our son with his siblings otherwise?" He wiped Marcia's tears away with his fingertips. Eamon wondered, not for the first time, if Niall was suffering from a mental illness. For the most part, he thought that Niall appeared to be devoid of emotion and lacking empathy. He pushed the thought to the back of his mind. He held Marcia at arm's length. "I will come up wit something!" He smiled thinly, trying to reassure her. Eamon's mobile phone rang. Taking the phone from his shirt pocket, he stepped back, holding his finger up to Marcia, he went to his office and locked the door. "Hi Dave!" he said to Big Dave Broadbent. "I will ring ye on the other phone!" He unlocked his safe and took out the mobile that he used to speak about private business matters.

Eamon had phoned Dave earlier, leaving a message for him to return his call. "One of my men has taken a crack over the head from a pair of young cunts that waylaid him in the early hours in the club car park. My man is in intensive care. Fighting for his life. His heavily pregnant wife is by his side. I am putting a couple of my men out there to try to find out if there has been any talk. Ye know how they tend to brag. If luck is on my side, and they are local, I want them dealt wit."

Dave Broadbent said that he would await Eamon's go-ahead.

Eamon moved round the large desk, slumping into the office chair, stretching his legs on the desktop. His thoughts went to Niall. He had tried various things with him each time he had stepped out of line. Eamon was at his wit's end as to how to deal with his son. He realised that some of Niall's personality traits were similar to his own. For the most part, Eamon did not wear his heart on his sleeve, although he had revealed more to Marcia than he had to anyone else. He had been taciturn from a young age. He had come to recognise that it was his father's brutality that had been the cause. But Niall came from a loving home where he was doted on. Eamon was a changed man ever since he began his relationship with Marcia – she had changed him. Her love had quelled many of his demons. How the fuck can I leave my family to live thousands of miles across the Atlantic? he asked himself wearily. Marcia would not be able to cope with Niall! he silently concluded.

The following day, Eamon stood by his car in the school car park waiting for his sons to finish for the day. Minutes later, the mass of young children came into sight. Quinn was among the group, laughing with another pupil. He spotted Niall lagging behind, appearing surly among the chattering youngsters. Quinn spotted his father, his beatific smile lit up his handsome features. Eamon grinned as Quinn spotted him and began running towards him. Eamon kept his eye on Niall.

As if he sensed his father, Niall glanced in the direction of the parked cars. Putting his head down, he sauntered towards them.

"Papa!" Quinn increased his pace, his heavy satchel dragging on the ground. He hugged his father's legs. Eamon ruffled his hair, continuing to observe Niall who continued to look down as he approached. Both boys clipped their seatbelts in, all the while Quinn chattered cheerily, while Niall turned to look out of the window. On the short journey home, Eamon caught Niall's look in the rear-view mirror. He momentarily held his son's dark eyes. He had no wish to intimidate the small boy. Eamon looked away.

"When youse two change out of yer uniforms, stay in yer room because I wish to speak to ye." Eamon smiled at Quinn, whose worried look quickly dissipated when Eamon patted his head kindly. Niall remained silent.

Eamon sent the boys upstairs, saying that he would be up in a few minutes. The two dogs followed him out on to the terrace. He smiled at the sight of his wife and twin daughters, all wearing leotards and sitting on yoga mats. Marcia was teaching them the moves, their three bottoms raised in the air. Marcia laughed when both girls rolled backwards. Catching Marcia's eye, Eamon winked, before retreating inside.

Eamon opened Quinn's bedroom door first. He smiled as Quinn sat on the edge of his bed, looking apprehensive. He had put his school uniform neatly away and had changed into a t-shirt and shorts. Eamon sat facing him. Quinn began twiddling his fingers. "Dadda would like ye to tell him what happened on Dom's boat. Dadda knows that Niall pushed ye. Quinn looked down. Eamon, with one finger, gently lifted his chin.

Quinn spoke quietly, "We were sitting outside on the deck looking for pods of dolphins, then Maureen went to get us a drink." He floundered. Eamon nodded, and Quinn continued. "Niall said that he had seen a dolphin break the water alongside and told me to kneel up on the seat to get a closer look…" He paused again. Eamon waited, face impassive. "I leaned over to see and then he hit my back hard and I fell over the side and my head went under the water. I thought that the dolphin would eat me!" Quinn's dark eyes filled with tears. "I was scared, but Dom jumped in and pulled me back into the boat. Maureen was crying."

Eamon stopped him, brushing his face with his fingers. "I will speak to Niall shortly, but first Dadda wants to talk to ye."

Quinn nodded, wiping the back of his hands over his wet face as tears continued to stream.

Eamon took his small hand in his. Quinn held it. "Dadda will always protect ye, Quinn. I cannot allow any of my children to go out in a boat again unless I am there too." He said softly but firmly.

Quinn sniffled, listening.

"Furthermore, I know that ye are a brave boy. Also, ye are a great swimmer." Eamon smiled. Quinn's eyes darted. "There has been tings in my life when I was a boy about yer age that had frightened me. However, ye are my son and strong like me!" he encouraged. "If ye are brave ye will not allow anything to frighten ye. Ye can conquer yer fears! Dadda will always be by yer side to help ye!" Waiting, observing his words sinking in, Eamon continued. "Do ye understand?"

Quinn affirmed, nodding. Eamon took the boy's other hand. "Ye have nothing to fear because I will always look after ye."

Quinn showed a reluctant smile. "Papa, I have missed you. I do not feel safe when you are away," the small boy confessed. Even though the dogs will bite someone if they hurt us," Quinn said in earnest. Eamon's heart melted. Quinn threw his arms around his father's neck and Eamon cuddled him, heart breaking as he knew that he would have to leave them again soon. He held him at arm's length, smoothing his coal-black hair. "If there are times when Dadda's business requires me to go away for a while, ye all can join me. In Florida, there is Disney World! Mummy and I can take all youse."

Quinn took a couple of seconds to think about it. He smiled. "My friend Robertson at school has been there, twice. To Paris and Tokyo!"

Eamon rose to his full height. "Ye will be able to tell him all about Disney in Orlando, Florida." Eamon smiled at him. "Would ye like to join me in the pool later? I need a swim. No racing. Ye boys always beat me!"

Quinn inhaled before answering, "I will change into my swimming trunks!"

"Grand!" Eamon stated. Then he left Quinn's room to go speak with Niall.

Niall stood up from where he was sitting on the bed when Eamon entered. Eamon closed the door and crossed the room. He sat at the end of the bed next to Niall and exhaled, shaking his head. Niall looked straight past his father's shoulder, avoiding his gaze. "Look at me, son," Eamon said, "I need to speak wit ye." Again, as he had with Quinn, he spoke gently but firmly. Niall held his father's eyes, without blinking. "I am not going to go over what ye did to Quinn while on Dom's boat in Marbella. Ye are aware of it. I am not going to listen to any excuses for ye behaviour, Niall, because there are no excuses for doing something like that. Do ye understand me?"

Niall nodded, unmoving, unblinking.

"How many times do ye tink that I am going to warn ye?" Eamon left the question hanging. "Do ye want me to separate ye from yer brother? Send youse to different schools? Would that suit yer?" Eamon saw Niall's dark eyes glaze over. "Answer me!" he directed, without raising his voice.

Niall said quietly. "No, Papa."

Eamon pressed on. "I am trying to discover what would make ye happy because ye do not appear to like Quinn. Perhaps if ye went to another school away from him, maybe ye won't feel as if ye want to hurt him?" Eamon paused for a few seconds. "I have a younger brother, Patrick. I would do anything for him, as he would for me." Eamon stood up. "The ball is in yer court, Niall. The decision is yers, because I will not tolerate any of my children hurting one another!" Eamon waited.

"I'm sorry!" Niall muttered.

"I hope that ye mean it, Niall. Ye've really crossed the line this time. Ye could have killed yer brother!" He let his words sink in before turning to leave. "Change into ye swim wear for the pool before yer evening meal!"

Niall nodded, looking down at the floor.

A while later, Marcia came out of the nursery. The girls had been bathed and were now asleep. She hesitated at the terrace doors. Eamon was swimming with Niall and Quinn all three were laughing as they splashed about. She knew that Eamon let the boys beat him in the race.

"Double or quits!" Eamon called out. They raced to try to catch up with him. She saw him slow down as both boys touched the end of the pool simultaneously. He nodded his head, smiling and said "Twenty euros each. See youse in my office later where I will pay yer winnings!"

Eamon walked up the steps and out of the pool. Marcia held a towel out for him. He took it and wrapped it around himself, following her to the table on the terrace. Marcia tilted her head. Eamon smiled at her, drying his hair. "How did you manage to convince Quinn to go back into the water?" Marcia asked cheerily.

"They are of my loins!" he laughed. "My sons will not be afraid of anything. Quinn agreed wit me!" he teased. Sitting down, he pulled her onto his lap. Marcia rained kisses across his face. "I am tired," he declared, kissing her lightly. "My night has not even begun. I am due at the club tonight. Dan deserves to have some time off wit Cindy. Both have been flat out wit me being away." He picked up his phone off the table and checked the time.

"I can give you a relaxing massage before you leave," Marcia said, pressing her breasts into his chest. "With extras," she added, smiling "It may rejuvenate you."

Eamon stretched, locking his hands behind his head.

"I will do all the work while you relax," she purred as she felt the bulge beneath her increase.

Eamon momentarily closed his eyes while Marcia discreetly fondled his forming erection. "I have a new black dress that you will like, with a top of the thigh hemline that will reveal scarlet-red silk ouvert panties." She cocked her head, eyebrow arched.

"Sold!" he smiled, opening his eyes. He glanced at the boys who were batting a ball to one another in the pool. Quinn hit it with force, Niall leapt, increasing the power of the return, skimming his brother's ear. Oblivious to Niall's intention, Quinn smiled swimming after the missile. Eamon glared when Niall looked his father's way. Eamon gave Niall a sharp nod, dark eyes fixed on his son with a warning. *The boy cannot help himself. He has always got to best his brother,* he thought, turning his attention back to Marcia.

Eamon lay on the bed, arms behind his head, waiting for Marcia to change into something more comfortable. He had checked on the children. All were asleep. Marcia had told him earlier that Martha, the eldest of the two Irish sisters who worked as dancers at the club, had confided in Marcia that she was pregnant. Benny Harris was the father, but he was in the dark regarding the pregnancy. Marcia had pressed Eamon to tell Benny. Billy had also informed Eamon that Benny Harris was contemplating leaving the Hawk Wind club security team. He aimed to return to the Middle East where he had a pal who offered him a job on a security team for a rich Arab. However, Eamon was reluctant to interfere in the couple's lives.

Billy also revealed that Brady, Sandy Lord's 16-year-old son was in a relationship with Martha's nineteen-year-old sister, Bridie, and that Scott Lord was not very happy about it, because Scott had discovered that Bridie was three months pregnant.

Eamon sucked air through his teeth. *I have enough on my plate to contend with without others' problems,* he silently concluded, when Marcia's entrance into the bedroom brought him back to the moment. He turned onto his side, elbow bent, hand supporting his head. "How long do ye tink that I will be able to last wit ye looking so hot in that skimpy dress?" he asked, running his eyes over her. "At a guess, I would judge that ye have no more than a yard of material on." A flash of red panties caught his attention. He turned onto his back, observing.

Marcia's stilettos clicked across the marble tiles. She smiled at his erection. "I have an oil that stimulates sexual desire." She held up the small bottle clasped in her palm.

"I tink that ye wasted yer money," Eamon said, indicating his rock-solid shaft. He adjusted himself.

She smiled and placed one knee on the bed. "Turn onto your front. Relax!" she directed.

Obeying, Eamon spread-eagled onto his front, head turned in profile. Marcia removed the high heels and straddled him. Eamon groaned with pleasure when her flesh made contact with his. Massage oil trickled down his back to the crevice of his buttocks. "Mmm," he murmured, barely audible when her fingers and thumbs expertly kneaded the knots in his back.

Marcia slid the shoestring straps off her shoulders, revealing a cupless bra. She shimmied the hemline of the dress above her waist as she moved up his body, rubbing the liquid into the nape of his neck. Eamon closed his eyes, sinking deeper into the soft mattress while she began to release the tension in his shoulders. Eamon relished the feeling that her fingers gave him. Leaning across his broad shoulders, she began to massage his head. He sighed at the sensual contact of her nipples brushing against his skin.

He slowly turned over, supporting her. "Marcia, ye could not imagine the amount of restraint that—"

She did not give him time to finish, rising enough for him to enter her, her hand guiding. As he gradually filled her, she began to move with slow deliberate movements, pelvic muscles taut, enhancing gratification, head thrown back riding him.

Eamon lay on the pillow, observing her, taking her hands in his, matching her rhythm. Then, in one swift movement, he pulled her into his chest, hands firmly clasping her buttocks and without withdrawing, he was above her, arms either side of her head. "There has been no other woman that can fulfil me as ye do!" he whispered in her ear. Tongue meeting tongue, heart rates rising, pace heightening, they reached the peak. Clamping her within his powerful thighs, increasing the measured motion, feeling them synchronise, he took her with him.

Eamon sat behind his desk at the Hawk Wind club. Although Dan was having time off, Eamon was expecting him to come in to discuss Scott Lord's attack. He had not bothered locking the office door. There was a firm rap at the door. Eamon called out to enter. Benny Harris came in and closed the door behind him. "Lock it!" Eamon smiled, proffering the chair opposite him. He thought that Benny appeared perturbed. Dark circles under his eyes indicated a lack of sleep. Eamon sat up, forearms resting on the desk.

"I think that I have done my time in Spain. Time to move on." Benny stated, shifting in his seat and giving a wistful smile, which Eamon noted was not that of someone eager to move on. "I hope that it does not inconvenience you, boss."

Eamon pursed his lips. He knew that Benny and Scott Lord had worked together in the past, renewing their association in Spain. The men, although not close, had a camaraderie. Eamon was surprised that Benny would up sticks, not knowing whether Scott would survive. Eamon guessed that his reasons for leaving ran deep.

"Ye are an asset to me, Benny. I cannot lie. If there is anything that I can do to keep ye on my payroll I will do it!"

Benny nodded, however, Eamon sensed that he had made his decision. "I am booked on a Qatar Airways flight in three days."

Eamon slowly nodded, wondering why there was a rush to leave so soon. He held his hand out and Benny shook it, smiling thinly.

"I wish ye all the best. Dan will sort out the money that yer owed." Eamon said. Benny rose to leave. Eamon exhaled, fighting with his conscience about enlightening him regarding Martha and the pregnancy. He leaned back into the office chair, studying Benny. "Ye can tell me to mind my own business. Nonetheless, my wife informed me that Martha the Irish dancer confided in her that she was pregnant. The girl was tearful!"

Eamon ran his fingers over his goatee beard. He continued, "Apparently, Martha told her that ye are the baby's father!"

If Benny was shocked, he did not show it, however, that did not fool Eamon. The two men held one another's look.

"Martha is with a young dark-haired fella," Benny countered. "I've seen her leave the club a couple of times arm in arm with him."

Eamon took note that Benny had not denied sleeping with Martha.

"The lad she has been seeing is her younger brother Liam. Martha told my wife. He found Martha by chance when he stopped off here, before continuing on his worldly travels." Eamon left it in the air. The ball was now in Benny's court. Eamon felt that he had done his bit.

Eamon observed Benny inhale. Benny slowly nodded twice. "I will sort it!" Benny stated with a fleeting smile. Both men nodded.

Eamon sent Marcia a text, I have done as you wished. I have passed on the information regarding Martha. Benny Harris said as he left that he would sort it, sending three emoji love hearts.

Marcia immediately replied, Thank you. I love you, including five love hearts. He smiled to himself. A loud knock on the door brought him back to the here and now. "Come in!" he said.

Dan entered, locking the door behind him and taking a seat. "The security team have seen the footage of the two assailants. No one recognised them. However, one of the men seemed to recall a lad getting mouthy with Scott, but nothing came of it after Scott gave him a warning. He said that was the end of it. Nothing to warrant a retaliation. Nevertheless, when these kids are 'coked up' who knows how their minds work!"

Eamon sucked air through his teeth, slowly nodding. "It's looking like that. Maybe the pair of wankers had taken umbrage at being given a bollocking from Scott. Hence the attack."

Dan took out his phone. Clicking on the photos, he passed it to Eamon. "I took some close-up pictures from the frames of the footage. Although it's dark, you can make out their faces."

After studying the pictures, Eamon said, "Send them to me."

Dan pressed send.

"Enjoy the rest of ye time off, and I'll speak to ye later," Eamon said.

Dan raised his hand, taking his leave.

After Dan left, Eamon sat with his forearms on his desk, fingers drumming and contemplating Scott's attackers. He decided that he would make another call when he returned home. Even though it would be an ungodly hour, he knew that Big Dave Broadbent would take the call. He wanted to arrange a meet-up with him and show Dave the pictures of the two attackers. Eamon used a few coastal areas early in the mornings whenever he met Big Dave. This time, he decided upon Cova del Barber, classified as one of the hidden gems for tourists along the coastline on the outskirts of Benidorm. Nevertheless, he knew from experience that in the early hours of their clandestine meetings, they would be guaranteed isolation.

5

Martha wrapped a dressing gown around her upon hearing the knock at her apartment door. She felt tired, as sleep was evading her. For the most part, Martha was a peacekeeper. She normally let her younger sister Bridie take advantage of her, due to the pair's unhappy childhood. Martha was the one who coped with any problems. However, of late, she felt annoyed at her sister's selfish ways. Bridie had taken to staying out late with new pals that she told Martha she had met in a café in Calpe. Martha sensed that she was lying but was trying to give her the benefit of the doubt. She wanted to chastise her for not taking her key with her, but she knew that she would not say anything. Bridie would just turn the tables on her, blaming her for bringing them to Spain from London. She would not upset her younger sister. Exhaling, she opened the door. Martha stood gobsmacked, mouth agape.

Benny cocked his head to one side, smiling. "Can I come in, Martha?"

Without replying, Martha stepped to one side, holding his look. Benny entered the small lounge and stood facing her. "Why didn't you tell me that you are pregnant?"

Martha looked away, without answering. He reached for her, fingers gently cupping her chin, easing her face towards him. "Martha, I am booked to fly out to the Middle East in three days. A new job, a new life!"

Martha's green eyes watered, and she looked down, remaining silent.

Benny continued, "Please, look at me." He raised her chin.

Her green eyes brimming with tears, she complied. "Martha, I would have left Spain without knowing that you are carrying my child!" He put a finger on her lips when she started to speak. "I know that I previously told you that I am too old for you, however, it didn't prevent you from getting into my head. I can't sleep at night since the time we were together. That was the reason that I was leaving. I also discovered that the good-looking fella that you have been leaving the club with is your brother." Pausing for two seconds, he plunged right in. "The anguish of wanting you was something that I have never experienced before! The only way that I thought to ease the pain was to bury myself in work thousands of miles across the globe. Not that I was not fooling myself that I wouldn't carry you in my heart no matter where I roamed."

Benny reached for Martha's red curls at the nape of her neck, which had escaped the top knot, playing his fingers in the silkiness of her hair, holding her look. "But now that I have discovered that I am going to be a father again..." When they had spent the night together he had told her about his ex-wife taking his young daughter with her when she had left him. "I am thrilled. I want us to be together, Martha!" That is if you want me in your life."

Martha stiffened, her voice taking on a serious note, "Benny, I planned to have your baby on my own, thinking that you did not want me." She hesitated, then confessed, "However, I knew I would always have a part of you in my life."

He smiled and replied, "I am pleased that you did become pregnant. It gave me the kick up the rear I needed. I was putting my principals before my happiness, which was due to my worries about our age difference." Smiling, he embraced her. "Although I am no catch for someone like you, I will care for and look after you and our child."

Beaming, Martha threw her arms around his neck.

Benny laughed at her enthusiasm. He lifted her, cupping her buttocks. Her legs clamped around his waist. Her mouth found his, as he carried her towards the bedroom.

....

Eamon smiled to himself as he drove home in the early hours of the morning after finishing for the night at the Hawk Wind club. Benny Harris had phoned him asking for his job back. He'd said that he had cancelled his move to the Middle East. He had sorted things out with Martha and was staying on in Spain. Benny had said that he and Martha were going to make a go of it.

Eamon was pleased that Benny had retracted his decision to leave his security team. He valued his loyalty, and Marcia would be happy that Martha's situation was now resolved. He remembered Marcia's previous prediction that his two security men Scott Lord and Benny Harris would end up in relationships with the two pole dancers Martha and Sandy. He had to admit that Marcia was spot on the money, although her mystical bent unnerved him. He hoped too that Scott would survive his ordeal, as Marcia had also predicted.

He rolled the window down even though the chill air of early October wrapped its tendrils around him while he drove up the Altea Hills. His baby girls' second birthday was approaching. His sons were seven and eight years old. He had lived on the edge for so long, forever being on the back foot, waiting to receive the proverbial tap on the shoulder from the Law. Although the drumbeat that informs the criminal world when any trouble looms had been quiet of late, Eamon knew that he couldn't ever let his guard down and he was constantly looking over his shoulder. He had been thinking about taking his family to New Zealand. The clean air of the beautiful country appealed to him. It was a fanciful thought though. Maybe one day in the future when the children have all flown the nest, he mused.

He put the key in the front door lock and opened the door. The two dogs were waiting for him, their tails wagging. Across the large lounge, he could see a low light filtering from under their bedroom door. Removing his shoes and suit jacket he quietly eased the ajar door.

He smiled at Marcia who was lying on the bed wrapped in a cream silk negligee embroidered with peacocks. She returned his smile, putting the book that she was reading on the bedside cabinet. He stood framed in the doorway, observing her. I would not trade this vision of her waiting for me for all my vast financial fortune, he thought, crossing the room. He sat on the bed. Neither of them spoke as they reached for one another.

....

Scott Lord had not been showing any signs of improvement, and the prognosis was looking dire as he remained in a coma. However, to Eamon's amazement at 23:46, twelve days after the attack, Scott's fingers slightly moved, touching Sandy's hand as she continually held it while she sat keeping vigil over him. A few minutes later, Scott had slowly opened his eyes. Sandy, crying tears of joy, had called for the nurse. An elated Sandy telephoned Marcia early the following morning to inform her of Scott's remarkable recovery. Eamon had teased Marcia when she had predicted that Scott Lord would soon return to health. The blood clot in his brain that was causing the problem had dispersed. He was now able to sit up and he could receive visitors.

Eamon had his security men, along with Big Dave Broadbent on the case. They had made numerous enquiries regarding Scott's two assailants, to no avail. Nevertheless, Eamon was not about to give up. He was tenacious in seeking the pair out. He would ensure that no stone would be left unturned.

Two days later, after closing time at the Hawk Wind club, Benny Harris invited some of the other security men to a drink at Irish Michael's bar to celebrate him becoming a father once again. Eamon and Benny's work colleagues had noticed the positive change in Benny ever since he had discovered that Martha was pregnant with his child. Dan, Billy, Jackie Cooper, Thomas Harper-Watts and a jubilant Benny Harris got out of a taxi outside of Irish Michael's bar on the seafront promenade. All the men were in high spirits, apart from Jackie Cooper, whose marriage had recently hit a sticky patch ever since he had relocated to Spain. Nevertheless, the rest of the men were in good spirits. They were all chuffed that their pal Scott Lord was on the road to recovery.

On the opposite side of the road, near the beach, a few blocks back from Irish Michael's bar, Kenny Whittle and his cousin Dwain Sherper were on their way home. Both young men were high on cocaine. Earlier the pair had been thrown out of a party. They were laughing and, Kenny, as per usual, was bragging about his sexual conquests earlier that night. The normally introverted and studious Dwain was no longer in awe of his good-looking, streetwise cousin Kenny from Liverpool, who had been staying with his family for six weeks. Dwain continued to feed his cousin's ego, but he knew that it wasn't going to be for much longer. Kenny's six-week visit was coming to an end. Dwain didn't normally smoke, drink alcohol or take drugs, but that all changed when his cousin came to stay with his family in Spain. Dwain had been in awe of Kenny when he first arrived, admiring his good looks, charisma and luck with the opposite sex. However, Dwain grew tired of the constant drama that Kenny instigated. That night at the party, two women had begun a catfight in the bedroom, both vying for Kenny's attention, until another girl burst in to see what all the commotion was about. Mayhem ensued when all three realised that Kenny had seduced them all, leading to his eviction from the party. Kenny Whittle had his arm around Dwain's shoulders and was going into detail about his sexual conquests that night when his attention was diverted by the men's laughter on the other side of the road. Stopping in his tracks, he slammed his free arm across Dwain's chest. "Fucking have a look at who it is!" Kenny exclaimed.

Dwain didn't look up. He wasn't wearing a jacket and his white shirt was being whipped in the strong gusts of wind that blew in from the Mediterranean shoreline. He felt cold and tired. All he wanted was to go home. Kenny grabbed his cousin's jawline, twisting his head, making him focus, pointing towards the group of men who were banging on the door of the Irish bar.

Dwain just about caught the gist of his cousin's Liverpool slang. He always struggled to decipher his cousin's meaning. Although Dwain's mother Brenda was raised in Liverpool, her scouse accent was watered down because she had left Merseyside at the age of seventeen when she had met Dwain's father Alec Sherper. In the early 1960s, Alec had come to the world-famous Cavern club with his dad and two pals from Brixton to see his idol Gerry and The Pacemakers play.

Kenny clenched his fists and fumed, "THAT FUCKING OLD HAS-BEEN PIT BULL!" Leaning closer, he forced Dwain to turn his head. "THAT'S THE OLD CUNT THAT JUMPED US IN THE HAWK WIND CLUB CAR PARK!"

Dwain flinched, twisting free of his hold when Kenny shouted in his ear. The howling wind carried his words away. To appease his cousin, Dwain looked towards the group of the last, as the men filed into the bar. Dwain was exhausted. He was unused to the late, narcotic-fuelled life that his cousin Kenny seemed to thrive on.

Kenny had invited himself to stay at Dwain's parents' home for a holiday. Although Dwain had at first enjoyed Kenny's company, Kenny's constant bragging about his powerful crime boss father in Liverpool, who, he said, reigned supreme, started to wear thin. Furthermore, Dwain had to endure Kenny's daily reportage about his girlfriends back in the UK. However, he had to admit that Kenny's good looks and charm had got them invited to a lot of parties with women, which he otherwise would have been too shy to attend.

Dwain wanted to return to the normality of studying to be a mechanic, as his father had been. His dad's wish had been for Dwain to become a racing driver. Dwain knew that his expertise in handling his father's vintage Mustang at high speed could put him up there with the top drivers. Dwain's mother, Brenda doted on her younger brother Kenny, and she was also very fond of his son, young Kenny. However, Dwain soon realised that young Kenny had flattery down to a fine art, which he used on his aunty Brenda. She fell for it hook, line and sinker.

"We are going to get your dad's gun that you said he kept in a drawer by his bed," Kenny said. Upon seeing Dwain's jaw drop, Kenny firmly held his cousin's arm, all the while coaxing. "Don't worry, our kid, I am only going to terrorise the bastard. Do you think that I'd be stupid enough to gun down that ancient prick? You and I have Whittle blood. I want to show him who he's dealing with!" Kenny said.

Dwain said nothing, he picked up his pace, trying to release himself from his cousin's grip.

"I promise that it'll be no more than a frightener," Kenny said.

Dwain reluctantly nodded his head.

Kenny added excitedly, "We will use your old man's motor. I'll fucking show them that they can't mess with me!"

Dwain stopped dead, adamant to make a stand, his voice quavering, he said, "There is no way that I am touching my dad's Mustang. That car is his baby!" Dwain's show of bravado wavered when Kenny angrily lifted him by his shirt collar and stood inches from his face.

"Do I need to keep reminding you about the Whittle blood in your veins?" Kenny shoved Dwain, causing him to stumble, then grabbed his arm to prevent him from falling. Changing tactics, he patted Dwain's shoulder, linking his arm through his. "Cuz, I'm going home soon. Play the game, our kid. Just help me with this one last favour," Kenny wheedled.

Dwain reluctantly agreed. "I mean this. I know how to handle the car, and I will drive it," he stated, while Kenny urged him on. Dwain just wanted to get it over with and get to his bed.

Kenny scoffed, "Fucking Lewis Hamilton the second. That's all I've heard ever since I arrived in Spain from dear old uncle Alec." Mimicking Dwain's dad, Kenny said, "My Dwain has what it takes to be a top Gran Prix champion. I taught my boy all there is to know about motors!" Putting his arm through Dwain's he coaxed, "Come on! I am only joking. I know that your dad is proud of your skills. Let's leg it quickly the mile to your mum's place! Once I pay that old has-been back, I am heading straight back to Liverpool!"

Dwain felt spurred on by the thought that his cousin would soon be leaving Spain. The pair hot-footed it along Altea's promenade to the Old Town so Kenny Whittle could carry out his revenge.

Dwain stealthily moved across his parents' bedroom. He glanced at the snoring couple, their mouths wide open, like frogs catching flies. He prayed that they wouldn't wake up. He opened the bedside cabinet drawer and silently pulled out the pistol. He knew that his dad kept it loaded in case they were burgled. He took two more bullets from the box beside the weapon. Retracing his steps, he quietly shut the bedroom door. At the front door, he took the Mustang car keys that were hanging on the rack. He quietly closed the door behind him. Kenny was waiting on the front steps, smoking a joint. He grinned when he was handed the Heckler & Koch USP German pistol.

"Be careful, it's loaded!" Dwain stated, moving to the garage.

Kenny smirked, admiring the weapon. "My old man has an arsenal of shooters!" he stated, weighing the compact firearm in his hand.

"Whatever!" Dwain muttered, nervously putting the key in the ignition to his dad's most prized possession the Ford fourth generation fastback GT coupe Mustang. He fired up the finely tuned V8 cylinder engine, and it purred to life as he skilfully drove out of the garage. Dwain felt exasperated to the extreme now that the effect of the cocaine had worn off. He just wanted to get this business over with. The only thing that motivated him was knowing that in a short while, Kenny would be leaving Spain and he could carry on with his ambitions. He was going to take his father's advice and become a qualified mechanic and take up professional racetrack driving. His dad had taught him all there was to know about vehicles. Dwain had become a skilled driver with his dad's tuition, and he could handle the Mustang like a professional.

Without taking his eyes off the road, he warned Kenny, "Remember the law in Spain. Being in possession of a weapon carries a heavy sentence. There is zero tolerance! Out here you will get the book thrown at you for having that gun on you!" Dwain tried to drive home the seriousness of what his cousin could face.

Kenny scoffed, "Do it look like I give a monkey's? I grew up around firearms. My old man trades in shooters with the Africans and the Middle Eastern!"

His boasting fell on deaf ears. No matter the subject, Kenny had to best it. Dwain just concentrated on the fact that soon Kenny would be gone from his life.

"This is a baby compared to what I'm used to!" Kenny indicated the gun, raising it towards the windscreen.

Nerves taught as a bow string, Dwain shouted, "Put that away. It's bloody loaded!"

Kenny laughed, placing the weapon on the floor. "Stop being paranoid. I know what I'm doing!" Kenny said, tapping Dwain's knee in reassurance. "Once you park along the promenade along from the bar, we'll have a clear view in the moon's bright light. We may be in for a bit of a wait, but we can have some 'white' to help keep us on our toes!"

Dwain, inhaled, vowing to himself that it would be the last time that he would use cocaine. However, he knew that he needed to be alert and that he would need the narcotic that his cousin had introduced him to. It hadn't taken Kenny long after arriving in Spain to meet a dealer when the pair had gone out clubbing.

The men in Irish Michael's bar had been reminiscing about their time in the Special Forces and some of their missions. Thomas Harper-Watts had been an officer and had been Dan and Billy's boss. They were all laughing and ribbing one another about the high jinxes that they had got up to, which Thomas Harper-Watts hadn't ever reported. They recalled the camaraderie that they had shared. However, for the most part, Jackie Cooper was just getting quietly drunk, keeping his thoughts to himself.

A while later, Jackie began bemoaning his lot regarding his marriage. Dan frowned, listening to Jackie Cooper's revelation about his wife Yvette's disloyalty. Billy caught Dan's look. Jackie, two sheets to the wind, leaned precariously on the barstool. To his left, Thomas held him up. Jackie grinned. "Men stick together!" he slapped Thomas on the arm. "Loyalty. That's all we ask from our women!" Shaking his head, Jackie slurred, "My wife Yvette is having it off with her Jamaican Muay Thai instructor. You don't need to use your imagination to know that he's not just giving her lessons in self-defence. I know for a fact that he's giving her far more than personal training! I tailed the pair!" he revealed to the room.

The men inhaled, remaining silent.

Jackie Cooper continued, "My wife's boss, Suzette at the Mystique beauty salon, covers for her. I have watched them on many occasions."

Dan intercepted, "Come on mate!" he smiled, moving alongside Jackie and putting his hand on his arm.

Thomas put a supportive arm around Jackie's shoulders. Jackie shrugged him off. "What sort of fucking stupid prick am I?"

Jackie's forefinger stabbed at his chest as he spoke. "Do you know what boys?" he asked, scanning the men. "I can't believe that I'm standing for it."

The men's sympathy for their pal's situation was palpable, although no one spoke. "I'd like to take the bastard out. I know that I should just walk out on Yvette." He looked at each man for confirmation. They gave none. "That's what blokes like us would do!" He pointed a forefinger at each of the men. His head slumped onto his chest. Thomas and Dan grabbed him, holding him fast. He leered into their faces. "I love the woman!"

Irish Michael mouthed, "Taxi."

Dan nodded as he and Thomas helped Jackie towards the door.

The promenade was deserted apart from the iconic white with two red-stripes, vintage Ford Mustang GT that could go from zero to 60 mph in 4.4 seconds.,

Dwain and Kenny sat in the car, watching and waiting. All eateries and bars were closed, and litter blew in the wind and tumbled across the road. White-capped waves tossed fishing boats in the bay. Kenny had insisted on giving Dwain more cocaine to keep him awake. Suddenly, Kenny sat bolt upright when the door of the Irish bar opened and a man came out and put a cigarette to his lips, keeping it there, without lighting it. Kenny punched Dwain's arm. "Fire it up!" he commanded, without taking his eyes from the bar, watching the man who was looking out to sea. A couple of minutes later, two more men, supporting a third who appeared to be in a drunken stupor, came out.

"That old cunt is occupied. Bad move!" Kenny guffawed as he reached for the gun. Positioning himself in readiness, left-hand finger on the trigger, he weighed up his target.

"Don't aim at them!" Dwain shouted.

"Fucking see to your driving. Leave this little mob to me!" Kenny snarled.

Dwain obeyed, the car silently crawling, the finely tuned engine quietly moving towards the unsuspecting men.

Benny Harris, who was struggling to quit smoking, took the unlit cigarette and threw it into the gutter. It was a habit that he was determined to break, now that Martha was going to have his child. He was going to get his act together he wanted to enjoy what years he had left with his new family. He had told Martha that they should get married before the baby was born, and she had eagerly agreed. Benny was suddenly shaken from his thoughts. A movement in his right peripheral vision caused him to look in that direction.

"DOWN!" he commanded. Two shots rang out as the other three men obeyed the order. Jackie Cooper's reaction time was slowed by the amount of alcohol he had consumed and he groaned as he took a hit.

Dwain, realising that Kenny was aiming, put his foot down on the accelerator.

The Guardia Civil officers patrolling the sea front heard the first shot. Tyres screeching, they flew along the promenade, and seeing a man slumped on the ground with others in attendance, guessed that he'd been shot. However, they could see that the other men were looking at his right shoulder. "No pares!" the officer in the passenger seat ordered his partner, who was driving. Glancing at the group of men, he could see that the one on the ground was moving. The officer put out an APB order, reading out the number plate of the car ahead while his partner gained ground on the speeding car.

Hands clapping, adrenaline pumping, Kenny turned round in his seat, laughing at the police car following behind. Heading northeast, the Mustang reached the N-332. Dwain did not require direction. He knew exactly where to go. He took the exit towards the A-150 for a couple of kilometres, then merged onto the AP-7. He was gaining ground as the chasing car dropped further back.

Kenny shouted, "Put your foot down my old Grand Prix Formula One expert!" egging Dwain on, not that Dwain needed any encouragement, knowing that they were in serious trouble. The thought of his father's anger at stealing the car, more than the trouble that lay ahead if they were caught by the Guardia Civil, is what pushed him on. The Ford Mustang V-8 American muscle car went from zero to 60 in seconds. Pressing on the gas pedal, Dwain used perfected driving skills that his dad would have been proud of in any other circumstances. He was certainly putting his expertise to the test. The clear AP-7 road in the early morning was to Dwain's advantage. Dwain shouted, without taking his eyes from the road, for Kenny to put his seat belt on. Although Kenny was whooping with excitement, he did not need to be told twice; the speedometer made its way towards 150 miles per hour. Dwain prayed that the Guardia would not be able to match his driving skills.

Pure adrenaline fuelled Dwain on towards Denia. The car flew around hairpin bends. There was no sign of the police car as Dwain approached Montgo mountain. Dwain's only hope had been if he could gain enough ground, he would be able to hide the car in a property that his father had previously purchased with the thought of moving inland. However, his wife Brenda, who wore the trousers in the marriage, had put the dampener on the move. Hence, it was up for sale. Seeing that he was clear of the Guardia, Dwain made a left. Driving through iron gates that remained open, he pulled into the driveway. Jumping out, he opened the double garage doors.

Kenny clapped Dwain on the back. Dwain ignored him. Dropping to the ground on all fours he vomited, then sat up, hands covering his eyes.

Kenny, who had begun to walk away, returned, dragging Dwain to his feet, and supporting him. "Let's get behind those trees! If we are spotted by the Law. We're in the shit!"

"I need water!" Dwain mumbled as Kenny rough-handled him. Upon reaching a thicket in the grounds, Dwain slumped against a large fig tree. Kenny shook him, saying "You're not the only one who needs a drink. Stop thinking about yourself for once!" Head flopping to one side, Dwain drifted into unconsciousness. Kenny, sneered, "Fucking stay there you selfish twat! Once I get back to your place, I'm getting a taxi to the airport. Don't forget to say that we haven't seen each other since the party!" Moving towards the gates, he turned and upon seeing Dwain appearing comatose, said, "Some fucking fun you are. Don't think that I will be returning to Spain. Give me Merseyside anytime!" leaving the dehydrated Dwain to his fate.

It did not take the Guardia Civil long to find Jackie Cooper in the local hospital. Dan had instructed Billy and Thomas Harper-Watts that if anyone was questioned by the police to say that they had not seen the shooter. The men would sort him out later. He instructed them to return home, saying that he would deal with any police enquiries.

The two officers appeared satisfied when Dan convinced the pair that the shooting happened too fast. He explained that the men were celebrating as one of their wives was having a baby. Dan knew that Spanish men were family oriented and loved children. Both officers smiled. The older of the two, who spoke clearer English, informed Dan that the offenders would eventually be apprehended. He said that the Guardia had the number plate of the Mustang.

Fortunately, the hospital was quiet. A surgeon was called, and Dan waited while Jackie Cooper underwent a shoulder arthroscopy to retrieve the embedded bullet. A while later, the doctor informed Dan that the surgery had been successful and the nurse was dressing the wound and putting Jackie's arm in a sling. Dan went outside and called Eamon's number.

Eamon and Marcia had had very little sleep. The time was 8:18 am and the beginning of the sunrise filtered through the bedroom shades. The boys were home from school for the weekend. Eamon cradled Marcia in his arms while she slept. The previous evening, Eamon had taken Marcia to the edge of ecstasy, controlling his desire to join her. After pleasuring her, he had raised her legs to his shoulders – tongue teasing, fingers aiding, bringing her once more to the point of no return. Marcia's body bucked beneath him as she cried out, urging him to enter her. He lowered her legs down from his shoulders, and positioned himself above her, eagerly filling her, tongue seeking tongue, deepening their pleasure. The finality of their frenzied lovemaking raised the heat in the bedroom. They remained entwined in the same position, him inside her, slowly shrinking after their powerful union. Eamon smiled to himself while he mused, "I have the complete package."

Marcia had told him "You have given me four beautiful babies. You protect us. To add to that, I desire you as much as I did from our first encounter."

Eamon felt guilty about not telling her that he would be leaving for the three-month stint in Miami. He didn't know how they would be able to withstand the separation. Eamon's mobile phone on the bedside cabinet rang, bringing him back to the moment. Sitting up, he saw Dan's number and sensed that there was a problem for him to call so early in the morning.

"Sorry to disturb you, boss. However, I knew that you would want to know that there was a spot of trouble when we left Michael's bar in the early hours. A drive-by shooter took a pot shot at us. Jackie Cooper was hit. Although, thankfully, it was only his left shoulder. I got a taxi to take us to Benidorm hospital. A surgeon was contacted and, within a couple of hours, Jackie was on the road to recovery. Nevertheless, he will be out of the game for a while, but no sweat. I'll find a replacement until he can return to work."

Shocked, Eamon eased his arm away from Marcia and got up from the bed. While supporting the mobile phone under his chin, he slipped on his dressing gown and tied the belt around his waist. He left the room quietly, so as not to wake Marcia and headed outside to the terrace. Both dogs followed. He shook his head at the turn of events. "Ye are fucking joking! How is he in himself? Poor bastard," Eamon asked, concerned. Eamon closed the doors after the dogs and moved towards the terrace table.

"Fortunately for him, he got off lightly. We all did. There were a couple of shots fired. Fucking unbelievable!" Dan said. "What with the attack on Scott Lord a while back, we now have a shooter!"

"Did you get a look at the guy?"

"It happened too fast. We all hit the floor on Benny's command. However, although it was only brief, I caught a glimpse of the shooter, as did Benny. Thankfully, Benny was the first one outside and had time to warn us. Thomas and I, along with Billy, were struggling to get Jackie out the door. He'd had had a skin full. He was legless. Benny had noticed movement from the corner of his eye, and, turning to look, he saw the car approach. Benny caught sight of the raised gun and the shooter. By then, we were all outside tending to Jackie who was having difficulty standing. Although we tried to cover him, he was slower to respond and he took the first shot. The other bullet hit the bar door frame!"

Eamon began pacing, running his fingers through his hair.

Dan continued, "Boss, I am not 100 per cent certain, but I would lay money on it that it was those two that I belted when they assaulted Scott Lord in the Hawk Wind car park. Benny is meeting me a bit later at the club to have a look at the video to confirm whether my instinct is right." Dan paused for two seconds. "I am concerned about Jackie." Dan paused again. "I took Jackie back to his place when he was out of the hospital. The villa was in darkness. His wife was not there to help him." Dan went on, "Earlier in the bar, while we were having a drink, Jackie began bemoaning his lot. His marriage is on the rocks. The more that Jackie drank, the further he went into detail about his wife's betrayal."

"Betrayal?" Eamon repeated.

Dan sucked air through his teeth. "Jackie told us that he was suspicious so he had been staking out his wife. He thinks Suzette is in cahoots with her and that she covers for Yvette when she has her clandestine meet-ups with Elliot!"

"The Jamaican Muay Thai trainer?" Eamon asked.

"That is who Jackie said it was, boss."

Eamon exhaled. "Let me know the outcome when ye check the video."

He turned upon hearing Marcia come out on the terrace with two coffee cups. She sat down opposite him, eyes questioning, sensing that something was wrong. She sipped the coffee. Eamon did not touch his.

"Have ye spoken to Suzette recently?" he asked her, flatly.

Marcia's eyes darted as she tried to read Eamon. "I went to the beauty salon to have a facial and body wrap yesterday. What is wrong?"

"Wrong!" he repeated. "Did Suzette let you in on her and Yvette Cooper's secret?" He held her eyes while she stayed silent.

"Eamon I—"

Eamon held his hand up, interjecting, "Marcia, please don't try to insult my intelligence, because I know that Suzette would have told ye. Don't dig yer own grave by lying!"

Marcia exhaled and Eamon continued. "While Jackie Cooper's wife and Elliot the Muay Thai trainer were having it off, yer pal Suzette covered for them so that she could deceive Jackie..." Eamon scoffed, "who, I might add, has been tailing his Yvette and her Jamaican lover. Jackie Cooper has been shot. Fortunately, it was only in the shoulder!" Marcia gasped, as Eamon continued coldly, "Dan took him home after Jackie had the bullet removed, and the villa was in darkness. That is what is wrong!" Betrayal!" he spat.

Marcia rose from the table, moving round to stand facing him. "Eamon, Suzette did tell me. But it isn't any of my business. You could not expect me to inform you. However, I asked her not to involve me by telling me the details!"

"But she did!" Eamon stated flatly, without wanting an answer. "Yer pal Suzette tinks that she is clever. Jackie Cooper has been trained in seeking out the enemy!"

Marcia knew that Eamon's anger was not directed at her. She moved a step closer to him, putting her palms on his chest.

He looked down at her and said, "I am not asking ye to betray a confidence, but please never lie to me. My men inform me of any misdemeanours within our circle, not to gossip. It enables me to run a tight ship."

"I understand," Marcia replied, raising a hand to the nape of his neck. He nodded, and his hand moved to her waist. "Is Jackie going to be alright?" she asked.

Eamon nodded slowly. He placed his other hand on the small of her back, holding her to him. Marcia felt his anger dissipating. He softly kissed the top of her head. Marcia knew that Yvette had been unhappy ever since the couple had relocated to Spain. Furthermore, she sensed that this crisis with Jackie Cooper would bring about a reconciliation and that Jackie would forgive Yvette for her indiscretion. However, Marcia knew that the men in their circle would not tolerate or forgive infidelity from their partners. Nevertheless, any dalliances among the men were swept under the carpet. She thought that this was unfair but she kept her thoughts to herself.

"I should tink that the man is broken!" Eamon stared out at the vista, appearing deep in thought. He slowly exhaled. "Suzette Greenaway is nobody's friend!" he declared. "The woman invites trouble!" he added.

Marcia remained silent, letting him get it off his chest.

"The children were sound asleep when I checked the monitor earlier. The girls were excited last night about their birthday party today." Marcia distracted him away from the subject of Suzette. "Quinn said that he had a surprise gift for them. He told me that he had saved his winnings from each race in the pool that he had beaten you at!"

Eamon smiled.

Marcia's fingertips moved along his jawline. "Do you want an extra hour in bed before the excitement begins?"

He exhaled, and took her by the hand, leading her back to the bedroom.

Slowly removing her dressing gown, she let it fall to the floor. Standing naked before her, Eamon lifted her small frame, placing her on the bed, covering her. Slowly paying homage down her body, loving her. Marcia returned the adoration. She was aware of Eamon's fear that she would betray him, as his dead wife, Eve, had. She aimed to quell any uncertainty in their relationship. There was no urgency, no observing from the floor-to-ceiling mirrors as they reached the peak. Synchronising, they flowed deeper into the chasm of their love.

....

Brenda Whittle-Sherper, Dwain's mother, was lying wide-awake in bed beside her still-sleeping husband Alec. She heard two distinctive, loud raps on the front door. She started, instinctively recognising the sound from her past when the Law beat the door at her parents' home in Liverpool to arrest her brother Kenny, who from a young age was a leader of a gang that the police were after. Alec opened one sleepy eye when she quickly rose from the bed. "Stay there!" she said.

Alec rolled over, returning to sleep. Snatching her housecoat, Brenda hurried, opening the boys' bedroom doors as she passed. Both beds hadn't been slept in. Mind racing, she went into acting mode upon opening the front door. Being brought up in Merseyside, with a brother who lived a life of crime, she had experience with dealing with the police. Fortunately, their mother regularly used the services of a local clairvoyant, who could prewarn of impending visits from the Law. Hence, nothing illegal was ever discovered. Not that it had prevented Kenny's arrest, but he was always released without being charged.

Brenda smiled. The two Guardia Civil officers standing on the steps, hands resting on holsters, did not return her warm welcome. Brenda prepared herself. "We would like to speak to Alec Sherper, the owner of..." the officer took out a notepad, reeling off the registration of a white Mustang.

Brenda put her hand up to her mouth, feigning surprise. "Don't tell me that the car has been stolen. I forgot to lock the garage and left the key in the ignition last night!" Her hand flew to her forehead "That car is my husband's baby!" She declared. "I take second place to his prized possession!" She smiled weakly. The officers did not smile back. "My husband is not a well man." She tapped the left side of her chest. Indicating her heart.

The officers' suspicious eyes scrutinised her. "The car was involved in a serious incident in the early hours, involving a shooting."

Brenda hid her shock.

"Two bullets were fired at a group of men outside a bar along the promenade. One man has been shot. The other bullet went astray," the older of the two officers who spoke English stated. He added, "However, this is an attempted murder offence!"

Brenda, slumping against the door frame, put both hands to her throat. "Good God!" she exclaimed.

The elder officer smiled smugly. "Whoever was driving the car outran our fast-response driver!" he said, shaking his head. "Our driver is one of the top men in that division. The driver of the Mustang was experienced in handling the vehicle, to the level of a professional racing driver." He took a notebook out of his top pocket and checked his notes. "It was reported that the Mustang reached speeds up to 240 kilometres per hour was reached!"

Brenda gasped for effect, however, she wasn't listening to him. Her mind was on her son Dwain and his cousin, young Kenny.

"The perpetrators have evaded us, for the moment," the elder Guardia threw in sternly. "I can assure you that we will leave no stone unturned in our search!" He gave Brenda a tight, half smile. Both officers sharply nodded and left.

Brenda shut the door and leaned against it for support, her mind in turmoil. She hurried upstairs to check Dwain and her nephew's beds once more. They had not been slept in. Her instinct informed her that Dwain was driving the car and young Kenny was the shooter. Sneaking across her bedroom while Alec soundly slumbered, she eased open the drawer of the bedside table where Alec kept the gun and bullets. The lid of the box was tilted, and the box was empty.

Brenda geared herself into action and went downstairs to telephone her brother Kenny in Liverpool. Her brother lived in the upmarket area of Beach Lawn in Liverpool in a Grade-2 listed, eight-bedroom Victorian property with his second wife, who had been brought up in the area, unlike Kenny. Victoria Whittle, upon marrying the big-time criminal, insisted that their two children go to private school. Also, Kenny, under Victoria's guidance, had dropped his Liverpool accent. Nevertheless, his snobbish wife did not insist that her man relinquish his position as the boss of the Merseyside criminal world. The rewards were too high.

Kenny Whittle answered his sister's phone call. Brenda reiterated what the Guardia Civil officer had just told her. She explained that both the boys had not been home. She said that the keys to the Mustang were always hung up on the hook in the hallway but that they were now missing. Gingerly, she said that Alec's gun was missing.

Dwain was Brenda's only child and she was prepared to fight for her son, and she knew that Big Kenny's pride and joy was his boy. Kenny was her brother's firstborn, from his first marriage. But Brenda wished that she had never agreed for young Kenny to stay with her family.

Kenny instructed her to try to discover who it was that was shot and to call him back. Brenda knew that it was young Kenny who must have coerced her introverted son into all this. She had previously thought that Kenny would bring Dwain out of his shell. The realisation set in as to how blind she had been, thinking that her brother's boy would have instilled confidence in her boy. Her eyes were now open. Young Kenny was a chip off the block. The apple had not fallen far from the tree, she concluded, gathering her thoughts. Brenda decided that she would break all family ties once her brother stepped in and removed his son from Spain.

Young Kenny had hitched a lift from a lorry driver who dropped him two kilometres from his aunty Brenda's home. Kenny spotted a police car up ahead parked on the same side of the road. He did not want to make it look too obvious by crossing over. Head down, he walked towards the vehicle. A metre clear of the car, Kenny heard a door slam. He continued walking.

"Detengase!" the Guardia officer roared his command.

Kenny did not speak or understand Spanish, however, he recognised the authoritative tone of an order. He stopped, turning and smiling at the officer, cocking an eyebrow. "Good morning!" he said cheerily as the policeman approached, hand on his artillery.

"English?" the officer questioned, dark-brown eyes holding Kenny's.

Kenny nodded.

"Address!"

Kenny reeled off his aunty Brenda's address. Unfortunately for Kenny, this officer was one of the two who had visited that same address a short while ago.

Kenny sat in the back of the police car, thoughts racing as to how to wriggle out of the predicament that he was facing. He acted dumb under interrogation by the officer. He said that he had been for an early morning stroll and got lost. The officer laughed in his face. Young Kenny was angry, and if this situation had been in England, he would have abused the policeman. However, his interrogator had a gun. He remained silent on the drive to the police station. Although Kenny knew that his aunty was savvy and streetwise, having been brought up in Liverpool, his aunt and uncle lived by the law. Nonetheless, his cousin Dwain was his aunt's Achilles heel, which he would use to his advantage.

At the police station, Kenny demanded to make a phone call. He was allowed one call. Kenny didn't want a lawyer. He phoned his aunty Brenda.

An ambulance arrived at the hospital with sirens wailing. Dwain Sherper was fighting for his life. He had been attached to a drip to prevent him from dying from severe dehydration. A man with his dog had gone for an early morning jog. At the gates to the vacant property, the Doberman's attention was drawn to a clump of bushes. The dog's barking brought the man to see what the animal was excited about. He was stunned by the discovery of a young lad by a tree in a comatose state. Feeling his pulse, the man immediately phoned for an ambulance.

Brenda Whittle-Sherper had received two phone calls in succession. One was from her nephew Kenny who was detained at the local police station, and the other shortly afterwards from the hospital regarding her son Dwain. She rushed to her boy's side. By the afternoon, Dwain rallied. He confessed all to his mother, who told him not to worry. Brenda placed a telephone call to Marcia O'Donally. Brenda had been a previous client. Marcia had previously predicted that there would be trouble with the Law. When Marcia answered, Brenda demanded to speak with her husband Eamon O'Donally. Brenda explained everything to Eamon, putting it to him that her brother Kenny Whittle would visit him in Spain to speak with him. Eamon agreed.

Benny Harris had identified the drive-by shooter in the Mustang from the club's security video from the night when Scott Lord was attacked in the car park. Dan confirmed that it was the same lad that had assaulted Scott Lord. Dan had beaten the pair in the Hawk Wind car park before they hastily retreated. Eamon sat at his desk in his home office, pondering on Big Kenny Whittle from Liverpool. He had heard of the notorious hardened dandy, whose son was locked up in Spain. Eamon knew that the Guardia Civil would not waste time in getting a confession about the shooting of Jackie Cooper. No matter how tough the lad thought that he was, the Spanish police had zero tolerance for firearms offences. They would use any method if the boy tried to resist questioning. Eamon realised that Big Kenny would want to return to the UK with his son. He sucked air through his teeth while placing a call to Dan informing him that he was calling a meeting at the club and to bring Billy, Benny, Jackie and Thomas.

The men filed into the Hawk Wind office; Dan locked the door. Eamon updated them on Jackie's shooting. Arm in a sling, Jackie appeared to be faring well. "Yous men have a choice as to which way this turnout with Kenny Whittle's boy is played. The lad's father is coming here to Spain to try to prevent his boy from getting a hefty prison sentence. However, if youse decide," he looked at Jackie, "to deny that it was his boy who fired the gun..." Eamon rested his forearms on the desk, hands in a small pyramid. All the men nodded. Eamon gave a tight smile. "I am sure that Big Kenny will be willing to compensate youse all, including Scott Lord, who thankfully is on the mend."

Jackie spoke up. "I have no problem with that boss!" The others agreed. Eamon rose to his full height. "I will keep youse updated." He smiled, checking his watch for the time. "I have a party to attend. My baby girls are two years old today."

Eamon parked outside the restaurant on the marina next to Marcia's Mercedes. He had booked the table for the twins' birthday party. Going to the boot of his car, he took out two wrapped parcels. Although Marcia had purchased the girls' presents, Eamon wanted to purchase a surprise gift. He had spoken to Jane for her advice. She had shown him the artist's work on the internet. Eamon had given Jane his specifications, and Jane placed the order. Eamon entered the restaurant, struggling with carrying the gifts. Marco, the maître d' held open the door for him.

Marcia looked up, smiling. He winked at her. "Daddy is here!" she said to the children who had their backs to him. Thomas Harper-Watts's two sons sat opposite Quinn and Niall. Quinn turned and clapped his hands excitedly. Aisling and Aine copied, fidgeting in their chairs. Aisling pushed Aye's hand away as she tried to prevent her from getting down from her seat to go to her father. Eamon stopped Aisling with a firm look when he saw her push Aye's hand away. Aisling smiled back at him and remained seated. Eamon sat at the head of the table watching his daughters rip the wrapping paper off of the gifts. Both girls were dressed in identical emerald-green and white checked frilly dresses, their copper-red curls tied in a top knot with matching green satin bows. Aye and Marcia helped with opening the boxes. The girls simultaneously squealed, their podgy hands clapping when the dolls in the image of each girl surfaced. Both girls hugged the baby dolls.

Eamon looked around the table. Niall was speaking with Atticus, and Quinn and Mathew had their heads down, smiling as they chattered. The table was laden with birthday gifts and treats. Marco approached the table with a large pink and white icing cake with four candles, two at each end of the cake for each girl. Eamon silently went back through the years to his and Patrick's childhood birthdays, which had passed them by with just a hug and birthday wishes from their mother. Their father did not remember their special days. For the most part, he didn't even recognise them in his drunken haze, until he took it upon himself for no reason to beat the boys. Eamon came back to the moment to join in and sing happy birthday when the candles were lit. Eamon's mobile phone rang. Checking the screen, he could see that it was an unknown caller. Pausing for a second, he rose from the table, nodding towards Marcia, and headed towards the door. He had given Brenda Whittle-Sherper his number so she could keep in with any updates from her brother Kenny.

"My brother and his associates will arrive in Spain early this evening. He wants to know where to meet up with you." Brenda said.

Eamon informed her that he would be at the Hawk Wind club from 10 pm. Eamon placed a call to Dan asking him to inform the men that Kenny Whittle was on his way to Spain, giving Dan the time of the meeting. Although Eamon would have his security on standby at the club, he intended to speak to Kenny Whittle alone in his office. He was not bothered that Kenny Whittle was bringing his henchman. The man had more to lose than Eamon did. He knew Whittle's son's get-out-of-jail card would be uppermost on his mind. Eamon held the key to his boy's release. Eamon had his hand on the restaurant door ready to return to the party when his phone rang. It was Diego, the manager of his haulage company. Stepping away from the door again, he answered.

"The dogs are urgently needed. There is a driver that I think has been taking drugs to the UK!" The old boy's tone was urgent.

Eamon said that he would be with him shortly. He phoned Dan again and told him to meet him at his villa and to bring Billy and the dogs. He shook his head. The haulage company had been running without a hitch for a while. Eamon realised that of late he had become complacent with the drivers.

The twins' ice-cream-smeared mouths puckered when Eamon came back to the table to kiss his daughters. Aisling held out her cherished Reborn doll for her father to kiss. Smiling, he tousled the silicone baby's hair, which appeased her. Aine hugged her Reborn doll to her chest. Turning to Marcia, Eamon said, "I have some urgent business to attend to at the depot. The dogs will be required."

Marcia nodded, placing her hand on his arm, squeezing reassuringly, realising that one of the drivers could be trying to smuggle contraband. She knew that Eamon would not miss his children's celebration if it was not imperative that his presence was required at the haulage depot with the Belgian shepherd dogs.

Eamon turned to his sons and said, "When I return a bit later, I will join youse both for a swimming race in the pool!"

"Double or quits, Papa!" Quinn chirped up, beaming. Eamon smiled, nodding. Niall smiled thinly. Eamon tousled both boys' hair. Kissing Marcia briefly, he left to see what was facing him with this latest episode of trouble.

Eamon sat in the back of the Land Rover with the two Belgian shepherds. Billy was at the wheel, Dan alongside in the passenger seat. The motor pulled into the haulage bay where a lorry was parked. The driver sat behind the wheel with his head down. Although the Polish driver appeared nonplussed when the men got out of their car and headed towards him, his demeanour changed to one of concern upon seeing the dogs. Alarm showed in his eyes, as he focused on the leashed animals. His eyes darted when the group approached the cab.

Billy pulled open the cab door. "Get the fuck out!" Eamon roared at the man in the cab. Gingerly, trying to avoid contact with the dogs, the driver climbed down, sidestepping, standing in front of Diego and his son Nicolas, who had taken over the management from his father, who was reluctantly easing himself into retirement.

"There you go, boy!" Billy held the door as Caesar leapt up and began searching the lorry. Dan moved around the outside of the lorry with the other dog. Within seconds after jumping onto the rear seat of the cab, the dog's attention moved up towards the cab roof lining. His body stretched, nose sniffing, excitedly barking, tail wagging. Billy called the dog to heel, rewarding him with a pat on the head. Billy clambered across the seat and patted the lining of the roof. He discovered two packages. He jumped down from the lorry as the driver tried to make his getaway.

He shoved Diego, who stumbled backwards. In the nick of time, his son Nicolas broke his fall, preventing any harm coming to his elderly father. When the Polish driver tried to make a run for it, Eamon made a lunge for him, but Billy beat him to it. Billy shouted the German command, "Fass!" to the

Belgian shepherd. The stocky driver yelled, struggling to break free as the animal shook his victim, fangs holding on to his jacket sleeve. The dog, eager for action, obeyed the command to refrain but remained on guard.

Dan returned from his inspection. Billy took control of both dogs while Dan, frog-marched the driver to the office, followed by Eamon. Billy stayed outside of the office doors.

The man, sweating profusely, wiped his brow with the back of his sleeve, eyes remaining fixed on Eamon who stood before him. Dan stayed near to the door.

"Who the feck is yer supplier?" Eamon jabbed his fingers in the man's chest. The man sneered at him and Eamon grabbed his jacket front, shoving him against the oak desk. The man glared back, remaining silent. "Ye Polish pox-balling cunt!" he spat. The Polish man's derisive look sent Eamon into a frenzied rage. Yanking him forward, he head-butted him. Blood spurted from the driver's nose. He screamed in a language neither Eamon nor Dan could understand.

"Understand this!" Eamon struck a kick with his right foot, hitting Janacek Kaminski on target. Kaminski yelled, falling to the floor and holding his testicles.

"Get off my fucking property!" Eamon shouted. Dan opened the door. The man bent over, hands between his legs as he crossed over the threshold. Dan kicked him in the rear, sending him sprawling. Billy smirked when he landed at his feet where the dogs were waiting. Kaminski stumbled on the way to his car, which was parked on the other side of the depot. "Billy ye and Dan take the dogs and go over the prick's motor. If ye find anything, confiscate it before ye let him go. He may not give up any names, but whoever he's working for isn't going to be happy with the useless cunt."

The men returned minutes later smiling, packages in hand. Billy had got Kaminski to confess that he was to deliver the other packages of cocaine for someone else after this run. Dan laughed. "I think it was the Brazilian roundhouse kick that Billy practised on him that made the man see sense."

"I have been itching to try out that move ever since Scott Lord showed us at the gym!" Billy grinned.

"Bring Diego and Nicolas in Dan," Eamon directed.

The old, Spanish manager and his son came into the office. "Ye shouldn't have to put up with this shite at yer age, Diego. However," Eamon turned to Nicolas, "if ye know anyone who can get rid of that," he pointed to the four packages, "ye will find that ye both will be more than pleased with the returns." Eamon saw the look of concern on his old manager's face. He placed a reassuring hand on his shoulder, although he spoke to Nicolas. "Don't ye worry about any comeback if ye sell it. Nevertheless, I would advise ye to use discretion." Nicolas nodded, while his father Diego smiled tightly. Eamon knew that his trusted manager and his family did not have any dealings with narcotics, but, at a guess, Eamon thought that Nicolas would find a way to sell the drugs.

Later that night, Eamon waited in the Hawk Wind club office. Earlier, Brenda had phoned him to say that her brother would meet him at the club at 10 pm Dan voiced his concerns that there could be trouble, however, Eamon thought otherwise. He knew that he held the ace card and that Kenny Whittle wanted his son off the hook. Young Kenny would be looking at a stiff prison sentence for attempted murder if Eamon's men IDed him as the shooter. Dan reluctantly agreed, although he wasn't happy knowing that Eamon would be alone with the notorious gangster, who Dan guessed would come mob-handed.

Right on time, there was a knock on the office door. Dan stepped aside as three men entered. Eamon, sitting at his desk, gave a nod to Dan, who retreated. Eamon stood to his full height, offering his hand. Kenny Whittle lightly but firmly shook it, taking a seat. The two men with him stood near the back wall.

Eamon did not know what to expect, however, the man who faced him was not what Eamon had envisioned. He had heard stories previously from Jimmy Grant regarding the man's notoriety. Eamon judged the tall, slim, fair-haired, immaculately attired man as a dandy. Eamon thought that Kenny Whittle would not look amiss on the streets of Paris.

"I am not here to make the situation worse. I just want to get to the crux of the matter. You and I are both businessmen," Kenny Whittle said, smiling. His steely blue eyes held Eamon's challenging dark pools. "I wish to have the situation concluded as soon as possible. We both do not want to encounter any more problems. Therefore, if we agree, I can return my son to his anxious mother."

Eamon had expected a Liverpool accent, not someone who spoke with an English middle-class vocabulary as Kenny Whittle did. Eamon smiled to himself, without letting on how ridiculous he thought the affected accent was.

Eamon sucked air between his teeth, nodding his head. He leaned back in his chair, resting easy. "I tink that ye are confused. I do not have any problem. The sticky situation that yer son is facing is yers!"

Kenny Whittle's jawline clenched. The men standing behind him changed stance.

Eamon continued. "Nevertheless, if ye don't mind me reminding ye," he said, smiling, "that it is ye who has the issue, not me," Eamon observed the henchmen stiffen.

Kenny's piercing blue eyes iced over. "Please let us understand one another. I am determined to take my son back home." His caustic smile did not go amiss. "Furthermore, I am willing to compensate your man. From what I hear, it is a superficial wound. No harm done." His smile softened.

Eamon flicked his brow, ignoring the intensity of the two men's glares from behind their boss. Eamon proceeded to counterattack. "Unfortunately, I am afraid that the shooting isn't the only incident which involves yer lad and another. There is another more serious incident that occurred before this latest one." Eamon observed Kenny's hard swallow. Eamon added. "Previously yer boy, along with another assailant, attacked one of my security men in the Hawk Wind club car park after my man finished work in the early hours." Eamon caught the flicker of surprise in Whittle's face. "The blow to the back of his skull put my man in the ICU for weeks. At one stage it looked like yer lad, who wielded the weapon, and the other one that was wit him, would both be facing a murder rap! Notwithstanding, the anguish that the stricken man's heavily pregnant wife must have endured." Eamon didn't mention that Scott was on the mend. There was no reflection on Kenny's face.

Kenny paused for a few seconds, then smirked. "If you are saying that my son was involved in this attack weeks ago, I find it difficult to comprehend why my son was not arrested earlier. It is obvious that this is all supposition!" Kenny stated smugly.

Eamon's smile spread, his eyes cold. "Supposition is not something that I would use to accuse someone that I knew for certain was the perpetrator!" Eamon countered. "We could not discover the identity of the two until yer son popped his head out of the car window, gun in hand, shooting one of my men! Hence the recognition!"

Kenny Whittle bristled, uncrossing his knees.

Eamon spoke, "I have the video recording of the assault." He paused for two seconds. "I can show it to ye if ye wish to see it." Eamon continued, "My right-hand man happened to look at the security footage when yer boy snuck up behind one of my fellas. However, my right-hand man upon seeing the pair skulking in the shadows of the car park on the screen, rushed out to try to prevent an altercation, but it was too late to prevent the blow. However, he did get in a couple of counter jabs, whereby they retreated!"

Kenny Whittle dismissed the offer to look at the recording with a wave of his hand, without replying.

Eamon held Kenny Whittle's glare. "How do ye put a price on a heavily pregnant distressed wife who has not left her man's side for the duration of her husband's life and death battle with a blood clot on the brain?" Eamon drove home the seriousness of the charges Kenny Whittle's boy would face. Eamon waggled his head and pursed his lips. "I should tink that three hundred grand, not euro, would appease my men for both incidents." Eamon waited for Whittle to barter.

Kenny Whittle stood up and scraped back the chair, smoothing down his trousers. "I will arrange with my sister for the money to be delivered to you here tomorrow afternoon." He smiled thinly, adding, "That will give enough time for your side to make it clear to the Law that it is a case of mistaken identity."

Eamon gave a sharp nod. "As soon as the transaction is finalised, I will instruct my men to make arrangements to attend an ID parade." Eamon stood and moved across the office to open the door. Stepping aside, he allowed the three men through. Standing sentry outside of the door was Aar the herculean, 165 cm tall, 108 kg Somalian security guard whom Dan had recently recruited. The three men side stepped as Aar threw them a hard look. Both men looked away.

"Nice setup you have here!" Kenny's smile was directed towards the two dancers on the stage, their legs hooked around the poles. Ada and Sunni, both stunning, smiled back. "They must have powerful thighs to be able to continue in that position!" Kenny remarked when Sunni winked at him. Nodding and smiling back, Kenny gave a soft laugh. "How do you get away with having so much temptation under your roof, O'Donnally? My wife would not tolerate it!" Eamon smiled, without responding. Giving one last glance in Sunni's direction, Kenny bade Eamon goodnight.

Eamon caught Dan's eye as he was talking to Cindy at the bar, signalling for him to join him back in the office.

Dan locked the door, taking a chair. "How did it go boss? I stationed Aar outside of the office door when I saw Kenny Whittle's bodyguards."

Eamon smiled, easing back into the chair. "There has been an agreement made, whereby, Kenny Whittle has offered to compensate Scott and Jackie, although Scott's pay out will be greater. Nonetheless, the rest of youse men are also entitled to recompense. More so ye, Dan. Ye were in the frame on both occasions. If it had not been for yer intervention and coming to Scott's aid, the situation could have been far worse for him."

"That is what my job entails!" Dan stated.

Eamon shook his head and held his palms toward Dan. "Loyalty does not go unrewarded!"

Dan smiled warmly, nodding.

"Tomorrow, the men will give their statements to the Law, swearing that the shooter was dark-haired and in his early thirties." This was the opposite description of young Kenny Whittle, who in the photos was fair-haired and in his early twenties. Eamon directed, "Inform the others," he instructed, "That way young Kenny Whittle will be released. The sooner that piece of scum leaves Spanish soil, the happier I will be!"

Eamon exhaled when Dan returned to the club floor. He unbuttoned his suit jacket, and sat back, hands locked behind his head, eyes closed, reclining in the big leather office chair, long legs stretched out on the desktop. His thoughts turned to Marcia and his children. He had had a demanding day and had not had the time to spend with his family. He'd promised himself that he would make it up to the boys tomorrow once he had completed the transaction with Kenny Whittle. Smiling to himself, he thought of his twin daughters. Marcia, along with Aye, had taken the birthday girls to a toy store in Benidorm town centre to purchase doll cots and accessories, although Aisling and Aine had not wanted to part with the life-like dolls.

Eamon checked his watch. Taking his phone from his pocket, he texted Marcia. *If you are not too tired, it would be nice to spend some time with you later.* Three emoji love hearts followed. A few minutes later, Marcia replied along with a picture of herself in black silk underwear, propped up on the bed. Blood rushed to his groin as he scanned her breasts and nipples in the cupless bra, his eyes slowly moved to between her legs. He zoomed in on the opening of the ouvert panties, widening the frame. Upon seeing her glistening, knowing that she would be waiting for him, he loosened his trouser fly. Getting hot under the collar, he undid his top shirt button. There was a knock at the office door, bringing him back to the moment. Quickly adjusting himself, he called out to enter, sitting up close to the desk to hide his evident arousal.

Ada, the sultry Spanish dancer came into the office, her beatific smile and almond-shaped, dark-brown eyes gazed at him as she shut the door. Eamon involuntarily scratched his earlobe. Eamon had been informed that Ada had been making a play for Jackie Cooper. Eamon was not ignorant of Ada's intentions. Married or single, Ada would go after what she wanted.

He took in the thigh-high leather boots, with only a short gap to the skirt hemline. Her second-skin top revealed braless full breasts straining against the thin fabric. As she sat down opposite him, she presented him with a flash of black panties.

"I wanted to speak with your wife. Although it is of no urgency," Ada said, parting her legs a little, giving him a clearer view. He was reminded of Marcia's photo and his groin groaned, bursting for release. He quickly regained control, fleetingly thinking back to his younger years, when a one-night stand would have sufficed to offload. "My wife will be in the club tomorrow night," he said with a touch of sternness. He wanted Ada out of his office. She cocked her head, smiling, slowly standing, moving to the corner of his desk, perching on the edge and crossing her long legs. He took in the perfume notes of lemon and bergamot. He sucked in air between his teeth, "I am a busy man!" he directed flatly, without trying to appear dismissive.

Ada continued to smile, standing up, without adjusting her short skirt, which had risen higher. "If you ever need some company throughout the long, boring night shift, I am available." Her dark eyes twinkled. "Good conversation is my forte!" She grinned, flashing even, white teeth.

"Like I said, Ada, my wife will be in tomorrow. If it's conversation that ye are after. 'Tis my wife that ye need to speak wit. Marcia is extremely eloquent." He spoke harshly.

Unaffected by his tone, she gave a soft laugh, turning to leave. Upon opening the door, she turned her head towards him and said, "You can always call on me. Out of pure interest, your handsome visitor earlier, is he local? Only I have not noticed him in the club before."

"He would be out of yer league. The man is English gentry!" Lying, Eamon stung her.

"They are all the same between the sheets," Ada threw back smiling, as she shut the door.

Shaking his head, he picked up the club's handset, calling Dan to his office.

"How busy are we out there?"

Dan replied, "Get off home, boss, and spend some time with your family. There is sufficient security to cover tonight. Furthermore, Aar can handle any difficult situations should they arise." Dan chuckled, "The punters quiet down when Aar is around. Only a fool would mess with that man."

"I appreciate it." Eamon made a mental note that he would make it up to Dan – give him a bonus, as well as time off to be with Cindy.

Eamon texted Marcia to say that he was on his way home.

On his return home, the dogs greeted him, tails wagging. He ruffled their coats in response. Remembering to remove his shoes, he placed his keys on the side table. He crossed the lounge towards the shaft of light beneath the bedroom door.

Eamon stood framed in the bedroom doorway; he began undressing. Marcia's dark-brown eyes reflected his. She was wearing a short, black silk negligee. She turned to face him as he stepped out of his underpants. "Give me five!" he said, as he walked to the shower.

Marcia's heart was racing as she admired the smooth plane of her husband's muscular back, the curve of his buttocks and solid thighs. She thought back to their first time together when she had first seen him naked. The night of Joey B's celebration, Eamon had escorted a young, blonde woman to the venue. Marcia recalled how her heart sank upon seeing Eamon with the pretty, young blonde. She had felt somewhat dejected because she had hoped that Eamon would attend alone.

She had wandered off to join the revelry in the marquee in Joey B's grounds. Some couples began to dance slowly to the sultry sounds of Lionel Ritchie. Eamon came to her mind as lovers swayed on the dance floor. From behind her, Eamon's Irish brogue had broken through her heavy mood. She remembered the touch of his hand on her shoulder, and his dark, smouldering eyes, which matched Eamon asked her to dance. She did not hesitate. Their powerful magnetism drew them together, clamping their bodies fast, so nothing could come between them. She had not shown any resistance to his kiss, one that sealed the completion of the couple's wandering souls. Marcia believed that Destiny had placed them together to bring back together their two souls that had wandered apart. That night on the dance floor, as she was encased in Eamon's strong but gentle hold, she felt that their lost souls had completed their roving.

However, before the music ended, all hell had broken out. The young, blonde who had come with Eamon stormed up to the couple, shoving Marcia with such force that Marcia toppled over, striking her head on the ground. It had all happened so quickly that Eamon hadn't had time to stop the angry blonde who was shouting abuse at Marcia, who was visibly shaken.

Eamon had ordered the young woman to leave. He had insisted upon taking Marcia to the hospital, as she appeared dazed by the assault. Afterwards, he returned Marcia to her and Suzette's rented villa. Suzette was staying over at her secret lover's villa that night and Marcia had invited Eamon in. Her state of disarray required her to shower and change out of her torn dress. She told him to help himself to a glass of wine while he waited.

She was in the shower and upon hearing the door slide open, she turned her head, then slowly faced him. His intense, dark-brown eyes held her transfixed. His maleness erect, within seconds he took her in his arms and gently entered her. Carrying her, he remained inside her, with her legs clamped around his waist. They kissed deeply, their lost souls reunited from a lifetime of separation. Marcia's longing for him was complete. Their unhurried love making throughout the night took them both to great heights. Then he had left her in the morning to go to Miami for two weeks. However, Destiny had other plans. The following day, Jimmy Grant's murder changed everything. Eamon returned to her the following day.

Eamon came out of the shower drying his hair. "I am going to check on the children. Then, my wee mystic, I am going to make ye pay for enticing me from work!" he winked, slipping on a towelling robe.

Eamon returned a few minutes later, adjusting the monitor near the bed that showed the children sleeping. "I am going to have a large bath put in with an overhead shower, as this en suite is the only one without a bath." It had been at Eamon's insistence that they used the ground-floor bedroom. It had previously been intended as a guest room. That was before they had the children. "I realised that we have been missing out on the enjoyment that spending time together in the bath would bring!" He smiled, dropping his robe, standing before her, erection evident. Kneeling over her, he began untying her silk robe, exhaling softly when her hand and fingers manipulated him.

"I will be able to massage you in the bath," Marcia purred.

Eamon was enjoying the stimulation of the light touch playing over the eye of his shaft. He nodded. "Ye are going to get the full brunt of me shortly," he smiled. "I can't get any harder!"

Marcia leaned towards him, tongue aiding. He threw his head back and groaned. Gently prising her head away, he said, "I want it to last." He lay her on the bed, raising her legs, parting the ouvert panties. "Ye are halfway there, my hot little mystic. I want to pleasure ye for a while, but keep control until we are both ready." She felt his warm breath and tongue flicking between her legs. She turned her head towards the mirrors, gripping and releasing the bedding with every stroke, fighting the rising heat throughout her body. "Eamon," she moaned.

Withdrawing, he covered her. She sank further into the soft bed upon his entry, clinging to him, biting the nape of his neck as the orgasm took her.

"I am going to stay wit ye. The next one will be deeper." He took her over the edge. His mouth took each bud in turn as he thrust, swathed in perspiration, their bodies clamped together. "Join me," he whispered into her neck. Bodies obeying, eyes closed, they both reached the soaring heights of their joint orgasm, hearts beating with exertion.

Eamon remained on top of her. "I am getting too old to have this much sex in one go!" Lifting his head, he slowly withdrew, pulling her to him in an embrace. Her fingertips played across his lips. "You are an extremely virile and fit man who needs regular sexual release."

"Extremely virile!" he repeated, smiling. "My virility is due to wanting ye. I admit that I do like sex, as much as ye do! My wee sex addict!" he laughed, lifting her face to kiss her.

"I also admit that ever since we met my libido has increased. How can you call me a sex addict, when you are the cause of my addiction?" Marcia said.

He rolled her on top of him, clasping her rear. "Ye may have fooled me in the very beginning, wit yer coy act and demure demeanour, however, ye tend to forget that I have ye on video. My wild, wanton woman!" He smiled. "Ye taunt me by sending provocative pictures of yerself. Fortunately for me, I was alone in the office when you sent that." He did not mention Ada's intrusion. "I zoomed in on the picture wit yer legs open wide. Ouvert panties enticing me. I could see that ye wanted me. What is yer intention but to entice me to yer bed, when I am supposed to be working?" He gave a sharp, playful nod.

"Has there been any more news about the shooting? The more that I think about it, the more disconcerting I find it. Jackie Cooper could have been killed, or any one of the men!" Marcia said, concerned.

Eamon exhaled. "The problem has been sorted. There is no need for concern." He didn't tell her about Kenny Whittle's visit or the trouble he had had that day with the Polish driver at the haulage company.

She played with his chest hair. "You encounter a lot of stress in your jobs, Eamon. However, sexual release is beneficial. Orgasm is said to aid the heart!" She giggled.

He gave a soft laugh. "Not at the same thrashing pace as the first time around, I hope. Both of us were tearing into one another!" He tapped the bridge of her nose playfully. "Ye were the instigator, my wee banshee! Howling as I took ye! Biting my neck and clawing my back," he accused, teasingly. "'Tis grand to see that I can continue to pleasure ye!" he said, before adding, "Some men encounter problems."

Marcia sensed that he was serious. "Eamon if there ever came a time when there was any problem, I would still love and want you."

He shook his head. "I know that dysfunction can affect some men…" He did not finish. She nestled into him.

"You are all I want. Sex has been a great part of our union, but, even if that should ever happen, we would still have each other." Marcia put her arms around Eamon's neck, kissing him lovingly. He smoothed her hair, returning the kiss.

Holding her face in his hands, he studied her features. "There is not any ting in this life that can break our bond," he spoke seriously.

Marcia, eyes searching, gently pulled away from him, sitting up. "Eamon, you are frightening me. Why do you say it? What has happened?"

"I am only making a statement!" He tried to make light of what he was feeling about having to up stakes for a period.

She shook her head. "Eamon!" she faltered, placing her hands on his chest, almost pleading, "Why do I sense that you are withholding something from me?"

Eamon drew her to his chest. "Marcia, stop yer fretting. We are a part of one another. Don't read into my meaning." He felt that it was not the right time to tell her that he was expecting a call anytime soon asking him to return to help Alphonso get his new venture off the ground.

Rolling her onto her back, he covered her, arms supporting either side of her face. He kissed away her fears and his member began seeking. Her legs involuntarily parted, yielding to the unhurried, soothing motion. Their deep love took them to the edge. Eamon clamped her with his powerful thighs and administered gentle but firm thrusts. Marcia clung to him, freefalling into the abyss.

6

The following morning after Brenda had dropped the money off at the Hawk Wind club, Eamon phoned Dan to organise the identity parade.

Two hours later, Kenny Whittle turned up at the Guardia Civil station along with some other men of varying physical appearances. The fast-response officer who had given chase to the Mustang had reported that the shooter was light-haired. Jackie, Dan, Thomas and Benny attended the line-up to identify the man who had shot Jackie Cooper. Young Kenny Whittle, standing second from the left in the row of men looked straight ahead without flinching as Dan's fleeting yet intense glare bore into the perpetrator's blue eyes. The four men made statements to say that the gunman was dark-haired, of swarthy complexion, aged approximately mid-30s, unlike the baby-faced 21-year old, fair-haired, pale-complexioned Kenny Whittle.

A few hours later, Eamon received a phone call from Big Kenny Whittle's sister, informing him that her brother sent his regards. "Mmmm," Eamon mumbled, hanging up the phone.

Eamon sat at his desk going over the club's bookings while waiting for the call from Dan to inform him of

Kenny Whittle's release. He contemplated the division of the three-hundred-thousand pounds compensation from Kenny Whittle. He knew that Scott Lord should get the largest amount. He had been released from the hospital and was convalescing at home. Nonetheless, although Jackie Cooper had been shot, his injuries were less serious and he was already on the road to recovery, unlike Scott who required medical assistance to aid his recovery. Jackie had thankfully gotten off lightly due to his men's quick response. Eamon picked up his briefcase and got up to make his first port of call.

Sandy Lord opened the door, stepping aside to let Eamon into the three-bedroom villa that Scott had begun renovating before his assault. Scott had been upbeat about the purchase of the property, which Eamon had helped him secure a mortgage for. Scott, who was sitting in an armchair went to stand as Eamon came into the lounge.

"Stay where ye are. Once that ye are rested and fit enough, ye can come back to work, which won't be too long by the looks of ye!" Eamon smiled. Sandy went off to make coffee. Eamon looked round the villa, which had been in a state of disrepair when Sandy and Scott had first moved in. Before the attack, Scott had begun renovating the place. He had planned to get the villa in order before their child was born.

Putting the briefcase to one side, Eamon took a seat. He thought that the armchair had seen better days. "I expect that ye have been kept in the loop by the men about Jackie Cooper taking a hit from a drive-by shooter? To cut to the chase, the gun man was the same guy that attacked ye in the Hawk Wind car park."

Scott frowned.

"Furthermore, I was paid a visit by the young prick's father from Liverpool."

Jackie sat up. Eamon smiled thinly. “However, the man was eager to get his toe rag kid off the hook. Fortunately, I was holding the get-out-of-jail card, which did not come cheap.” Eamon smiled. “I struck a deal wit him.” He paused for a couple of seconds and continued, “Compensation!” Eamon grinned, pushing the briefcase towards Scott. “Open it!” Eamon directed.

Appearing perplexed, Scott lifted the case, just as Sandy returned with two cups of coffee. “I will leave you two to it.” She turned to leave. Eamon stopped her. “Sandy, can ye stay, as this concerns ye as well as Scott?” Looking at Scott holding the case, the heavily pregnant woman sat on a chair at a pine dining table.

“I want youse both to have a break when ye are both up to it. There is no need to travel any distance at this stage,” Eamon said, smiling warmly at Sandy. “Just somewhere local.” Dan had told him about a hotel that he and Cindy used for the occasional break, which he highly recommended. “Javea has a grand hotel a stone’s throw from the beach!” He added, “I can call in a favour and get some help wit the alterations to yer home.” He looked at Scott. “Time is of the essence. Ye don’t want yer child to come home to disorder!” He smiled at Sandy, who looked bewildered. Eamon stood up. “There are times such as this when ye could use some help. I will cover your building expenses as my gift to show my appreciation for ye loyalty.” He glanced at Scott. Eamon knew that Scott would not turn down any request from Eamon, no matter the situation. Sandy sat with both hands on her baby bump, speechless.

“That will clear ye mortgage.” Eamon threw a look at the briefcase in Scott’s hands and nodded as he opened it, looking at the thousand-pound bundles inside. “Remember, this is not charity.” Eamon knew how proud Scott was. “Like I said earlier, it's compensation." Eamon turned to leave. "We can get the legalities sorted out for ye later." Eamon could help Scott to launder the money from Kenny Whittle via his contacts.

Dumbstruck, mouth agape, Sandy rose from her chair. She stood next to Scott who took her hand, his free hand to Eamon. "I can't thank you enough boss!" he enthused.

Sandy stepped forward, trying to hug Eamon, but her baby bump got in the way. Eamon put his arm on hers, smiling warmly.

Giving a sharp nod to them both, jangling his keys, Eamon turned to Scott and said, "To be sure there will come a time in the future when ye will have the opportunity to return any favours."

He left the villa. Sitting in his car, he made a phone call to Greg's construction manager whom he had dealings with in the past, before Greg's demise. The business was now Suzette's. She ran the show. No matter, Eamon went over her head and contacted Sebastian, who agreed to take on the renovations of Scott's villa. He also gave Sebastian the order to install a large bath in his and Marcia's ground-floor en suite bathroom. Then he made a phone call to Jackie.

Jackie Cooper entered Eamon's office at the Hawk Wind club, his arm in a sling, looking like the cat that had eaten all the cream. It was not the look of a man whose wife had betrayed him and who had recently been shot in the a rm, Eamon thought, indicating for Jackie to take a seat. "How are ye?"

"All is great. This is a bit awkward though." Jackie raised his arm in the sling slightly, smiling. "However, Yvette has become my Florence Nightingale. It appears that you need to get someone to take a pot shot at you to turn your relationship around!"

Eamon had to hand it to Jackie. He must really love Yvette to be able to forgive his wife's indiscretion. He's a better man than me, Eamon thought to himself.

"In the near future, Yvette and I will be renewing our wedding vows," Jackie revealed.

Eamon remained passive, placing his forearms on the desk. "The reason I have asked ye here is to give ye this!" He slid the large envelope across the oak desk. Jackie looked at it without reaching for it. "There is some compensation for yer injuries from the kids' father who shot yer."

Jackie picked up the envelope smiling. "I appreciate your help boss!" scraping his chair back, standing, preparing to leave. "I will take Yvette away for a few days." He smiled. "Another week or so and the doctor said I will be up and running!"

Eamon nodded.

"Thanks again boss!" Jackie said, raising the envelope.

Eamon reflected, leaning back into the office chair after Jackie shut the door. 'He couldn't understand how Jackie, a hardened man who had fought in war-torn territories as a trained killer could so easily forgive his wife's disloyalty. It went beyond Eamon's comprehension. He shook his head. If he had been in Jackie Cooper's shoes, there would have been no forgiveness on his part. His pride wouldn't allow it. He would raise hell and high water for Marcia. In his book, she was his, he was hers. There was no room for any in-between.

He thought back to the time when he had read his ex-wife Eve's diary and the explicit details of her affair with Jimmy Grant. The crushing blow wiped out any pain of bereavement that he had felt at the time of her death.

However, when Marcia came into his life, he discovered the true meaning of love. Her devotion to him was unwavering, nonetheless, he had learned not to become complacent. He was always on the alert. In his heart, he felt that Marcia reciprocated the depth of his feelings that he had for her. However, he was constantly battling with the voice in his head that whispered not to trust anyone. He knew from experience that Marcia wouldn't forgive him if he crossed that line. She had previously mistakenly thought that he had betrayed her. He had returned home in the early hours to find that she had left him. He momentarily felt a pang of anguish as he recalled finding their bed empty.

The rapping at the door brought him back to the moment. Eamon called out. "Enter," He was expecting the visit – Dan, followed by Billy and Thomas, and a few minutes later Benny Harris entered the club office. "I won't keep ye boys long!" He slid an envelope towards each man. He had given 20,000 to Billy, Benny and Thomas. Dan received 30,000. "For the inconvenience of the other night," Eamon declared. Grins spreading across their faces, the four men nodded in appreciation.

"Thankfully the young prick's father, Kenny Whittle, has taken him back to the UK. From what I hear, Kenny Whittle's sister's boy was wit the shooter at the time. Her boy was the driver. The family plans to leave Spain for an unknown destination." Eamon returned the men's smiles. "At a guess, it will be to get her boy away from the influence of his Liverpudlian cousin. Brenda had mentioned to Eamon when she made the cash delivery, that her young lad had been easily led by his cousin. She said that their family would be relocating, making a new start and breaking all ties."

7

Marcia had dropped Niall and Quinn off at school. She pulled into the parking area and got out of the car to hug the boys. She stood watching the pair join the throng of pupils. An ominous cloud descended upon her and fear gripped her solar plexus. She suddenly felt the urge to run after her sons. Holding on to the car door for support, her heart racing, she scanned the building, spotting Niall walking in alone. She homed in on him. The memory of the blood moon came flooding back to her – the day she had received the news that her son Reuben was lost to her. Marcia thought of the recent blood moon. A foreboding filled her senses as she watched Niall disappear through the doors. She tried to shake off the feeling, telling herself that her fears were unfounded. Today was like any other school run. She saw one of the school masters standing by the doors as the last group of pupils entered, closing the doors behind him. Marcia sat in her car for a few minutes trying to make sense of the overwhelming feeling that Niall faced danger.

Exhaling, Marcia started the car and headed towards Suzette's villa. She had the car roof open, with the wind blowing through her hair, trying to clear her mind. Although her heavy mood lifted slightly as she drove further away from the school, Marcia could not dismiss the feeling that a crisis was looming.

Marcia observed the backdrop of the Sierra de Bernia mountain range looming behind Suzette's villa. She felt that with Suzette living alone there she was vulnerable. However, Suzette had previously told Marcia that she felt protected by the range. When Marcia had tried to encourage her to put the isolated villa on the market, Suzette said that the memories of her cherished years that she had spent with her husband Greg there prevented her from moving.

Suzette stood beaming, glamorously attired in a pale blue, capped-sleeve fitted dress and royal blue stilettos. Her black bobbed hair had ben coiffured and her make-up professionally applied. Lloyd had shown Suzette the art.

"Marcia, you look chic and radiant. I recognise the designer, it is Zimmerman!" Suzette stated, admiring the floral, long-sleeved silk and linen shirt coupled with a cream lace, tiered midi skirt, off set with cream leather wedge heels. "It is an exotic look that suits you!" Suzette complimented.

Both women pecked one another on the cheek. "I don't need to ask you if you are happy with your life with that man of yours!" Suzette said, looping her arm through Marcia's. They ascended the villa steps and stepped into the lounge. Marcia moved towards the floor-to-ceiling windows and terrace doors. The vista in the distance never failed to make her realise why both she and Suzette had relocated to Altea Hills from the UK.

The two friends had previously arranged for a catch-up for a couple of hours. Aye and Bonita were at home entertaining the twin girls. Marcia went through the doors onto the terrace while Suzette made them coffee. Although the two women lived a short distance apart and Marcia regularly visited Suzette's Mystique beauty salon for treatments, Suzette's busy business life prevented her and Marcia from being able to spend any amount of time together. Suzette, on occasion, would ring Marcia with the latest gossip from the salon, however, Marcia preferred not to become involved, especially if it concerned any of Eamon's men.

"I have so much to tell you!" Suzette said excitedly, placing the cups on the large garden table under an awning. Although it was late October and there was a soft breeze lowering the temperature, both women used high-factor sun protection and did not sit outside without shade.

"First things first!" Suzette grinned. "Brady, Sandy Lord's 16-year-old son is an apprentice brick layer. When I spoke to Sandy about how Scott was faring, she confided in me that her son had just left school and that Bridie, the younger of the Irish sisters who danced at the club, was pregnant by her young son. I telephoned Sebastian my manager at the construction company and asked him to take Brady under his wing. Sandy phoned me later, thrilled."

Marcia had wondered why Bridie had given up pole-dancing at the Hawk Wind club. She sipped the coffee while Suzette continued.

"You know that Yvette had this thing going on with Elliot, the hunky Jamaican Muay Thai trainer? That is now over, ever since Yvette's husband Jackie Cooper was shot. It shook her to the core." Suzette's tone became hushed and she whispered conspiratorially, "However, Yvette told me that she felt guilty because she was in bed with Elliot at the time of the shooting!" Suzette shook her head. "To my surprise, Yvette has agreed to retake her wedding vows with Jackie, which is apparently going to take place shortly. Jackie is pressing for them to make a new start. Furthermore," she smiled, "Everyone in our circle is invited to the party. I must say I do like celebrations of any type. It does give one a chance to mingle."

Marcia smiled. She knew that Suzette meant to find a man. Marcia remained silent throughout. Suzette sighed. "I know that Yvette had been unhappy with the move to Spain until she began working for me at the salon. Then she encountered Elliot! Can you imagine that handsome and fit stud?" she said grinning. "The thought makes me hot!" She fanned herself, swooning.

Marcia could not help but chuckle at Suzette's antics. "However, Yvette said that her husband is in the dark about her dalliance." Raising both hands, she said, "No harm done!"

Marcia took a large gulp of her coffee. She did not reveal that Eamon had informed her how Jackie Cooper had divulged to the men how he had followed his wife and seen her with her Jamaican lover.

Marcia moved to the subject of Suzette's private life. If there was not a man in her life at the moment, Marcia knew that her friend would have her eye on someone. "What is happening in your social life?" Marcia knew that Suzette often went to the clubs with Lloyd and Keiron. All three loved the night life.

Suzette smiled, dark eyes twinkling. "Although I have taken heed of your previous predication that there is an older, handsome, foreign man waiting in the wings of my destiny until he shows himself, I have been seeing a younger hunk. Nothing serious! Only a stop gap!"

Despite herself, Marcia smiled, but she was concerned. "How much younger?" she asked.

Suzette grinned. Replying without giving her new man's age, "I met him in a nightclub in Javea a few weeks ago. Romano visits me at the villa a few nights a week. We have an understanding. He is a stud in bed. So much energy in the bedroom!" She winked. "He is, as I said, just an interlude."

Marcia laughed, cocking her head. "He sounds very young!"

"He is mature for 28. It is only a bit of fun!" Suzette threw in when Marcia shook her head.

"Enough about me. What about you Marcia? How are the children? Is Niall behaving? I know that you have had your problems in the past with him." She included, "However, your two sons are handsome like that man of yours and the twins are copper-headed, green-eyed stunners. It was a blessing in disguise that you underwent sterilisation after the twins because your randy Irishman would have had you barefoot and pregnant as soon as you were able!"

Marcia smiled. "Niall, of late, appears to be keeping his jealousy in check, for the most part. Eamon and I are aware that Niall is a withdrawn child. He is deep like Eamon. Although Eamon adores his younger brother, Patrick, Niall does not have the same bond with his siblings," she confessed sadly. "However, we are both hoping that Niall will improve as he matures. We are not going to give up on him." She smiled wanly. "I dropped the boys at school before I came here. Normally, Eamon drives them, but he was busy this morning. When the boys got out of the car, it was like an ominous cloud descended over me. Watching Niall go towards the entrance…' she faltered. "I sensed a feeling of a portent of things to come. I had to prevent myself from running after Niall to protect him!" Marcia ran her thumbs back and forth across her fingertips. Suzette reached for Marcia's hands, clasping them.

"You told me when I phoned you when Eamon was out in Miami, that Niall had become out of control, being rude to Aye and Bonita with his father away." She added, "This feeling that you experienced may well be a subconscious thing because you are concerned about Niall." Suzette tried to allay Marcia's fears.

Marcia smiled thinly, nodding, although she did not believe that it was just her concern regarding her son's nature making her feel like that. She sensed that it was a warning.

Suzette checked her watch; she was meeting a rep at her beauty salon in an hour. "Between us, I have made enquiries regarding a few tweaks, one must not age gracefully!" She nodded, smiling sagely. She lifted the skin around her eyes, then cupping her breasts, she raised them. "I must be ready for my new man that you foresee in my future. One must take care with the aid of an excellent surgeon." She grinned. "Furthermore, I will need to ask Cindy and Yvette to stand in for me. Lloyd, along with Keiron, will manage the hair and beauty side, while the girls will take over the bookings for a few days."

Marcia, of late, had been thinking along the same lines of having breast implants. She also thought that crow's feet were becoming visible. However, she sensed that Eamon would not agree to her having surgery for the sake of vanity. Suzette had no one to answer to.

"The surgeon has come highly recommended. My young lover will appreciate my new enhancements!" Suzette laughed.

Marcia laughed with her. "I am certain that he will!"

"Marcia, you have had five children, and I am childless. How have you retained your amazing figure, whereas I now require a surgeon's aid?" Suzette giggled.

"Suzette, I have practised yoga for many years and swim regularly. However, since the twins have been born, I can see the signs of ageing!" Marcia replied.

"Ageing!" Suzette exclaimed, repeating Marcia's declaration. "Marcia, please believe me that you look as young as you did when we first met over eight years ago. You have kept that man of yours in your bed, throughout. Therefore, you do not need to go under the knife! Unlike me, who will need help for when I will be meeting this new man that you predicted for me in the not-too-distant future."

Suzette took on a more serious note, taking Marcia's hands in hers. "We have so much to be grateful for. Look at how our lives have turned out compared to a decade ago when I booked a tarot reading with you."

Marcia pressed her lips together in a warm smile.

"I remember the warning you had given me about the police raid on my home. When I told Max of your warning he brushed it to one side as rubbish. However, he did stash his money." Suzette grinned wickedly. Suzette later stole it when Max was in prison. "The day your prediction came true when the police beat our door in and handcuffed Max, I made my plans!" She raised both hands, beaming. "The rest is history. Our journey together began. I have so much to thank you for, Marcia!"

Marcia went to speak but Suzette interrupted. "Before you say anything. Without your gift, guiding me from day dot, I would have none of this." She splayed her hands towards the large property and grounds. "I never envisioned my life as an independently wealthy woman. Although, step by step you counselled me with your predictions. I know that there have been times when I did not heed your advice." She smiled weakly. "I am learning not to be impulsive with men," she threw in, laughing gaily.

Marcia doubted that her friend would be able to resist when an attractive man caught her eye. However, she kept her own counsel.

Marcia was deep in thought about Eamon on the way home from Suzette's. She decided that later when she felt that the timing was right, she would put it to him about her thoughts on having surgery.

Eamon was in the pool with Aisling and Aine when Marcia came out to the garden with the dogs following. The Belgian shepherds both greeted her when she had parked up. The girls squealed with delight, clapping their hands. Aisling, arms in armbands, splashed and moved through the water towards her. Aine followed with Eamon close behind them. "Swim, mummy!" Aisling called, wanting Marcia to join them.

"Mummy will change into a swimsuit," Marcia said, going back into the villa.

Eamon winked his approval when Marcia came out onto the terrace in the high-cut, multi-coloured swimsuit that she had purchased from the Zimmerman designer label. As she walked down the pool steps, Eamon embraced her, his free hand exploring under the water.

"Me daddy!" Aisling cried, mouth puckering, wanting a kiss. She clutched his arm. Eamon laughed. Obliging, he kissed both girls. Marcia played with the girls for a while, while he swam. A while later, Aye appeared, and the two excited girls struggled to reach her. They knew that her presence meant dinner was ready. Hand in hand, dressed in robes, they trotted alongside Aye towards the terrace doors.

Eamon smiled as Marcia swam towards him, into his embrace. He cupped the exposed flesh of her rear and he pulled her to him. "This swimsuit doesn't leave much to the imagination!" Eamon said, caressing the curve of her buttock.

Marcia put her arms around his neck, clamping her legs around his waist. She kissed him along the jawline, while his fingers explored.

"We need to finish in the bedroom. Leave the swimsuit on," Eamon breathed, lifting her out of the pool.

She knelt on all fours and he parted the crotch of the skimpy swimwear. He worked his way down her inner thigh, tongue teasing, teeth nibbling, exciting her, as he reached his destination.

Marcia gasped, raising her buttocks to meet him, head thrown back, enjoying every second that he slowly filled her. They held each other in a deliberate synchronisation. In one swift movement, Eamon flipped Marcia on her back. Then he peeled off the swimsuit, covering her, kissing her. There was a gasp of pleasure as he took her. They locked together in ecstatic fulfilment that deepened with the soul kiss that bound them.

Feeling Marcia's heart racing, Eamon smiled. "We would probably have had even more babies, what with the way we can't keep our hands off each other. There was no way that we would have been able to use precautions. Ye meet me with my wanting of ye, my lustful wee mystic!"

Marcia put her arms around his neck sensing a touch of wistfulness in his statement. "Are you disappointed that I cannot give you any more children?"

"Not in the least. I was stating a fact – that we both enjoy the pleasure that we get from making love. We have never used precautions against ye getting pregnant. Nothing would have changed that between us. We would have continued until we had a houseful!"

She ran her fingers along his jawline. "From the beginning, when you first made love to me, feeling you deep inside of me, I had hoped that you would give me your baby. Although, I thought that I couldn't fall pregnant because I had difficulty before I met you. However, much to my surprise and joy, I discovered that I was pregnant with Niall. Little did I realise how quickly I would fall pregnant again. Six weeks after giving birth to Niall, you gave me Quinn. I was thrilled! Two beautiful boys – one right after the other. I had assumed that our family was complete when I did not fall pregnant again for a few years. Then you gave me two beautiful daughters."

Eamon brushed her mouth with his, hardening inside of her. He had previously thought that he would never have any children. He had had two previous marriages. His short marriage to Aye's younger sister lasted only eighteen months – her premature death was brought about by malaria. Eve, his second wife had been having an affair with his boss Jimmy Grant, which Eamon only discovered after her death in a car crash. She had lied to Eamon about not being able to have children. He had discovered her contraceptive pills hidden in a drawer, and her diary revealed that she was planning to get her claws into Jimmy by having his baby. But then he met Marcia, and they had two sons in quick succession. A few years later, beautiful twin daughters completed his family. "Ye have given me so much pleasure, and to top that off, you gave me our children. Also, to have a wife who is up for sex anytime…" he smiled. Hands cupped her rear, holding her close, his movement measured. "Ye cannot ever leave me!" he directed, seeking her mouth.

8

Marcia was early for her hair and beauty treatment appointment with Lloyd at Suzette's Mystique beauty salon. Cindy was on reception and had told her to wait in the staff room. Marcia returned the beaming smile of Violet, the Jamaican cleaner who was sitting at the table drinking a cup of tea. She stood up, proceeding to make Marcia a cup of coffee. Although Marcia didn't want one, she accepted the jovial woman's offer and took a seat. It had never ceased to amaze Marcia how the heavily built woman tirelessly cleaned the large building. It was beyond Marcia how she heaved her bulk without puffing and panting. "How are you and your family?" Marcia asked.

"We all good!" Violet shook her head, loose flesh wobbling. She returned to the table, placing the cup in front of Marcia. The chair groaned under her weight as she slumped on to the metal, tubular-legged chair. "Sad wid Yvette!" The Jamaican woman appeared to be speaking more as a directive, than wanting Marcia to answer.

Marcia remained silent, slowly sipping the coffee rather than becoming embroiled in a difficult situation. She knew that Elliot, Yvette's former lover was Violet's nephew. Her sister

Josephine, Elliot's mother, who matched her sister in size, came to the salon on occasion for beauty treatments.

"Dat woman she was tearful. Yvette telt me dat she heartfelt!" Violet placed her free hand on her ample chest, taking a large mouthful of tea. "Me did not telt her not to jump dat broomstick wid her man again. Her man bin a cheatin' on her!"

Marcia was taken aback by the revelation, however, she continued taking small sips and did not reply.

Violet continued, "My man, he done been taking oder women to his bed!" She held up three podgy fingers vehemently shaking her head. "Dem women come to me door wid babies. I shut da door on dem all. Dat man dey do ye wrong!" Violet grinned showing white tombstone size teeth. "Dat man he upset and a wailing when I slammed dat door!" Marcia tried to keep up with Violet's patois. "I jus telt dat girl da positives. I ask Yvette is da heart wid da man or dat lover?"

Marcia could not look away from the earnest, dark eyes of the woman. "'Tis da lover!"

Lloyd poked his head around the door, curling his forefinger at Marcia. She smiled at the Jamaican cleaner. Violet nodded back.

Marcia lay on the beauty-bed while Lloyd tied on a blue apron to protect his clothing. Preparing the creams to begin her facial, he said "I have so much to tell you, Marcia, about our night out at the Discoteca Nocturna club in Murcia with Suzette and Yvette!" He spoke in a conspiratory manner. Marcia closed her eyes when he applied the cleansing cream. "It was Yvette's hen night, and we were having a ball, dancing and drinking, although Yvette was not overly excited about retaking her wedding vows. Nevertheless, we convinced her that she was doing the right thing to break it off with her Jamaican stud. Mind you, I would not mind a bit of that hunk myself!"

he chuckled, continuing, "Furthermore, after a few drinks, Yvette revealed that her husband wanted a clean slate." He lowered his voice and said, "Jackie confessed to a one-night stand with Ada the Spanish pole dancer!" A wicked smile spread across his face as Marcia's eyes flew open. Lloyd pursed his lips and said, "Ada is a predator. Keiron and I see many things when we are working at the cocktail bar. One needs to lock up their man when she is around! Getting back to Yvette, she eventually let her hair down and got into the swing of things. Until later when she sat down while we continued enjoying the dancing. The next thing I spotted was Yvette heading towards the club exit!" Lloyd paused for two seconds for effect. "Our darling Yvette had the Muay Thai hunk trailing two feet behind her. We do not need to have a vivid imagination to glean a picture of what occurred..." He left it hanging.

Marcia closed her eyes, inhaling quietly. While she was working at the Hawk Wind club, Marcia had observed Ada on the stage doing her routine, glancing in Eamon's direction when Eamon had been standing at the bar speaking to Billy. There had been a couple of occasions when Ada's gaze lingered on Eamon. Marcia was aware of the dancer's intentions. Marcia thought Eamon must have been made aware of Jackie Cooper's fling with Ada. Nevertheless, she knew that Eamon would sweep it under the carpet, as the rest of the men would. However, Yvette was demonised due to her tryst with the Muay Thai trainer.

9

Marcia was leisurely swimming, deep in thought regarding the phone call she had received earlier that morning. The number on her mobile phone had been withheld. This was the second time within two days that it had occurred. She had dismissed the first one as a wrong number. However, her senses were alert and she knew that whoever was on the other end of the line was listening to her voice.

Due to her past experiences of being attacked, the phone calls unnerved her, even though she knew that she was protected by the Belgian shepherds watching over her while Eamon was not home. Glancing up at her were two pairs of intelligent, almond shape eyes – her canine protectors, heads resting on forepaws, were observing her.

She pushed any negative thoughts to the back of her mind. Marcia wasn't going to let anything mar her excitement about her upcoming surgery. She had convinced Eamon that she wished to have a breast enhancement. He had at first baulked at the idea. He felt that her vanity was being placed before her safety. She had argued that since she had given birth to the twins, she felt that her breasts required some uplift. Reluctantly, he had acquiesced to her wish on the understanding that she was to go to a highly reputable surgeon. Marcia had one in mind. She had booked her appointment. She was to undergo the operation while Eamon was in Miami. Unexpectedly, Alphonso Gabrette had asked him to return for a couple of days. Marcia felt that she could not begrudge the old Italian Eamon's help with his new club. Alphonso Gabrette had previously stepped in to help Eamon with the problem that Marcia had caused when she did a tarot reading for Joyce Grant and revealed that her son-in-law, Matt, was involved with narcotic dealings. Joyce's daughter had informed on Matt and Matt went to prison along with his partner in crime, Franco Gennaro junior, of the powerful New York mafia family. After that, the Gennaro family had it in for Eamon and Marcia believing them to be the original informers, but Alphonso Gabrette made the problem disappear. Marcia would not allow herself to imagine what steps had been taken to disperse the threat. She knew that the world she and Eamon lived in had its own rules. Legality did not come into the methods that she knew were used. There was an unwritten law among their families.

She neared the edge of the pool and was suddenly alerted to movement behind her. Marcia turned her head abruptly and smiled as she saw Eamon swimming towards her.

He had returned from his appointment with his bank manager and had quietly commanded the dogs to remain quiet as he'd slipped into the villa to change into swimwear. He was intrigued by Marcia's faraway look. He felt that something was bothering her. "Ye appear to have something on ye mind!" He placed his arms on either side of her holding on to the edge of the pool, eyes smiling, holding hers, waiting for a reply. "Marcia?" he asked after her hesitation. "I don't want to leave for Miami if ye are feeling troubled. It is enough that ye are going to have an operation, and one, I might add, that will inflict unnecessary risk to yerself, let alone pain. What for?" he quickly added.

She put her arms around his neck. Marcia did not want to go over the subject again. She had a devil of a task the previous night trying to convince him that it was minor surgery. "I am not concerned about anything. I am running through in my mind the checklist of what I need to prepare for tomorrow."

He nodded slowly. "Like I said previously, I don't need for ye to have big breasts. And ye will certainly not be putting them on show for anyone else," he threw in.

She placed two fingers on his lips, kissing him lightly. "Whatever I have shown, and no matter how seductive I have been, you are the only one that I have ever wanted to entice."

"Entice!" he repeated cocking an eyebrow, with a drawn-out smile.

"You are my stud!" she chuckled.

"Stud!" he nodded his head, laughing. "Ensure that ye don't forget it!" He kissed her briefly "Ever!" he threw in, eyes smiling.

"After my swim, we can have lunch on the terrace, and if the girls don't wake, I could mount ye for an hour!" he slapped her rear playfully, releasing her.

Marcia put on a towelling robe and went inside the villa. She walked towards the refrigerator. Aye had previously prepared a salad, Eamon's favourite, sticky Thai rice. Her mobile phone on the lounge table rang. She stopped in her tracks for two seconds, hesitating, turning to look to see if Eamon had heard the phone. He was ploughing through the water, doing laps. Her instinct warned her that it was the unknown caller. Marcia felt compelled to pick up the phone, even though she knew she should leave the call unanswered. She saw the withheld number flash up on the screen. Heart racing, she turned once again to look out the terrace doors at Eamon doing his regular forty lengths. Gingerly, she pressed the green button without speaking, waiting. There was an eerie silence at the other end. Determined not to allow herself to be intimidated by the call, she braced herself and firmly said, "Hello!" trying to project confidence. Nevertheless, unnerved by the non-reply, she immediately cut the call dead, dropping the phone on the table. She exhaled, fighting to overcome her anxiety, trying not to allow whoever it was to invade her mind.

Eamon stepped from the refreshing cool jets of the shower, grabbing a towel and drying his hair. Marcia turned on her side, the mirrors capturing 360 degrees of his toned physique. Inhaling softly, her eyes rested on his tight testicles and bobbing flaccid penis as he walked towards the bed. "I gather by yer smile of satisfaction that ye like the mirrors. I am going to add to our enjoyment!" He picked up her mobile phone from the dressing table and pressed record on the video app. Marcia was thankful that she had deleted the three previously withheld phone calls. Rolling onto her back, she involuntarily opened her legs. Eamon smiled, glancing at their reflection above the bed. "Nice," he murmured, running his fingers down the inside of her thigh. His fingers toying at the entry of her moist opening.

Marcia bucked as Eamon began teasing between her legs with his tongue. Reaching into the drawer of the bedside cabinet, without ceasing, he held up the handcuffs. Raising her arms, he secured her wrists to the brass headboard. "At a guess, I'd give ye a few minutes before ye come. For the first time!" he said, smiling. "However, enjoy it, let it take ye. The next time will be slower, and deeper!"

Marcia thrashed against the restraints as Eamon moved down her body with his tongue and teeth tweaking, softly moving across each taught dark bud. She moaned, breathing rapidly. He increased the pace, clamping his thighs on either side of her body, finding her mouth, tongue meeting tongue. Head thrown back, she held him fast from within.

A short while later, he nodded, smiling, continuing upon feeling her release. Unclipping her bonds, he set her on all fours, adjusting the angle of the phone as he re-entered. "Watch in the mirrors," he directed, "It will aid ye enjoyment!"

Marcia observed all angles, recording their intimacy in her mind. Hands clasped on either side of her buttocks, Eamon continually and slowly entered and withdrew. "It will record as we flow together." Eamon felt Marcia orgasm again.

They both watched their movements in the mirrors. "It is so sexy! I can feel you throbbing deep inside of me," Marcia said in a heightened whisper as their juices began to flow simultaneously. Both enjoyed watching the finality of their coupling. Eamon held her in his arms, while he replayed the recording. "I tink that it is the most beautiful thing to observe us making love. To see us in the act from beginning to the end, coming together is such a turn-on!"

Marcia tilted her head. Eamon smiled into her eyes. "We made our babies from the vision that we have just seen!" Eamon pulled her to him. "That is why I don't like to just have a quickie." He kissed her. "When I make love to ye, it is meaningful. Not a two-minute release," he stated, smiling, smoothing her face with both hands, brushing her lips with his. "This, my wee mystic is going in my safe," he said of the video recording that had captured their intimacy.

Marcia had dropped the boys off at school after seeing Eamon off at the airport early that morning for his flight to Miami. Although she would have preferred that Eamon was home while she was undergoing surgery, she knew that it was important that he help Alphonso with his new business venture. The surgeon had informed her that it was minor surgery, but she was still filled with trepidation. Suzette, who had previously undergone the procedure, told her that the slight discomfort she would experience was worth it.

Marcia smiled to herself, as the vision of Suzette's enhanced breasts came to mind. The surgeon had done skilled work on her friend as she truly looked amazing. She heard her mobile phone ringing as she approached Altea Hills Golf club. Without taking her eyes from the road, she took her phone from her bag and glanced at the screen showing a withheld number. She took a quick look in the rear-view mirror. All was clear behind her. Marcia pulled over, feeling annoyance mixed with apprehension. She answered, "If you think…' She didn't get any further.

"Mum!" the voice interjected. Marcia's mind momentarily fought to recall from the recess of her mind where she recognised from – the voice that she had locked away for nearly a decade.

"Mum, it's Reuben!" Trapped emotions burst the dam. Tears spilled forth, and uncontrolled sobs mixed with rivulets of pent-up heartache prevented her from answering.

"Please don't cry. I am desperate to see you before I relocate with my new family."

Scrabbling for tissues that she kept in the glovebox, she wiped her tears. She put the call on loudspeaker, not wanting to miss a word. "Reuben, how did you find me? I live in Spain."

He gave a soft laugh. "Mum, my girlfriend and her young son used to live in Spain. Her son's father is a Jamaican guy who is a Muay Thai champion and has a gym out in Costa Blanca. Michelle, my girlfriend told me that she had a tarot reading from you before she left him to return to England.

When she described you, I was ninety per cent sure that it was you. She went on to say that you conducted your work from a beauty salon where she had her appointment."

Marcia was silent throughout, absorbing her eldest son's voice. "She also said that you had told her that you had briefly attended Elliot's training and that you practised Hatha yoga, and you also swam daily. She found your business card, after I informed her that I may know you." He paused for a couple of seconds. "Mum. I did not mean to scare you with my phone calls. I was trying to pluck up the courage to speak to you."

"Please don't concern yourself. I am fine. It is you that I am worried about, Reuben. I am in a financial position to help you. I can send you money to help you and your family," Marcia said. "Is there any chance that I can see you?" She tried to hold back her feelings of loss. It's been so long, Reuben, since I have held you!" She threw in before he replied, "Do you have a passport?"

"Yes, Mum. I only have two weeks before we leave this life behind and make a new start."

"Give me your bank details and I will get the money transferred. If you book a hotel near to me in Altea Hills I can meet you. I have to tie up some loose ends here. Then we can meet up." Marcia said, knowing that she would have to make do with the free time she would have the day after her operation. She informed him that she would head to the bank and complete the transaction. He said that he would immediately text his details then confirm once his flight and hotel were booked.

Mind and heart racing, Marcia phoned Aye to say she would be an hour as she had business to attend to. She turned the car around and headed to CaixaBank where she held her personal and joint business accounts.

Outside the bank in her car, Marcia jotted down her son's banking details, which he had sent a few minutes earlier via text.

Gael Martinez, the bank manager, welcomed Marcia into his office. She gave him the details, instructing him to send 10,000 euros from her personal account via international transfer. Gael Martinez was familiar with Marcia and Eamon O'Donally. The bank manager was aware that her husband's 150 million euros was in off-shore accounts in various overseas hideaways. Gael Martinez received regular financial stipends for keeping Eamon O'Donally's vast fortune a closely guarded secret. Because the bank manager's clandestine family was known to his client Mr O'Donally, the two men had an agreement that suited them both.

Marcia knew that what she did with her personal account would not affect her joint business account with Eamon. She took a silent intake of breath as she left the bank, relieved that the money was on its way to her son.

On her way back home, Marcia's mind was spinning. She realised that she would require help to get her plan underway. Time was of the essence. Marcia rang the only person that she knew she could trust to keep a secret. Jane answered on the second ring. Although Marcia did not go into detail, she explained to her friend that in a couple of days, she would be late in collecting the boys from school. She said that she would telephone the head of the school if it came to it. Jane knew that Marcia was having surgery. Jane did not hesitate to help. She asked no questions as to Marcia's reason. Such was the women's bond. Marcia reasoned that if it came down to it, she would tell Jane all so that she could help her.

Marcia winced. She knew that the painkillers that the doctor had prescribed would soon kick in to ease the post-op discomfort. The drive to meet her son Reuben in Benidorm was only 11 km. She had the address of the hotel. Marcia knew that it was not far from Benidorm's municipal market, where she had previously driven Aye to purchase Thai herbs and condiments for her cooking. Her heart was racing, from nerves and excitement. However, she also felt a sense of guilt because she knew she was doing something behind Eamon's back. But this was her son who she would go through hell and high water for. Marcia knew the risk that she was taking as Eamon had eyes everywhere – no matter that he was overseas. Nonetheless, her heart pushed her towards the clandestine meeting.

The small hotel car park was empty bar for a minibus with the hotel's name on the side. She hoped that tourists who flocked to Benidorm would want to be closer to the popular town and not outside, where this hotel was. She clicked the fob, locking her car. She slung her white leather bag over her shoulder and straightened the soft pink, above-the-knee skirt of the suit that she wore. Adjusting her sunglasses, she entered the reception area. The tapping of her stiletto heels on marble flooring brought the young man on the reception desk to attention. He smiled warmly as Marcia approached. She observed him run his eyes over her ringed hand. "May I be of assistance?" He said in flawless English, beaming a smile at her.

Marcia thought his smile was beguiling, although her interest was not with him. "I am meeting a resident here. Can you direct me to the pool area please?"

He pointed to a sign to his left. "I will send someone to bring you a beverage," he said.

Marcia smiled, nodding.

Marcia spotted the young man, dressed in a white, long-sleeved shirt and dark trousers at the far end of the pool area. He was sitting at a table with his long legs stretched out.

He was speaking to a waiter who placed a half-pint glass of beer on the table.

Containing the impulse to run to him, Marcia walked briskly. It was surreal to see this young man, her son, who, the last time she had seen him, was a mere lad of eighteen years. But here was a man. He had olive-toned skin and black hair, so like his half-brothers, Niall and Quinn, Marcia thought. She passed two middle-aged women on sun loungers, both engrossed in their books. The waiter turned to her and smiled.

Reuben turned to look. Pushing back the chair, he moved towards her. He had a handsome, chiselled jawline. He smiled, showing white teeth. It was the face that she had longed to see once again for nearly a decade. The hovering waiter bowed, retreating. Reuben held her face in both hands, removing her sunglasses and placing them on her head. He held her at arm's-length, beaming, then drawing Marcia into his embrace, hugging and kissing her.

Stoically, she bore the pain from his strong clasp. Silent tears fought for release from the over whelming joy that she felt at being able to be with him. Marcia smoothed back his hair. Mother and son's dark eyes lovingly held one another's. "I have booked the Italian restaurant in the hotel, Mum. They serve vegetarian food," Reuben said, smiling. "I can't imagine that you have become a meat enthusiast!"

Marcia shook her head, laughing, slipping her arm through her son's. They walked back to the table. Sitting opposite one another, Reuben took her hands in his and said, "Mum, I can't thank you enough for your financial generosity. I did—"

Marcia cut him off. "Reuben, I am in a position to help you." She took his hands, running her fingers across the back of his hand. He smiled, looking at the diamond and emerald ring on her left hand.

"Your husband obviously cares for you. I have never seen such large precious stones! I can see how radiant and glamorous you look. I am pleased that you are happy with your life."

Marcia inhaled softly, a wry smile on her face. She did not want to speak of the deep love that she had for her husband out of respect for her son's memory of his father. As a young boy, Reuben had worshipped his father, before his untimely death.

"Mum, when I told my girlfriend that I had spoken to you and informed her about the large amount of money that you sent to help us. She told me that she knew that you are the wife of a powerful man. Her ex-boyfriend Elliot told her about him. He said that you had a family together!" Marcia caught a hint of wistfulness, although he was smiling.

"He is a wonderful man. We have four children – two boys and twin girls." She did not elaborate on her life. "Tell me about your newfound family. You have a ready-made son?!"

Reuben grinned. "He is a character. Very clever. So, like his mum!" he said proudly. Marcia could see that her son loved the woman. "Once we are settled, if all goes well, Michelle and I plan to have a baby."

Tears of happiness spilled forth and Marcia squeezed his hands. "I can send money to help you out."

Reuben leaned forward to kiss her. "Mum, you have done enough. I intend—"

Marcia interjected. "Reuben I am wealthy. I have no financial worries. I have a joint share in a nightclub that is extremely successful." She was not bragging. Marcia wanted him to understand that it would be no hardship for her if he allowed her to aid him. "You are going to benefit from my good fortune." She smiled warmly, kissing the back of his hand. "I do not want to hear any more refusals," Marcia spoke firmly. Then her cadence softened. “I won’t see my son struggling while I live a life of luxury. Please, indulge me,” she implored.

Reuben nodded in acceptance.

From a balcony overlooking the pool, a mobile phone camera focused on the couple at the far end of the pool. It clicked with each embrace. Without taking her eyes from the subjects, the woman spoke harshly. “I am telling ye. That’s her. It’s Eamon O’Donally’s wife. The bloody stuck-up bitch. The snooty cow who drives the latest Mercedes. Money is no object to her.” Leaning further over the balcony, she focused the screen and carried on snapping photos of what appeared to be a lovers’ meeting. “It seems that her toy boy is more to her taste! She can’t keep her hands off him!” The woman sneered. “She’s not satisfied that her old man bungs her money. Slag!” She called out over her shoulder, keeping the camera focused on the couple. The sound of the shutter clicking continued as she bemoaned her lot to the young man propped up on the bed in the room. He was bored and wished that he hadn’t agreed to take her away for two days. She was treading on thin ice with him, he thought to himself. He despised her constant criticism of others. It was like she was always spitting venom, her biting remarks fired at any female that took her attention. He had found her exciting for the first few weeks of their relationship, then she told him that she was pregnant. Everything changed. The great sex became a thing of the past and now became a chore to her. She used the pregnancy as an excuse.

“For fuck’s sake, why do you have to stick your nose into other people’s business all the time?” he asked testily, exasperated with her perpetual nastiness. “It could be an innocent meeting. An old friend from the past.” He was fed up with holding his tongue. He turned on her, ready for war. “Why do you feel the need to rain verbal abuse on anyone who gets on in life?" Brady spilled forth. He abhorred the bitterness she harboured due to her early life experiences. It grated on him. "You are not the only one that had a crap childhood!" Brady fired at her. He wouldn't accept it as an excuse for being nasty any longer.

Face aflame, she marched towards him, hands on hips. Her face, which he had once thought pretty, now appeared ugly with bitterness.

"What has ever gone right for ME?" She poked a finger at her chest, glaring at him.

Remaining silent, Brady inhaled. He decided that this would be the last day with her. He made a mental note that he would call Joanna, the young woman whom he'd met on his early morning run along the beach. It had been on the second early morning routine exercise that Brady Lord had asked her for her mobile phone number.

Laughing gaily after spending five hours together, Marcia, with her son's arm around her waist strolled towards her car. Reuben was gazing at his mother while she told him that she would send him further financial help, insisting that he keep in touch. Reuben, holding Marcia at arm's length, smiled into her eyes and nodded in agreement.

He hugged her, and although earlier Marcia had taken two pain killers to help relieve the post-op discomfort, she inwardly bore the pain of his strong hug. Marcia opened the car window, Reuben leaned through, hands on either side of his mother's face, embracing her. Both waved when Marcia reversed the Mercedes. She blew her son a kiss before leaving the car park.

"Got ye!" Bridie said aloud. She was sitting in the reception area waiting for Brady to sort out the hotel bill. The room service that Bridie had ordered had gone way over his budget. Bridie had been angry that they were leaving early. She purposely ordered a three-course meal to bump up the room service bill. She had asked Brady to show her the text from his stepdad to say that he was urgently needed at home. Although he had shown her the message, the street-savvy Dublin girl felt that it was a conspiracy between Brady and his stepfather. Bridie knew that Scott Lord did not approve of his stepson's relationship with her. She grasped another opportunity to capture Marcia O'Donally and her handsome, young lover on camera. Standing from a vantage point near the hotel doors, she discreetly captured the evidence that she intended to put away for a rainy day.

Martha had not believed a word of what Bridie had told her on the phone about Marcia O'Donally having an affair with a young lover in the hotel that Brady Lord had taken her to. She assumed that it was either a case of mistaken identity or Marcia had met up with a friend. Martha knew that her sister was vindictive. Her previous hardships had embittered her to the point that she directed her venom at anyone who appeared to have a better life than her. She had experienced the sting of her sister's jealous remarks regarding her man, Benny Harris, who was attentive and generous to her. When Benny had purchased the villa for her, Bridie took her envy to a new level. However, Martha had made a stand when she started to smear Marcia O'Donally's character. Not to be outdone, Bridie demanded that Martha should come to her apartment, and she would show her proof. Reluctantly, Martha acquiesced.

Martha was stunned as she looked at the evidence, although she did not show it. She could not deny it. It was plain to see from the numerous damning photos on her sister's phone. More to the point, however, Martha wondered why her sister felt the need to interfere in other people's business.

"Ye are not defending that Jezebel now, are ye?" Bridie spat, snatching the mobile phone from Martha exhaled and sat down, looking sadly at her sister. "Brady did not come home again last night. But I put a stop to his little game. I found a phone number in the back pocket of a pair of his jeans in the wash basket. I rang it. The girl who answered was informed that I am having Brady's baby. I warned her to stay away from him. He will pay when he returns!" Eyes ablaze with fury, she began pacing. Although Martha loved and protected Bridie, she would not blame the young lad if he did not return to her. Who would want to listen to her constant railing?

"Please delete those pictures, Bridie. Don't get caught up in others' affairs." She wanted to say to mind her own business and try to rescue her own relationship, but she didn't.

"Fucking delete them? These are going to be printed. I will put them away until I need them again!" Bridie grinned caustically. "Ye have everything now since ye grabbed yerself a sugar daddy."

Martha sighed, standing to leave. She felt the void widening between them. Martha hoped that her sister's state of mind would ease once she had her baby. If she used the photographs to cause trouble, Martha knew that she would not be able to stand by her. Benny would not allow it. Benny had come home early and heard Bridie ranting on the phone. Martha had been ruffled by the call. Benny had gone out of his way to welcome Bridie into their home. However, Martha knew that he would only tolerate so much from Bridie. Under normal circumstances, she would have invited Bridie to dinner at her home, but she could not bring herself to feel compassion for her sister and she knew Benny wouldn't want her there either after hearing that Bridie had upset her.

Later that night, the house phone at Martha and Benny's villa rang. Martha switched her mobile phone off at night at Benny's request because Bridie was constantly ringing at all hours. Benny placed his arm on Martha's, preventing her from getting up. He answered the call. "Phone an ambulance!" he directed derisively to the caller, putting the receiver down.

"Bridie has lost the baby. She is blaming young Brady for not coming home." Martha insisted that she must go to her sister. Overriding Bridie's demands that she only wanted her sister there, Benny said he was going to accompany Martha. He would not allow Bridie to bully and cause upset to his pregnant woman.

Benny and Martha followed the ambulance in their car. They waited until the doctor said that Bridie was fine after her miscarriage before taking her home. Benny would not allow Martha to stay with her for the rest of the night, as her sister had wanted her to. Bridie was seething at what she felt was abandonment by Martha.

Bridie was on her own. A few days later, she paid a visit to the Hawk Wind club to ask Marcia O'Donally for her pole-dancing job back. Bridie was informed that she could have her name put on the list with the other girls who were waiting for a vacancy. However, Bridie had derived a plan.

Bridie telephoned Martha, whom she had not seen since the night of her miscarriage. She was itching to tell her the news. Bridie cut to the chase, informing Martha that she would be leaving Spain. "How will ye survive?" Martha asked, concerned. "Don't ye worry about me. Ye only care about the old fella yer shacking up wit. And his kid that yer having! Don't try to pretend now that ye care about me!"

Martha did not try to defend herself, she just asked, "What about money?" She paused for two seconds before adding. "I will ask Benny..."

Bridie jumped in. "I will have a couple of grand to tide me over until I get a job. I've looked on the internet for rooms to rent. No problem. And I am going to cash in on my assets!"

"Assets?" Martha repeated, not comprehending.

"Marcia O'Donally has cooked her fucking goose. She had her chance, but foolishly, when I went to get my job back at the club, Mrs High-and-Mighty put my name at the bottom of a waiting list. Let's see how far she falls by the time I've finished wit her!"

Martha gasped. "Please don't do anyting stupid. Tink of her husband's pain if ye send those pictures to him!"

Bridie guffawed. "Send him pictures?" I should not tink so!" Bridie ended the call, cutting off her sister's pleading.

"I hold the ace card!" Bridie angrily shouted to the four walls after the call to Martha.

....

Eamon returned to Spain after three days in Miami, knowing that he was not off the hook and was required to return to Miami shortly. He made his way to the club office after speaking to Billy and Benny Harris who had been standing by the bar. They had been discussing Scott Lord who was returning to work in a couple of days. He had been informed that Scott was his old self and had been working out at the gym with Billy. That night at the club had been easy. There hadn't been any trouble, even though there was a stag party in attendance.

Sitting at his desk, he sent a text message to Marcia to ask if the children were asleep. Soundly, she replied. Photo attachments followed. He relaxed into his chair, holding the phone up, scrolling through each picture, blood rushing to his groin at the vision. Surgically enhanced bare breasts, nipples erect, reflected in the bedroom mirrors while she put on a show for him. She lay on the bed, legs akimbo, skimpy, red silk ouvert panties revealing her desire for him.

Eamon shook his head, smiling, not being able to take his eyes off her. Zooming in, he studied her breasts. Although he hadn't liked the idea of her having surgery, he now did not argue. He was the only one that benefitted from admiring them. He would not allow her to flaunt them. Marcia sent another view, her buttocks facing the mirrors, legs wide. He homed in, releasing his fly button.

Give me half an hour. I am going to reward you tonight for the exhibition. Hopefully, you are not tired. It will be a long night. He sent four emoji red hearts. He called Dan on the walkie-talkie, informing him that as it was quiet, he would be heading home.

Bridie had waited along the road from the Hawk Wind club for the second night running. From her vantage point, she had a clear view of the car park where Eamon O'Donally parked his Maserati when he was working. She smiled to herself upon seeing the car drive in earlier. She had waited for an hour. Thomas, Aar and Billy returned Bridie's smile as she approached the club doors. "I want to speak wit Eamon!" She said. Thomas nodded, holding the door open for her.

Glancing around the busy club, she headed towards the office door.

"Come in!" Eamon replied to the rap on the door. Bridie, unsmiling, entered, shutting the door behind her.

Eamon pursed his lips trying to read her. He proffered a chair and wordlessly she took it. Eamon sitting up, forearms on the desk, held her look. He was surprised to see her as she no longer worked at the club. He remained passive. Billy had informed him that Scott Lord was pleased that his stepson

Brady had a new girlfriend, one nearer to his age. He told Billy that Bridie had lost Brady's baby. Scott was relieved that Brady appeared happier now that Bridie was no longer in his life. "What brings ye here at this late hour?" Eamon asked, cocking his head at the sullen girl.

Bridie, clenching her jaw, stiffened. "This is not a social visit!" Bridie stated.

Eamon's look hardened as he scrutinised her face and read her body language. She appeared to be preparing for battle. "Then tell me what is yer reason," he said, calmly.

Opening her shoulder bag, she took out a large envelope. He observed her icy look as she slid it across the desk. He sucked air through his teeth without taking his eyes from her. Taking hold of the envelope, he weighed it in his hands before opening it. Sitting back into the chair, he tore the seal open. His look gave nothing away as he glanced at a couple of the photos within. Throwing them on the desk, he glared at her. "'Tis not a very nice game that I tink ye are intending to play. Blackmail?" Cocking an eyebrow, Eamon waited for a reply, slowly running his fingers across his goatee beard.

Her eyes took on a look of defiance, ready to face off. "They are photographs, what I thought should be brought to yer attention. Nobody likes betrayal!" Bridie stated.

"Ye appear to be concerned about others' lack of morals, yet ye come here intending to blackmail. It's rather like calling the kettle black. Or maybe your lack of intellect cannot decipher the difference!" Eamon smiled caustically.

Bridie exploded at his jibe and stood up. Before she had time to speak, Eamon rose to his full height. "Obviously, ye want money. Hit an all-time low ever since yer lad's new girl has found herself yer old jockey to ride." Firing insults at her was the only thing that prevented him from striking her.

"Brady has got himself a new mare. I hear the boy is happy with someone his age." Eamon continued firing insults at her.

"YE SHOULD LOOK CLOSER TO HOME. LOOK AT YER WIFE SHAGGING A GOOD-LOOKING BLOKE. HALF HER AGE. OBVIOUSLY, YE ARE NOT ABLE TO PLEASE HER!" Bridie shouted.

Eamon's eyes were like ice-cold steel as he leaned forward across the desk. Bridie stepped back. "Ye are fortunate that ye are not a man. How much are ye asking for?" he growled.

"I want two thousand pounds. Not euro!" she demanded.

Inhaling, he turned towards the safe, slapping the bundle on the desk in front of her. She viewed it. Picking it up, she held it out to him. "This is only a thousand euros!" she screeched.

He nodded. "Count yerself lucky that ye are walking out of here. Now fuck off out of my sight before I change my mind!" he commanded.

Bridie snatched the cash, stuffing it into her bag.

"I wouldn't have taken yer for a 'sleeveen',[1] however, it proves how wrong ye can be!" Eamon said.

She stuck two fingers up at his insult, slamming the door behind her.

Eamon locked the door. In a zombie-like fashion, he moved to pick up the envelope, slumping into the chair. Exhaling, bracing himself, he removed the pictures. All emotions within him died as he looked at Marcia smiling in the embrace of the young, dark-haired guy, whose hands were placed on either side of her face. They were kissing and hugging one another, then they were arm in arm. He studied her. He could see that she had had the surgery. Her breasts were straining beneath the pink jacket that she was wearing.

[1] Irish word meaning untrustworthy or cunning person.

Eamon rose and moved to the filing cabinet. He removed one of the two bottles and a glass that were kept for guests. He poured a tumbler three-quarters full of brandy. Knocking it back in one go, he picked up his phone. Finding the number he was looking for he dialled. It was answered after three rings. Refilling the glass and downing the golden liquor, he put the evidence back into the envelope and left the club.

"Good night boss!" Dan and Billy called after him as he marched towards his car without turning, raising his hand at them.

"Was that my imagination, or did the boss stagger?" Billy asked Dan. Dan had taken note but kept his own counsel. Both men watched the car pull out. However, to their amazement, the Maserati headed in the opposite direction to Eamon's home.

"What the fuck is going on?" Billy stated, frowning. Dan, perplexed by Eamon's erratic behaviour, began to ponder on his boss's last visitor. Bridie had entered the club earlier, smiling. Upon her exit, she exuded fire and brimstone, her face like thunder. He wondered if there was a connection.

The manager on night duty stood at the small hotel reception desk. Smiling, he said, "Good evening, sir!"

"I phoned earlier and booked a room."

The night manager checked the name. "Room twenty-one," he said. He turned to take a key from the row of hooks behind him. "May I take a bank or credit card for a deposit? It's company policy against damages, should they occur."

"Cash!" Eamon grumbled. He counted out the amount, pushing it forward on the desk.

The man nodded his head, taking the five hundred euros. He was not going to argue the toss. His trained nose could detect alcohol on the immaculately dressed man.

Although he recognised couture, the night manager was not fooled. He judged the man in front of him to be no gentleman.

"Have ye got a bottle of Hennessy-VS?"

Irish! the man thought, smugly. "Certainly, sir. I will have one sent to your room."

Watching the big man retreat to his room, the night manager tried to rationalise the man's one-night booking and the smell of alcohol. Most probably had a fall-out with his wife, he thought. He had noticed the wedding ring. He went over to the computer to look at the camera that had captured the car park at the back of the hotel. "Maserati!" he said aloud, impressed. "Hopefully a big tipper!"

Marcia could not understand what was keeping Eamon. It had been just over an hour and a half since his text saying that he was returning home early from his shift at the club. She knew that with the club, anything could happen to change things at the last minute. Fights could break out at any given moment. Although there was enough security staff to deal with any trouble that should arise, Marcia knew that Eamon would not walk away and leave his men to it. Wrapping a towelling robe around her, she went into the lounge, heading for the terrace doors. Both dogs fell in behind her. She slipped on a pair of flip-flops that she kept by the doors. Sharp tendrils of cold air encased her. The palm fronds rustled as they were buffeted by the strong gusts of wind. She sat at the garden table, eyes searching the vista, listening for Eamon's car.

Two hours had passed since she had received his message, and she felt that she could not wait any longer. She sent him a text message and waited ten minutes to make sure it was delivered, but it remained unanswered. Consternation gripped her solar plexus. Marcia rang Eamon. There was no answer and the automated voicemail kicked in. Marcia left a message for Eamon to ring her. After leaving three more voice messages over the next hour, with no reply, she began to panic. She rang Dan's number and Dan informed her that Eamon had left the club earlier. He told her not to worry, that he would phone Eamon. A short while later, Dan phoned her back, confirming that he could get no answer. He reassured her that the club was about to close and that he and Billy would go out to look for Eamon's car.

Storm clouds were building out at sea. The first raindrops splattered over the swimming pool. The dogs shook their coats and Marcia shivered. She returned to the bedroom. Time and again she rang Eamon's number. Tears fell on the last call when she received an automated message that the number was unavailable. She silently prayed to the Spirit world to bring Eamon home safely to her.

....

Eamon's mind was in turmoil as he lay on the hotel bed. He had been down this road before when his ex-wife Eve had deceived him. His love for Eve turned to hate. He could not believe that it was happening to him again. It had taken him a long time to trust Marcia. If he had not seen the photos with his own eyes, he would have called the girl out as a liar. However, when he had first looked at the photographs of Marcia in the arms of a young lover, he knew the anguish that he was experiencing was incomparable to anything that he had experienced before. Although he hadn't revealed it in front of Bridie. Eamon thought back to how Marcia had duped him into believing that he was her soul mate.

Earlier, he had felt a murderous rage at being betrayed by Marcia. After her last call, he had thrown the mobile phone across the room, smashing it against the wall. Something told him that he could not confront her. He would not be able to answer for his actions. He picked up one of the strewn photos from the bed. Marcia was wrapped in the young guy's arms, looking adoringly into his eyes.

"What a prize cunt I am. I paid for her breast enhancement and the eyelift that she said she needed. FUCKING SURE YE DID!" he shouted to the four walls. "When ye have a young fella who's half yer age to entertain! YE SLATTERN!" he spat the insult. "YE ARE GOING TO PAY. I PROMISE YE THAT MY PAIN WILL BE NOTHING LIKE WHAT YE ARE GOING TO HAVE WHEN I TAKE MY CHILDREN FROM YE!" he threatened aloud, poking a forefinger at her face in the picture, then ripping it in two.

He scoffed at his stupidity. He had returned to Miami for three days to oversee the delivery and fitting of the four Baccarat crystal chandeliers from France that Alphonse paid a small fortune for. He pondered if Marcia had purposely set the ball rolling for the deception when she had made the prediction about Joyce Grant's son-in-law Matt.

Alphonso had stepped up and alleviated the problem. Nonetheless, she would have known that Eamon would be required to return the favour. He concluded that she must have purposely set things up for him to be absent in Miami so she was free to sneak off with her lover. "There was me concerned about leaving her for three months. Could not bring myself to tell her!" He laughed aloud again, chiding himself at being hoodwinked by his wife.

Propped up on the pillows, Eamon leaned across the bed to pour himself another drink from the half-filled bottle on the bedside cabinet. It slipped from his hold, spilling the contents on the carpet. He laughed at his foolhardiness. How could he allow himself to be drawn in by her? He watched the alcohol seep into the pile. He pulled himself up, staggering towards the small fridge. He smiled upon seeing the row of miniature bottles of alcohol.

Raising a bottle, he made a toast. "Here's to ye Josephine," he said, recalling the woman that he had met on the flight to Miami. "At least ye are honest in yer game." He guffawed. "What a loser!" he spoke of himself. "I was handed it on a plate. I turned Josephine down flat. I vowed never to be disloyal. The game is about to change. I'll put her on the back burner. Two can play that game!" He picked up another photo of Marcia, glaring at her the young man leaning into her car. "Two can play yer game! No more Mister Loyal. YE WHORE!" he shouted, stabbing a finger at her face that was being held by the young lover's hands.

Downing the last dregs of every bottle, he retched, leaning over the side of the bed and projectile vomiting across the floor. He wiped his mouth with the back of his suit jacket sleeve and fell back on the pillow. The alcohol took him to the dark void where he could escape from the reality of what his life had become.

Mr Smythe-Carter, the night manager had been standing outside room 21 with an ear to the door, hesitating to knock. He had received a complaint earlier about shouting and the sound of furnishings being smashed. He heard the man inside, slurring, railing abuse against someone. The manager knew that he could not allow the disturbance to continue. However, he could not muster up the courage to face the man.

Suddenly, the noise subsided. Exhaling, he stealthily moved along the corridor. The night manager returned to the reception area to phone the gentleman who had made the complaint, informing him that he had dealt with it. He breathed a sigh of relief that he hadn't had to confront the drunken Irishman. He was not brave, nor foolish. He hoped that there was not too much damage to the furnishings. However, he concluded that judging by the Irishman's attire and his expensive car, he would not have too much of a problem retrieving any costs.

Marcia had hardly slept. The snatched hours of sleep came after she had exhausted her tears, sobbing into the pillow. When the Hawk Wind club had shut, Dan and Billy had searched for Eamon's car, but there had been no sighting. The men were going to resume their search for Eamon, however, Marcia had insisted that the pair return home to get some rest. Dan told her that they would continue in the morning.

Marcia put on a brave face in front of the children. She did not want them to think that there was anything amiss. Aisling and Aine would usually vie for Eamon's attention first thing in the morning before he drove the boys to school. Eamon had only returned from Miami a couple of days ago. She had found it difficult to be without him, and the children also missed his presence.

Marcia explained to the boys that Papa needed to attend to his business. Aye distracted the twins by allowing them to help her in preparing a gingerbread cookie mixture.

Marcia returned from the school run to find Aye and Bonita, the Spanish housekeeper, playing with the girls in the grounds. The dogs were on the terrace, heads resting on forelegs, observing, and turned their heads when Marcia came into sight. They then returned to sentry duty, eyeing the ball that the women were throwing back and forth to the giggling girls.

Marcia had hoped to see Eamon's car parked in front of the villa on her return. Fighting against despondency, she went inside to make another phone call.

A short while later, Marcia buzzed the intercom to let Jane's Land Rover through the gates. Both dogs wagged their tails upon seeing Jane. They ran to greet her.

Jane had her fair hair in a ponytail and was dressed in jodhpurs that showed her curvaceous figure. "I have an hour to spare. Dogs and horses are fed and watered," Jane stated. She waved to the girls as they played. Both waved back, resuming their game. "They are beautiful," Jane remarked, continuing to observe them.

Aisling stamped her foot in Aye's direction, "Rib khun!" the small girl demanded loudly, impatiently telling Aye to be quick. Aye waggled a finger at her in playful chastisement. Marcia shook her head. Jane laughed. "As beautiful as they are, you can see how strong-minded those little females will become. I think that Billy and I made the right decision not to have children. I will stick to my animals," she said, grinning.

Both women sat under the awning on the terrace. Marcia put Jane in the picture about Eamon's sudden disappearance. Jane said that Billy had phoned her from the club last night around 2 am to let her know that he would be home late. She said that upon his return he said he would have a couple of hours of sleep and then he was going out again. "I never question Billy, however, now that you have told me about this situation, I should think that Billy and Dan are on the case!"

"Dan had told me that after their search for Eamon's car, they had phoned numerous hotels, but Eamon had not registered with any of them. For the life of me, Jane, I am perplexed. Why would Eamon just disappear like this?" She sighed heavily. "Dan has assured me that they will continue to look for him until they discover his whereabouts."

Marcia's hands fidgeted as she spoke, and Jane took hold of them. "There must be some logical explanation, Marcia.

You said that he had sent you a text message to say that he was returning home to you?"

Marcia smiled thinly. "I had enticed Eamon with my previous texts." She did not go into details; she knew that there was no need.

Jane smiled, then looked serious. "I do not understand. It is mind-boggling. Something must have happened after he had texted you."

Marcia exhaled. "I asked Dan the very same thing, but he is in the dark as much as I am." She looked away. Jane patted her hand.

Turning towards Jane again, Marcia continued, "I am frightened, Jane. He could be lying in a ditch somewhere, injured!"

Jane shook her head and leaned back in her chair. Marcia pressed on, "Scott Lord was sneaked up on and attacked in the club car park, and then, a while later, Eamon's men were shot at outside of Michael's bar. Thankfully both men are now recovering, but it can be a dangerous job working in a night-club, Jane. Our men are prime targets to be attacked by irate men who have been evicted from the club. You work there. You have seen first-hand when drunk and high men have been frog-marched out of the building, shouting at the security guards!"

Jane nodded and said, "However, Marcia, just think about it, Eamon's car would have been seen on the search. It is not only the fact that the car is a Maserati, it also has very conspicuous number plates." She tried to reassure her that Eamon had not been waylaid by anyone. "Marcia, I feel certain that something must have happened after Eamon replied to your texts, something that had upset him. There is a possibility that he could have driven off somewhere to cool his heels! Maybe someone or something had upset him and he needed some time on his own to calm down so he booked into a hotel, or a bed and breakfast."

Marcia shook her head vehemently. "Eamon would not do that, Jane. If Eamon has something on his mind, he takes immediate action. Eamon is spontaneous. His temperament is explosive. Dan and Billy would have known if there had been any trouble at the club."

Jane inhaled. "I know." She replied heavily.

"Jane, Eamon and I were looking forward to spending some time together last night. He was eager to return home. Eamon cut his night shift short."

"Then there has to be a really good reason for his disappearance, Marcia. Eamon may have received an upsetting phone call before he left the club. It has to be something along those lines. Otherwise, there is no rhyme or reason."

Marcia sighed. Jane rose to leave and hugged her. "Leave it to the men. They will find him."

"I will ring you as soon as I hear anything," Marcia said as Jane took her leave.

"I don't think that we should bother phoning any more hotels," Dan said to Billy, tapping the side of his left temple with his forefinger. "Something is telling me that if the boss is in a hotel, he has most probably given a false name. Let's go and try to find his Maserati." Dan sat behind the wheel. "I don't think that he would choose a big hotel. Get up a list of small places – three or four stars," Dan directed Billy.

They tried three hotels that were situated near one another. Then Billy directed Dan towards the two-star hotel. That hotel car park was empty. The sat nav then directed them to the four-star hotel on the Avenida de Ruzafa in Alicante. They drove around to the car park at the back of the hotel. There they spotted the Maserati. Both men smiled as Dan parked next to it.

Mr Smythe-Carter, the hotel night manager was in a quandary. Not only had he received a phone call from the day manager, Informing him that he was sick and could not take over the day shift, he knew that around midday, the Irishman would be required to vacate room 21. He had knocked on the door earlier, albeit lightly, and listened for movement behind the door. Silence. He tapped his pen on the wood counter, contemplating his next move. Mr Smythe-Carter stiffened when the two men entered the reception area. Dan and Billy approached the desk. The manager looked down his nose at the pair, straightening his tie.

"May I help you, gentlemen?" he asked.

"I want the room number of the owner of the Maserati parked out the back," Dan stated.

"Do you have the name of the vehicle's owner?" the manager said haughtily, taking a step back as Billy stepped closer, leaning towards him.

"There is no point in giving names." Billy pointed at the computer screen on the reception desk. "Look at the computer for the booking registration. That motor belongs to our friend and we wish to speak to him." Billy paused, glaring. "It's not a request. Do you understand me?" Billy growled through gritted teeth.

Giving a sharp nod, Smythe-Carter smiled thinly. He had no intention of making an issue out of the request. Without hesitation, the manager opened the screen in front of him. "Mr Smith is in room 21. I tried earlier to rouse him..."

Billy jumped in, holding his hand out. "Give me the key!"

It was against company policy to allow anyone other than a member of staff to use the universal card to gain entry, however, the manager thought it wiser to not argue the toss.

Dan and Billy stared him down. He took the card from a side drawer, handing it over. "Please return it," he said, giving a show of his authority. He held the door card out gingerly towards Billy. Billy snatched it, giving a sharp nod in reply.

Dan pointed to the door halfway along the corridor. He listened at the door for movement. He looked at Billy and placed his finger to his lips as he put the card in the slot. When it flashed green, Dan noiselessly pushed down the handle.

Both men shook their heads at the mess as they entered the room. Billy pinched his nose. The stench of vomit and alcohol was made worse by closed windows. Billy stood by the door to allow a shaft of light in as Dan moved silently across the carpet to pull back the curtains. The light revealed the extent of the disarray. Billy quietly clicked the door shut. They moved towards the bed where Eamon lay on his side. The empty miniature bottles of alcohol were strewn across the bed, among the photographs. They peered closer, scanning each one and recognising Marcia.

Billy, shaking his head, mouthed to Dan, "Poor fucker!" Then he noticed the smashed mobile phone near the wall. He retrieved it, handing it to Dan.

Dan saw that the cracked screen showed missed calls from Marcia and himself. There were numerous unread text messages. Dan inhaled, putting the phone in his pocket, picking up the empty Hennessy bottle from the floor next to the bed. On the bedside cabinet lay Eamon's wedding ring.

Eamon was comatose. Dan tapped his face. No response. Dan no longer whispered. Eamon was out for the count. "Help me get his suit off. He has puked on it. By the look of the amount of drink that he consumed and how much he vomited, it was fortunate that he didn't choke. Fortunately, by looking at the large stain on the carpet, he had lost a lot of the brandy."

"Leave the underpants on!" Dan instructed. Billy had found a towelling robe hanging in the wardrobe. "Once we get him under that shower and clean him up, we'll get him into that robe. You can book him in for another night. Get jobs-worthy on the desk to have the suit and shirt express cleaned. Bring a pot of strong black coffee. Wait for it and bring it yourself. We don't want any nosy bollocks in the room. Also, inform the manager that any damage will be paid for."

Billy nodded. Both men heaved Eamon's dead weight to the shower cubicle. "Stand back!" Dan stated once they had left Eamon leaning with his head slumped against the tiled wall. Dan turned the dial to cold and stepped back as the powerful icy torrent hit Eamon's face.

Eamon groggily struggled, arms raised to defend himself from the onslaught. He gradually opened his eyes. Both men smiled warmly at him.

Dan had gathered up the photos strewn over the bed and returned them to the envelope on the bedside cabinet. They threw the miniature bottles along with the Hennessy bottle in the bin. They wrapped him in the robe and aided him as he staggered to the bed from the shower. Billy took Eamon's clothes and went to speak to the manager.

Eamon silently sipped the second black coffee, staring at the liquid while Dan sat back on a hard chair at the small pine desk, giving his boss time to clear his head. He had sent Billy back to the Hawk Wind club with the photographs. He instructed him to put them in Eamon's office safe and to bring back the spare mobile phone that was kept in there.

Dan contemplated the situation, trying to piece the jigsaw together. Last night, Eamon had been in high spirits before the Irish girl Bridie went in to speak to him. Eamon had said he would be leaving early and asked Dan to take over.

Dan thought back to a short while after that when Bridie came storming out of the club with a thunderous look on her face. A while later, Eamon appeared to stagger to his car, getting in and speeding off in the opposite direction to his home. He thought of how over an hour later Marcia had rung him concerned because she had expected Eamon to be home by then. Dan pondered the photos of Eamon's wife. He sensed that something did not sit right. He judged himself to be a pretty good judge of character. Marcia did not fit into the box of a player, even though the photos made it look otherwise. She had been photographed in the embrace of a much younger, good-looking guy. However, Dan's gut feeling was telling him that all was not as it appeared in the pictures. The missing piece of the jigsaw was Bridie. Blackmail, he concluded.

Eamon inhaled, stretched and looked around the room. He turned to face Dan. "I don't need to ask if yous two saw the pictures."

Dan did not comment on the context of the photographs. "Billy is putting them in the club safe. He is bringing you the other mobile phone that you keep there. You are booked in for another night here just to give us a bit more time." He glanced at his wristwatch. "The hotel's express cleaning service will return your clothing within two hours."

Eamon nodded, rising from the bed and heading towards the bathroom.

Coming back into the room, he wiped his mouth after brushing his teeth with the hotel-issue toothbrush. "I need to ask ye a big favour. I have decided to return to Miami for a while. It will be a lot on yer shoulders to keep the business running and keep an eye on my children, however, I will look after ye, once I sort tings out that end." He paused for two seconds. "We'll take it from there."

Dan nodded without replying. He got up to answer the knock on the door. He stepped out of the room, closing the door discretely behind him. He returned with Eamon's laundered suit. Handing it over, he said, "I will sort everything out with the men, boss. Billy will agree to step in to share the workload. There will be no problem," Dan assured him.

"I need my passport from my home. When Billy returns wit the phone I will phone Miami. Afterwards, I will book a flight as soon as possible."

Billy returned to the hotel room and Eamon put him in the picture about his plans. Billy didn't hesitate to fall in with his boss's wishes.

Marcia had phoned Dan. He had told her that he was on his way to speak to her. She pressed him about Eamon. He replied that he had found him and that he would speak face-to-face with her when he arrived.

Pressing the button to open the villa gates and let Dan's car through, Marcia stood framed in the doorway. She watched Dan get out of his car and tried to read his body language. Her multi-coloured, floral, ankle-length, Indian-style dress billowed with the strong breeze when she descended the steps towards him. The two dogs wagged their tails upon recognising him.

Dan smiled thinly. "May I speak to you somewhere inside where it is private?" Without conversing, Dan followed Marcia into the lounge. The girls were napping, Aye was in her room, and Bonita had finished for the day. The sense of awkwardness was palpable. Dan moved toward the far side of the large room and stood by the terrace windows, briefly looking out. He turned to face Marcia. Her dark eyes searched his. He inhaled and said, "I have spoken to the boss. He has asked me to come here to get his passport." Dan could see that Marcia was struggling to comprehend his request.

"Eamon's passport?!" she repeated, eyes darting, trying to understand why Eamon would be going overseas without seeing her or the children.

"This is no easy thing for me to have to come here. Please understand. I am only the messenger."

Marcia moved towards him and said, "Dan, I don't understand. Please tell me where Eamon is. I must see him to talk to him," she pleaded, her voice rising.

He shook his head sadly. "I cannot go above the boss's orders. He requires the passport immediately."

Marcia clutched at his arm. "Dan, please tell me what has happened," Marcia said as she fought the tears.

Gently but firmly, he released her grip without replying. He looked at her, then continued, "I have been instructed to oversee the business for a while. If you encounter any problems, I was told that you are to call upon me."

"Is Eamon going to Miami without speaking to me?" Marcia asked incredulously. Dan held her desperate look without confirming her question. Marcia forlornly shook her head. Rivulets of tears cascaded down her face. Appearing defeated, she slowly turned, head down, and went to get Eamon's passport.

Upon Dan's return journey back to Eamon, he gave Marcia a great deal of thought. To his mind, she would need to be a very good actor to appear to be in the dark as to why Eamon would leave her. *Surely, if she had a lover,* he mused, *Marcia would realise that Eamon had discovered her secret.* Although Dan had seen Marcia in the photographs, in what appeared to be an intimate encounter with a younger guy, the whole setup seemed unlikely. He thought that he needed to get to the bottom of it.

Later that evening, Dan dropped Eamon off at the airport. Eamon had changed flights so he could leave for

Miami earlier than planned. He was moving along the queue to board the plane for Miami at Charles de Galle International Airport. Eamon carried no hand luggage. He would purchase whatever he required on the other side of the Atlantic He had phoned Alphonso Gabrette to inform him that he was returning to help out with the management of Alphonso's new nightclub. However, he had not mentioned anything yet to the old Italian about his change of circumstances, or that he was making plans to bring his children to live with him in Miami. Eamon was determined that Marcia would pay heavily for her betrayal with another man.

A jubilant, although somewhat curious, Alphonso had questioned Eamon about his change of plans. They had agreed that Alphonso would give Eamon the nod when the club was ready. There were still a few finishing touches to make before the opening date. Eamon said that he had everything wrapped up earlier than expected in Spain. The old Italian was satisfied with his answer.

Marcia had been unable to sleep since her encounter with Dan after he had informed her that Eamon would be leaving Spain. She had been sitting outside on the terrace since the previous evening trying to make any sort of sense of why Eamon had left her and the children without any notice. She knew that she hadn't been the cause of his sudden departure. There wasn't anything on her part that she could put her finger on.

She had hoped that Eamon would have made contact by now to explain what was going on. The suspense was tormenting her. Marcia felt the need to talk to someone, however, she realised that Jane and Cindy wouldn't have any answers either. Their partners, Dan and Billy were Eamon's men, and she knew that their lips would be sealed. Marcia heard her phone ping as a text came in. She eagerly picked it up. She sighed with disappointment to see that it wasn't Eamon's number. It was Suzette saying that she had some free time and would like to visit. Marcia replied that she was at home and would be pleased to see her.

Marcia did not want to say anything to Suzette regarding Eamon's departure because she would have railed against him. Suzette breezed toward Marcia who was waiting to greet her at the top of the steps up to the villa. Suzette looked as glamorous as ever – nails painted, make-up flawless. Suzette made no secret that she had Botox and filler injections to aid in holding back the years. Her dress was no doubt from one of the hottest designers that she favoured. The women hugged, and Marcia stepped back to let Suzette through the door.

"I love your dress," Marcia complimented her cap sleeve, slash neck, green, knee-length dress.

"This is the mantis-green dress that I spotted in an up-and-coming Italian designer's collection while browsing through Vogue."

Suzette stopped in front of Marcia and studied her face. "Although you look as gorgeous as ever, you appear drained. What's wrong?"

Marcia said she would explain after she had made them a drink.

Marcia made them both coffee and they sat down under the terrace awning before she went into detail from beginning to end.

"Passport!" Suzette declared. "Do you mean to say that he has gone abroad without a goodbye to you and the children?" she asked, shocked.

"It appears that way. Dan informed me that Eamon has left him in charge of the business and also to look after his family if there are any problems," Marcia said downheartedly.

"Who the hell does he think he is?" Suzette stated indignantly. Her face flushed with anger. "Calling himself the big shot. What sort of coward would hightail it from his family, instead of trying to sort out with you whatever the problem is? Because there obviously is one!"

"I'm perplexed, Suzette. I feel tormented."

Suzette reached across the table to take Marcia's hand.

"Listen to me. You and I have faced many obstacles in our time, and no man is going to destroy us. Let him carry on. Wherever he is!" Suzette threw in. "Work will take your mind off him. I will make the phone calls to your previous clients in the address book and start getting them booked in. Show him that you are not going to be treated like a doormat!"

Marcia inhaled, and said, "I won't be able to concentrate!"

"Please, Marcia!" she put her hand up to prevent her from continuing. "You have great powers of mental control. For as long as I have known you, you have practised yoga. Try putting into practice for yourself what you preach to others. Dig deep, you told me in the past," Suzette teased. "Do not allow negativity into your mind. Do not give another your power of control. Get your life back, Marcia!" Suzette directed. "You have Aye and Bonita to help you. You are in a strong financial position. If Eamon O'Donally imagines that he can pull your strings like a puppet..." She waggled two red-painted talons. "Suzette's dark-brown eyes flared. "Teach him a lesson. Fight back, Marcia. Think about all that you have put into your relationship with him. You have devoted your life to him and given him four children! Look where it has got you!"

Marcia nodded slowly, smiling weakly. "Okay! But only two days a week." She realised that Suzette was right. Going back to work would help to take her mind off Eamon leaving.

After all, to take his passport, Eamon must be serious about their separation. She had to think of her future.

"That's my girl. I will get the ball rolling at the salon." Suzette grinned in triumph. "Keep yourself busy. Sort your wardrobe out. Retail shopping is a great therapy. You and I will take the twins with us. I will take us all out to lunch this week – the girls will enjoy it!"

Marcia felt more uplifted after Suzette had left. She sat down to lunch with Aisling and Aine, although she hardly ate any of the salad that Aye had prepared for her. Aye had chastised her. She had spent time in the pool with the girls. Later, while the twins napped, Marcia had some spare time before she went to collect the boys from school. She decided to sort through her wardrobe, as there were some items that she needed to take to the dry cleaners. She took out four dresses. Then she looked at Eamon's suits. For the most part, they were black, his favoured colour, however, he had had three made by his tailor in dark grey. Marcia remembered how they had suited him. She reached up to where they hung, taking the sleeve and holding it to her face. Taking in the scent of his cologne. She took it down to have it cleaned.

She remembered to check the pockets to make sure there weren't any coins or anything else in them. She pulled out a purple business card embossed with gold lettering. Marcia went rigid with shock as she read and reread the woman's name. The phone number told her that this woman lived in the US. Leaning against the wall for support, card in hand, she slid to the floor and sobbed with the realisation that she had discovered the reason why Eamon had left her.

10

Eamon had asked not to be disturbed throughout the nine-hour flight. He clipped his seatbelt and kept his seat in an upright position, knowing that if he reclined the seat to a sleeping position and there was turbulence, the flight attendant would have to disturb him. He was awoken by the flight attendant before the impending descent into Miami. He used the bathroom, splashing water on his face, trying to clear his groggy mind. He returned to his seat. Thankfully, the seat next to him was vacant. He remembered part of a dream. Marcia and his four children were at an airport. He ran towards them as the group disappeared through the departure gate. He had no ticket or passport. A feeling of loss overcame him.

The familiar cacophony of the traffic filled Eamon's senses. Miami's shopping mall was but a short distance from the airport. At this time of day, shoppers added to the mix. A lorry braked, blasting a horn, cars screeched to a halt, taxi drivers joined the mayhem. He noticed Joey raising his hand in greeting. Eamon briskly moved toward the waiting limousine. He knew that once he was inside the car, the noise would be muted. Eamon slid into the passenger seat, clipping the belt in.

"I bet ya haven't missed this!" Joey said, grinning, as he shut the driver's door, indicating the ensuing ruckus on the street. Cabs and cars blasted their horns as Joey nipped into the flow of traffic. Joey had passed no comment on the fact that Eamon had no luggage.

Joey brought him up to speed regarding the renovations to Alphonso's watering hole. Although Eamon had been away from Miami for a few days, Joey said that the builders were making good progress. On the 18-mile journey to Golden Beach, Dade County, Eamon slipped into the conversation that at some point he would need to pick up a few things. Joey nodded, stating that the following day he would drive him downtown to the mall. Joey also informed Eamon about the deterioration in Alphonso's health. "It appears that each time you return to Spain, Alphonso loses his inspiration." The previous times after you left Miami, I found the old man sitting in his recliner in the early hours, gazing out at the Atlantic."

Eamon felt guilty for previously deserting the old Italian. However, he would now have time on his hands to sort his and his children's future out in Miami.

Joey's cadence softened. "To be honest with ya," he paused for a few seconds as if it was difficult to say. "I don't even think that when the club opens, it will fill the void that Marcella has left in his life with her passing! But..." he said, smiling, "he's perked up since ya phone call. Al enjoys ya company!" He took his eyes off the road for a second to smile at Eamon. "It pleases me that he is fond of ya. He told me that he thinks of ya as a son!"

Eamon nodded, turning to glance out the window. A vision of Marcia and his children rose before him and a black void filled his heart. Dismissing the moment, he turned to Joey. "How long do ye tink it will take before opening night?"

"Not too long," he answered. For the rest of the drive, Joey spoke in depth about his concern for Alphonso and the fact that although the old Italian's mind was as sharp as ever, it was his physical health that was rapidly on the decline. Joey told Eamon that out of his three daughters, the youngest, Chiara, was the only one who regularly looked out for her father. He spoke of Alphonso's generosity to his girls, whom Joey judged to be selfish, apart from Chiara.

Eamon kept his own counsel about Alphonso's daughters. The old Italian had previously remarked about the rivalry between the two elder girls. Victoria and Aria had been at one another's throats since their teens. He spoke of their husbands, who he thought were both well-matched to his two eldest girls. All were, in his estimation, money grabbers. Chiara was Alphonso's favourite. She openly adored her father, phoning him daily and visiting him twice weekly. Whereas he had said that he rarely spoke to the two eldest daughters.

When Eamon arrived at Alphonso's home, he could see the deterioration in the old Italian, although it had only been a few days since he had last seen him. His eyes and smile welcomed him. Alphonso held out his hand. Eamon took note of the slight tremor, which was not notable previously. He reverently kissed it, taking the proffered chair opposite. Alphonso adjusted his recliner to the upright position. Studying Eamon, he pursed his lips, noticing he wasn't wearing his wedding ring. "Problems?" he queried.

Eamon inhaled. He had removed his wedding ring in the hotel. He had it in the inside front pocket of his suit jacket. At both airports, he had been searched after the detector had picked it up going through security. He did not want to discuss it. He would deal with the situation. However, Alphonso, eyebrow crooked was waiting for an answer.

"Ya appear to be travelling light. No luggage! Ya wedding band has been removed. And yet ya told me on the phone that ya had it all wrapped up in Spain." He scratched his nose, pushing his glasses up. Leaning into his chair, he held Eamon's look. He continued, elevating his brow when Eamon did not answer. "I am not prying into ya private life, son. But how can ya move forward if ya come here with a burden weighing on your mind?" He pressed on. "The last time I saw ya, when ya left here, ya appeared to be a man who was content with his lot. What's changed so quickly?"

Eamon shook his head slowly, running his thumb and forefinger a few times through his goatee beard. "I don't want to burden ye, Al." Eamon gave a small smile.

"Offloading is good for the soul…" Alphonso left it hanging, waiting for Eamon to explain.

Joey brought Alphonso his regular golden liquor. Eamon waved away his offer of a drink.

Sucking air through his teeth, Eamon waited until they were alone before confiding in Alphonso. He inhaled. "I have seen photographs of my wife with a fella." Eamon gave a sardonic laugh, adding, "Who appears to be half her age."

The old boy pursed his lips, making himself comfortable, taking a small mouthful of his drink while Eamon went into details about the situation that he said had torn his marriage apart.

Alphonso let him have his say without interruption. Joey returned, topping up his boss's glass. Alphonso did not touch it for a while. "Tell me a bit about ya woman's history."

Eamon nodded, informing Alphonso about Marcia's early marriage and how she had been widowed when her young husband died unexpectedly. He talked about how she had devoted her life to her young son who had been seven years old at the time of his father's death, until he turned eighteen. Eamon included all he knew about Marcia's son – the back-packing trip to Asia, the drug smuggling, the incarceration and the deal that was brokered with the Law, whereby he gave them names and he was released from prison under a witness protection programme. Then Marcia came to Spain." Although he felt uncomfortable relating his private life to Alphonso, he left nothing out, trusting his fatherly concern. "My wife Eve died in a car accident shortly afterwards." He gave a caustic smile. "Whereby I discovered a few home truths from a diary that she had kept with all the sordid details of her love affair with Jimmy Grant. To be honest, the revelation paved the way for me to move forward. Shortly afterwards, Marcia and I got together. The rest as they say is history! Although…" he paused for two seconds, "history has repeated itself with Marcia playing me as Eve did." Eamon tried to smile.

Eamon went into detail regarding Bridie's blackmail and her demand for money in exchange for the photos of Marcia with the young guy.

The old man vehemently shook his head, frowning, taking a large mouthful of whisky and swirling it on his palette, taking in its bouquet. Placing his glass on the small table next to his chair, he leaned back into the recliner. "This boy of your wife's that she had from her previous marriage, does she have contact with him?"

Eamon shook his head. "Not since he went underground. She does not speak of him. Although, I don't doubt that she must tink of the lad."

"How old would ya say that her boy is now?"

Eamon pursed his lips, shaking his head. "He has got to be roughly late twenties. We have been together for ten years. Marcia said that he was eighteen when we first met."

The old Italian pressed on with his queries. "Your woman, has she ever given ya reason to doubt her loyalty? Is she flirty around men? Has she ever turned ya away in the bedroom?" Alphonso sat up, reaching for the glass. "Her actions over time would give ya some indication if there was any reason to doubt her loyalty."

Eamon inhaled. "If I had not seen the evidence of her betrayal..." he shook his head, "I would not have believed it of her. As I said to ye previously, Marcia ticked all the boxes. She fulfilled me in every way. Nevertheless, she certainly fooled me!"

"From the time when she was widowed, did she ever speak of past relationships?" Alphonso dug deeper.

Eamon shook his head. "She said that I was only the second man in her life. She was only seventeen when she first married, and she was widowed at twenty-three. Like I said, Marcia devoted her life to her boy until their separation. Then she met me!"

"Her history doesn't speak of a woman who's a player," Alphonso said. He paused for a long moment while he took a swig. "What was this guy like in the photos with ya wife? Describe him." Eamon cocked a brow. "Humour me!" Alphonso directed.

Eamon sucked air through his teeth. "Mediterranean appearance, dark hair, olive skin tone, young. Much younger than her."

The old man played with his ear lobe. "Put an age on the guy in the photo."

"At least a good fifteen years younger than Marcia." He threw a hint of a smile at the old man. "Where's this going, Al? There is no getting away from it. I could see that they were intimate. She won't get another chance to play me!" His neck and face flushed with anger.

"Don't be too quick to judge her. Go back and weigh it all up. In my opinion, ya got it all wrong. I'll lay a thousand bucks on it that's her boy. He's contacted her. Maybe he was down on his luck – needed money. Whatever the reason, your wife went to see him. Furthermore, it was unfortunate for her that some lowlife who had a grudge for whatever reason spotted her and snapped a few pictures. Thinking as ya would if ya did not know any different, that they were lovers, not mother and son."

Eamon's eyes darted as Alphonso stared at him. "Think about it. Her boy and the fella in the pictures are about the same age. Ya wife has played it straight with ya throughout ya marriage. Ya not telling me that a previous loyal wife and devoted mother suddenly goes off the rails." Alphonso vehemently shook his head. "Sort this mess out with her because to my reckoning, ya have done her an injustice, son."

Eamon was silent, deep in thought. Alphonso persisted with his interrogation. "There is always some indication when things go wrong in ya marriage. Did ya not look back to when ya discovered that Eve was playing around with Jimmy Grant? Was there anything that might have given you an indication of her tendencies?"

Eamon slowly nodded.

"Don't throw in the towel before ya allow the woman to defend herself!"

"To my mind Al, there is no defence!" Eamon replied harshly.

"Give ya self time to calm down. However, don't leave it too long. I can't have ya with only half ya mind on the new venture. Ya not only dealing with your wife but ya family of four babies. Ya need a clear head, son." Alphonso smiled. "Do ya want to take a thousand buck wager that is her boy in those photos and not someone that she is seeing behind ya back?"

Eamon smiled thinly, giving a small nod.

After showering, Eamon donned the robe that hung on the bathroom door. He knew that he had to have a glass of wine to try to put a halt to the swinging back and forth with his decision to phone Marcia. His feelings were hurt and the anger was still raw. He returned to the lounge where Alphonso kept a wine rack with a bottle of sauvignon and a glass. He settled into the overstuffed armchair by the floor-to-ceiling windows. His phone was on the coffee table. He resting his long legs on the top of the table beside it, while taking a large mouthful of wine. He let it trickle slowly down his throat and felt the relaxing effect begin to take hold. He allowed himself to think about Marcia. He checked the time on his mobile phone; Spain was six hours ahead of Miami. He batted back and forth with the thought of ringing her. However, he concluded that once he had questioned her, and found out it wasn't her son as Alphonso deemed him to be in the photos, he would be faced with the finality of a life without her. He knew that the alcohol was forcing him to admit to himself that he wanted to be wrong and for Alphonso to win the wager. Knocking back the rest of the wine, he punched in Marcia's number.

Marcia had taken the children to Jane's the previous evening, hoping to keep them occupied so that they would not question where their father was. Jane had asked if the boys would like to help clean out the stables and feed the horses, which she knew they loved doing. Aisling and Aine had also wanted to help, and under Jane and Marcia's watchful eyes, they had picked up small handfuls of hay to give to the ponies while Niall and Quinn toiled with their large forks.

Marcia had opened up to Jane regarding the card that she had found in Eamon's suit pocket. She had shown Jane the purple card with the woman's name and cell number in gold lettering. Marcia lay in bed that evening contemplating her conversation with Jane. Jane had pressed home to her that the card was not evidence that Eamon was being unfaithful. In Jane's opinion, Eamon was too much of a family man. Marcia wasn't convinced. She knew she had to throw herself back into giving tarot readings. Suzette had phoned her the previous night to tell her that she already had three month's worth of bookings.

Marcia felt that she could not face going to work at the Hawk Wind club. After she had gone to bed and cried to the point of mental exhaustion, she had managed to get four hours of sleep.

She rose from the bed and headed to the bathroom. The previous day, the builders had finished installing the large stand-alone Jacuzzi bath that Eamon had ordered. She removed the robe that she had fallen asleep in. Her mobile phone rang. She moved naked across the bedroom to answer it. She glanced at the screen and saw it was a withheld number. "Hello?" she answered.

"How are the children?"

Marcia sank onto the bed upon hearing his voice, all thoughts of another woman gone. "Eamon," she breathed softly, "the children miss you!" There was a long, drawn-out silence. "Eamon—"

Eamon cut her off. "Who was the guy that ye met up wit in the hotel behind my back?" he interrogated, flatly.

Marcia faltered. "Eamon, it was my son, Reuben. I could not deny him. He is my child!"

Eamon did not reply for a few seconds. "Why in hell did ye not tell me? I had to hear it second hand, without knowing that it was yer boy." He didn't go much further. He could hear Marcia crying.

His cadence softened. "Marcia, this situation could have been prevented. All ye had to do was inform me, instead of leaving yerself wide open for scum to take advantage of the situation." He inhaled, knowing that her tears continued to fall. "Marcia, when we got together, ye told me about yer boy, but there has been no mention of him for a decade. Then some lowlife takes pictures of ye with a fella that ye met up with in secret. Ye lay yerself wide open for blackmail and for someone to rock our marriage."

"Blackmail?!" Marcia exclaimed.

"I was paid a visit at the Hawk Wind club before my leaving to come home early to ye. There were various photos of ye in the embrace of a younger fella by a hotel swimming pool and by yer car. Money was demanded in exchange for those photos. How did ye expect me to react?" He spoke testily.

She gasped. "I am so sorry, Eamon. I did not plan to deceive you. Reuben contacted me while you were in Miami. It may have been my last chance to see him as he is relocating with a young woman and her child. She lived out here in Spain. Elliot, the Muay Thai trainer is the father of her boy. Reuben had met her when she returned to England. Upon their meeting, she mentioned that she had had a tarot reading from a woman named Marcia, without knowing that I was Reuben's mother. She had kept one of my business cards. Reuben realised that it was me!" She continued, "Eamon, I transferred money to his bank account to help them financially – from my personal account."

Eamon sucked air through his teeth. "Marcia, we can discuss yer lad and his future wit the girl and child later when I see ye. I am committed to Alphonso's project out here in Miami for a few months."

He paused for a moment when he heard her sigh. "However, ye can come to me. Arrange wit Aye and Jane to have the children for a couple of days. Bonita will also help. Dan and Billy will watch over them. Marcia, I need ye wit me!"

Marcia's thoughts went to the purple card with the woman's name and cell number that she had previously discovered in his suit pocket. "I will be with you as soon as I have everything arranged." She paused, then said, "I love you, Eamon."

"I love ye!" Eamon threw in. "Get the earliest first-class flight possible, no matter the cost. I want ye to feel rested on yer arrival."

Eamon finished the bottle of wine while he sat for an age deep in thought about Marcia's son, trying to imagine how it must have been for her not to have had any contact with him over the years. He couldn't go there. Nothing could ever prevent him from seeing his children. Except for incarceration, which he did not want to envisage. He'd been looking out the windows at the storm clouds building out in the Atlantic. Furious winds tossed vessels to and fro. It reminded him of his own fury when he'd imagined that Marcia had betrayed him with another man. His rage would have destroyed her, yet she was innocent.

Returning to the huge bed, he lay on top, allowing his mind to envision Marcia in his arms. Aching for her embrace, he released the robe belt, his shaft thickening as he imagined her joining him in the age-old method of sexual release.

The following morning, Eamon joined Alphonso for breakfast. He was seated in his chair by the window with his breakfast tray before him. He had instructed Joey to bring the same for Eamon.

Without a word, Eamon put money on the small table next to the old man's chair.

Alphonso crooked an eyebrow.

Eamon smiled. "Yer wager. Ye won the bet. It was her boy!"

The old Italian laughed, pointing with his knife toward Eamon. "My body may not be as it was, but my mind is still sharp. I knew it. That gal is no player." He took a large forkful of scrambled egg and salmon. "Now we can move forward!" He gulped a mouthful of his favourite Italian coffee from the company Volcano Coffee Works, which his daughter Chiara had introduced him to. Marcia used the company after Eamon had sent for a batch when he had tried it on a previous visit to Alphonso's. Joey placed Eamon's breakfast tray on the table. Eamon nodded and thanked him. Addressing Alphonso, he said, "My wife is joining me for a couple of days. I thought that she could see Miami for herself." He began to eat.

Alphonso grinned, continuing to devour the rest of his breakfast. "I don't doubt that she will aid ya comfort. After the rocky last few days, there's nothing like making up!" He winked. Eamon gave a small smile.

"Joey informs me that ya will need to go downtown later. I will ring my tailor. Antonio will sort ya out."

"Just a couple of suits and accessories. I need to keep up wit yer style, Al!" Eamon smiled.

Alphonso nodded, then said, "I have made a couple of phone calls this morning to the builders that are putting the finishing touches on the club. Hopefully, if all goes according to plan, the furnishings will be arriving today and installed within two days. Then it will be the grand finale! The opening night. It would be great if ya wife is here to see it."

Joey drove them to the central district in downtown Miami, north of Biscayne Bay. They passed the iconic

Dupont building and the Freedom Tower, stopping along 1st Street just outside of the tailors. Joey said he would go look for a hot dog stand and await the call for them to be picked up.

The tailor was a tall, slim, suave-looking man, with a chiselled jawline and wide, full mouth that revealed perfect teeth when he smiled, which complemented his defined eyebrows and almond-shaped, chestnut eyes. Eamon took note of his muscular physique, straining beneath the silk shirt under his open suit jacket. His appearance spoke of someone who took great pride in their overall appearance. His attire was immaculate. *The guy's got class,* Eamon mused. He judged the silver-grey-haired tailor to be in his early sixties. Eamon thought that he would not look out of place in Paris or Rome, in some elegant setting, not downtown Miami.

Eamon did not usually take much notice of how other men looked, however, he couldn't but admire the man. The tailor held out a manicured hand to Eamon, after kissing the back of Alphonso's and greeting them both. The Italian accent sat well with the man's overall appearance.

Alphonso and Antonio conversed briefly in Italian. He ensured that Alphonso was seated, comfortably before beckoning for Eamon to follow him across the tiled floor.

Throughout the time it took for Eamon's measurements to be taken, the two Italians continued to converse. After a while, Antonio apologised. "Please forgive me for appearing rude. It is not often that I get the opportunity to speak to someone from the mother country."

Eamon raised a hand. "'Tis understandable. When I meet up wit someone from my birthplace, Dublin, I find that I tend to slip into using words and phrases that we used back home, which most would find difficult to comprehend." He smiled.

"I see from your suit, the cloth, that you favour Canali," Antonio said, running an expert finger through Eamon's Kei wool suit jacket. He reached across to a rail. "Perhaps this would appeal to your taste." He held up a dark blue suit. "It is by the designer Alfredo Corneliani. The slim fitted, waisted jacket was designed for men such as you, who have the physique of Adonis," he complimented.

Eamon allowed him to remove his jacket, replacing it with the recommendation. Antonio buttoned it, standing back while adjusting the full-length mirror. Eamon nodded at his reflection. "One in each colour."

Antonio handed a black suit to him of the same design. Eamon slipped the jacket on, giving a sharp nod of approval.

"One moment," Antonio said. He went to another rail on the other side of the room. He returned with a black suit. "This is one of my most favoured designers, which I often wear. My partner also."

Eamon's look remained passive upon the revelation that the tailor was homosexual. It did not surprise him.

"The cut of the fabric and the design will enhance your physique. You are a big man with broad shoulders that require attention." He smiled. "The designer, Zegna, had men with your physique in mind.

"Elegante!" Antonio kissed two fingertips expressing his delight when Eamon came out of the dressing room after trying on the suits, standing in front of the mirror. "Perfecto!" Antonio raised his hands, turning towards Alphonso, who smiled, nodding his approval.

The tailor handed Eamon two pairs of John Lobb City 11 handmade shoes in mid-brown and black. While Eamon tried both pairs on, Antonio returned with a selection of various coloured Canali designer silk gauze neckties. Eamon chose four.

"The lad will need four white shirts," Alphonso piped in, "underpants and half a dozen pairs of the merino wool socks that I wear." Antonio went to the far end of the room to fetch them.

Eamon returned to the changing room. Once out of earshot, Alphonso turned to Antonio. "Put the bill on my tab." Antonio smiled, returning to the long, glass-fronted cabinet that housed tiepins and cufflinks to add to the bill.

Eamon took out his bank card when he approached Antonio. "Alphonso has settled the bill," he beamed, turning toward the old man.

Eamon tried to insist on paying, but the old man rose from his chair. Antonio stepped forward to aid him. "I dare say that ya will earn it!" Alphonso said, smiling at Eamon. Eamon took Alphonso's arm to support him. He thought, not for the first time, that a walking stick would be of an advantage to the old man, but he did not voice it. Both men thanked Antonio.

"Head to Giuseppe's!" Alphonso ordered Joey. "Our next port of call is only a short distance along SE 1st Avenue to my barbers," he explained to Eamon. Joey dropped them off outside the shop. Car horns blasted as two other drivers who had the same idea vied for the same spot. Joey ignored them as he waited, keeping the engine running while the men alighted from the car to go to the barber's shop.

Giuseppe Logan snapped his fingers at a young barber to take over from him when Alphonso came into the shop. Only two clients were being treated to shaves in the row of six chairs. Kissing the back of the old man's hand, he shook Eamon's. "The rush is over, thank God!" The big, red-headed man helped Alphonso to a seat. "I want my friend here to have ya special treatment. Ya can tell him all about ya Irish heritage. Eamon is a Dubliner." Eamon removed his jacket. Giuseppe passed it to a waiting assistant while another started on Alphonso's shave and haircut.

"Do ya just want ya goatee and hair trimmed?" he asked the reflection in the mirror while tying a protective cape on Eamon. Eamon nodded. After listening to the barber's rapid-fire regaling about his parent's early life in Ireland, Eamon closed his eyes when Giuseppe wrapped his face with a hot towel in preparation for his shave.

The man had not come up for breath as he told Eamon the tale of his parents' marriage. He spoke of how his mother's family were against the union as they were protestant. His late father was a catholic from Belfast in Northern Ireland. He went into how the pair had broken away from the troubles of the Shankill Road area in the late 1960s. When he came to how his father was a heavy drinker and would regularly beat his mother and the boys of the family, Eamon switched off. He did not wish to return to that place in his mind that lay hidden in the depths. He thought about Marcia and his children. Without appearing rude, he occasionally nodded.

Eamon opened his eyes, returning to the moment when Giuseppe was finishing. "My old mum said that when they had immigrated to New York on Cunard, she had loved every moment on the 3,140-mile voyage."

Eamon sighed with relief that he had survived Giuseppe's cutthroat shave, as the barber had seemed to be concentrating more on telling his life history than on the shave. Eamon concluded that he would stick to his electric shaver in the future.

Alphonso chuckled in the car on the way home. "Ya may think that Giuseppe don't pay attention. I know that he talks a lot. However. The man's an expert!"

"That cutthroat blade was a bit too close for comfort!" Eamon confessed.

"Same here!" Joey piped in. "I'd rather take my chances with someone holding a gun on me than Giuseppe Logan's blade, while he hovers over ya jugular with that cutthroat without paying attention, 'cause he's continually talking!" he chortled.

That night, Alphonso received a phone call from the works manager. His men had worked overtime and everything was complete ahead of schedule, from the electrics and plumbing, down to the gas fittings for the cookers and kitchen appliances for the restaurant. The nightclub was ready for the opening night.

Eamon went up to his room, taking the list of successful candidates that Alphonso gave him after the staff interviews. Eamon removed his jacket and hung it in the wardrobe. He decided to shower before sending some emails. He sat in the overstuffed armchair and poured a glass of cabernet sauvignon from the bottle that Alphonso had pressed him to take to his room while he worked. He put his feet up on the coffee table by the floor-to-ceiling windows and turned on the laptop that Joey had purchased for him on the instruction of Alphonso. He fired off emails to potential employees: a manager, who would come under his training, to take over when he returned to Spain; hat-check girls, bar staff, chefs – two were required, six had applied; commis chefs and waiting staff – the applications had been numerous; washer uppers – ten applied. Joey had men in mind, who he knew personally, for the security team.

It had taken him until nearly midnight to send all of the emails. There was a long list of Alphonso's contacts: distillers who were on standby to fulfil the orders of barrels and cases of wine; caterers; suppliers for the bone china and cooking utensils; Alphonso's tailor for the security team suits; and the designer of the uniforms for the hat-check girls, waiting staff, chefs and commis chefs, and kitchen help. Eamon ticked off each one. The old Italian's long tentacles had reached out to people who could return a favour from somewhere down the line in the past; people Alphonso had helped in one way or another. Although Eamon judged that the cost of opening the venue would run into six figures, as the Hawk Wind club had, he knew the old boy was not counting the cost. This was not about earning money from the venue. Eamon knew that this was Alphonso Gabrette's last wish to go out in a blaze of glory – something on his bucket list. Eamon was determined to see it to its fruition. He felt it was the least that he could do in return for the massive favour that Alphonso had done for him.

He inhaled, reaching down to the coffee table and picking up his mobile phone. There had not been any messages from Marcia since their last conversation. He had given a lot of thought to Marcia's clandestine meeting with her son. Although the way was clear in his mind, he would speak to her about his decision when they were together. He wanted to find a way to ensure that in the future, there would not be any further opportunity for anyone to rock their marriage. He had hoped that Marcia would have sent him photos of herself. He toyed with the thought of texting her, however, he baulked at the idea due to the way that he had left things with her. He realised that he had caused her pain and done her an injustice by up and leaving Spain without confronting her. He knew that he had gone about it the wrong way. He contemplated his reason for running from the situation. Digging deep, he concluded that he had not wanted to have to face losing her. He found it difficult to sleep without making love to Marcia each night while they were apart. He could not fathom never being able to hold her in his arms.

Stripping off before his shower, he glanced at his naked reflection in the wall-to-wall, ceiling-high mirrors. He had had the same kind installed at his villa. Marcia enjoyed observing the reflection of their lovemaking, as he did. His mind went to the videos of them making love, which were locked in his safe at his villa in Spain. Despite this, he was not interested in pornography. When he was younger, he had viewed a couple of videos. It had not appealed to him to watch couples having sex on film. It had made him feel like a voyeur. It was not his thing. However, he and Marcia both enjoyed watching their lovemaking on film.

He felt the blood rush to his groin as he thought of the last time Marcia knelt before him, her tongue stimulating him, accommodating him, ensuring that he received deep satisfaction when he involuntarily released. He had repaid the pleasure that she had given him that night three-fold.

He thought back to the time when circumstances had divided them in the past. He drifted back to the time when Marcia was pregnant with Niall. The joy of discovering that he was to become a father for the first time was marred by drama, with the threat of him being given up by a whistle-blower who was naming men whom Eamon had dealt with in the past when he was Jimmy Grant's right-hand man. Eamon had sent Marcia out of reach of the Law. He was concerned that she would have been interrogated if he had been apprehended. He sent her to Thailand under the watchful eye of Aye. He thought back to their enforced separation. The mental and physical ache of longing for her had been torturous. Nevertheless, he had to suffice with the regular pictures that Marcia had sent him of her naked body, baby bump expanding.

As he entered the shower, turning it to full power, his mobile pinged. He jumped out of the shower and hurriedly crossed the room, grabbing his phone. He went back and switched the water off. He read Marcia's text, *I miss you,* followed by three emoji love hearts. He replied, *I love and long for you,* followed by a row of emoji love hearts.

A few minutes later, she replied with a message and an attachment, *I hope that you like it!*

He opened the attachment. Marcia videoed herself naked in the bathroom. She walked past the newly installed free-standing bath, toward the shower cubicle. Eamon slumped into the armchair by the windows without taking his eyes from her. Marcia switched the jets on, her back to him. Cascading water ran from her shoulders down to her curvy buttocks, between her legs as she leaned over, slowly she turned to face the camera, and her dark-brown eyes held his. Tearing himself away, he travelled to the contours of her breasts – fuller, dark nipples erect. He became rock solid, his breathing heavy. The vision reminded him of the time before they had first got together when he had taken the risk of stepping naked into the shower to join her.

Her back turned to him. As the scene played out, his eyes remained transfixed on his phone's screen. Marcia put on quite a show for him. She cupped her breasts, fingers manipulating, and rivulets of water from the overhead shower trickled down her body. The water sparkled across her mound, disappearing between her thighs, where he longed to go. He noticed that she had waxed down there. Her fingers, in a slow, measured pace, tweaked her dark buds. Her hand moved down to between her legs.

His desire for her throbbed in his hand, firmly clasped, yet controlled. Her words aided his pleasure. *I need you Eamon!* she purred with light gasps. Softly calling him, legs parted, she inserted her finger. Eamon groaned with her every movement, reaching his peak as she continued to call his name. Finally, she cried aloud for him, simultaneously releasing. The video stopped. His heart pounded. He leaned back into the armchair, inhaling, smiling with satisfaction.

He sent her a text message. *Beautiful, I could not ask for more when you are not with me. I love you. See you at the airport tomorrow.* Five heart emojis followed.

Normally he would have sent any videos or explicit photos of Marcia and him together to another phone, locking the SIM card in his safe. However, being in the US, he was unable to transfer it. He did not like the fact that the explicit footage of Marcia was on his phone if for any reason his mobile phone was confiscated. This was Miami and he was about to mingle with the city's elite crime bosses. Nevertheless, he couldn't bring himself to delete the video of Marcia.

Alphonso was sitting at his favourite spot by the window in his vast lounge. "I have reserved us a table at my restaurant for tonight. It will give ya wife a taste of superb Italian cuisine. Another reason to persuade her is that Dade County here in Miami has superior living to Spain. That is without the lure of the designer shops to help draw her across the Atlantic!" He grinned, waggling his head. "Okay! We may have the odd hurricane, however, there is always plenty of warning given. Dade County is firmly structured. Biscayne Point is a neighbourhood of North Beach, an upmarket area with nice properties. It is on three islands which are accessible from 77th Street, and from 85th Street by vehicles. There is a pedestrian bridge at 80th Street. Tell ya wife there are good schools for ya kids!"

Eamon smiled, nodding without replying.

"I will wait here for ya while Joey drives ya to pick ya wife up from the airport."

Eamon checked his watch, standing to leave.

"I am looking forward to meeting this woman of yours," Alphonso said smiling, leaning back into his chair, raising the leg rest.

Eamon could tell that the old man wanted a nap. He thought that he looked tired. Eamon left with Joey to meet Marcia who was arriving within the next hour and a half.

Eamon pointed, speaking to Joey. "My wife is coming through the doors!" Joey pursed his lips and gave a sharp nod of approval, observing her. Eamon stepped from the limousine, moving towards Marcia, who wore a black, knee-length suit, pulling matching black luggage. The Hermes bag that he had purchased her was on her shoulder.

Marcia smiled, spotting him. He took her case. They briefly kissed – a kiss that had more depth to it than any onlooker would have noticed.

Joey came forward to put the case in the boot of the car. A yellow cab blasted its horn, impatient to park in the limousine's spot. Joey, without turning, raised the back of his hand towards the driver. Smiling at Marcia, he said, "Welcome to Miami."

Marcia entered the lounge behind Joey who had her luggage. He took it to the bedroom where she would be staying with Eamon. Eamon closed the lounge door. Alphonso adjusted his chair to a sitting position, beaming his welcome at her. As she came towards him, he appraised her, running his eyes from her head down to her stiletto heels. He held his hand out and Marcia took it. Turning hers over, he kissed the back without taking his eyes from her. "Please!" he directed to the chair opposite him. "This is such a pleasure to meet ya, Marcia. I hope ya don't mind entertaining an old man while ya man and Joey attend to work at the club. I intend to have you in attendance for the opening night!"

"I would enjoy getting to know you. Eamon has often spoken fondly of you and your family."

Alphonso grinned. "That is one beautiful English accent." He turned his attention to Joey who came back into the lounge with Eamon. Both men smiled when he waved them away.

"Your man has a lot of interviewing and phone calls to contend with today. He must get everything organised in preparation for the opening night in two days. I hope that ya will be staying for it?"

Marcia smiled. Eamon had texted her to say that Alphonso wanted her in attendance for the opening of his nightclub. "It will be a pleasure. Exciting!" Marcia added. The old man beamed.

Marcia excused herself while she went to change into something more casual. She decided on a cap sleeve, royal blue dress. The neckline dipped in a heart shape, showing no cleavage but which defined her full bust line above a nipped-in waist. She chose matching blue, low-heeled, open-toed wedges that complimented the look.

Marcia walked towards him. Unabashed in his admiration, Alphonso nodded his approval. "I can understand how the lad wants ya by his side!" He smiled. Marcia blushed. She sat down opposite him, and Alphonso made himself comfortable. He indicated to the bottle of Voss mineral water and the glass on the table next to her chair. "I have a stock in of the water that Eamon said ya favour."

"Thank you, that is very considerate," Marcia said. She poured herself a glass and took a sip. Under Alphonso's watchful eye, she crossed her legs and faced him.

"That is a beautiful ring. That is some stone!" Alphonso said, indicating Marcia's engagement ring. "The emeralds are a nice touch. The boy has a good eye all the way round!" he threw in, smiling." He held Marcia's look. "However, ya can't be too careful… muggings in Miami," he said no more.

"Eamon insists that I wear my rings, although I am cautious," she replied.

The old man nodded, adjusting his position, leaning back, hands clasped on his stomach. "Do ya mind Marcia if I touch on the sensitive subject regarding the difficult situation that arose with the Gennaro family in New York when ya had indirectly set the cat among the pigeons?" He asked candidly, holding up his hand, palm facing her. "This is not about blaming ya!" He smiled reassuringly, observing her unease. "I'm intrigued!"

Eamon had not told Marcia that Alphonso had a hand in alleviating what could have been a very difficult situation for Eamon with Franco Gennaro. However, she sensed that Alphonso must have aided him and thought it justifiable that he would be interested. "Do you wish to know how it came about?" Marcia asked.

Alphonso nodded. "I would like to hear your side of the story. How did ya really know what was occurring thousands of miles away? Was it a coincidence that ya hit the nail on the head about Jimmy Grant's son-in-law being involved with the New York mob?"

Marcia inhaled softly. Shaking her head she said, "No not a coincidence. If I had not been certain, I would not have said anything to Joyce Grant. She was aware that my predictions are always accurate. Previously, I had revealed a life-changing situation to her. Joyce knew that I had also advised Jimmy. Joyce had welcomed me to her home, so when she requested a tarot reading, I felt the need to repay her kindness." Marcia put her palms together in a pyramid, resting under her chin. "Alphonso, when someone makes a kind gesture, I like to return it. I can't explain how I can predict future events. I, myself, find it perplexing and can't offer any explanation, but I have accepted it. I have used tarot cards for many years to guide my intuition. They are a part of me. Reading the cards is as natural to me as breathing. Maybe coincidence does play a small part. I am not saying that I have never been wrong in the past. I only know from clients that they have been satisfied."

Alphonso had not taken his eyes from her. Marcia had his full attention. "Returning clientele have informed me of how the information I passed on prevented situations that would have otherwise negatively impacted their lives. It came to my ears on more than one occasion that I have been accused of working with the police! Someone who could not come up with any other logical reason of how I could know such sensitive information concluded that I must have been part of the setup of a police raid!" Marcia gave a soft laugh. "Which is ridiculous, because if I were helping the police, why would I impart a pre-warning to someone about a dawn raid?" Marcia smiled.

Alphonso pursed his lips, nodding. He cocked an eyebrow and ventured, "You have given people the heads up that there would be a police raid on a particular day?" He looked astounded, splaying his hands and shaking his head in disbelief. He continued, "Did ya give out warnings to Max Greenaway in the UK and Jimmy Grant when ya got to Spain, seeing as those two were related? Because if my memory serves me right, about ten years back Max Greenaway turned Queens Evidence. You were on the scene then? That was the time Eamon came to Miami to set up a business deal for Jimmy Grant with my son Carlo." He dug deeper, piecing everything together. "You mentioned that you and Eamon were together by that time and you said that you spoke to Eamon while he was in Miami about the concern of Jimmy Grant going missing."

There was a long moment of silence before Marcia answered Alphonso. She was aware of his sharp mind, which his aged body belied. She did not wish to go back to the past but felt that she could not avoid it.

Alphonso's eyes held hers. "Take it back to how ya came to Spain. It intrigues me."

"Max Greenaway's wife came for an appointment to my home in the UK. Someone had recommended me to her. We had never met before then. It was during the tarot reading that I gave her a warning regarding an unexpected police visit. I advised her that if she had anything of an incriminating nature in her home to remove it before a certain date I felt that the police raid would occur. However, I was to learn that Max Greenaway had not believed my prediction when his wife had told him until it was too late and he was arrested on the date in question during the police raid. Suzette later informed me that she had taken measures to remove a substantial amount of money before the visit by the Law since she had believed my warning." Marcia hoped that would be enough to satisfy his curiosity.

Alphonso adjusted his seating position. He leaned back, hands clasped across his stomach, eyes darting and continued questioning. Marcia sensed his alert mind ticking over while he studied her. She got the feeling that he would not let her off the hook just yet. She was right. The wily old Italian smiled. "It strikes me, Marcia, that somehow ya became involved with Max Greenaway's wife. It can't be a coincidence that ya visit Spain where Greenaway's cousin Jimmy Grant lives. There must be a connection." He did not wait for a reply. "It seems to me that for ya to become embroiled in the life that these two men lived, there had to be a good reason. Marcia, I am a good judge of people. Had to be throughout my life. I don't think that ya are the type of woman who chases money. Ya are too classy!"

Marcia had not expected to be interrogated in such depth. Alphonso studied her for a long moment. "Were ya somehow coerced into stepping into the life of crime that these men were living?" He paused a moment and then threw in, "However, knowing Eamon, once ya two became involved, my guess is that he would have stepped in and put a halt to ya being used!"

Marcia inhaled. "Eamon changed my life. Our relationship took off rather quickly. Eamon protected me." Alphonso smiled as Marcia continued enlightening him. "I cannot deny that I was unnerved by Eamon's world. It was a world away from my previous sheltered life. However, I fell in love with him and a short while later we started a family."

Alphonso nodded.

"Although, Alphonso, at that time, things were difficult. Eamon feared that he would be arrested and he sent me out of the country for my own protection."

Alphonso pursed his lips. "That is understandable. I remember that there was a 'canary' singing at that time. Many were arrested before the rat Max Greenaway was dealt with!" He smiled and continued. "I know that there is a downside to living with a man who has a criminal past. I understood that with my wife and my children. I knew that they would have lost my protection if I was ever incarcerated. However, it goes with the territory. When a couple love one another, as Marcella and I did. And I don't doubt that Eamon feels the same way about ya. There is only one way – to stand by each other!"

Marcia nodded. "Eamon and our children are my life, Alphonso."

"There is one thing that I would like to get straight in my mind, Marcia before I stop my probing," he smiled, "Do ya have control over imparting the information?"

She paused for a couple of seconds sensing that he was inferring that she had purposely informed Joyce Grant about her son-in-law's criminal dealings with narcotics connected to Franco Gennaro. "I do have that control to withhold or to reveal. Although in the beginning, many years ago, I was not as tactful, for want of a better word. I did not realise the caution that was required during a 'reading'. Bear in mind that I was a novice with the information that I was relaying. I learned to become eloquent and cautious with what I imparted to a client. There are numerous reasons why someone might want their cards read, for example, suspicions regarding a relationship or business, or health or money. They may be caught up in a legal entanglement and want to know the outcome.

However, in certain circumstances, for instance with Joyce Grant, who I class as a dear friend. She had some worries regarding a situation with her daughter. I was faced with a choice: to withhold what I could 'see'. Or reveal the truth." Marcia said, firmly pressing home her point of view. "I find that honesty is the best policy in close relationships. Furthermore, before the revelation, Joyce and I came to an understanding that the revelation would remain between us." Marcia smiled wanly. "Unfortunately, it did not work out that way. However, I don't blame her. She was protecting her daughter."

Alphonso sighed and said, "Although I think that there are times when the truth can cause problems. This must have been a difficult call. It was a difficult position that ya found yerself in. But, to put myself in her position, if I asked for the truth, knowing, that my close pal could give me the answer, I would expect nothing but the truth. Honesty among friends is something that I value." Alphonso gave a sharp nod. "I can understand ya predicament, however," he smiled, "hopefully, that situation is water under the bridge." Alphonso shifted in his seat. "It's an area that I have stayed away from in the past – spirits, ghosts, another life beyond this one, although my wife Marcella and my youngest daughter often watched TV shows where people supposedly contacted the dead. I suffered it in silence. I thought it was a load of baloney. However, can ya explain how ya come to know these things with such accuracy?"

Marcia smiled."I can only tell you that it comes from my experience and my spiritual beliefs. The voices in my ear from an unseen realm guide me,"

Alphonso inhaled taking it in. "Do ya believe that when we leave this life we go to another?"

Marcia nodded. "I have had proof many times throughout my life, which leaves no doubt that our loved ones' energy remains connected to us, even though their physical presence cannot be seen by most."

Alphonso looked away to the window out towards the Atlantic Ocean. "Do ya think that my wife and son are with me?" He turned his head to face her.

"Love bonds us, Alphonso."

He gave a soft smile. "I can't say that I was the perfect husband. There are regrets." He did not elaborate. Continuing, he said, "However, Marcella was the love of my life. It brings me comfort to hear ya say that she is still with me. I don't mind leaving, knowing that Marcella is waiting." Marcia noted that he did not speak of his son who had been murdered.

Alphonso tweaked the tip of his nose a few times with two fingers. Pressing on, he said, "Did ya foresee Jimmy Grant's death?" Marcia nodded. "I warned him of imminent danger, a threat to his life. I saw a boat and the sea. I also gave him the description of two men from overseas. I recall that I distinctly heard the bagpipes of Scotland, linking the pair. I advised him about dubious business transactions that I felt would take place within a few days of the tarot reading."

The old man slowly nodded, absorbing her words. Marcia went on, "Eamon was in Miami at the time, not realising that Jimmy was missing. I informed him when he telephoned me that Joyce had told me that Jimmy Grant hadn't returned home. Nonetheless, I informed Eamon that I sensed that he was not going to be found. I felt certain that he had been killed. Eamon had said at the time that he would try to phone Jimmy, but when he did, it had been disconnected. That's when Eamon returned to Spain."

Alphonso adjusted his chair to an upright position, supporting himself on his elbows. He made a pyramid with his hands and rested his chin on his hands, studying Marcia. "Ya appear to have been thrown into the deep end from the beginning. However, you and Eamon have four babies together. Life with Eamon must have suited ya."

"Eamon is a wonderful father and husband," Marcia said.

Alphonso smiled. "Men are not the easiest to live with. We tend to dominate. It goes with the territory. When ya live in the type of world that we do, ya cannot differentiate. The worlds collide – business and private life."

"I understand that," Marcia said. "Eamon lives under a lot of pressure. I try to ease his burden by understanding that he requires some private time away from the family and away from work."

Alphonso nodded sagely, "Like I said earlier, the man has good taste. My Marcella was of the same mould. She gave me and the children priority. It's hard to find good women."

He pointed towards the window. “This was Marcella’s favourite spot. She would sit where you are in that chair, gazing out across the Atlantic for hours, in the days after our son Carlo was killed. I knew that she went somewhere deep into her mind where I could not reach her. Even though I knew that she loved me deeply, the anguish of the loss of her child overshadowed our relationship. Marcella’s barriers were raised after that. A mother’s bond with her offspring is not to be underestimated.”

Marcia held his eyes. She sensed that Eamon had spoken to him about her son Reuben. She smiled warmly.

They had been talking for hours. Marcia had insisted on making him lunch. Alphonso had eaten the sliced beef sandwich before returning to his room for a few hours. He told her that he was going to take them to his restaurant that evening.

Marcia closed her bedroom door and changed out of her dress. She entered the bathroom, feeling relief as the powerful jets of the shower played over her shoulders, releasing her tense muscles. Closing her eyes, she thought about Eamon. He was a man of powerful emotions and sexual desires. He exuded a commanding presence. His silver-fox handsome features were attractive to women. Marcia had seen it first-hand with the females that vied for his attention at the Hawk Wind club. Her thoughts went to his reaction when he had assumed that she had had a lover. Marcia knew that she could not confront him about the card that she had found in his jacket pocket. She did not want to delve into something that would germinate a seed in her mind that he had been unfaithful to her. However, she pondered over how he had come to have the card. She envisioned Eamon having sex with another woman but pushed the thought to the back of her mind.

She slipped on the towelling robe that was hanging on the back of the bathroom door, taking in the familiar scent of

Eamon. She lay on the large bed. She had slept on the long flight for a few hours, but the six-hour time difference from Spain began to take its toll. Marcia thought about her children who were under the care of Jane and Aye. Billy had eagerly stepped in to help with Niall and Quinn. The boys loved him. Billy had endless energy and was great with entertaining them after school, whether it was swimming races in the pool, football or seeing to the horses. Marcia knew that she did not need to be concerned. Aine and Aisling had not looked back after waving goodbye to Marcia. Aye had sat in the passenger seat when Jane strapped their car seats into her Land Rover. Marcia let sleep take her.

Slowly opening her eyes, Marcia could hear water running in the distance. The dark skies cast shadows across the room. She rolled over onto her back. Eamon moved towards her, dropping the towel as he approached the bed. "I have missed ye!" he said as he knelt above her, clamping his thighs against hers, untying her robe. He ran his hands over the contours of her breasts. His fingers reached her nipples. Marcia smiled and reached her hand down, fingertips playing across the end of his evident desire. He began to relax, inhaling, allowing her to continue with the measured motion of her hand. "We have two hours before we go out tonight," he breathed. "I could not get the image of you out of my mind after you sent me that video."

"Did it help?"

"Hmm..." His erection thickened – rock solid. Marcia leaned forward. Both hands clasped his shaft as she took him in her mouth. Her tongue began lovingly pleasuring him.

They both lay side by side, satiated by the hour-long session of passionate lovemaking. "My wee mystic has turned into my porn star! That was a first to record ye pleasuring yerself!"

Marcia blushed but laughed. “I wanted to show you how much I missed you.”

“It certainly worked,” he smiled. “I felt as if ye were here wit me when I joined in wit ye.”

He waggled his head and his tone became serious. “We may have to tink about making some big changes in our lives soon. Alphonso wants us, as a family, to relocate to Miami.”

Marcia stiffened.

“However, we can deal wit that later. I want us to have a clean slate. Have tings out in the open. If there are secrets between us, it bodes for trouble in the future.”

Marcia thought of the card that she had discovered in Eamon’s jacket pocket. She did not mention it. He cupped her face in each hand. “When ye next speak to yer boy I want ye to tell him to look for a home wherever he and his new family are going to settle.” He paused for a long moment. “I will fund it.”

Marcia beamed and threw her arms around his neck, kissing him. He returned it. She realised what it took for Eamon to come to that decision.

“Let’s not keep the old man waiting. Alphonso told me how impressed he was wit ye,” Eamon said.

Alphonso stood back, allowing Marcia to walk ahead of him into his restaurant, named ‘Marcella’s’ after his dearly departed wife. The maître d’ welcomed them, showing the group to their table. There were only a few tables occupied by other customers, however, Alphonso knew that later the popular eatery would be busy. The table for six at the far end of the room was Alphonso’s favourite. He could sit facing the door to see who entered the restaurant.

Earlier, Alphonso had complimented Marcia on her outfit. She wore a black, Karen Millen body con dress with long sleeves, and full front zip that opened just above her cleavage. Eamon, within the privacy of the bedroom, had approved of the high-collared, belted, knee-length black dress that she wore with black stilettos. The diamond and emerald studs in her ears complimented the rings on her left hand. Although she had previously worn the dress when dining out with Eamon, he did not fail to express how 'horny' she made him feel.

They had only kept their lovemaking to an hour as they knew they had to join Alphonso, otherwise, Marcia would have been a willing participant in relieving Eamon's erection. Tearing himself from her embrace, he had told her to keep the dress on upon their return home later that night.

Alphonso nodded when the waiter asked if Alphonso wanted his usual. Eamon ordered a bottle of Barbaresco Asili Reserva 2011, asking for two glasses. He pressed Marcia to try the wine. She accepted and took a small sip, putting the glass back on the table, smiling her approval at Eamon. Alphonso took a large mouthful of the Eagle Rare Bourbon whisky.

He looked at the couple. "Ya are a fortunate man, son!" He held the crystal glass in both hands leaning back into his chair. "Not that I think that ya don't deserve good fortune!" He smiled, keeping his eyes on Eamon. "To have ya life turned around when ya met Marcia, a woman with intelligence and good looks – keeps a man interested." He winked, smiling at Marcia. She returned his smile. Eamon nodded, taking a long draught of his wine.

"Marcia has given me some food for thought regarding my doubts about life after death," Alphonso admitted.

Eamon cocked an eyebrow, a smile played at the corners of his mouth. "My wife has talents. Some that I find a wee bit intimidating," he laughed. They placed their orders with Alphonso's recommendation, asking the chef to swap the meat for fish for Marcia. Alphonso nodded, looking over Eamon's shoulder.

Eamon realised that Alphonso must have recognised someone coming in. He recognised the voice without turning to see who it was, even though the man spoke in Italian.

"Please join us," Alphonso indicated towards Ricardo Barossa and the woman by his side. Eamon turned and gave a slight nod in Barossa's direction. Ricardo dismissed him.

"My friend Josie and I came in to have your chef's wonderful Italian cuisine before we retire for the night. I see you have company. I don't wish to intrude." Ricardo's eyes rested on Marcia and he smiled.

Alphonso jumped in. "There is no intrusion. Please!" he indicated the seats. Ricardo took a chair, followed by Josephine. Marcia noticed the woman's fleeting glance at Eamon. She did not see his reaction, however, Ricardo did.

"Have you two met before?" he smirked, looking at his companion, who flushed.

"Mr O'Donally and I were seated next to one another on a flight from Paris to Miami." She spoke in an offhanded manner.

Marcia realised that this beautiful Latina woman was the owner of the card that she had found in Eamon's coat pocket. Eamon had not responded. Marcia observed the woman shift uncomfortably in her seat without looking at anyone and she noted the dark look that passed over Ricardo's eyes.

"Mr O'Donally!" he said with mock humour and cold menace. "Come, Josie!" She looked up at him. "You spend many hours with a passenger…" he threw a glance towards Eamon who held his look, and then turned his attention back to Josie. "Do not take me for a fool that you are not on first-name terms." He threw her a look, eyes fixed on her, smiling caustically. Ricardo appeared to let the moment go. "It appears that you have already met Josie, so I don't need to make any introductions," he said in Eamon's direction. "Please introduce me to this very attractive woman." He smiled at Marcia.

Alphonso's foot tapped Eamon's leg under the table when Eamon glowered. Alphonso jumped in. "Marcia is Eamon's wife. She is visiting for a few days. Marcia will be here for the opening of the club that Eamon is overseeing for me until I find someone to run the place."

"I have heard good things about your club near to Little Havana in downtown Miami. It's near my residential hotel suite. Which will be convenient, Alphonso. It will also be a pleasure to get together with like-minded people from our stable!" He threw Eamon a sideways glance.

Eamon did not respond, taking the comment to mean that Eamon was not Italian or from Miami – an outsider. The waiter took their drinks and the food orders. Ricardo wanted to eat at the same time as them.

"I have heard your name mentioned by friends in New York," Ricardo said to Marcia. She felt uncomfortable, without realising why. He continued. "Franco Gennaro senior from New York and I often keep in contact."

Marcia's unease heightened, she felt Eamon tense up next to her. Ricardo took the stage. "Franco spoke to me of your wife's 'gift'," he said to Eamon while keeping Marcia under his gaze. "It was an interesting conversation. One that not only captivated Franco senior's attention but mine as well." Eamon knew that a man such as Ricardo Barossa would have made enquiries about him and Marica, being so close to Alphonso Gabrette. "To have someone with a gift such as you appear to have…" he smiled, "would be beneficial."

Marcia adjusted her position. Facing Ricardo, she smiled thinly. "The ability that I have used in the past to unveil certain situations is something that I no longer use!" She stated flatly, wanting to put an end to the one-sided conversation.

"Hmmm. That is as maybe. It would be a travesty if your abilities were locked away and some important situation cropped up where they could help." He shook his head." I am sure that your husband and I can come to an agreement, whereby I could use your services. If I could impose upon you to visit my hotel room tomorrow, I require advice regarding my business. I will send my driver to collect you. I assume that you are guests at Alphonso's home?"

Eamon's jaw clenched. He felt another tap on the leg from Alphonso's foot, warning him not to react.

The three-waiting staff finally arrived with the dishes, relieving Marcia and Eamon from the awkward atmosphere around the table. "I see that you have chosen one of my grandmother's favourite specialities." Ricardo smiled a sickly-sweet grimace towards Eamon's plate as the *pollo alla cacciatora* chicken stew, a classic dish from Tuscany, was placed before him. "You should try *costoletta alla Milanese* as well. The veal cutlet is coated in breadcrumbs and fried in butter. It's one of my wife's specialities. Her Italian cooking is superb, although not up to the standard of Alphonso's chef here."

While Ricardo openly bragged about his wife's cooking skills, Josie appeared as if she wanted to be anywhere else but at the table with Ricardo Barossa. "Eat!" he ordered Josie, pointing at her with his knife. She obeyed.

Eamon caught Alphonso's glance. He ate in silence and Marcia picked at the baccala mantecato, salt cod with grilled polenta, a traditional Venetian dish that she was usually fond of. Even though she thought the chef had cooked it superbly, she felt sickened by the thought of the woman sitting opposite her having some connection with Eamon. But not just that – she felt put out by Ricardo's demands that she visit his hotel suite the following day to give him insight into a business matter. Marcia felt his malevolent energy directed at Eamon. She would not want to be in the woman's shoes. Marcia sensed that she would pay heavily for lying to Ricardo. Marcia could not bring herself to sympathise with her though. She knew that this woman wanted Eamon. She was unsure if Eamon had met her after their flight. Marcia thought that Eamon was interested in Josie, though. There could be no other reason for him to have her calling card in his suit pocket.

Marcia said very little on the way home. Eamon had his hand on her knee, while he discussed the opening night with Alphonso. She sat staring out of the window throughout the journey. The numerous designer shops and palatial homes dotted around Dade County held no interest for her. She knew that she would return to Spain shortly. Josie would be free to have Eamon in her clutches. Marcia did not underestimate Josie's lure to the opposite sex. Her looks and figure reminded Marcia of a young Sofia Loren.

Upon their return to Alphonso's home, Alphonso asked Marcia if he could have a private word with Eamon. She smiled, wishing him goodnight.

Joey retired to his room after getting Alphonso a night-cap of bourbon. Eamon refused an offer of alcohol. Unbuttoning his suit jacket, Eamon waited for the old man to savour the liquor.

"Ya had something going on with Ricardo's woman," Alphonso said. Eamon frowned. "Ya woman and Ricardo both have the notion that there is something between ya! He could tell his woman was hiding something when she referred to ya as Mr O'Donally. If you're sitting next to someone on a long flight, you introduce yourself using your first name. It's not as if it is a business situation." He took a small mouthful of amber liquid, eyeing Eamon. He continued, "She has a free hand with Barossa. The woman is renowned for spreading her wares outside of Barossa's domain. They have an agreement. However, if ya have, or if ya thinking of going there with her, I would be very careful. The man is extremely powerful, with no love of ya. He made that clear tonight."

Eamon scratched his earlobe. "Al, we spent nine hours on a flight talking. Josie did give me her calling card," Eamon confessed.

"Ya took it?" Alphonso said.

"Not with the intention of contacting her." Eamon elevated his brows. "I did not want to offend her. I put it in my suit pocket then forgot about it."

"Did ya dispose of it after?"

Eamon gave a small laugh at Alphonso's interrogation. He shook his head. "It is in my suit jacket hanging in my wardrobe at home in Spain. If I had thought of it, I would have ripped it up. I told ye, Al. I have no need or desire for another woman."

Alphonso tapped his forefinger on the side of his nose. "Marcia is not a stupid woman. Certainly no fool. Sort it out with her. Before the morning," he directed. "Otherwise, I promise ya that ya won't have an enjoyable time with her here."

Eamon opened the door to their bedroom. The chandeliers cast a soft glow. Marcia had changed into her cream silk kimono. She was gazing out of the window into the blackness. She did not turn as he approached. He placed a hand on her shoulder. She flinched. He turned her head to face him. Her eyes were glazed over – she was near to tears. "Marcia don't turn away from me. I have done nothing wrong."

"Eamon, I found that woman's calling card in your suit pocket at home. I discovered it when Aye was taking them to the dry cleaners." She stepped away from him. He held her fast.

"Marcia, the woman did give me her card on the Paris to Miami flight. However, there was not a thought in my mind to call her. I took it intending to throw it away. I knew of her past. The woman had given me her history with Barossa. What do ye take me for? I have ye. Do ye tink that I would fuck up our marriage? What we have is special. You are the only woman who interests me. You must believe me," He implored. "Ye don't know me, Marcia. Ye and my family, my four children – I don't want to be away from yous all, ever. I want to be able to come home to my wife each night, not to jump into another woman's bed because she gives me her card. Have ye ever been given a flyer in Benidorm and ye take it even though ye have no interest in whatever it is selling? Well, it's the same ting."

Marcia softly inhaled. "Promise me that you have not slept with her."

"Marcia, ye are the only woman that I have slept wit since the time that I stepped into the shower wit ye a decade ago!"

She stood up and moved towards him. His hands slid down the silk of her kimono over the contours of her buttocks. "Do you want me to put the black dress back on?" she said, pressing against his mounting erection.

"The geisha girl look does it for me, maybe coupled wit a few positions from the Karma Sutra that ye perform wit ease!" He lifted her, taking her to the bed. He stripped off his suit, the rest followed, hastily thrown over the armchair.

Eamon untied the belt of Marcia's silk kimono. He caressed her full breasts, fingertips fluttering over her nipples. She rested one of her legs on his shoulder while the other encircled his waist. As he slowly went deeper she bucked, meeting him. He observed her, head back, breathing heavily with each measured stroke. His teeth nipped at each dark bud. He felt the beginning, joining her they united.

Eamon lay awake while Marcia slept in his arms. She had spoken to him of the danger that she felt that he was in with Ricardo Barossa. He knew that he was out of his depth on the man's territory. Barossa's tentacles stretched across many countries. But, as much as he did not want Marcia to go to the man's hotel suite to give him a tarot reading, he knew that to keep the peace he must agree to it. Eamon told Marcia that Josie would probably take the brunt of Barossa's jealousy if he believed that Josie was interested in Eamon. Alphonso had told him that Ricardo and his son Angelo were renowned for slapping women around. However, Alphonso convinced Eamon that Marcia would be safe and to allow her to go to Barossa's suite of rooms. Alphonso informed him that Barossa spent a lot of time entertaining at the Mandarin Oriental hotel, which was centrally located on the three-acre island of Brickell Key.

Marcia dressed in a black, knee-length suit with matching high-heeled shoes, her tarot cards in the Hermes bag slung over her shoulder. She sat in the back seat of the chauffer-driven limousine with blacked-out windows. She looked out the window without taking in the sights as the car sped towards its destination. Her mind drifted to the time, over ten years ago, when Suzette Greenaway had sent Mikey, Max Greenaway's right-hand man to collect her. She felt that history was repeating itself. Although that time the emotional blackmail had involved her son Reuben, this time Marcia knew that it involved her husband. Marcia knew that Barossa was a powerful drug baron, but this did not faze her. She had mentally prepared herself to pit her wits against the Miami don.

As the car crossed the bridge to the man-made island, Marcia observed the tranquil oasis. She thought it looked like a location where, under different circumstances, she might like to stay for a few days with Eamon. She took in the stunning views of Biscayne Bay and the Brickell skyline, although she thought the view at home of the Altea Bay and surrounding hills was far superior.

The place had everything that she held dear – the magnificent home that Eamon had Greg Davison build for their growing family. It had been a wedding present from Eamon, however, they had not married or moved to the new home until later when she was pregnant with Quinn, Niall but a babe in arms. She was not prepared to throw her precious memories away.

Marcia followed the man out of the lift on the penthouse floor. She did not show any recognition to Josie waiting by the lift doors, who smiled thinly in her direction. Marcia did not miss the bruising on her cheekbone, covered with foundation.

Ricardo, dressed in a white dress jacket, white open-neck shirt and black trousers, opened the door to the driver's knock. He gave the man a firm nod of dismissal as Marcia entered the vast room. The balcony doors were open and she felt a soft breeze from the sea.

"Please!" Ricardo guided her towards the balcony.

"It is rather beautiful!" Marcia stated.

"This is where I find that I can relax best – to get away from the constant to-and-fro of my heavy schedule. There are five bedrooms, to accommodate guests."

Marcia thought wryly to herself, Away from your wife and family, to enable your mistress to entertain you. She glanced out at the magnificent view and down over the balcony at the swimming pool. Unimpressed, she turned towards him. She wanted to get this appointment over with quickly.

He studied her with a bemused look on his face. She knew that under most circumstances it would be intimidating to have a man like Ricardo Barossa in front of you. However, she judged that he desperately required her advice. Given the opportunity, Marcia would turn the tables on him.

Stepping back into the room, Marcia looked at the eight-seater mahogany dining table. She moved towards it.

"May I offer you some refreshment before you begin, Marcia?"

She politely declined. She had drunk a bottle of Voss mineral water before she left. Talking made her thirsty. However, she wanted nothing from him. He proffered a chair. Marcia placed her bag on the table, removing the cards, which were wrapped in silk and encased in a small wooden box. Ricardo pulled out a seat opposite her.

"Ricardo, I must ask that please refrain from asking any questions until after I have completed the reading."

He directed her a disarming smile. It washed over her. Business-like, she passed him the pack of cards and asked him to shuffle. "Upon feeling the need to stop. Pass them to me."

Ricardo, lips pressed together, did as she asked, while observing her.

The silence in the room was palpable as he placed the shuffled pack on the table in front of Marcia. Her eyes focusing on the deck, she slowly turned over the first of the twenty-two major arcana cards. She laid down three cards more cards diagonally, followed by another three.

Ricardo's dark eyes scanned over the cards as she tapped the top two, jumping to the four beneath. "I normally ask for a client's astrological birth sign. However, you appear to be a Capricorn. He gave two slow nods, without replying.

She concentrated on the cards and then said, "Within the next fourteen days there will be disruption regarding a business transaction. I see a vast expanse of water, islands, boats and the sea – possibly the Caribbean. The battle that will ensue involves a powerful man from distant shores." She circled a forefinger around the four cards. Moving her hand down, she tapped the card beneath. "There will be the wrath of a family connection. A partnership will be broken if the warning is not heeded."

Ricardo sat upright, listening intently.

"A younger male will try to move in if you are not holding the reins," she said. "Because this," she touched the Capricorn signifier, "this indicates that you have turned your back on this situation. I don't mean literally." She paused, looking at the cards, then said, "You have allowed another to take over – this family youth."

Marcia looked up when Ricardo's chair scraped. He leaned forward on the table, resting his forearms, eyes questioning, remaining silent. She delved further. "Although I see deception regarding this set of circumstances, the betrayal is not against you. It is for personal acclaim to beat the opposition in a business partnership. The personality is someone who wants to run before they can walk. They are not ready for such responsibility." Marcia enlightened him further. "There will be an explosive outcome if you do not watch out for signs. I am not saying that you are blind, however, you may be blinkered due to a family connection."

The chair scraped again and Ricardo placed his hand over the deck. Marcia stopped. Ricardo nodded twice, breathing heavily, looking between her and the cards. He leaned back into the chair. "Do you see if there is a threat to me once this situation that you speak of is rectified?"

Marcia glanced back at the layout. She shook her head. "Immediate action is called for. Regain your control and the crown will remain upon your head."

Ricardo stood up, smiling in admiration at Marcia. "You are a remarkable woman. Please take a more comfortable seat." He indicated the two large floral sofas on the other side of the room. "I won't take up too much of your time," Ricardo said upon seeing Marcia's reluctant look. Crossing the room, he disappeared through a door at the far end. When he returned, Marcia was seated on the edge of the sofa, back rigid, her bag placed in front of her on the marble coffee table.

Ricardo sat down opposite, leaning forward, holding out an envelope. Marcia stiffened. "I want to repay you for your advice."

Marcia smiled, shaking her head. "Ricardo, it is of no inconvenience to me. I can assure you."

He smiled, his handsome features lit up, although she thought his dark eyes retained their shark-like look. "I have no doubt that you do not need reimbursement." He threw a glance at her rings and bag. "Diamonds and emeralds of such quality and the Hermes bag do not come cheap. Your husband obviously appreciates you. He would be a fool if he did not."

Marcia did not respond. The compliments were wasted on her.

"Take it!" he pressed further. Marcia gave a curt nod. She put the envelope in her bag. She would give the money to Aye for her family in the village in Thailand.

He relaxed on the sofa, arm resting on the armrest. "I would like you to attend a party in two days with your husband and Alphonso. They have already accepted the invitation. As we speak preparations are being made on my yacht which I keep in Vice City Marina. I want to show you the beauty of Biscayne Bay from the deck as we cruise past Virgin Island!"

Marcia nodded as Ricardo went on. "It will be beneficial for your husband to be introduced to my associates. It will help to alleviate any problems that he may encounter as a stranger during his stay in Miami." A smirk played on his lips. "During Josie's encounter with Eamon on the flight from Paris to Miami she said they had a long conversation. Josie is an attractive woman. A head turner. Although somewhat…" he waggled his head, "overly sociable!"

Marcia retained her composure. She knew Ricardo was implying that his woman and Eamon had something going on. Marcia had believed Eamon when he swore that she had been the only woman that he had slept with since their first encounter. She trusted Eamon's word.

"Could you ask your driver to return me to Alphonso's home, please?" Ricardo nodded. Rising, he strode to a side table, picking up a mobile phone.

Marcia set her plan in motion. She had informed Eamon and Alphonso that she would be returning to Spain the night after the opening of Alphonso's nightclub, due to the twins becoming fretful by her absence. Eamon had booked her on the late-night flight. Before she was due to depart they spent a couple of hours together in the privacy of the bedroom engaging in some steamy farewell passion. Marcia dressed in a thigh-high, red, low-cut dress. She knelt above his face with her legs wide while Eamon's tongue teased through ouvert silk panties. Later, their naked bodies lay entwined, paying homage to one another, not knowing when they would unite again.

Eamon walked with Marcia to the first-class check area. Earlier, Marcia had spoken to Jane who said that she would ask

Billy to pick her up from the airport. Jane reported that the children were fine and kept busy by taking care of the horses. Billy had been entertaining the boys with water sports and football. Marcia had twisted the truth about the reasons for her early departure from Miami. She didn't want to hang around the Midnight Club for too long after the grand opening and signalled to Eamon that she wished to leave.

Eamon put his hands on her waist, pulling her towards him. "I noticed that ye were having a deep conversation wit Lucca in the club earlier. It appeared that ye held the man's attention." He said, cocking an eyebrow.

"He was talking to me about his wife. He told me that she suffered from a heart defect that prevented them from having children. It would be a risk to her life if she became pregnant. He was asking about our children. He appeared wistful. I was going to withhold what I felt, however, I informed him that he would have two children. Two sons."

Eamon elevated his brow, then nodded. "My little mystic appears to enthral all these powerful men out here." He cupped her chin, looked into her eyes and said, "Stay safe for me. Kiss and hug the children."

Marcia's arms went around his neck and she kissed him deeply. She stepped back and said, "I will see you soon." She smiled and turned to walk towards the departure area. Halfway there, she turned and saw he was still waiting, watching her. She blew him a kiss. Eamon smiled with two slow nods.

11

Marcia could hear a ringtone in the distance. Sleepily, she opened her eyes and realised it was her mobile phone. Propping herself up on the pillows, she reached for the phone. Eamon's number flashed up on the screen. Her heart began to race as she pressed to answer. It was news that she was expecting.

"Marcia!" Eamon said before she had time to speak. "Ricardo and his boy Angelo have been shot. Both were gunned down outside the Midnight Club only a short while after ye left and before Joey and I returned to the club. There was mayhem. Police had cordoned off Little Havana. Ambulances and medics were on the scene. The place was heaving wit Cubans who were irate about the destruction of Alphonso's club. They are not bothered about Ricardo and his boy, only Alphonso, their old friend, who I got Joey to take away from the scene."

Marcia gasped without replying. Eamon gulped. She thought that he was drinking. "The restaurant windows and front of the club were sprayed wit bullets from AK-7 rifles. Two of Ricardo's henchmen took a hit after they gave chase to the shooter's car. Lucca was fortunately inside the club. He told me that he thought that it had been a ruse that had drawn Ricardo out of the club. He said that Ricardo had received a call to say that there had been an explosion on his boat. Father and son immediately left, walking straight into the shooter's path. Ricardo's two men threw themselves on the floor. Lucca said that his brother's and nephew's faces were ripped open, their bodies riddled wit bullets!"

Marcia rose from the bed while Eamon was talking, picking up and wrapping a silk negligee around her, phone held under her chin. "Eamon, please leave Miami. It's too dangerous. We need you here!" She pleaded.

"Marcia!" he breathed deeply. "I am at the club trying to get some semblance of order." He paused for a couple of seconds. She heard the weariness in his voice. "How can I walk away from the old man now? He is mentally and physically broken. His last dream has been dashed. The club looks like a bomb site. The front has been practically blown off. The club licence will be revoked after this. The Law will class it as narcotic gang warfare and they won't tolerate it. Lucca has taken over from his brother. There will be a full-scale war wit the Columbians, who Lucca tinks are behind it!"

Marcia heard Eamon take another gulp, then the sound of a glass being placed on a hard surface.

"Eamon, please come away from there."

He interjected, "Once the workmen Lucca has summoned arrive on the scene to make the club secure from plunderers, I will return to Alphonso. I'll call you back later when I'm at his home."

She stood looking out the window. Her mind was on the deaths of Ricardo and his son. Marcia had taken the risk of withholding what she had seen in Ricardo Barossa's tarot cards – the threat to his life that she had known was imminent. She had not revealed that he would be dead within 48 hours of his reading.

Nonetheless, she had felt no obligation to Ricardo or his son. All the powerful men that she had come up against over the past decade had underestimated her when they thought that they could use her skills for their own gain. She may have been obliged to go along with their demands, however, she held the key to their destinies and could share or withhold what she thought most suitable. Her ability gave her the upper hand in that with a little bit of information, she could influence any given situation in their lives. These men misjudged her. She was no puppet. Marcia wielded power in her hands. For the most part, she was careful with how she used it.

Marcia realised that once Eamon had gathered his thoughts, he would question her about Ricardo Barossa's tarot reading. She knew Eamon was no fool. He was aware of Marcia's ability to foresee danger. He would want to know why she had not warned Ricardo Barossa about the threat to his life.

Marcia changed into a swimsuit. She needed to swim to clear her mind. She walked quietly across the marble tiles towards the terrace doors. The children and Aye were asleep and the only sound came from the tapping of the dogs' claws on the floor as they followed Marcia across the large lounge.

The early November air carried a cool breeze that threatened rain at any moment. Although this time of year was the wettest on the Costa Blanca, it was times like this that reminded her of England where she swam regularly in the outdoor pool at her health club. It was the only luxury that she had allowed herself back then. That life before she met Eamon, seemed like a distant memory. The first raindrops hit the water as she stepped into the water, holding her face up against the soft wind that sent droplets onto her skin. If Eamon had been at home, she would have swum naked. She silently sent up a prayer to the Universe to those that she knew protected her.

Marcia had put her trust in the unseen realm that she believed guided her to protect her family. She felt that Eamon would come back to her unscathed.

Eamon had been in Miami for a further eleven days after the murder at the Midnight Club. He had stayed on to be by Alphonso's side. Eamon had informed Marcia that the old Italian's health had hit an all-time low, but it had not been entirely due to the shooting of Ricardo Barossa and his son. When Alphonso was told that the Midnight Club had lost its licence and that there would be no chance in the future of reapplying, he sank into a deep depression. He had not been concerned about the financial loss – rather, it was his dream that had been shattered. The drinking hole where the once all-powerful Alphonso Gabrette could spend time with his old associates was now boarded up. Eamon had told Marcia that Alphonso's era had come to an end. He said that Chiara, Alphonso's youngest daughter, was arranging for her father to spend his last days at her home. She was hiring medical staff to attend to his needs.

Joey and Eamon had sat talking through past times with the old man the day before his move. Eamon said that Alphonso's mind was drifting throughout. His train of thought mixed. The old man's words were jumbled. He spoke of his dead wife, Marcella and son Carlo, at times mistakenly believing that they were both still with him.

Marcia was excited that in a few hours, Eamon would be back in Spain. He had phoned her from Paris when he was about to get his flight to Alicante. Dan was going to pick him up at the airport and he was going straight to the Hawk Wind club to check on the men, then he was coming home. She had not told the children that their father was returning from Miami. She knew the girls would be overly excited and not go to sleep, as they continually asked for their father. Quinn had been his sweet self throughout Eamon's absence, swimming and playing with the girls in the pool after school. However, Niall did not join in with the other three children.

Marcia had swum with him at times, trying to get Niall to interact. Nevertheless, he remained his unresponsive self. She was concerned for Niall. More so than usual. He appeared withdrawn. Furthermore, Marcia still encountered the feeling of portent of things to come. Each time that she dropped the boys off at school and collected them, the building seemed ominous to her. She tried to convince herself that her fears were unfounded. She knew that her sons were protected at the school. Marcia hoped that once their lives settled down when Eamon returned she would become less anxious. She put the perturbed feelings down to Bridie trying to wreak havoc on her marriage. There was also the feeling that she had encountered in Miami when she felt that she had fed Ricardo Barossa to the lions. Although it was not guilt that she felt. It had been the apprehension for Eamon's safety.

Marcia had returned to work at the Mystique beauty salon. Suzette had eight bookings for her, spread out over two days. Marcia's diary began to fill up as her past clientele clambered for appointments. Suzette had sent emails to inform them that Marcia would be working from the Mystique once again.

Keeping herself occupied by working had helped. Nonetheless, Marcia spent each night struggling to get to sleep, knowing that she would have to face a barrage of questions from Eamon regarding Ricardo Barossa's tarot reading. She could not lie to Eamon. That would not be an option. Her concern was that she hoped that Eamon would believe her that she had done it to protect him.

She had not gone to the Hawk Wind club to work due to Eamon's absence. Cindy and Jane had stepped up instead. Cindy took over the managing of the pole dancers and also worked at times behind the bar. Jane worked alongside her. Marcia had given them both a large bonus, insisting that they accepted it when they tried to refuse. Marcia had given the unopened envelope that Ricardo Barossa had given her to Aye.

Upon opening it, Aye had been stunned at the amount – 5,000 US dollars. She could not comprehend that anyone would pay such a large amount of money for a tarot card reading. She had told Marcia that a family member in Sisaket who 'read' tarot cards charged 200 baht, which was approximately 4 euros. Aye had said candidly, as was her wont, that she thought that 5,000 dollars was a disgusting amount of money to pay for advice. Marcia smiled when Aye thanked her for the money, which would go towards helping the local school where Aye's great nephew and niece were pupils.

Eamon was met by Dan at Alicante airport. Eamon had slept on the flight from Miami to Paris without interruption. He had pre-warned the flight attendant that under no circumstances did he want to be woken. He had kept the first-class seat in the upright position and his seatbelt fastened throughout the flight, knowing that if there was turbulence, he would not be woken up. He had given a lot of thought to the events in Miami over the past couple of weeks. He understood the reason behind the murder of Ricardo Barossa and his son Angelo. From what Alphonso had told him, Angelo Barossa had been dealing with Ricardo's Columbian contacts. However, Alphonso said that the lad had thought he could pull the wool over the Columbian bosses' eyes by saying that part of their narcotic delivery was useless.

The thing that bothered Eamon was that he knew that Marcia would have warned Ricardo Barossa of the impending danger. Eamon knew from experience that Marcia would have been spot on the money. However, what was unclear to him was why Ricardo had not acted upon it. The man had given her a wad of money for her advice. Marcia had told Eamon that she had given Aye the money. Five thousand dollars was not to be sneezed at. Logic told him that for the man to pay such a large amount, he must have been pleased with the information that Marcia had given him. He was bewildered, knowing that the pair's deaths could have been prevented. Nevertheless, he had kept his thoughts to himself when Alphonso was giving him the background on the trouble that Angelo Barossa had caused.

Eamon wanted answers from his wife. He put his thoughts to one side as he got into Dan's passenger seat. Dan had told him on the phone earlier, when Eamon checked in with him from Miami, that the Russians were trying to take over their turf. There had been a group of them that had taken out membership to the Hawk Wind club, although as yet they had caused no trouble. Their heavy drinking at the bar had seen a couple of them become loose-lipped.

Dan headed the car south, picking up from where he had left off the conversation. "Cindy overheard the Russians' conversations. Their boss, who was flying into Spain that week, was interested in buying a club – more upmarket than the Hawk Wind." Dan grinned. "The drunken words of the Russians. Billy said that he picked up a Bulgarian accent from one of the group as they left the club one night."

Eamon nodded.

"They have been drinking mid-week in Michael's Irish bar. Michael had told Billy and Jackie Cooper when they dropped in to have a couple of drinks the other night after work.

I thought about sending Scott Lord, Thomas Harper-Watts and Aar to the bar to see how the land lies. The Somalian lad is fitting in nicely with the boys," Dan added.

"Do ye have a name for this Russian boss? Any information on who he is? Or maybe someone is up behind him. Financially backing him?"

Dan shook his head without taking his eyes off the road. "I dare say that it will come out soon. Maybe the lads will hear something when they join them at Michael's. I have warned them not to get into any altercation with the boss."

"I would tink that the Somalian's herculean presence would quell any thought the Russians may have of starting trouble!" Eamon laughed.

Dan's tone took on a more serious note as he kept to the right at the fork following the signs for the A-70 Alicante/Benidorm/Valencia/Madrid before merging onto the A-70. He momentarily took his eyes off the road. "Cindy and I are getting married!" His attention returned to the road ahead.

"That's grand!" Eamon stated, pleased. Dan was a private man, not unlike Eamon. Both men did not speak about their private lives to others.

"It is about time that I made a decent woman of her. Cindy deserves it," Dan added, looking ahead.

"If ye would consider having ye reception at my villa, it will be my gift to host it for ye both. I could not run my business without ye, Dan."

Dan nodded his head. "I am sure, Boss, that Cindy will be pleased by your offer. Although I will need to run it by her. Nevertheless," he faltered, "thank you."

Eamon nodded to the security staff as he entered the Hawk Wind club followed by Dan. Eamon was pleased to see that the club was packed. He looked across at the cocktail bar where Lloyd and Keiron were juggling cocktails. Their audience of admirers was laughing. Eamon had to hand it to the pair. Men and women alike were drawn to the flamboyant pair. Eamon turned his attention to the stage where the dancers were doing their routine. He took note of a new face. She smiled at him from her upside-down position, her long limbs wrapped around the pole. He looked away without responding. The dusky skin spoke to him of mixed heritage. She was young with a perfect figure. The men hugging the stage had their full attention on her. Eamon knew that Marcia had not been working in the club while he had been away, so Cindy or Jane would have employed the new dancer.

Billy approached, breaking Eamon's train of thought. He smiled, indicating the dusky dancer. "Cindy gave the girl a job. Apparently, a little birdie told me that she has a Bulgarian boyfriend who comes to the club with a group of Russians."

Eamon turned his back to the stage, as did Billy. Eamon pursed his lips, scratching the side of his nose. "Why is it, Billy, that I smell trouble? Or is it just my suspicious nature that tinks she could have been planted here?"

Billy nodded. "Time will tell boss."

The dogs heard Eamon's approach before Marcia noticed that he was inside the villa. Marcia was standing near the terrace doors, waiting in readiness for Eamon. The house was quiet and still, as the children were all asleep. Aye had prepared Eamon his favourite Thai dishes earlier before she retired to her room and left them in the kitchen ready for him to enjoy on his return.

Marcia turned upon hearing the door shut. She hurried towards Eamon. The cream, Asian wisteria embroidered, skirt swished around her ankles. The black, long-sleeve blouse with gold, chain-link belt, which enhanced her small waist, complimented the look.

"Ye look as exotic as ye did in the video that ye sent to me." Marcia had sent him some footage of her doing a strip tease for him while he was in Miami, wearing an outfit from the Asian designer Rina Dhaka. The camera caught the reflection in wall-to-wall mirrors in their bedroom as she slowly removed the red blouse, giving him a 360-degree view.

Eamon smiled, leaving his suitcase near the door he moved towards her and scooped her up in his arms. All his ponderings about what went on in Miami were forgotten for the moment. Marcia threw her arms around his neck. They both hugged without kissing.

"I have desperately missed ye. To feel ye in my arms is what I have longed for." He breathed into Marcia's neck, taking in the fragrance of the Indian oud oil with the scent of juniper berries, vanilla and sandalwood, which was one of Marcia's signature perfumes that he never failed to recognise. It went with her, exciting him, drawing him to her. Blood rushing to his groin, he kissed her, carrying her to the bedroom.

"Marcia, I can't leave it until after I shower." He undressed after laying her on the bed. She sat up, smiling, beckoning him with her finger when he stepped out of his clothing. Rock solid, he knelt over her, inhaling softly when her light clasp encircled his penis. Her hand moved in slow motion as he throbbed in her grasp.

Unbuttoning her blouse and removing the chain-link belt, he took in her full breasts in the cupless bra. His mouth engulfed each bud, his tongue circling, teasing. He raised her skirt above her waist. Her legs widened when he covered her, allowing him entry via the ouvert panties. He cupped her buttocks with both hands as he filled her. Marcia tightened her pelvic muscles, meeting his deliberate thrusts. Their soul kiss began the ascending climax. He took her up with him to the plateau – frenzied soft but firm biting on both parts as they flowed together into the abyss of their powerful orgasms.

Hearts racing, he stayed within her, gradually shrinking. Supporting himself on his forearms, he smiled. "The vision of ye performing yer strip tease for me was professional quality. It certainly filled a gap!" He smiled. "But nothing can fulfil me unless I am inside of ye."

Marcia's fingers played along his mouth; they both briefly brushed one another's lips.

"I planned to give you a massage. To help you relax. I can run a bath for you."

Eamon nodded, "I will check on the children." He had glanced at the baby monitor while he undressed before their lovemaking. "I will shower. That way we will have more time. A seductive massage from my woman on the bed is an enticing prospect. Not that I would not enjoy ye joining me in the bath."

Eamon had stood looking at Niall for longer than he had at Quinn when he had checked on them. He had sorely missed his children. However, Niall was never far from his thoughts. He sensed that his eldest son was troubled. Although in slumber, head in profile, Niall appeared at peace. Eamon felt as if he was looking at himself as a child. He too had been a troubled youngster. However, his childhood circumstances were very different to his son's The variance was incomparable. There had been poverty and hunger, which for the most part was down to his father sinking beer down his gullet in the pub daily with no thought for his family. He and his brother Patrick had endured frequent beatings from their drunken, violent father.

However, Niall, on the other hand, was showered with love from the moment that he made his dramatic entrance into the world. Eamon had paid a small fortune to rush by private jet from Spain to Thailand to watch his child's dark thatch emerge while Marcia was giving birth to his son. From then on, he vowed that his child and subsequent children would live under his protection.

Eamon's heart lurched, soaring at the sight of the identical chubby toddlers with their abundance of copper-red curls. Aisling was asleep on her back, arms splayed and Aine was curled up in the foetal position. He stood a few feet from their cot beds in awe at their beauty. They bore a striking resemblance to his grandmother with their milky skin tone and fiery head of hair. He also recognised in them both her strong temperament. More so in Aisling than in Aine. Aisling, as young as she was, commanded attention, although Aine had her moments. They had Eamon wrapped around their podgy little fingers. He marvelled at how even at such a young age, they sensed that when they shed tears their father would soften. Marcia broke him with her tears. It had to be something inherent to the female psyche which enabled them to win over males, he concluded, smiling warmly and closing their nursery door.

Marcia lay encircled in his arms after she had massaged him. Both had pleasured each other again. Marcia had completed releasing the knots of built-up tension from Eamon's neck and shoulders. Upon reaching his buttocks, he turned in one swift movement placing her above him. Marcia had other ideas. Kneeling before him, she took him deeper. A short while later he had returned the favour.

He had waited to speak to Marcia about Miami. He did not want to ruin their private time, but he could not leave it any longer. "Marcia I need some answers!"

She ran her fingers through his chest hair, looking at him without replying. He held her dark-brown eyes with his. "I cannot get my head around Ricardo Barossa and his boy's murder." He paused for a short moment. "Lucca Barossa told me that his brother Ricardo had spoken highly of ye as to how ye had given him sound advice." Marcia remained silent. "The man had rewarded ye wit 5,000 dollars for the reading, no mere pittance. He had to have heeded the advice that ye gave him. But what is throwing me is the fact that I know first-hand that ye are always spot on the money wit pre-warnings!" He shook his head, cocking an eyebrow. "What went wrong?"

Marcia looked down. He cupped her chin in his hand, eyes searching. "Did ye know that was going to happen and ye kept it from him?" Marcia inhaled quietly. He adjusted his position, vehemently shaking his head in disbelief. "Do ye realise that once Lucca Barossa puts two and two together he too will want answers? The man is no eejit!" He sat up staring at her. "What did ye say to Ricardo for the man to pay ye such a great deal of money?" He paused for a moment. "Marcia, there had to be something that ye said that resounded wit him. The man was a powerful mafia don. He did not get to that position by being stupid."

Marcia held his look. "I told him about betrayal. I described a man who was linked to someone in a high-ranking position within the Law. The insignia on his uniform confirmed it. There was a family member who was a Judas to Ricardo. Not his son Angelo. I gave him the man's initials and description. I required Ricardo's trust," she added, pleading her case.

Eamon shook his head again. "Ye told me that ye had made some predictions for Lucca when he spoke to ye about his wife's heart condition. Did ye say to him that he would have two sons?" Eamon repeated what Marcia had previously told him. Marcia sat up facing him.

"Eamon, Ricardo Barossa hated you. I could see the malevolence in his eyes. He had the look of a shark that would devour its prey. At that moment, I knew that you would not stand a chance with him. He ruled that territory. You were on his turf. I know that you are powerful in Spain, but not in Miami. When Ricardo and his woman sat with us at our table that night in Alphonso's restaurant, I knew above anything that he would have had you killed." She hesitated, then continued, "I could not allow him to harm you. I saw the threat to his life in the tarot reading that I gave him. I sensed that it would occur at any given moment. When it came down to it, I had to decide to help Ricardo or save you. I had no compunction about withholding the outcome I could 'see'. I seized the opportunity to remove the threat to your life." She exhaled. "Eamon, I know that you protect me and the children. I understand your concern about me trying to outfox these powerful men. However, in the past, I have dealt with Max Greenaway and Jimmy Grant. Both men tried to overpower me and use me as their puppet, however, my gift of foresight is my power over them. I am able to manipulate their destiny."

Eamon nodded slowly. "Ye premeditated Ricardo's and his son's death by not informing him!" He gave an incredulous laugh. "Do ye realise what type of people ye were dealing wit?"

She placed both hands on his chest. "Eamon, please don't judge me for wanting to protect you. I knew what I was up against with Ricardo. You are my life. Our children would have suffered if he had had the opportunity to remove you. Therefore, the hand that I played was to win. Eamon, I would not allow Ricardo Barossa or anyone to destroy our world. I knew that you would not be harmed the night of the shooting." She stated firmly, "You may be physically more powerful than I am, however, my strength is in my gift of foresight. I have always used it to help many people, although there has been the odd occasion when it has caused problems, like with Max Greenaway and Jimmy Grant's son-in-law Matt. But for the most part, I only wish to guide others with my advice. It is as natural to me as breathing to call upon my spiritual guides."

Eamon cocked a brow and smiled. "Do ye class murder as being spiritual? Or, more to the point, do ye friends in unseen realms approve of ye aiding in someone's demise to enable ye to have a clear path in yer own life?" He waited for her answer.

Marcia inhaled. "I only know that I cannot put anyone before you or my children. If you and I must pay the price when we return to the spiritual realm for our misdeeds, so be it, if it means we will be together for eternity."

He looked at her for a long moment. She knelt on the bed before him. He took her face in his hands, slowly nodding.

"Not only did that man underestimate ye," Eamon said, "I did too!" He drew her into his chest, holding her to him. "My wee mystic warrior may hold a powerful tool in her hand wit her gift of foresight. Nonetheless, please don't get too comfortable. These people are not eejits." He brushed his mouth with hers. "I have enough to deal wit."

"Eamon, I will do anything to protect you and the children. As you do."

"That's as maybe. However, in the future, before ye tink about knocking anyone from their pedestal, make strategic plans, as I do..." He kissed her again. "...to ensure, my wee Boudica, that there will be no comeback." He smiled when she straddled him. He tapped her mouth. Lifting her, placing her beneath him.

"Now we have put that to rest. We are going to enjoy some slow loving." He threw his head back upon feeling her mouth engulf his erection. Marcia's tongue teased. She caressed his scrotum, empowering him. Eamon surrendered to her.

12

Bridie had decided to go to Barking in Essex as there were some vacancies in Barking Hospital and nearby schools for cleaners. Bridie didn't care how she earned her living, whether it was scrubbing floors or bar work. She knew how to make her way in life. While she was still in Spain, she sent various applications via the internet. She was thrilled to be invited for three job interviews the week after she arrived in the UK. She was confident that she would secure work. She was also looking at rooms to let at reasonable rents. She had the directions from Gatwick airport. The journey was an hour and twenty-six minutes. Two changes on the train would take her to her destination.

Bridie had not realised that the high cost of living in London would drain the money that she had been given by Eamon O'Donally. She cursed him time and again as to how he had robbed her. She had demanded two thousand pounds from him for the damning pictures of his wife and her young lover. He had halved it. However, her life began to look rosy after that. Nothing fazed the young girl from Dublin. She had purchased a SIM card for her mobile phone and gone into an internet café in Barking to submit online enquiries for rooms.

She had no problem with securing work at Barking Hospital. She had altered the cadence of her voice when applying for a room in a shared house. Everything fell into place. With the 1,000 euros left over from O'Donally and another 500 that Martha her sister had given her, and her wages from her new job as a cleaner at Barking Hospital, she would be able to live well until she found something more suitable. Bridie aimed to work in a club as a dancer. The tips that she would receive from the punters was the draw. Bridie planned to make well of her life in Essex as the starting point. She had easily found new accommodation in a large, Victorian house, ten minutes walk from her job.

The beginning of her new life was enhanced by one of the young male tenants, who rented the room next to Bridie's. By chance, he happened to work at the same hospital, in the hospital cafeteria. A romance quickly blossomed. Within a few days, he succumbed to her charms. Bridie began to encourage him to sneak food out of the café, whereby, their food bill was cut down. Bridie and Terry were able to purchase cannabis, which was easily attainable from the lads who worked at the hospital. Their supplier was a barman at the local pub. Smoking until the small hours became a regular thing. Their clocking-in time at work became later by the day. Both were given notice on their jobs if they continued to arrive late to work.

Bridie had no other means of income, but there was no way she was going to sleep on a park bench, which is what happened to some of Terry's associates. She may have been down on her luck, what with her rent due and her cash flow dwindling to a few quid, however, Bridie always had her sister Martha to fall back on who was living the high life in Spain with a man who provided her with a nice lifestyle. She rang her.

Martha, heavily pregnant, sat resting on the sofa with her feet up on a footstool, taking the strain off her swollen feet.

Benny Harris was outside cleaning the pool. When the phone rang, Martha reached across to the side table to pick up the phone. Such was Benny's concern for Martha's welfare, that he made sure everything was accessible and within reach to prevent her from over-exerting herself.

Martha said hello, but before she had time to say anything more, Bridie screeched down the phone. "Martha, ye have got to help me. I am going to be kicked out on the street because I have no money to pay the rent. I have lost my job." She sniffled for effect.

Martha adjusted her position, pushing the cushion further into the curve of her back. Benny had recently put it there to help ease her aching back, which was due to the weight of the baby.

"Bridie, I have been worried about ye. There has been no contact since ye took off from Spain." Martha had given Bridie money just before she left Spain for London. I can't help ye again. Benny has been renovating the villa and the garden. Our baby is due soon. Why don't you come back to Spain and live wit us? There is a spare room, Bridie. I won't be able to sleep at night to tink of my baby sister on the streets of London!" Her tone was warm and caring, no matter that Bridie had screeched down the phone at her. She was tolerant, quite the opposite of her sibling.

"Fucking come back to Spain after O'Donally ripped me off for the photos of his Jezebel woman wit her young fella?" Bridie scoffed. Martha rested her head on the back of the sofa, closing her eyes, while listening to her sister blaming others for her problems. Martha's anguish for her younger sibling's welfare far outweighed her fears that Bridie would wreak havoc on her and Benny's relationship if Bridie decided to take up her offer and came to live with Martha.

"Get yer sugar daddy to give ye some money. He works for O'Donally. That's crap that he's skint!"

Martha exhaled. She was weeks away from her due date – she felt tired.

"Ye have got to help me!" she sobbed into the silence. Martha had not responded. There was no point. Bridie realised that her demands were not going to be met. She screamed into the phone, "YE PROMISED TO LOOK OUT FOR ME WHEN WE LEFT DUBLIN. NOW YE GOT AN OLD MAN TO KEEP YER, YE FORGET ABOUT ME!"

"Bridie, please don't say that!" Martha pleaded, placing a hand on her baby bump. She had hoped that her contented life with Benny Harris would continue as it was. Nevertheless, listening to her young sister railing, she despaired for her new-found happiness. "Ye are my baby sister and I love ye!" Tears ran like rivulets down Martha's face onto her neck as she promised to try to help her.

Benny had been standing by the terrace doors and he stepped into the lounge. "Martha, get her bank details and her address," he directed without any tone of caring for her sister's welfare. He knew that Bridie would use emotional blackmail on Martha.

Martha had her bank details. Benny went to fetch a box of tissues. He bent over her, wiping her tears, cupping her chin. "Ye are such a good man, Benny!" She took his hand in hers.

"I am not going to allow anyone to upset you, Martha!" He kept his tone light, belying what he felt. He was not going to stand by and watch his gentle woman be used. "If your sister does not want to come to live with us, then there is nothing that we can do. She will survive. I will help her out this one time," he reassured her. "Don't worry your pretty redhead," he said, kissing her.

Benny had the full measure of Martha's sister Bridie. He knew about how she had blackmailed Eamon, demanding money for the photographs that she had taken of Eamon's wife Marcia with a young guy. She had been behind the rift caused in his boss's marriage. However, it did not take long for it to become clear that Marcia O'Donally was innocent of the charges of being unfaithful. Scott Lord's stepson Brady had told them about his hotel stay with Bridie before he had had enough of her and ditched her. Brady had gone into how Bridie had taken the pictures of Eamon's wife with a young guy in the hotel grounds. Before she had left Spain, Bridie had phoned Brady to tell him that she was on the rise, going into how she had shown Eamon O'Donally the incriminating photos of his wife. Bridie bragged that she had extorted money from him. Scott informed Dan and Billy. He did not want anyone to think that Brady had anything to do with the extortion. Dan had informed his boss. Eamon confided to his men that Marcia had met up with her son from a previous marriage. He did not want his wife classed as duplicitous.

This would be the last monetary gift that Benny would send to her. He made a vow to himself that it would be the last time. He helped Martha reposition herself on the settee, lying next to her, he played his fingers around the gleaming red ringlets that had escaped from where the crown of curls was tied up on the top of her head.

13

Bridie did not want to part with the money that Martha had sent, but she needed to pay her rent. She had a few days before her eviction warning would be executed. However, she changed her mind upon a chance meeting. That evening on her way to the newsagent to top up her mobile phone credit, she passed a young guy huddled in a shop doorway. Bridie slowed her pace upon seeing him snort some white powder from the back of his hand. He did not have any blankets or sleeping bag. She studied his appearance. He did not have the black teeth or look of a drug abuser, although his dark-brown eyes were red-rimmed. His clothes looked expensive. A Stone Island jacket does not come cheap. His shoes were of good quality leather. Bridie concluded that the young lad had not been a user for long. He was a bit grubby, not filthy, his hair styled. She was intrigued.

Curiosity got the better of her. Bridie stopped and introduced herself. She received a well-spoken reply. When he told her his name was Rupert Mendez, she smiled and sat down next to him as he relayed his story. He was an only child, private-school-educated. His family holidayed three times a year in the south of France. But all that bored him. His stepfather was very wealthy. Rupert said that he had purchased a yacht that was worth over three million pounds. His stepfather had been a general in the army, and Rupert had found his strict, regimental upbringing intolerable. He had it drilled into him at every given opportunity that his wealth was gained through hard work.

Rupert despised his arrogant stepfather, who often berated him for smoking dope. Then, when his stepfather had discovered his hidden stash of cocaine, he evicted him from the house. His mother had stood by and allowed it to happen, giving her son a weekly allowance, which he spent on drugs.

He confided that he no longer respected his mother for staying with the man for his money. He continued to say that he had been introduced to drugs by a student at his school. He confessed that the narcotic was only an escape.

On hearing Rupert's story, Bridie had a gut instinct that this could be an opportunity to turn her luck around. She sympathised with his plight. Bridie told him that she would be his friend, offering to help him by giving him shelter in her rented room for a few days.

Bridie was out of Rupert's league – she led him like a lamb to slaughter. The young lad would rue the day that he was taken under the wing of the pretty girl from Dublin. Bridie Murphy would lead him to a far worse place than a shop doorway.

He ended up being kicked out of his family's luxurious home just past Devil's Dyke in a village in the Sussex Downs. He had told Bridie that the property was shut up while his parents were holidaying for two months in Cannes. Rupert bared his soul to Bridie. He informed her that he and his mother had previously been close. She had confessed to Rupert that she had a nest egg hidden away in a tin under the floorboards beneath her bed. Although his stepfather was generous to his mother with monetary and jewellery gifts, she was wary as she had been burnt in the past by Rupert's father who had left them for his young secretary when Rupert was ten years old. She wanted to ensure that she would not end up poor again. He told Bridie how he had visited his cousin in Spain on occasion. Rupert stated that Ramone and his father were Spanish, however, Ramone's father had died a few years ago from a heart attack. Rupert said that his cousin was working as a janitor at an exclusive private school where the wealthy send their children. It was near to where Ramone lived in Altea on the Costa Blanca. Rupert went on to say that his handsome cousin had plans to better himself. He was on the lookout for an older, wealthy woman. He labelled his cousin Ramone a 'Don Juan' without malice. Bridie's smile beamed. She was going to introduce Rupert to her world and show him how to get revenge on his stepfather. She intended to kill two birds with the proverbial stone.

Two days later the pair came out of Brighton train station after getting away without paying the train fare. Bridie followed Rupert to the taxi rank. He directed the cab driver to take them to Fulking, a village nestled in Devil's Dyke on the Sussex Downs. Rupert ordered the cabbie to stop near The Shepherd and Dog pub. His home was but a short distance from there. Walking along hedgerows, they came to the magnificent home. Rupert punched in the code to open the gates. He knew how long it would take before the alarm went off as he accessed the front door. Bridie hurried him to the bedroom. Within minutes, the pair pushed the bed away from the wall and rolled back the carpet. Rupert lifted the small floorboard. Bridie lunged forward, lifting the large tin from its hiding place. Bridie did not need to look inside until later, she could tell by the weight of the contents that there was a vast sum inside.

Within three hours, the pair were back in Barking in Essex. On the return journey on the train, Bridie asked Rupert for a favour. She knew that the besotted Rupert would agree to anything just to please her. Rupert had promised to contact his cousin Ramone in Spain. She gave Rupert some names and asked if Ramone could check if they were pupils at the elite school near Altea in Spain. Even though Rupert had blanched at the idea at first, he went along with it.

However, as luck would have it, Rupert later revealed that his cousin Ramone's casual girlfriend was the school's undersecretary, and she had gone through the registry for him. Bridie had wanted to speak to Ramone to ask him to join them in their quest after he had come back with the affirmative that the two students in question were enrolled at the school. Furthermore, to Bridie's advantage, Rupert had previously stated that Ramone was down on his luck and in dire need of money. He had purchased a car with the money that his late father had left him, but a car crash had written his vehicle off and he was using the school laundry delivery van. Ramone had jumped at the chance to go along with Bridie's plan when she had offered him a ten thousand pound down payment. However, a further fifty thousand pounds was promised to Ramone once the plot was finalised. Ramone did not hesitate. Without any thought about getting caught.

Bridie had paid the rent that was due, and for two months in advance. Although she hoped to be out of the area earlier, she was not concerned if she lost the money that she had paid in advance to the landlord. If her plot went according to plan, she would be sitting on eighty thousand pounds. There had been forty thousand in cash in Rupert's mother's tin. The rest was from the money that they got from selling the jewellery that was contained within the hoard – diamond rings, bracelets, two diamond-encrusted watches and a necklace, also rare diamonds that were in a velvet, pull string pouch. Bridie had sold the jewellery to various dealers in precious stones. Each dealer had tried to undercut her, but Bridie had haggled, raising the price, even though she had no idea of the value of the items. She was savvy, streetwise and knew how crafty people could be.

Furthermore, Bridie had stopped smoking dope. She wanted a clear mind to carry out her plan for her next move, although, she had purposely increased Rupert's cocaine supply. He was constantly out of his head on the narcotic, which was easy to come by from the lad in the local pub who they had previously got dope from. She required Rupert's mind to be frazzled. Her thoughts were on the big picture and the money that would set her up for her future. She intended to have the last laugh on Eamon and Marcia O'Donally. She intended to teach them both a lesson – him for ripping her off with the money for the photographs and Marcia for not giving her her job back

She intended to turn her back on her sister Martha, once she was in a financial position to do so. Bridie's vision was that she would be on the first available coach out of Victoria Station. The open ticket that she had purchased and kept out of sight from Rupert guaranteed her flight to freedom. Her dream was to eventually head to the Caribbean alone.

14

Tanya Green had been on the Costa Blanca for a few weeks before she applied to work at the Hawk Wind club. She liked the woman who had employed her. Although Cindy said that she was standing in for her boss, Marcia.

Nevertheless, when Cindy had seen Tanya in action around the pole at her interview, she knew that the beautiful, mixed-race girl, would be an asset to the club. She immediately gave her a job. Tanya had been raised on a council estate in Harold Hill in Essex. The cul-de-sac in Daventry Gardens with the car park and green out the front of her mum's council house had been her haven, as was Harold woodland near St Ursula's Catholic Infant and Primary School, which Tanya had called her second home. She had been a perpetual student, soaking in information like a sponge. She excelled at most subjects, including sports. It was a close-knit estate that she lived on. There was no concern for the children's safety. The neighbours were classed as family. Everyone's parents looked out for one another's children. Front doors were left unlocked during the day with no fear of theft or problems. However, Tanya's mother, Maggie, who was a single parent, was the local dope dealer and dealer of stolen goods – anything that could earn her cash to supply her alcohol and substance addictions.

Maggie Green had a blue Doberman pinscher, its colouring due to a gene. Although he was known to be fearsome with strangers that came to the home, especially anyone who tried to not pay, one look at the dog from Maggie was all that was needed, and the canine would become like a pussy cat with the local children.

Maggie had given birth to a mixed-race child. Her Barbadian lover, Winston, father to Tanya, went AWOL when Maggie was four months pregnant. Her family and the neighbours stood by her. For the most part, they were tolerant of Maggie's behaviour due to her having a kind heart. Maggie would help those who were down on their luck.

Nonetheless, Maggie's elder sister Joanie had given up on her younger sibling, but, not so with her child. Tanya became her prodigy. Joanie was determined that her adored niece would not end up like her mother Maggie. She stepped up, looking out for her. Tanya grew to be a stunning, long-legged, blue-eyed, Afro-haired beauty. She was also a girl with a brain. She was not going to stand by and see Tanya's life go down the drain. Joanie had instilled in her niece that she had to have broad shoulders. Tanya took onboard what her aunt taught her. The girls at the catholic school were jealous of the attention Tanya received from the opposite sex, although, it was uninvited and unwanted. Tanya put it on the back burner, under the guidance of her aunt Joanie.

The physical resemblance between Maggie and Joanie was obvious, but the similarity stopped there. Joanie also lived on the estate, in Serene Mews. She had been married at a young age but had no children. Mick, her husband of three years, had had a low sperm count. He died in bed after choking on his vomit in his sleep with Joanie sleeping alongside, unaware of his demise. The love of her life lay dead for hours until she tried to wake him.

There had been no other that could match her man. She remained a widow. Joanie was devoted to her beautiful niece. She pressed upon Tanya the value of having a good education. Tanya, at 15 years of age moved in with her aunt after a drug raid at her mother's home. Tanya had opened the door at 6 am to the detectives and police with protective shields, due to the dog. The Doberman was put out on the green in front of the house by a dog handler.

Under instruction from her aunt Joanie, Tanya had packed her bag while the police were searching the rooms for drugs and stolen merchandise. The police discovered numerous small bags containing cannabis, alongside weighing scales and new clothes with labels on in a pile on an armchair. In the fridge, there were twelve packets of sirloin steaks and eight boxes of king prawns that had only arrived the evening before the raid. Maggie's protests that she had purchased them from the supermarket fell on deaf ears with the policeman who removed the loot.

Joanie had stormed into her sister's living room and announced that she was taking Tanya to live with her. A detective held four bottles of gin with security tags on still on them, which he found in the cupboard along with other various bottles of alcohol. A plastic shopping bag lined with foil to prevent tagged goods from setting the alarm off was to the side.

Maggie agreed with Joanie that Tanya would be better off away from her bad influence. When Joanie had been informed about the raid, she asked one of the local lads to drive her to her sister's home. Although she lived on the same estate, only a short distance from her sister's home, she had difficulty walking and her breathing was laboured, due to heavy smoking.

However, when Tanya came to live with her, Joanie switched from smoking rolled tobacco to chewing nicotine gum while wearing a patch on her arm 24/7. She encouraged her niece not to smoke or take any form of narcotic substances. Tanya abided by her aunt's wishes. She became her aunt's carer, although she did not discontinue studying.

What Tanya did not learn from books she devoured from the internet. Near to her 18th birthday, Tanya learned that her aunt had six months to live. Joanie had emphysema and required oxygen bottles to help her breathe. Her body was riddled with cancer. Joanie refused to go to the hospital, saying that she would not leave Tanya.

Arrangements were made for the MacMillan Cancer Support nurses to attend to her in her front room. Tanya stayed by her side to the end. Her dying wish was for her educated niece to get away from England, get a job in Spain and find herself a wealthy man, one that would appreciate her. Before her passing, Joanie begged Tanya to start taking the contraceptive pill. Tanya listened to her wise aunt. "You must take control of your life. Have kids when you want them." Tanya obeyed.

With four thousand pounds gifted by her aunt before she died and a new passport, Tanya, carrying a rucksack, boarded the bus from Harold Hill Community Centre. She felt nervous standing at Gooshays Drive in Harold Hill waiting for the bus that would take her on the one hour and forty-one-minute drive to Gatwick airport. She kept her promise to her beloved aunt Joanie and stepped onto the bus. Heading towards Romford, she looked out of the bus window. Her thoughts were with her dear aunt Joanie who had made this life-changing trip possible. It was when the bus crossed over the Dartford Crossing that she began to relax, her past doubts and apprehensions dissipating. She recalled her dear aunt Joanie's daily mantra, "Above all, value yourself. Use your looks to get what you want. Do not trust anyone. A friend today can become your enemy in the future." Joanie pressed upon Tanya the importance of keeping her plans and dealings to herself. "Aim for the top rung on the ladder of life," she had instilled in her. "Never succumb to any form of narcotic substances. Do not allow a man to control your life. Be in command of your destiny." Joanie had told her to repeat the words daily.

The young detective that had been on the last raid to Tanya's mother Maggie Green's home would rue the day that he had encountered Tanya Green. When Tanya had opened the door to him at 6 am.

15

Tanya had rented a one-bedroom apartment in L' Alfas del Pi in Valencia with nice views of the Mediterranean Sea in the near distance. Tanya had haggled with the landlord for a good deal on the six-month rental. She put on the charm and struck a deal, although she had used half of the money that her aunt had given her as a deposit. She had also managed to get a bar job on only her second day in Spain. She was hoping to get enough money to buy herself a car. For the time being, she enjoyed walking to keep fit, but she liked cars and her aunt had paid for her driving lessons, so it was something she planned to do.

There was a Bulgarian guy who had become a regular at the bar ever since she started working there. She had on several occasions politely refused his offers to buy her a drink. He persisted in asking her out, but her answer was always the same. She repeatedly declined, stating that she wanted an early night. It was not that she didn't think he was good looking, he was. He had mid-brown hair, pale blue eyes, a wide, full mouth, with a distinctive 2.54 cm scar on his left cheek. He had nice, white teeth, although she had noticed that the bottom four were crooked when he smiled. He was over two metres in height with a well-proportioned body, but she thought that his dress sense left much to be desired. She judged his age to be in the late thirties. She discovered later that he was forty – twenty-two years her senior. Tanya thought that he was passable for an older man, although she was hedging her bets with him. She gained a lot of attention from the other male customers in the bar. She would bide her time to see how things panned out.

A week later, Tanya agreed to his offer of wine and dinner. He drank vodka – Tanya was teetotal. The Bulgarian did not impress her, although his car did. He drove a late-model, black Mercedes. His phone seemed to be constantly ringing when she joined him in his car. She took note that he would bark orders in Russian, despite being Bulgarian. Tanya had previously tried to learn the Russian language when she lived with her aunt. It had been before her aunt's rapid decline in health. She had given up when her aunt became too ill and required constant attendance. Tanya pondered why he did not speak in Bulgarian when he was giving directives. She concluded that he was dealing with Russians.

After keeping him at arm's length for three weeks after their first date, Tanya decided to invite him to her apartment. She confessed that she was a virgin and was waiting for the right man. Tanya cooked him a meal and afterwards, they kissed but nothing more.

It bolstered Mitre's ego that he would be the one to take Tanya's virginity. The following day, he gave her a gift – a one-carat, solitaire diamond ring. In return, she gave him her virginity that night. Tanya became Mitre Akulov's woman. She was to discover that he was the right-hand man to a wealthy Russian called Tolya Fedorin. Mitre changed her life for the better overnight. It did not take her long to learn how to pleasure him. The more pleasure she gave him, the more she got from him. He was generous, bestowing Tanya with gifts of jewellery and money. She began to stash away the money that he gave her. The tips from the punters and her wages would cover her rent.

Tanya kept a supply of Grey Goose vodka at her apartment, although Mitre's preference was Russian Stolichnaya and Beluga Gold Line Russian vodka, which he said his boss had introduced him to. One night, after their lovemaking, he wanted a drink. After downing a few glasses of vodka, he enlightened her about his favourite tipple. He told her that the expensive Russian vodka was only attainable to him in bulk when it was smuggled in on the boats.

She wanted to find out what he was up to. She sensed that smuggling was on the list. She would bide her time with him. She used her capacity for learning in the art of pleasing him. Tanya excelled in the bedroom with her Bulgarian lover. He fell for Tanya and began to trust her. She pressed him about his boss Tolya Fedorin. Mitre informed her that his boss owned a property in London, but for the most part, he resided in St Petersburg. He proudly said that he had visited his boss's home in Russia. He drunkenly told her about the history of St Petersberg and its founder Peter the Great. She pretended to listen, but she was already quite knowledgeable of Russian history, having excelled on the subject at school. She could have further enlightened him about the Mariinsky Theatre and the Russian State Museum, which showcased Russian iconic religious paintings as well as Kandinsky's works, but she did not. His ego required boosting. She played dumb, asking innocent-sounding questions about his boss. She realised that he was narcissistic and controlling, but it suited her for her next move up the ladder.

One day he had asked her for a favour. His boss would be visiting Spain soon. Mitre told Tanya that he was going to open a rival club to the Hawk Wind. He said that there was no limit on the cost of the upmarket adult club. Tanya learned that Tolya Fedorin was extremely wealthy. She began to form a plan. She wanted to climb to the top rung. Mitre had told her that the Russian boss required a plant in the Hawk Wind club, an informer to pass on information about the owner of the club.

16

Tanya got a job as a pole dancer at the popular Hawk Wind club. She found the other dancers friendly. She had been open about having a boyfriend because Mitre often came to the club to take her out to restaurants. Lloyd and Keiron took Tanya under their wing after she relayed her earlier life to them. She left nothing out about growing up around her mother's criminal life on the estate in Essex, although she left out the part about her beloved aunt Joanie leaving her a nest egg. She wanted pity for the moment. Tanya went out clubbing and bar hopping with the two flamboyant men when she wasn't working.

On one occasion, Lloyd told Tanya about his boss, Suzette, at the other job he had at the Mystique beauty salon, who was Marcia O'Donally's best friend. Suzette, he stated was stuck up her own arse at times, nevertheless, she was a great laugh and also very generous. Tanya learned that Marcia and Eamon O'Donally were business partners in the Hawk Wind club. Lloyd had gone into detail about how Suzette, on one drink-fuelled night out clubbing with them, had informed them that she had gifted her half shares of the Hawk Wind club to Marcia O'Donally on the condition that her husband never takes full control of the club. Suzette's wealth was due to her dead fiancé's legacy to her. Suzette was worth millions, Lloyd had informed Tanya, after making her swear under oath not to pass the information on. Tanya swore her allegiance. She wanted to get friendly with Lloyd and Keiron's boss, Suzette.

Tanya booked an appointment with Lloyd for a facial and full body wrap. He told her that he would treat her afro-Caribbean curls to a special hair wrap that would tone down her wild locks. Tanya moved closer into the circle.

Suzette was speaking to Cindy when Tanya came into the Mystique beauty salon for her appointment. Although Tanya had not yet met Suzette, she could tell who she was from Lloyd and Kieron's description of the elegant woman with the dark bob.

Tanya beamed as Cindy recognised her. Tanya had taken an instant liking to Cindy. She spoke straight from the hip, as her late auntie Joanie had. Suzette turned her head, stepping forward. "I have an appointment," Tanya said, aiming her smile at Suzette. Suzette introduced herself. Cindy waved, returning to her client in the chair, wrapping her hair in foils.

"The boys speak very highly of you. They both said how glamorous and attractive are. Your dress looks amazing on your lovely figure. I should imagine that it has to be from one of Italy's top designers," Tanya complimented. "Not that I could ever afford anything like that."

Suzette beamed, her red lipstick matched her manicured talons. "Darling girl. You may have taste and not the means at the moment." She patted Tanya's arm, smiling. "However, as my dearest friend Marcia taught me, the page of the book that you are on now will soon turn. One never knows what Destiny has in store. My friend is a mystic." Suzette paused. "Do you believe?" Tanya nodded.

"With your heritage…Jamaican?"

"My father was Barbadian," Tanya answered.

"I should imagine that your father's family are 'believers'. You must meet Marcia. She works from the salon conducting tarot readings two days a week. The boys said that you are joining us for a night out!" Suzette patted Tanya's arm affectionately. "I will look after you. Those two will lead you astray!" Suzette smiled as she said it so that Lloyd could hear.

He winked at Tanya. "The girl needs to find herself a rich sugar daddy. I have connections!" Lloyd said.

Suzette shook her head and cast a look of warning at Lloyd. She did not wish to continue with the banter as there were other clients in the salon. Although clients found Lloyd entertaining, he sometimes got carried away and did not know where to draw the line.

Tanya smiled but did not mention that she had never seen her father. However, she thanked Suzette for the offer to take care of her.

When Tanya gave Mitre the information about Eamon O'Donally and his wife Marcia being joint owners of the Hawk Wind club, she omitted telling Mitre how Marcia had been gifted the fifty per cent share of the club by Suzette. After all, she had taken an oath to Lloyd. Tanya did reveal that Marcia was a mystic who worked at the Mystique beauty salon two days a week conducting tarot readings. Pleased with what he could pass on. Mitre gave her some money to go shopping for new dresses, shoes and a handbag. She did not dress provocatively. She had no need. Her hourglass figure could be defined by whatever she wore. Tanya was aware that physically she had everything in the right places. According to her auntie Joanie, Tanya had inherited her looks from her absent father. Tanya bore no resemblance to her thin, fair-haired, pale-skinned mother. Tanya soon discovered that Mitre was obsessed with her. She realised though that he was no fool, so she did as he wished to keep him happy.

17

Eamon had spent more time with the children since his return from Miami. The girls coveted his attention. He had taken them, along with Marcia, to his restaurant. Upon their return, he had joined them in the pool. Eamon had received a call earlier from Joey to say that Alphonso had passed away in his sleep at his daughter Chiara's home. Joey said that she wanted a small funeral with only family in attendance. Eamon's heart went out to Joey who had been by the old man's side for a lifetime, and now he was excluded from the funeral service. He was thankful that he was not required to attend. He had enough to attend to in Spain.

His thoughts were also on the news from Joey that Lucca Barossa was to become a father, despite Lucca's wife's heart defect. He mused upon Marcia's prediction that they would, against the odds, have two sons in quick succession. Joey had confirmed that Lucca was running the show since his brother Ricardo and nephew Angelo's murder. Eamon realised that Lucca would have taken onboard Marcia's prediction about his future children. Furthermore, Lucca would conclude that Marcia had not predicted accurately for his brother Ricardo. Or that she purposely withheld telling him of the imminent threat to his life.

"Daddy, watch me!" Aisling demanded Eamon's attention, breaking his thoughts. He swam with her as she kicked her legs, banging the water with her arms supported with armbands. To his side, Aine gripped his swimming trunks. Pulling them down a little too far for decency. Behind him, Marcia came to his aid, laughing, cocking an eyebrow and smiling while she pulled them back up. "Papa, can we race later?" Quinn called out. He and Niall were at the far end of the pool, jumping from inflatables.

Before he had time to answer, Aisling angrily retorted. "No Papa, Daddy!" she corrected Quinn calling her father Papa. Quinn laughed at her. Aisling started to cry, tears streaming down her face. Eamon shook his head when Quinn sped towards them to comfort her. He cuddled and cajoled. Referring to Eamon as daddy. Aisling sniffled, then carried on splashing fiercely, trying to make her way to the steps. Marcia took both girls out of the pool for a nap and Aye took over from there.

Eamon was head-to-head with both sons. This was no performance on Eamon's part. It was for real. Quinn and Niall's energy far outstripped their father's. Eamon was beaten in every race. He paid up their winnings. Both boys were thrilled. Billy was picking them up to stay overnight at his place. They went inside to change and get their overnight things. Marcia had laid out what was required.

"My boys have thrashed me every time. This is getting expensive!" Eamon laughed, walking out through the terrace doors after showering and changing into a white shirt and black trousers. Marcia smiled, sitting at the garden table and adjusting her sunglasses. She was dressed in an azure-blue, ankle-length, flowing skirt with a long-sleeve blouse embroidered with peacocks, cinched at her waist with a silver chain belt.

"Ye look exotic." He eyed her up.

"Once the boys leave for Billy and Jane's and the girls are in bed, I thought that I could entertain you before you leave for work tonight. I have been studying my small book." She looked up at him and smiled.

"Are ye wanting to try out some Karma Sutra moves?" Eamon asked.

Marcia nodded, smiling. "You know that I give in to you easily." She laughed softly. "If I can remind you of the first time that I welcomed you without hesitation." Her eyes followed his expanding bulge as he adjusted his trousers.

"If I had realised that ye were that easy to take, I would have made my move on ye long before. It would have prevented ye flirting wit the Texan." He threw in, jealousy flaring in his eyes.

Marcia knew that Eamon was serious. It had been a bone of contention with Eamon when the Texan had come on to Marcia just before she and Eamon got together. She let the mention of Brandon pass.

"I tink that if I had not snapped ye up when I did, the Texan would have whisked ye away to his ranch. He was persistent wit ye!" He paused for a moment. "I remember how I had watched the pair of ye in a restaurant one lunchtime. Ye was giving him the come-on. Leaning across the table so that he could have a clearer view of yer cleavage. He could not get enough of ye. I had a vantage point on the other side of the eatery. I could have easily wiped the floor wit him. However, as angry as I felt at that time, I had no claim on ye. Therefore I left without eating my lunch. Fifty euro I wasted!"

Marcia knew that Eamon did not let go of anything, but she did not realise how much it still bothered him about Brandon. She could hear it in his tone. She had not mentioned that she had gone out with Brandon at the time because she thought that Eamon was not interested in her. When Eamon had danced with her, they had kissed. However, Eamon had walked away from her – dropping her and leaving her feeling humiliated.

"Eamon, he would not have enticed me to be with him. It was you that I wanted. We were only friends."

He scoffed, "Marcia!" he leaned his forearms on the garden table, "Please don't take me for an eejit. The night of the party ye both were line dancing. He had his arm around ye waist. Ye had yer head back laughing with him. He was coming on strong to ye. Ye lapped up his attention!" Eamon's dark eyes grew more intense. "The following day, he was wining and dining ye. I can describe the low-cut dress that ye had on that day. It was like a second skin on yer. It did not leave much to the imagination of what was on offer." He cocked an eyebrow.

Marcia exhaled, holding his look. She could not deny that she had worn that dress to capture Brandon's attention. She needed a way out of Spain after feeling rejected by Eamon.

His cadence softened. "Why do ye tink that I made my move on ye that night when ye were in the shower? I knew that I had to seize my opportunity. Even though I fleetingly weighed up the risk as to what I was doing. Ye could have cried rape. I had stripped off and opened the shower door. My heart was pounding, but I could not resist ye any longer. The stakes were high. I was going away the next morning for two weeks to Miami for Jimmy Grant. I would have lost ye if I had not taken the chance!"

Marcia rose and moved to stand in front of him. He sat back in the garden chair. "Eamon, when we danced the first time and you kissed me, you walked away and left me on the dance floor. I felt humiliated. But you haunted my dreams. My every waking hour. You had just become a widower. I thought that I was just another woman to you."

He gave a soft laugh. "Let me get this straight wit ye, my wee mystic. Once I discovered that she (he did not mention his last wife's name) was playing the field. She was history to me. I was the eejit that did not see what she was up to wit Jimmy Grant. If it had not been Grant, another man would have come along. After her betrayal, I did not want to become involved in a relationship again. I had decided to play the field," he confessed. "Nevertheless, I did not reckon on the impact that ye would have upon me!" He locked his hands behind his head as he spoke candidly. "It was something that I had previously never experienced!" Giving a small laugh, he said, "Our first kiss terrified me. I fought the strong feelings that I had for ye right after our encounter on the dancefloor. However, the night that we first made love, ye wrapped yer mystical tendrils around my heart. I took ye home after that hassle ye encountered from the woman I had taken to escort me. Ye said ye needed a shower to clear ye head. I wasn't sure if I was reading the signals right, but I took the bull by the horns and joined ye in the shower. It paid off dividends. The sex was great. I was not going to throw away what I had found wit ye."

Marcia smiled, moving closer to him. He placed her on his lap, her arms encircled his neck.

"I did not blame her for lashing out at me that night. She was your date. I could see that she was all over you. She let the women know when we were talking together that she had her claws in you. the impression I got from speaking to her was that it was not your first date. If you had treated me as you did her, I would have left you standing. You would not have had a second chance to humiliate me." She said firmly.

He smiled, cupping her chin in his hand. "She was no date!" He shook his head. "Certainly, she meant nothing to me.

I invited her to accompany me because I did not want to go to the party alone."

"Are you saying that it was the first time that you had been with her? It did not look like it to me. I observed her linking her arm through yours as if you were a couple," Marcia said with a touch of indignation.

Eamon laughed out loud, holding her tight to him.

He sucked air between his teeth. "Had you previously slept with her?" Marcia pressed.

Eamon leaned back, shaking his head. "What difference does that make? The girl was known to be obliging. She was nothing to me. Forget her." He paused, then continued, "Marcia, as ye knew from the beginning, I had a fucked-up head at the time. However, ye and the children have helped to sort my thoughts out. Looking back at how I reacted, I went and got blethered at Michael's Irish bar after I observed ye wit the Texan. I remember how I bent Michael's ear that night about my feelings for ye. I was offered a woman that night and I turned it down."

Marcia stiffened. He tightened his clasp. "I did not touch her. In fact, while I am laying my cards on the table to ye, I aided the young woman and her child and sent her to Ireland."

"Ireland?!" She repeated, confused. The penny dropped. "Do you mean that you could have slept with Anna?"

"After I had turned her down that night, I suggested she go to live in County Armagh wit Patrick's family to help wit the children. Anna and her child had been abandoned by the child's father. Anna was on a one-way ticket. She accepted my offer to pay her expenses. The rest is history. Patrick's wife died, and Anna gave him a son – my name's sake. There is no need to say more."

Marcia knew that he had sent Anna and her child Chloe to Patrick's family home in County Armagh to help with his autistic daughter and young son. But she did not know the story of how they had become acquainted. "Eamon, there are many things that I don't know about you." She looked long and hard at him. "There are times that I feel concerned, like now! I did not realise that Anna wanted you before Patrick!"

He put his arms around her waist. "Ye have nothing to worry about. Believe me. The only reason that I did not tell ye or my brother about the circumstances under which we met, was because nothing happened. There was no need to mention anything. My brother loves the woman. What I am trying to make ye understand is that from the beginning I only wanted ye. There has not, nor will there ever be any other. Only ye!"

Marcia's dark eyes continued to question his. Although she was surprised by his candour, she was pleased that he had told her. There had been a time in the not-too-distant past when he kept everything from her. She inhaled quietly.

"I know that ye have had a great deal to contend wit and putting up wit me and the life that I took ye into. Don't tink that I don't realise how naive ye were when we first met. We have had a roller coaster ride over the years. Nevertheless, not for one second have I ever thought or wanted to betray ye!"

Marcia softened. She pursed her lips. Eamon smiled. "Ye look like the baby girls look when ye pout." They both smiled. Eamon ran his hands up her back. "Mmm," he murmured when she kissed him and began to fondle him. She released the button of his trousers and undid the zip, sliding her hand inside. "You are becoming damp." Her fingers played across the end of his growing bulge, while she nibbled his ear lobe.

Eamon said, his voice husky with desire, "This has got to stop. Billy will be here soon to take the boys for their overnight stay." He breathed without moving, holding her close, shielding her in case Aye or the boys interrupted.

Gradually easing her hand from his crotch, she zipped and buttoned his trousers back up with one hand, while holding her to him with the other. "'Tis a shame, as I am enjoying yer administrations. However, my lovely temptress, I want to experience this Karma Sutra position that ye have learned before I go to work tonight. Then I will show ye a few positions that I have up my sleeve." He gave her a big kiss.

"Hiya boss!" Billy faltered, smiling, jauntily moving towards them. He wore Levi jeans and an open-neck, denim shirt, which suited his tall, lean, muscular frame. He was still the cool, good-looking man that Marcia had first been introduced to when he had flown in from London to work for Eamon. It was at the time when Eamon had taken Marcia to Marbella to visit Maureen and Dom and had surprised her by taking her to the jeweller, Amos, who was to design her beautiful diamond engagement ring.

The two dogs stood like sentries on either side of Billy. "I hope that I am not interrupting?" His cheeky grin spread and his eyes sparkled with mischief. Eamon shook his head, lifting Marcia from his lap and placing her feet on the ground.

"Aye let me in through the gates. These two beauties met me at my motor." He ruffled the coats of both dogs; their tails wagged happily. "Can I have a moment boss?"

"Aye has made various takeaway dishes for everyone tonight," Marcia told Billy as she made her way inside to let the men speak in private.

"The boys were snacking on Aye's banana and fresh shredded coconut cake as I came in. Aye gave me a slice. Delicious!" Billy rubbed his stomach, pulling a chair out from the table opposite Eamon. "That woman can cook!" Once alone. Billy took on a more serious note, his cadence indicated concern. "I spotted the new pole dancer with a guy in a restaurant in Benidorm today. Jane and I had popped in there for lunch. I took a table on the other side of the restaurant with a view of the pair. She did not see me, but I heard snippets of the conversation, which was more one-sided. The guy did most of the talking. Nothing of interest, he was too wrapped up in her. Although he spoke pretty good English, his Bulgarian accent was unmistakable. The man appeared loved-up with the girl; his eyes did not leave her. He was holding her hand across the table, running his fingers across her left hand. She wore an impressive size solitaire diamond ring on her fourth finger. However, I took note that when she is at work her fingers are bare." He waggled his head, lips pursed. "On the one hand, it could be that she does not want the punters in the club who she is performing for to think that she is unattainable. But what that valuable-looking ring tells my suspicious mind is that she is up close and personal with the Eastern European. Furthermore, for him to put that ring on her left hand, fourth finger so early into the relationship means they are a serious item. Whirlwind courtships do occur. Nevertheless boss, the girl's demeanour and her body language told a different story."

Eamon nodded. The start of his relationship with Marcia had been a whirlwind affair. Within weeks of him returning from Miami after Jimmy Grant was reported missing, he had put an engagement ring on her finger. He had no intention of losing her. However, their love was reciprocated.

Billy continued. "From my observation of the couple, I picked up that it was not a two-way street. She appeared disinterested. She's merely tolerating him." He gave a soft laugh. "Not that her man noticed. He was enamoured with her. Mind you, the girl's a looker. There's a touch of the Caribbean genes in her. In my opinion, the Bulgarian is punching way above his weight. He must be twenty years her senior. His looks are non-descript. He has a nasty, red, raised scar about an inch long on his cheek, without saying that the man is ugly," Billy said, grinning. "Nonetheless, what with him splashing out on her with the ring, he drove a late-model, black Mercedes. I snapped the registration discreetly – Spanish plates." He smiled, taking his phone out of his shirt pocket, flipping through his pictures, showing Eamon. "Certainly not cheap by any means."

Eamon knitted his brows and looked closely at the photo.

Billy continued, "Jane would have wondered what I was up to if she had seen me but she was preoccupied with discussing a dog that she was training for a guy in Moraira." Billy relaxed into the chair, locking his hands behind his head. "My gut instinct tells me that the new pole dancer is a game player, boss. She is telling everyone at the club some sob story about growing up on a council estate in Harold Hill in Essex prior to her coming to Spain a couple of months ago." He cocked his head to one side and said, "She has admitted that she has a boyfriend, but she has told Cindy and the two male hairdressers that the Bulgarian is only a stepping stone!" Billy and Eamon both elevated their brows.

"I will find out where she is living when I go to work tonight. There will be an address for her in the office at the club! That's if she's not given a false one," Eamon said.

Billy nodded.

Eamon stretched, without standing and gave a sharp nod. "Aar informed Dan that he was in Michael's bar the other night." Eamon took out his phone, flipped through it and showed the screen to Billy. "That is the picture that Aar took of the same car that ye have a photo of. He had stopped by to quench his thirst in Michael's Irish bar. There was a group of men drinking at a table. He reported back to Dan that two of the men were Spanish, one was Russian and one was a loud-mouth Bulgarian with a distinctive scar to the left side of his mouth. Aar had a bit of a run-in with them after defending one of the girls that frequent the bars. The Russian pulled the woman down on his lap as she passed the drunken men's table. She slapped him and he became abusive, calling her derogatory names. Aar got off his bar stool and went to her assistance. Fortunately for them, the four backed off!" Billy and Eamon laughed. "Dan said that Aar said that the group did not want any argument with him. However, the big Somalian was curious as to who they were. There was only one car outside the bar. From the photo that ye took of the car, Billy, it's the same Bulgarian that is playing footsie with my new employee!"

Billy's lips pinched together, nodding. "She needs to be watched, boss. My feelings are to not trust her. I could be wrong, but I don't think that I am, boss."

"Same here," Eamon agreed. "The Bulgarian could be involved with the Russian who I heard is planning to open an upmarket adult club. I tink that they want to know how the land lies wit the competition. Hence the Bulgarian sends his girl in to spy." Eamon sucked air through his teeth.

"The dancer's boyfriend appears to not be short of cash, what with the diamond ring he gave her and also the expensive motor he is running around in. Why would a man who appears so besotted allow his woman to flaunt her wares on a stage in front of other men?" He threw in, "She's got some form. Not that she would be my type!" He smiled, as did Eamon. Although Billy had had his fair share of women in the past, he did not have a roving eye. That stopped when he met and married Jane. "It don't add up." Billy shook his head. "She must be after information for him."

Eamon nodded. “I agree. Aar told Dan that the Bulgarian was footing the bill in Michael’s bar. I need names. See what ye can do wit that car registration.”

“I will get straight on it!” Billy said, standing up. “I need to get back. Your boys are going to have riding lessons tomorrow morning. They both have a natural seat!” Billy said of their riding ability.

“How is Niall wit Quinn? He tends to be jealous of his siblings. Fuck knows why, Billy. Marcia and I treat them all the same. Maureen tended to spoil him when the boys stayed wit them in Marbella. However, she is getting on a bit now and they are getting older. Too much for her to cope wit since Don’s health went on the decline.”

“Niall is fine. I am aware of his rivalry with his brother. Not that Quinn gives him any call. To be honest, boss, I think that it’s in the lad’s nature to be number one,” Billy said. “Jane and I curb the tendency as I have seen you do. Yesterday, when he was helping me clean out the stables, he told me about a disagreement that he had had at school with Thomas Harper-Watt’s lad, Atticus.”

Eamon knew that Niall on occasion disclosed snippets to Billy of what was going on at school, which pleased Eamon. He did not want his son to keep things to himself.

“The disagreement started when Atticus stated that his grandfather is a Lord, and therefore more powerful than Niall’s father. Niall was put out by the statement. Niall appeared to me to be indignant when he told me. He declared to Atticus that his father was powerful. Niall informed me that he was annoyed and confused because he could not understand why he did not have any grandparents as Atticus did.”

Eamon exhaled, running his fingers through his hair and shaking his head. Briefly glancing out into the distance, he leaned back in his chair. "Both mine and Marcia's parents are dead. My only sibling lives away wit his family in County Armagh. It did not occur to me that the children would need relatives. They have a grand life. Ye and Jane have taken to my boys. What can ye do Billy?"

"No more than what you are doing, boss. However, he asked me if I could be his grandfather!" Both men smiled. "I said I would prefer to be known as his uncle because I was not old enough, but Niall said that I looked old!" The pair laughed.

"Billy, if Niall opens up to ye, I am thankful. He is of concern to me. I know that his mother worries about him. Marcia lets him have his way, for the most part. However, I keep him in line. If I allowed him to bully his younger brother, as he has in the past what hope would I have at controlling him when he hits his teens?" The chair scraped back as Eamon stood up, rising to his full height. "I have been looking into taking the family on holiday to France for the Christmas break. I am going to ask Thomas to join us with his family. I would like ye and Jane with Dan and Cindy to accompany us too. All expenses paid!"

Billy raised an eyebrow, smiling.

Eamon laughed. "Before ye get too enthusiastic, it's Disney World Paris!"

Billy slapped his hand on his knee, laughing. "That will be brilliant. Thanks boss. Jane says that I am a big kid in men's trousers at times. I will have the opportunity to prove her right when I join the kids on the rides!" Billy chuckled.

"There will be Dan and Cindy's wedding beforehand. The reception is being held in my villa grounds. Dan said that Cindy has the plans underway. We can kill two birds wit one stone. Once Dan and Cindy are married, they can go on their honeymoon from Paris to wherever they plan to go. I have not told Marcia or the children yet. However, once I get the okay from Dan, I will book it."

Eamon was sitting on the terrace, glass in hand, taking a long gulp of Rioja Gran Reserva. He began to unwind after Billy had taken the boys to stay at his and Jane's villa for an overnight stay. Aisling and Aine were sleeping soundly. Aye had retired for the evening to her room. The sky was overcast, cirrocumulus clouds were forming rippling patterns out in Altea Bay, a pre-warning of rain in the early evening. He stretched his long legs out. He had previously promised the boys to take them to Disney World in Florida, but with him no longer being needed in Miami, he would take them to Disney World in Paris instead. He would not break a promise to the boys. Eamon did not want the children to have bad memories of their childhood as he and his younger brother Patrick had.

Long-buried thoughts of his early life that were locked away in the recesses of his mind suddenly resurfaced. Eamon took another large mouthful of wine to aid him in confronting his memories. The vision showed him the cowed child of his yesteryears, hearing the slam of the door and the unintelligible slurred roaring. Eamon was a skinny lad of no more than seven years old, lying in bed, alert for his father's nightly entrance. Posthaste, his thin legs would take him down the stairs and he would quietly open the kitchen door, then close it, heart thumping. Futile prayers were wasted as he scurried towards the garden toilet. But no one came to save him from the monster who carried out the ritual beatings most nights after the pub turn out. He would squeeze between the toilet bowl and the wall of the outside toilet, hands covering his face for protection, fighting nausea from the stench of urine where his father would miss the bowl and no one cleaned the mess.

His fear of the blackness was overcome by the terror of knowing that at any moment shovel-size hands would reach in and grab him, throwing him onto the hard, muddy ground. Hobnail boots aimed and hit the target for the most part. He heard his father's drunken cursing to no one as he stumbled. Eamon's mother would stand in the kitchen doorway with tears streaming down her face, although she never offered a mother's protection.

It had taken Eamon from the time he was a boy to a man to forgive her abandonment at a time when he needed her the most. He later realised that his mother had been helpless. She was as frightened of his father as he was. He could never envisage hurting his sons. His children and Marcia were his life.

He came back to the moment when Marcia's hands, from behind him, caressed his chest. She planted a kiss on the top of his head. Taking her arm, he gently pulled her to his side, leaning in to meet her kiss. Marcia sat on his lap, arms entwined around his neck. He inhaled her scent, both silently looking into each other's eyes.

After a long moment, Marcia, sensing his heavy mood, said, "You appear concerned."

Eamon smiled warmly. "There are times when I tink of my childhood. Although for the main part, I tend to let it be. For the life of me, how can a full-grown man beat his defenceless child?"

Marcia was aware that it was not a question. She knew about his childhood and how his father physically abused him by kicking and beating him from an early age. Her fingers moved down either side of his goatee beard, he watched her. You did not follow in your father's footsteps."

"Eamon you are an exemplary father. "That's as maybe. Even though I would not raise a hand to my children, my selfishness has put them in danger. They live under the threat that someone could take out their revenge on me by using them. Also, I live with the fear that one day they could lose my protection if the Law caught up wit me for my past misdeeds," he spoke solemnly. "Hindsight is a wonderful ting!"

"You must not reproach yourself. We cannot change the past! You and I would not have met under different circumstances. There would be no us. We would not have made four babies. Would you still change your past to be without us?"

Eamon smiled weakly, cupping her chin, answering her with a deep kiss.

There had been no Kama Sutra positions that night. The lights were turned down low and the shutters were drawn against the rising storm. Marcia gauged Eamon's lingering pensive mood and gave him a soothing body massage before their lovemaking.

Eamon lay on his back running his fingers through Marcia's hair while she lovingly took him deeper. Their reflection in the wall mirrors was being recorded on Eamon's phone for their later pleasure. He observed Marcia's nakedness as she knelt before him, mirrors reflecting each caress. There was nothing sordid, only the beauty of the scene as her mouth brought him to the edge. He flipped her onto her back in one swift movement. Rock solid, he knelt over her, she reached to encircle him, fingertip teasing.

Gently prising her grip, he smiled. "I want ye to be first. Then I will join ye on the deep one when we come together." Eamon made love to her, mouth moving slowly from the base of her neck, making his way to each erect bud, tongue teasing. Her fingernails sank into his flesh, arching towards his erection, pressing for him to take her. Pleading, calling for him as his tongue flittered warm between her legs. He smiled, observing her as he slowly began to fill her, measured motion taking her higher.

Marcia reached for his face, soaring to the summit of pleasure and then freefalling into the bliss of their union. Still, he stayed with her, holding back until her head dropped back as she rose from the plateau.

"Relax and join me," he directed. His powerful thighs clamped on either side of her. Imprisoned within, Marcia held him with her pelvic muscles. He gradually moved their position without withdrawing. They both turned their heads to watch their reflections in the mirrors. Eamon raised Marcia's legs so she could gain a better view of him inside of her. He felt her release.

18

Eamon was in his office at the Hawk Wind club going through the bookings when his mobile phone rang. He answered it, seeing it was Thomas Harper-Watts's number. Eamon had given Thomas the night off, so he was wondering why he would be calling so late at night. "Thomas!" he paused for two seconds, sensing that the call was not good news.

"I received a telephone call from my father a few minutes ago. The reason that he hadn't called me earlier today after he met up with Chief Inspector Ross Lowe is that he was waiting for the names of the people who are under surveillance with Special Branch."

Eamon undid the top button of his shirt and loosened his tie, listening intently.

"The Chief Inspector was unexpectedly called away from the meeting with my father just as he was about to pass on the information. However, they decided to meet up again afterwards. Upon the Chief Inspector's return to the club, he was plied with alcohol. Lowe was inebriated and revealed all."

Eamon braced himself – he sensed what was coming. He had the terrible feeling that his past misdeeds might be about to catch up with him. "Your name and Billy and Dan's names are on the enquiry list in the investigation into the deaths of the Bulgarian brothers and the woman that was involved with them. The guy who was smuggling drugs via your haulage business was recently apprehended by the UK border force for importing narcotics using a UK haulage company. Sniffer dogs discovered cocaine in his lorry as he returned from Belgium at Dover. To save himself from a very long prison sentence, he named everyone involved. And by association, he also implicated you three in the murder of the Bulgarian brothers and the woman and the burning of their cottage. The information he provided about your connection is only a supposition, and he offered no hard evidence. However, Special Branch has put two and two together. Because you pulled the perpetrator over the coals for using your business for smuggling, they looked deeper into it and discovered that the two Bulgarian brothers and the woman who were behind it all had been killed in Spain. The Chief Inspector said that intensive inquiries were made and they know that you were involved somehow. However, they must gather concrete evidence against you all. Hence an undercover officer has been sent out here to the Costa Blanca to try to infiltrate your world."

Eamon sucked air through his teeth, running a hand through his hair. "Thomas, I can't tank ye father enough for the information. Lord Arthur is no young man to put himself out like this for no reward."

Thomas chuckled. "Boss, my father finds it all terribly exciting what with his mundane, retired life. His exact words to me."

"I will reward ye, Thomas. Ye should take yer wife away for a couple of days. Ye are due a break."

Thomas replied candidly without elaborating. "I don't think Isabella would appreciate spending time away with me at the moment."

Eamon thanked him again. He did not know the details of Thomas's marriage troubles, although Billy had told him that Thomas had indicated that he was finding it difficult to please Isabella of late.

He summoned Dan to his office. He would tell Billy in the morning as he was at home with Jane, and Niall and Quinn were sleeping over. Dan knocked sharply and entered the office. Eamon told him to lock the door. "Take a seat. Eamon knew that there was no right time to impart what he had been told. Dan was shortly to be married. "It looks as if we have a problem."

Dan took a seat leaning back and crossing a leg over his left knee. Eamon relayed the information. Dan shook his head when he finished listening. "Boss, if you think about it, the Law can only surmise from the information that they have received about us. Okay, it's a pain that we are on their radar. But they require more to go on. Therefore, they have sent an undercover agent out here in Spain to try to work his frame in. We know that they are only clutching at straws."

Eamon nodded. "To be sure, Dan. I know that there is no proof of our involvement in the removal of those Bulgarian brothers and the woman. It was years ago. The Law would have come calling sooner if there had been any clear link to us. Nevertheless, we can't get too comfortable. This is a wake-up call! I know that ye marriage is pending and ye have a lot on yer plate, however, I want ye and Billy to consider a backup plan. Don't ye worry about the cost. I will sort ye and Billy out. Thomas will be included. I can arrange it for our families to hightail it from Spain at short notice. Then we can go from there. Dan gave a sharp nod, sitting upright. "Thomas's father will give him the nod before anything goes down." Dan rose, preparing to go back to the club. "Can ye speak to Billy in the morning?

My boys are staying over at his place tonight and I don't want to spoil their fun."

Eamon remained in the club office, pondering his next move. Eamon's wealth of 150 million euros in laundered money that he had gained from overseeing Jimmy Grant's last consignment eight years ago had grown considerably over the years, through investments in various areas. He sent his bank manager and business adviser a regular stipend. He was the only other person who had any real knowledge of Eamon's fortune, although he would have no idea how Eamon had amassed it in the first place. No questions were ever asked. Eamon knew that the bank manager knew better than to pry into his affairs. Gael Martinez was only interested in saving his own skin.

Eamon had made him aware of the information that he had regarding the bank manager's clandestine life. Furthermore, Eamon reminded him that he was aware that his father-in-law was the bank's CEO. But Eamon knew that the situation could change at any given moment. New cycles begin. The time would come when Gael Martinez would retire. His eldest son Filipe Martinez would one day step into his father's shoes. But Eamon had already done his homework. He had been made aware that the son also had a secret lover. Furthermore, the lover was male. Eamon had intimate photographs of the gay couple and an address of an apartment that they jointly owned. The evidence, should it ever be needed, was locked in his safe at his villa. The son had a new young wife, whose family were also big investors in the bank.

In order to avoid the ups and downs of Wall Street, investments were made in valuable artwork and rare gemstones – opals that were found in Australia. At some point, Eamon was going to have some earrings and a ring made for Marcia with the rare opals. He owned some top-quality gems: alexandrite, which was emerald by day and ruby by night. Alexandrite is well-known for displaying one of the most remarkable colour changes in the gem world. It is green in sunlight and red in incandescent light.

Eamon thought about where he might go if he relocated. He had been considering moving his family somewhere new. Years back, he had purchased a property in Ireland so his brother could take his family there and escape the criminal path he had been on. Ever since Eamon had purchased the smallholding for him in County Armagh, Patrick had turned his life around.

A few days later, Eamon was in his office at home and the boys were at school. Aye and Bonita were occupying the twins in the kitchen making gingerbread men .Marcia was in the bedroom doing her yoga routine. He sat at his desk and perused the property sales on his laptop. A secluded property in County Wicklow, Ireland caught his eye. It was located between Kilmacanogue village and Enniskerry village, on the Glencullen river in the foothills of the Wicklow mountains in the east of the island, minutes from the Dublin border and a mere 24 km south of Dublin city centre. The airport in Dublin, which had flights to 195 destinations was another attraction for him.

He could arrange for his brother Patrick to safeguard his family. He knew that he could rely on Patrick. He would be able to get them out of the country at any given moment if the need arose. Eamon mapped out the distance from Patrick's smallholding in County Armagh. Within a car journey of two hours, Patrick could be on hand to help oversee the building work that would be required. He zoomed in on an aerial view of the five-bedroom house, which was set on an acre of lawned grounds. He could arrange to have an indoor swimming pool built for Marcia and the children. He realised that it would be an upheaval, more so for the boys with having to change schools. County Wicklow's cold, wet climate would be a shock from the warm weather they were used to in Spain. However, Eamon felt that he had no choice. His family's safety was paramount. He looked for a local school. There was a suitable catholic private day school for junior and senior pupils that had excellent academic achievement ratings and was within a short distance from the property. He browsed information about Ireland's Wicklow Mountain National Park and the 129 km walking trail, which took in the beauty of the Powerscourt waterfall just outside the village of Enniskerry. He pondered on living out his latter years in County Wicklow – just him and Marcia. Eamon would not allow himself to envisage his life without her.

He was satisfied that his family would be safe in County Wicklow. His accountant Santiago Emil dealt with Eamon's legitimate businesses. On paper, Eamon's money was all legal. Even though the taxman took nearly half in taxes, he had no problem with that. The haulage company and the restaurant were in Eamon's name. The Hawk Wind adult club, although in joint names with Marcia, came under the same taxation umbrella as it was classified as a family business. The club and the haulage company were both 'gold mines'.

He made a phone call to his bank manager who dealt with his laundered money. He reassured Eamon that there would be no problem with the transaction. Eamon's legal income that went through the system via his successful businesses would cover the purchase of the new home and the building work it would require.

Eamon took note that the property had been on the market for sixteen months. After speaking to the estate agent. He placed an offer of 400,000 euros in cash, Just under 200,000 less than the asking price. The agent informed him that the family was eager to sell due to a bereavement. Eamon instructed the agent to inform the seller that he wanted an answer within the hour, otherwise, he would withdraw the offer.

Eamon wanted the property and would have been willing to pay the asking price, however, he thought it was worth taking a gamble, knowing how long the property had been on the market and how eager the owners were to sell. He knew he would come out as the winner.

Thirteen minutes later, the agent gave him the good news. Eamon instructed him that he did not wish for his name to be known to the seller. The agent agreed. Eamon knew that the man would carry out his direction to the letter to gain his commission. Eamon was confident that his plans would be kept under wraps. No one else would know, apart from his brother Patrick, whom Eamon had telephoned earlier. He had informed Patrick about the situation with the London Special Branch sending an undercover agent to Spain to try to infiltrate his circle, hoping to slap a murder charge on him and two of his men. Eamon went into detail about the Bulgarian brothers and the woman. He did not need to tell his brother about how he conducted his retaliation though. Patrick knew his brother enough to realise that Eamon would have dealt with the problem in a way that would allow no comeback from the Eastern Europeans.

Eamon gave Patrick the rundown on the property that he had purchased in Wicklow County, asking if he would be able to help him oversee the extension work, although Eamon did not want to pressurise him. He knew that he could rely on Patrick. His brother could be trusted to ensure that everything would run smoothly. Eamon told Patrick that he realised that the work would be a burden, what with tending to the animals on his smallholding. However, Patrick said that Anna, his wife, was more than capable of handling the horses and the livestock, the chickens, ducks and geese. Without hesitation, Patrick reassured him that he would oversee the project. Eamon said that he would reimburse him for his trouble, brooking no argument.

Eamon would also require someone local to keep watch over the house. The agent was instructed to employ a trusted gardener/housekeeper. The agent said he had someone in mind who had worked for the previous owner.

Next, he needed a builder. The agent stepped up. He could recommend a trusted construction company. Eamon gave instructions to the firm to build an extension to house an 18-metre indoor swimming pool and stables for six horses. The agent said that he would get on to finding a reputable architect.

Satisfied with his plan of action, Eamon phoned Dan and Billy, who were going with him to pay a surprise visit with the detection dog to his haulage company. The Russians and Bulgarians were trying to infiltrate any avenue to export narcotics. His HGV delivery drivers were an easy target. The drivers he employed had families, for the most part. Eamon was aware that he was required to protect both his business and the men who worked for him, as they were easily intimidated by the Eastern Europeans. Although having the Belgian shepherd dog aided in the prevention of drug exportation, he was aware that he could not avoid some smuggling slipping through. He would need dogs working on site 24/7 to avoid it completely.

However, Eamon was firm yet fair with the drivers. They respected him and no one wanted to lose their job. Eamon offered every company employee a bonus at the end of the year to keep them sweet. To outward appearances, it appeared to be working, however, Eamon was not a man to get too complacent. His previous lifestyle as Jimmy Grant's right-hand man had taught him that vigilance pays off.

19

The following evening, Billy parked along the Altea beach boulevard near the old town and headed to Irish Michael's bar. Eamon had told Irish Michael that there was an undercover cop from the UK operating in the area, and to let him know if anyone new arrived at the bar. Michael had revealed to Eamon that there was a new barman who was renting the flat above the bar, who had been asking questions about the owners of the Hawk Wind adult club.

Billy had been feeling excited as it was not too long before Christmas. He was looking forward to accompanying Eamon and his family on their trip to Disney World in Paris. However, when Dan had dropped the clanger about the undercover agent being in the vicinity, he put his business head back on.

Billy raised his hand as he stepped into the busy bar. Irish Michael called out, "Yer usual, Billy?" Billy nodded, smiling. He noticed that the barman did not smile back, although he nodded in a friendly welcome. Billy gave a sharp nod without missing that the barman quickly registered him before turning away again. You're our man, Billy thought to himself, sensing that the man had figured out who he was. Sitting at the bar with his back to the customers, Billy took a slow, leisurely gulp of his beer. The new barman stood to one side drying glasses.

"Have you been in Spain long?" he asked Billy. "Only I noticed that Michael appears to know you. Obviously, you are a regular." He moved in front of Billy, wiping glasses and stacking them beneath the counter.

"Michael makes it his business to know all his customers. Regular or otherwise." Billy responded, entering into the game he sensed the man was playing. "In answer to your first question, I intended to pass through the Costa Blanca and then head elsewhere, however, a lovely female kept me here." Both men laughed.

The new barman put his hand out introducing himself, "Leyton Borewood."

Billy shook it and introduced himself. The barman had a firm handshake. His pronounced biceps under his shirt sleeve suggested that he frequented the gym.

"My situation is the opposite." Leyton Borewood disclosed. "I landed here due to being dumped by a female a couple of months ago in the UK. Heart-rending coming home to a 'Dear John' note to say that she was not coming back. I had no ties." He lifted his shoulders in a shrug. "Therefore, I threw a few things in a rucksack and headed for the sun." He put the glass down that he was drying and headed to the end of the bar to serve a customer. Billy knew that he would return. A few minutes later he was back.

"You look as if you work out. In fact, you look like ex-military. Or is it the woman that keeps you fit?" The barman threw in, laughing.

Billy smiled thinly and raised an eyebrow. "Bit of everything." He took a larger mouthful of his drink, neglecting to answer the query regarding the military. Billy held Leyton's hard stare as he fed him snippets. "We have dogs and horses. Kennels and stables that constantly need repair tend to keep you active."

"What kind of horses and dogs do you have? I was brought up on a farm in Kent as a boy. I didn't move away until I married a girl from Middlesex."

Billy was going to put him to the test by asking him about the area in Kent he was from, but he had a feeling that it was part of his story and let it slide.

"Various breeds of dogs." Billy had no intention of telling him that Jane trained dogs in narcotic detection. "My wife trains dogs in obedience. We have two Andalusians for our leisure. We like to ride out." Billy picked up the glass without drinking. He wanted to make the beer last until he finished trying to suss the man out.

"Training dogs in obedience," Leyton repeated, nodding. "She sounds like she has skills with animals, to handle Andalusians and dogs. No wonder you were attracted to her. Does she have any sisters? She is the type of strong woman that I need. One that takes control beneath the sheets," he joked. Billy did not respond. "A man can get lonely," he said on a more serious note.

Billy thought it didn't sit quite right for a guy to say that was heartbroken over the recent breakup of his marriage but that he was eager to find another woman so soon. However, he kept his own counsel.

"Do you live nearby?" Leyton asked Billy. "Michael has rented the room above the bar to me. To be honest, the sound of the waves at night helps with getting to sleep."

Before Billy had time to answer, Irish Michael interjected, "Leyton!" He indicated that he needed help with customers wanting refills.

"See you later!" Billy called out after taking out his phone on the pretext of calling a taxi. He discreetly snapped a photo of the barman's profile while he was distracted serving at the far end of the bar. He took his leave, waving a hand without bothering to look back. He had what he wanted – a near certainty that Leyton Borewood was the undercover agent.

Billy went to visit Dan at his home. The two men sat on the terrace while Cindy retired to the lounge. "In my opinion, the man is the Law. He wanted to know the ins and outs of a cat's arse. Talk about the Spanish Inquisition!" Dan nodded. Billy continued," I think that he will turn up at the Hawk Wind club for a membership. The thing is that he will see that I work there."

Dan replied, "I will speak to the boss. It may be better if you stay away from the club for a week. We know that if he is the one, then he will have the rundown on the three of us. I know that we can't do anything about getting him off our backs, so we'll need to play it by ear."

As Billy had predicted, Leyton Borewood's had called the club to take out a membership. Dan had taken his details and visa card number over the phone. That evening while he was outside in the car park speaking to Thomas and Scott Lord he caught sight of the man in Billy's photo from Irish Michael's bar alighting from a taxi in front of the club. Dan nodded as he approached the club, opening the door for him. A few minutes passed before Dan entered the club, heading towards the office.

Eamon sat upright when Dan stepped into the room, locking the door and taking a seat. "Our man in question has just come into the club."

Eamon leaned forward, sucking air through his teeth, forearms resting on the desk. "Billy informed me earlier that the contact he uses to track a paper trail hasn't found anything to prove Leyton Borewood's existence. Therefore, I need him to be watched. Keep yer eye on him. Take note if he gets into conversation wit any of the staff. I sense that the man is looking for someone who will give him information."

Dan nodded, rising. "I will keep you posted, boss."

Tanya Green was on the stage performing the splits upside down on the pole. She ignored the wolf whistles from the men crowded around the edge of the stage. Her attention was drawn to the man at the bar sitting on a stool with his eyes trained on her. He winked his approval. She smiled at him, giving him her full attention. It was not because she felt an attraction for him, rather her response was due to recognition.

She thought that his appearance hadn't changed much since she had last seen him five years ago when she had opened her mother's front door to the dawn raid in Harold Hill in Essex. He was one of two of the detectives with the group of police officers that had searched her mother's council house. The police officers had discovered multiple bags of cannabis weighed and ready for sale. The back room was stacked with stolen property. Tanya's auntie Joanie, her mother's elder sister had intervened, coming to Tanya's rescue and removing her from the criminal life that Tanya was forced to live under.

Joanie insisted to Detective Aaron Birchwood that Tanya would come to live with her on the other side of the council estate at Serenity House. Detective Birchwood agreed. Tanya's mother was facing a long-term custodial sentence when it was found that she paid local shoplifters in drugs for their stolen goods. Tanya had grown up with her mother being either drunk or off her head on drugs all the time. However, Tanya threw herself into her studies, excelling at most, including outstanding sports achievements. Joanie had also taught Tanya the ways of men and how to survive in their world.

Tanya kept the man at the bar interested until she finished her routine. On her way out of the club, she passed him by. He placed a hand lightly on her arm and stopped her. "May I buy you a drink?" Tanya hesitated. He pulled up a stool for her.

Tanya smiled. "I am teetotal. I live a clean life. I work hard with not much time to play." She hoisted the Fendi bag on her shoulder. He glanced at her bag. "You must not waste your life working too hard for expensive items. Or perhaps you have an admirer who presents you with such gifts?" Tanya smiled. He pulled the spare stool closer. "Let me get you a cordial. Orange juice perhaps?" Tanya took the seat, facing him. He ordered her drink and held his hand out. "Hi, I'm Leyton." Tanya did not give hers. He cocked his head. "A beautiful girl like you must have many admirers." He passed a ten euro note to the barmaid. Tanya sipped the pure orange juice. "Are you attached to anyone?" Tanya shook her head, placing the glass on the bar. He smiled. "Does it mean that I could be in with a chance?" Cocking his head, he asked, "Dinner one night perhaps?"

Tanya could tell that he did not recognise her. He had not changed one iota over the past five years. She judged him to be in his thirties. He had mid-brown hair and dark-brown eyes that spoke of intelligence. He was also very fit and looked like he worked out. The stubble on his chiselled jawline gave him a sexy look. She imagined that he would be good in bed. However, sex was not what she was after. She wanted to find out who he was spying on in Spain. She pondered if her boss was on the wanted list by the Law in the UK. Mitre and Eamon O'Donally would both be interested in this man.

"If you give me your telephone number, I can call you to find out when you are free." He took a long draught of his beer, watching her.

"I don't give my telephone number out to clients at the club, or anywhere else for that matter. However," she said smiling, "maybe, I will call you at some point." He produced a pen from the inside of his jacket. Taking a beer mat from the bar, he scribbled his details on it, passing it to her. "Please don't forget me," he said, holding her gaze.

Tanya dropped the mat into her bag. Standing to leave, she adjusted her shoulder bag and said, "I assure you, Leyton, that I will give you some thought." She waved goodbye. Tanya fully intended to ring him. She wanted to keep in contact. She knew of two men whom she would mark their cards about the identity of the undercover cop. If her intuition served her well, both men would reward her.

Tanya had three thousand euros stashed away to put into her bank account from Mitre. She had pleasured him that day and had imparted the information about the undercover cop, which had pleased him. He had told her that he would investigate it. Tanya knew that Mitre was proud of the fact that he had been her first lover. Tanya was also a good actress. Her feigned cries of ecstasy were proof enough for his ego that he had fulfilled her. Mitre would easily part with his cash after every time she rode him crying out his name.

The following evening before Tanya was due to go on stage, she entered the Hawk Wind adult club and headed towards the office. She had seen the Maserati in the car park and knew that her boss was working that night. She knocked on the door.

"Come in," Eamon said. He wore his black frame spectacles, perusing the club members' registration book, which was open on the desk in front of him. He removed his glasses and shut the ledger, leaning back into the office chair when Tanya closed the door behind her. Dan had already informed him that he suspected Leyton Borewood was the undercover cop. Had been chatting up the new dancer. Dan had observed him talking to Tanya at the bar. A short while later, he had seen him scribbling on a beer mat and passing her what Dan assumed was his telephone number. He had watched when she deposited it in her bag. "What can I do for ye? If ye have any problems, my wife will be in the club tomorrow evening," Eamon said.

She took the chair opposite the desk. "It's you that I want to speak to," Tanya said, placing her bag on the floor next to the chair leg. It did not go amiss with Eamon that the bag was Fendi, a designer that Marcia at times favoured. He knew it was expensive – far beyond the reach of a pole dancer's wages. He pursed his lips, giving two nods.

"How can I be of help to ye?" He asked again, sensing that although she was young, she was artful.

"I wish to give you some information about the identity of one of the club members."

Eamon held her look.

"I am sure that there may be a few members that do not disclose their true identity for various reasons," he countered.

"I am positive that this man has a very good reason for not making his true identity known – or his true profession," Tanya said, smiling.

Eamon pressed his lips together. He was intrigued and let her continue.

"He asked me out. He didn't recognise me from our last encounter five years ago when he raided my mother's home in Harold Hill in Essex." Eamon did not respond. "His name is Aaron Birchwood. Although he was a detective back then, he may well have climbed the ladder." Eamon gave two slow nods. "I have his name and phone number. He uses the alias Leyton Borewood."

"What makes ye tink that this guy would be of interest to me?"

Tanya smiled. "I was brought up on a council estate with criminals that ranged from shoplifters to bank robbers. I lived by my wits. My instincts inform me that the undercover cop is here on a surveillance mission for the Special Branch in the UK."

Eamon was impressed with her reasoning, although he was sure that she had an ulterior motive. "What benefit do ye gain by informing me?" he asked.

Tanya reached for her bag and placed the beer mat on the desk. Standing to leave, she said, "I have taken a picture of his details." Eamon did not take his eyes off her. "There may come a time when I might require your help. I was taught to help those who will hopefully return the favour if needed. If I can be of further assistance, let me know," Tanya said, smiling. "I am to go onstage again shortly."

Eamon gave a sharp nod without replying. Exhaling, he picked up the beer mat, studying the undercover agent's details. "Aaron Birchwood, let's discover yer paper trail," Eamon spoke to the room. He knew that his plans for the relocation to Wicklow County could be brought forward at a push. He would pass the information about Birchwood to Billy so his contact could find his paper trail. However, he knew that his hands were tied. If any harm came to the agent through his intervention, he knew the Law would leave no stone unturned to find the perpetrator.

Eamon knew that Tanya's Bulgarian boyfriend worked for a Russian. He would lay money on it that Tanya would also inform him about the undercover agent in their midst. He gathered that she was game-playing – what game, he was unsure of for the moment. Eamon called Billy to his office on the two-way radio.

Billy knocked once, opening the door and then locking it.

"I need your computer pal's expertise," Eamon said, holding out the beer mat. Billy pulled out a chair, lips pursed, nodding at the details. "This is our undercover agent's alias, but his true identity is Detective Aaron Birchwood!"

"Was it by chance that the pole dancer IDed him? What I find puzzling is why would she mark your card, boss?" Billy suddenly had a lightbulb moment. "To my mind, the girl's playing a game, intending to kill two birds with one stone. She has the Bulgarian by her side. The girl must intend to gain from you both."

Eamon smirked. "My thoughts entirely. Although she is young, the girl is clever. She is hedging her bets on who is going to be her ally when she makes her move." Both men grinned, nodding in agreement.

"I'll get right on it. My hacker pal does not sleep." Billy checked his watch. "I will call him now."

"Pay him whatever his fee," Eamon said, moving to the safe and handing Billy a wad of cash.

"This undercover cop has entered a hornet's nest boss. He may think that he has come here to infiltrate us, but he will have the attention of the Eastern Europeans. I don't think that they will have any qualms about removing an interloper." Billy stood by the door. "I should be back with some info before you leave boss."

Just before midnight, a grinning Billy returned to the office and passed Eamon a printout. Eamon smiled thinly at the photograph of Detective Aaron Birchwood that accompanied details of his service with the National Crime Agency. He was married with two children – a boy and a girl. His home was in Hertfordshire. "Good night's work, Billy."

Billy placed money on the desk. "Leo wanted 500 euros." Eamon slid the remaining 500 euros back across the desk towards him. "Take Jane out for a meal. ~~Ye have~~ earned it!"

Billy thanked him.

Eamon could see the low light under the bedroom door when he returned home. The dog walked behind him, he opened the terrace doors to let him out. He went back inside to check on the children, all sleeping peacefully.

Pushing their bedroom door ajar, he smiled warmly at Marcia's sleeping form. Curled in the foetal position with an open book on the pillow beside her. Quietly retreating, he went to the cabinet, taking a wine glass. Opening a bottle of Barbaresco, he half-filled it before taking a slow draw, savouring the rich, delicious cherry fruit and the notes of cedar. He topped the glass up and walked out through the terrace doors. He noticed the dog was sniffing around the boundaries. Taking a garden chair at the table, he sat observing the animal. Jane had a young Belgian shepherd that she was bringing to him that day. He was 18 months old and trained in detection work. Jane was going to introduce the dogs, to make sure the older dog would tolerate the younger one.

He scanned the immaculately kept grounds. His Spanish gardener, Federico, had previously worked for Joyce Grant, and Eamon took him on after Jimmy died and Joyce moved to the US. The man came early in the morning before the sun got too hot, and Eamon paid the man cash in hand as Joyce had recommended. Eamon had no argument with that. Although he had never had a conversation with the gardener, he had made enquiries about his personal life, discovering that he lived hand to mouth with five children. Eamon doubled his weekly wage. He knew that Marcia gave him the children's outgrown clothes as he had youngsters of similar age.

Eamon turned his head upon seeing movement out of his peripheral vision. Marcia tightened the belt of her negligee as she came towards him. "You look troubled," she said, moving alongside him. He slipped his free arm around her waist, pulling her into him.

"I am grand. These late nights are taking their toll. I am not the young man I used to be who was able to burn the candle at both ends."

Leaning into him, she brushed his lips with hers. He returned her kiss, putting the glass to one side, sitting her on his lap, caressing the sensual silk around her naked form. He nibbled her neck, taking in the fragrance of saffron and top notes of mandarin oil. Memories of their holiday in Lake Como in Italy came flooding back to him. They had made love after Marcia had massaged him on the bed in full view of the mountain opposite the lake. He remembered how tired he had felt on arrival at the hotel, sleeping for hours, while Marcia patiently waited for him to wake.

Her arms went around his neck. A south-westerly wind blew sudden gusts, and the fronds of the surrounding palms in the grounds danced in unison. The chill in the early morning air indicated rain on the way. "I love to hear the wind among the trees. I feel as if they are calling me." Marcia said, cuddling into him.

Eamon smiled. "I should tink that ye have enough voices in yer ear witout trees calling ye, my wee mystic." His hands roamed sensually and lovingly down her back, resting on her buttocks. Cupping them without taking his eyes from her, he asked, "What time did ye fall asleep?"

"About eleven. I swam tonight after the children were in bed. Then I read a book. Without realising, I fell asleep."

Brow elevated, he said playfully," I hope that ye did not swim naked?"

Marcia shook her head. "I only swim naked when you are at home. Although we will have another dog later today, so soon it will be safer."

"The rules won't change," he said, smiling.

She covered his mouth with hers, then whispered, "Would you like me to massage you? It will help to release the tension."

"I dare say that ye are not going to play fair wit me. Ye are naked beneath that silk robe. Once ye straddle me it'll be game over!" he laughed, standing with her in his arms, brushing her mouth with his.

"I will shower. Then put some panties on – and not ouvert ones, my little vixen," he directed, as he carried her across the terrace "That will allow me a given amount of time to enjoy the massage before I ravish ye."

Heavy rain hit the windows in a torrent as Marcia concentrated on loosening up Eamon's tight deltoid muscles, getting in between the shoulder joints and his biceps. Her fingers and thumbs pressed into the contours of the tight muscles.

"That feels so good," Eamon murmured. He had his eyes closed and was naked, spread-eagled on top of the bed.

She continued working down his back. From his steady breathing, she thought that he was asleep. She kneaded the warm oil into his buttocks. Eamon shifted, but his eyelids remained shut. Her manipulation of the inner thigh muscles brought no reaction. Then she added gentle caresses and fluttering movements with her fingertips on his scrotum.

He turned around, supporting her as he laid on his back, fully erect. "We need some slow loving," he whispered groggily. Marcia leaned into his chest, breast and nipples making contact with his skin. In one swift movement, he moved so she was beneath him. His powerful thighs covered her. "Ye and the children are my everything," he said, running his forefinger along her top lip. Taking his weight on his forearms, he held himself above her. They kissed deeply and their souls united upon his entry. Each measured movement was synchronised until they both gave in to the final release, falling together into the abyss. Eamon held her to him without withdrawing, their hearts pounding against one another's chests.

The monitor suddenly crackled. Eamon leaned across to adjust the screen and saw Aine sitting up coughing. He shot out of bed, snatching his bathrobe and heading towards the nursery. Marcia hurriedly followed. Aisling slumbered while her sister gasped and then coughed. He felt her head. "Her temperature seems high."

Marcia took a thermometer from the chest of drawers where it was kept. Aye entered the bedroom, concerned. "It is her back teeth," she stated. Marcia showed her the reading on the thermometer – it was higher than normal, but not high enough to cause alarm. "No problem!" Aye declared, shaking her head and taking over administering the medication to Aine to bring her temperature down. Within minutes her coughing subsided. Eamon cradled her in his arms and took her to their bedroom, where Aine slept contentedly in between her parents. Eamon smiled as he smoothed her red curls that were damp with perspiration.

The monitor sounded again. Eamon got out of the bed, returning with a tearful Aisling, her head buried in the nape of his neck. "Make room for one more," Eamon said, smiling. "Aisling was crying for her sister." Aisling snuggled down, arm around Aine. "It's fortunate for us that I purchased this big bed. However, once they are in a deep sleep, I will slip in behind ye on the other side of the bed and we can finish off wit another round of slow loving." He winked.

20

Seventeen young heads bent down towards their desks, busily writing down what they had learned in their history lessons about Henry the Eighth and his wives. Niall had included the birth and death dates of the king, and also the disagreement he had had with Pope Clement VII because he would not agree to an annulment of his first marriage to Catherine of Aragon. Niall completed his assignment before the others. He had remembered every detail of what he had learned. He raised his hand. The master shook his head in exasperation and exhaled softly, speaking quietly so as not to disturb the rest of the class who were still busy trying to complete their tasks. "What is it, O'Donally?" he mouthed.

Quietly, so as not to disturb the class, Niall barely whispered, "May I be excused please, sir? I have finished the paper."

The master tutted, more to himself. "Can you not wait?" The normally brusque teacher kept his voice low.

Niall shook his head.

"Do not dally!" the teacher directed in the same low voice, his eyes glaring over the top of bifocal spectacles.

Niall was bored. He found history tedious as with most lessons that he absorbed with ease. He would prefer to be with

Billy and the horses. Billy was fun – good at playing football. He was pleased that Billy was now his uncle. He sauntered towards the boys' toilets at the end of the corridor. The school was quiet. All pupils were intently engrossed in their end-of-term exams. As Niall passed the janitor's cupboard he had no time to cry out. A hand clamped over his mouth and taped it shut. His small hands were secured behind his back and he was thrown into a cart full of laundry. The odour of dirty laundry filled his senses. He had caught a fleeting look at the man, whom he recognised. He had seen his abductor working in the grounds of the school on numerous occasions. Niall felt movement after he heard an engine start up. He realised that he was inside a vehicle. Towels encased him as he struggled to a sitting position. He did not cry, even if he had wanted to, knowing that his papa would protect him. Niall had told his father about Boswell, the boy at his previous school who had tried to extort money from him and Quinn. Papa had told Niall that he was to be told about anyone who tried to hurt him or Quinn.

However, his young mind was perplexed as to how he could contact his father right now. He knew that his father would be angry at the man when he discovered what he was doing. Niall did not doubt that his papa would hurt the man. Niall remained quiet. However, he was feeling hot, too hot, and he had the pressing need to urinate. He was no longer able to hold it in. Tears of humiliation trickled down his cheeks, knowing that he had soiled his school trousers. Feeling frustrated, Niall glared at the man's back who was at the wheel.

Niall found himself sitting on a chair in a room with an unmade bed and bare floors. The curtains were pulled closed, showing only a crack of light. Niall stared at the man, who removed the tape from his mouth and, smiling, offered him a bottle of water. Niall took it out of necessity.

Niall's dark eyes bore into the man as he offered him a sandwich. Crouching down before Niall, he said, "You are not going to be harmed. Once your wealthy daddy pays up, you can go home to your family." He smirked. "It won't be long!" He stood up facing the small boy. Niall remained unresponsive.

The head of school had been informed that Niall O'Donally was missing from school. A search party had been sent out, with pupils and teachers joining the search. The head teacher was in a quandary. He didn't know if Niall had wandered from the school. He could not imagine that he could have been abducted. That was something that just would not occur at his school.

An hour after Niall's disappearance, the alarm went up and the Guardia Civil and Eamon O'Donally were notified.

Eamon's Maserati screeched to a halt in the school car park. Six Guardia Civil officers, along with a dog handler were making their way through the school. Eamon wasted no time in joining them. The spaniel stopped outside of the laundry room. The officers followed the dog inside the janitor's cupboard. The dog barked, wagging its tail, but the trail seemed to stop there.

The security cameras showed Niall sauntering along the school corridor until he reached the laundry room. Although the officer zoomed in on the arm that snatched Niall, he couldn't make out any other features. The abductor's profile was obstructed by a cap visor that was pulled down, obscuring his face. A small, white van appeared on the screen leaving the school grounds shortly afterwards. The head confirmed that it was used by the janitor for the school's laundry. A call to apprehend Ramone Mendez was put out with the licence plate numbers of the small, white Fiat van.

Eamon had wasted no time in contacting the Guardia Civil superior. The comisario agreed to see him. Eamon had phoned Billy giving him the rundown, asking him to take

Quinn home with him. He would need to inform Marcia. Nonetheless, it was of the utmost importance, to ensure Niall's safety, that Eamon speak to the comisario first.

The big man's powerful presence was set off by his physical build. His looks suited his high position Not a single steel-grey hair was out of place. His eyebrows were black, almost meeting in the middle above an aquiline nose, giving him the look of a bird of prey. The comisario rose to his full height from behind his desk, proffering Eamon a seat. "It is highly unusual for me to speak to anyone that has been offended. My men are professionals. Their expertise in dealing with any emergency is second to none," he stated firmly, eyeing Eamon with his intense smokey grey eyes.

Eamon went to speak. The comisario put his hand up to stop Eamon from speaking. "However, Mr O'Donally, I am willing to give you a few minutes out of my busy schedule." He sat down, leaning into his office chair.

Eamon adjusted his position. "I am grateful for ye time comisario. However, I am willing to donate a quarter of a million euros to yer Guardia Civil fund." Eamon caught the man's renewed interest. "Or anyting else that ye deem fit," Eamon added.

The comisario nodded twice slowly. "That is generous of you, Mr O'Donally. I can reassure you that I will personally see to it that your son will be returned safely to you within a short time."

Eamon thanked him. Offering his hand, Eamon leaned across the desk and both men shook on it. "My name is Comisario Anton Rodriguez. I can assure you that this undesirable will be apprehended and severely dealt with." Eamon gave a sharp nod. "I will instruct my top men to prioritise the situation. The child's safety is of the utmost importance. If you leave me your phone number, I will keep you updated." Leaning forward, both hands resting on the desk, the comisario gave a thin smile. "However," his tone serious, "just one thing of importance." Eamon held his stare. "Do not allow your men to interfere. It is my job to apprehend criminals," he stated, brooking no argument. Eamon gave a sharp nod in agreement and left the Guardia Civil station.

Eamon phoned Dan on the way to his car, giving him the rundown of the situation. He instructed him to ring Benny Harris and Thomas Harper-Watts and to meet at the club in an hour. He said that Billy had taken Quinn back to his place where he would occupy him. He told Dan that he was going home first to break the news to Marcia. Then he phoned Billy, asking for Jane's help, as he knew that Marcia would require support while he sorted the situation out.

Marcia sat up from the sunbed under the canopy when Eamon came through the terrace doors. The new, young Belgian shepherd, Raj, came towards him, wagging his tail, followed by Roman. Putting her book to one side, she removed her reading glasses. "Where are the boys?" she asked with a hint of concern. Eamon hastened his step towards her without replying. She stood up from the sunbed as he approached her. He reached for her, holding her tight. He went into detail.

"NO!" she cried out, tears streaming down her face. She slumped in his arms, wailing like a wounded animal. He tightened his grip on her. "Eamon, you must find him!" Marcia begged.

"Marcia, I promise ye that everything is being done. I have the chief of police on the case. The comisario has assured me that they will apprehend the kidnapper in no time. His men have the culprit's details and they know his identity from the security camera. I promise ye that no stone will be left unturned!" His tone was stern, although inside he was crumbling, fearful for his son's safety.

"WHY Eamon? Why take my small son?" Eamon sat with her in his arms on the garden chair, smoothing her face and wiping her tears. "That school building gave me ominous sensations. I spoke to Suzette about it – how I couldn't shake off the sense of portent when I dropped the boys off at school. There was a sense of foreboding, a warning that I had not heeded! I allowed it to happen! Time and again I felt that it was somehow linked to Niall. How could I have left him unprotected?"

Marcia's tears dampened his shirt as she sobbed into his chest. He cupped her chin. "Marcia ye are not to blame."

"Eamon, I did not tell you because I did not want to cause concern. How could I stand by and allow this to happen to our child?" The pain in her dark-brown eyes nearly broke him. Eamon could not make her see reason.

Jane came round the side of the house; the two dogs moved towards her, their tails wagging in welcome. She hurriedly made her way to the far end of the terrace to console Marcia.

Eamon nodded, smiling wanly. "Marcia, Jane will stay wit ye while I meet up wit the men."

....

"I am going to leave you for a while," Ramone Mendez said to the stoic Niall, who glared into his captor's eyes. "Don't be scared," he cajoled. He had never encountered a child who seemed as if he could see right into your soul. Niall's dark eyes bore into his, directing hatred. He reminded him of the psychotic killers that he had watched documentaries on. Ramone shrugged it off. This was a mere kid who he would be glad to get rid of as soon as the payment was made. He unlocked the door, glancing back. The child's eyes, unflinching, continued to watch him. Pulling his baseball cap visor down to hide his face, Ramone went out to make a phone call. The school laundry van was hidden from view two roads away from his apartment. He decided to walk the mile to the bar. He knew that there would be few customers this time of day.

Bridie answered his call. Ramone said that all was going to plan. He had the boy hidden away in his mother's apartment while she was in Alicante visiting her sister for the week. Bridie said that she would send the ransom letter by express first-class post from overseas. Bridie said that it would leave on a flight for Spain that evening. Downing two bottles of beer while sitting in the corner of the bar, with his back to a couple of older Spanish men, Ramone felt exhilarated by the thought that within a few days, he would be sitting on the white sands on some Caribbean island. He was not fussed about which one. He had his passport at the ready for his escape when they received the payout.

Ramone had picked up a pizza for him and the boy. Entering the living room of his mother's apartment, Ramone noticed the silence. When he opened the bedroom door, Niall was sitting in the same position that he had left him in. The boy directed laser beams of hatred from his eyes at Ramone.

"I have food for us," he chirped, ignoring an almost palpable violent energy emanating from Niall. "I need the bathroom," Niall directed. Although his trousers were wet, he did not want the humiliation of urinating in them again. Ramone showed him the door, waiting outside until Niall finished. Ramone lay on the floor eating, while flicking through the channels on the small TV screen. Niall had refused food, however, he drank the proffered mineral water. He pondered on how his papa would find him. He knew he would be very angry at the man who had taken him away from his school.

The crashing sound of splintering wood brought Ramone to his senses. Startled, he jumped up and opened the bedroom door to find the front door on the living room floor. He froze, fearful of being shot. He raised his arms above his head at the sight of the guns pointed at him as men dressed in black piled into the room. The Grupo Especial de Operaciones aimed their Mauser SP66s at their target and shouted warnings. He took a step back, trying to back away when the leader of the group rushed him. A military boot struck between Ramone's legs, lifting him inches from the floor. He was pounced upon, pinned to the floor and handcuffed without resistance. The officer stepped into the bedroom. Putting the firearm to his side. He smiled at Niall. Speaking to him in English, "Do not be frightened, I am taking you to your papa!"

Niall responded in Spanish. "Estoy bien. Gracias!" The officer smiled, taking him by the hand. "Bravo!"

Eamon had finished speaking to his men behind closed doors at the Hawk Wind club. He directed Dan to go to Billy and get him to contact his pal who was an expert in IT. He wanted a paper trail on Ramone Mendez and information on all of his contacts.

"Do you think that this is a ransom case?" Benny Harris spoke up for the first time after listening intently to his boss.

"I am hoping that it is money that is behind it." Eamon could not bring himself to say that it could be someone out to harm his child, although he thought it. He would pay any amount to bring Niall home safely. Nevertheless, once his son was under his protection, he would have the perpetrator hunted. No matter where they ran to escape.

His men left the club. Eamon placed a call to Dave Broadbent bringing him up to speed. Dave Broadbent said that he would make Eamon's situation a priority once Eamon gave him Ramone Mendez's background.

Eamon leaned back in the office chair, long legs resting on the desk, pondering on the school janitor. The school head had explained that when Ramone Mendez applied for the job, he had a police check and no previous criminal past had been flagged up. Eamon felt that there were others involved in the plot to kidnap Niall. Fingers drum rolling on his desk, he was at a loss as to which way to go.

Three long hours later, Eamon's mobile phone rang. He felt a lead weight in his gut when he heard the comisario's voice.

"Your son is safe!" The words brought tears of joy to Eamon's eyes. Although the comisario informed him that Niall would require a medical check-up. Eamon grabbed his car keys and told him that he was on his way. He placed a call to Marcia as he sped towards the local jefatura de policia in Altea. He then phoned his bank manager to arrange a meeting with him, making it clear that it was urgent. Eamon knew that he would have the two-hundred-and-fifty thousand euros for the comisario within a few hours.

Comisario Anton Rodriguez sat behind his desk as Eamon entered. He proffered him a seat. Eamon smiled. "I cannot thank ye enough. The donation, as promised, will be available by late afternoon."

The comisario gave a slight nod. "Ramone Mendez took little persuasion in revealing to my officers who was involved in the kidnapping plot." A hint of a caustic smile played on the corners of his mouth. Eamon was under no illusion that the Spanish Guardia would use any means to garner information from anyone who violated the law, especially with crime against children. Spanish men held children in high regard.

The comisario pressed on, "Apparently, there are two others involved. We believe that there is a ransom behind it for a million euros" A long moment passed. "Although the other two perpetrators reside in England and are out of my jurisdiction." A smug smile formed while he continued, "Nevertheless, I have informed my colleague in London's Special Branch of the situation. They have all the details. As we speak, arrangements are being set in place for their arrests."

Eamon leaned forward, elbows placed on the desk. "Comisario, I am eternally grateful for yer expedience in this matter." Halting for two seconds, knowing that he could not overstep the mark with the powerful law enforcer. "If ye could see fit to giving me the two names, I will raise the donation by fifty thousand?"

Both men held a look until the comisario broke his. He pressed his lips together, then nodded, saying, "I sympathise with your plight, Mr O'Donally. I am also a father of two daughters." He exhaled, placing both hands on the arms of the chair, returning to fix Eamon's look. "Seeing that the pair in London who are involved in this serious crime are out of your reach," he smiled, "I cannot see any harm in it!" He opened a folder and scribbled on a piece of paper, which he passed to Eamon.

"Eamon was taken aback when he read the woman's name, although he did not show it. "Are these relatives of Mendez?" Eamon queried without mentioning the woman's name.

"Apparently they are cousins," the comisario stated. "According to Ramone Mendez, the woman is the girlfriend of his cousin, Rupert Mendez. Mendez claims she is the instigator behind the plot to kidnap your son." A wry smile formed as he continued. “However, once they are apprehended, the truth will be out.”

Eamon did not reply, he was seething that Bridie Murphy was behind the kidnapping plot. The former pole dancer at his club had previously tried to destroy his marriage and extort money from him. Making a silent vow, he prayed that he could get to the pair before the Law arrested them. No matter that it was a woman. She would receive the same punishment as her accomplice. Eamon would place the call to have Bridie Murphy hunted. She would not have the opportunity to inflict pain upon anyone else again.

Niall was putting his shoes on when his father came into the medical examination room. The doctor and the female assistant smiled warmly. The doctor spoke, “Niall is in great shape. Such a brave young man.”

Eamon crouched down before his son, eyes questioning. There were no answers from the stoical boy. Eamon tussled his hair. “I will let ye into a secret that ye are the first to know. Mummy has not been informed yet.” Niall perked up as he continued. “Dadda has planned a holiday for us to go on a plane to Disney World in Paris over the Christmas holidays.” Niall nodded. “I invited Billy and Jane to join us on the trip.” Niall smiled. Eamon stood to his full height.

“Uncle Billy will be excited to go on the rides!” Niall said as Eamon took his hand. Eamon thanked the doctor and the assistant and he and Niall left the hospital to go home.

Eamon opened the car door for Niall. While Niall was attaching his seatbelt, Eamon texted Marcia to say that they would be home in ten to fifteen minutes. Heading northeast on C. Comte d’Altea /N.3 towards Carrer Clot del Mingot, Niall found his voice. “I was waiting for you to collect me. Did you get lost, Papa?” Before Eamon answered, Niall quickly threw in,

"I did not tell that nasty man that you would hurt him because I was afraid that he may have become angry. Although I knew that you would once you discovered that he had taken me."

Eamon inhaled. He felt that he had let the boy down. He was at a loss for an explanation. Momentarily taking his eyes off the road, Eamon turned to face his son. Not for the first time, Eamon was taken aback by his son's perception of him – that he assumed his father would resort to violence. Eamon had never given him any indication that he used violent methods of retribution. Furthermore, he and Marcia rarely argued and if they did ever have any disagreement they always discussed it behind closed doors. His children were heaped with love and affection. It baffled him.

Eamon felt remorseful as he looked into his child's innocent, dark-brown eyes. How could he have allowed this to happen? He would demand that the school never allow his son to be left unattended. Returning his attention to the road ahead, he reassured Niall, "Dadda will ensure that nobody will ever harm ye or yer siblings." He did not know what else to say. He placed his free hand on his son's shoulder, gently squeezing. "The Guardia Civil will put that man in prison for a very long time." Niall appeared appeased, although Eamon knew that his son did not fully comprehend the meaning of prison.

"Two of the pupils at my school said to me that you own a nightclub where ladies remove their clothes. Their mothers were angry, they overheard them shouting at their fathers for going to your club, Papa! I know that you own a club, although I did not realise that ladies removed their clothes."

Eamon silently inhaled. He could not deny it. Nor did he feel that it was the right time to try to explain to his eight-year-old son who had been held captive for hours. He changed the subject. "If ye feel up to it, in a while after yer meal, want to race me in the pool for a hundred euros?" Niall's dark eyes sparkled as he nodded. He added "How about if I raise the stakes? Two out of three wins could see me doubling it to two hundred euros."

Niall clapped his hands. Eamon smiled to himself, relieved that the moment had passed for the need to explain to Niall about the adult club. Even though Niall had previously been shown around his club, Eamon had not gone into details about what went on there. He realised, however, that it was inevitable that his name and association with the Hawk Wind adult club would eventually be tossed around by his son's friends at school. However, he had not expected it so soon.

Marcia's flowing skirt and blouse whipped around her form as she hurried down the steps with the two dogs following behind her when Eamon's Maserati came through the villa gates.

"Would ye like to inform mummy about our secret holiday?" Eamon asked before Niall got out of the car. Niall nodded, smiling thinly. Eamon nodded his go-ahead.

Crouching before him, Marcia took Niall in her arms, smothering him with kisses. Eamon saw the tears brimming in her eyes as she struggled not to cry. Niall looked up in askance at his father, who gave a sharp nod. Niall turned back to his mother and said, "Papa is taking us all on an aeroplane to Disney World in Paris for the Christmas holiday!"

Marcia beamed, holding him at arm's length. "Darling, that is wonderful!" she enthused, taking his hand in hers. "How long have you and Papa been keeping this wonderful secret?"

He turned his head towards his father for confirmation. Eamon smiled. Niall answered, "When Papa came to collect me from the doctor's office." Niall added, smiling "Billy and Jane are being invited to join us!" He then frowned and said, "Papa, you did not mention that Aye would also be joining us."

"Of course, Aye is included in any of our family gatherings."

Marcia held Niall's hand while they walked towards the steps. "Aye is busy cooking many of your favourite dishes while the girls sleep," she said.

"I am hungry!" Niall stated, looking ahead. "The man offered me pizza. However," he paused looking at both of his parents, "I refused it." He faltered. "But I did drink bottled water."

Eamon shot Marcia a glance. Marcia squeezed Niall's hand affectionately. He responded cheerily. "I am going to race Papa in the pool later." He looked up at his father. "Papa is going to pay me double if I win two races out of three. That will be two hundred euros I will save for our holiday."

"If ye eat yer meal that Aye has prepared and ye rest up for an hour afterwards," Eamon said, "Then, I dare say that the odds of ye winning will be high."

Niall smiled. "Carbohydrates will refuel my body!" he declared. Eamon elevated his brow in awe at his small son's ability to absorb information.

Aye came away from her cooking when they entered the vast lounge. Hugging Niall, she informed him in Thai that she was preparing his favourite dish. Niall did not reply, however, he held his small palms together and bowed his head in gratitude.

Marcia knew that as soon as the girls awoke they would want Eamon's attention, leaving him no time for swimming with Niall. Aye had come up with the answer. She would feed them, then allow them to help her mix banana and coconut cakes. Aye had small cooking utensils and pinafores for the girls. Eamon and Niall were both changing into swimming trunks. Billy and Jane were entertaining Quinn at their home.

Billy informed Eamon that Quinn was happily helping to clean out the stables.

Marcia sat under the canopy at the garden table on the terrace watching Niall race ahead of his father. She knew that Eamon would allow him his moment of victory. Her thoughts were saddened, thinking about Niall's uniform that he had placed in the laundry basket after his shower, before eating his meal. Marcia had noticed that his small trousers, although dry, were stained. The smell of ammonia filled her senses as she held them. At that moment, she could have cried. She could not rid herself of the guilty feeling that she had let her child down. The vision of the blood moon came to mind. She remembered that red globe hanging in the sky at the time when Reuben had been taken from her. The second time it appeared she recognised it as a warning to which she had paid no heed. Her heart ached as she realised how close she had come to losing Niall.

Her thoughts went to Reuben. She occasionally received texts from him thanking her for the money that she regularly transferred to him. He wrote that all was well with his new family. Marcia had to be content with that for the time being.

She was brought back to the moment by Niall's clapping. She smiled seeing Eamon raise his hands in defeat, allowing Niall to win his trophy. As if on cue, Aye stepped through the terrace doors with Aisling and Aine, holding her hands. They were dressed in matching sun hats and pink cotton dresses. Aine squealed with delight, trying to tug away from Aye's hold upon seeing her father coming up the steps to the pool. "Swim, Daddy!" both girls said in unison.

"Mummy will change into her swimsuit," Marcia said. "Come with me. Daddy will join us later." She knew that he would need time out from the demanding time that he had faced with Niall.

Niall asked if he could go to his room to play with his game console. Eamon agreed. He was thankful that the boy didn't seem traumatised. He knew that Niall was stoic, a trait that he also had as a child. Nonetheless, the physical abuse that he had experienced as a small boy at the hands of his father had left mental scars that he carried throughout his life. He went inside the villa, returning to the patio with a large glass of wine. He adjusted his sunglasses, easing back on the sun lounger, taking a long-deserved pull of the wine. The relaxing effect was instant.

Marcia came out onto the terrace holding the hands of the smiling girls, all in their swimsuits. As he watched them walk down the steps into the pool, Eamon reflected on the plan that he had in mind. A thought came to him. He had not checked the post. The two dogs came behind him while he headed to the front of the villa to check the post box. He stared at the airmail letter, without opening it as he made his way to his office. He locked the office door and ripped the envelope open.

A burning furnace of rage hit his solar plexus when he read the typed demand for a million pounds to be left in a locker at Altea railway station. There was a code written for the locker. He punched the desk with his fist, heart thumping. Going to his safe, he retrieved the mobile phone that he only used on rare occasions. He made the call to Dave Broadbent giving him the details of the address in London that the comisario had given him. There was not much he could do about Ramone Mendez as he was in police custody, but he would guarantee that the masterminds behind the plot to kidnap his son and extort money from him would be exterminated.

21

Bridie Murphy was in a jubilant mood. Her plan, with the help of Ramone Mendez, Rupert's cousin, had been executed. She adjusted the weight of the rucksack on her back. The precious baggage was causing a strain on her neck. She was within a short distance from the flat that she shared with Rupert. Rounding the corner, she stopped in her tracks. Six armed police officers dressed in black were standing behind one of their colleagues who was using a battering ram to break down the door to her flat. She stepped into a shop doorway. Bridie could hear the splintering of wood. A crowd began to gather along the pavement observing the commotion. Regaining her equilibrium, without a moment's hesitation, she turned on her heels and headed towards her next destination. She was going to need to bring her plans forward.

She arrived by taxi and joined the queue at London Victoria coach station, her one-way ticket to Liverpool in hand. Bridie wanted to be near to the river Mersey. It brought back memories of the seven-and-a-half-hour ferry journey from Dublin to Liverpool when she and Martha had hurriedly fled their homeland and the excitement upon hearing the fog horns as they approached England. She longed to hear once more the ferry's seven short blasts from its fog horn before she left English shores for warmer climes.

She thought about her two siblings. Martha was having a baby and had settled down with an older guy in Spain and her brother Liam was travelling the world in a luxury yacht with his new girlfriend and her wealthy father. Settling in the back seat of the coach, her precious cargo secured between her legs, Bridie smiled to herself. She had forty-six thousand pounds in her rucksack from the sale of Rupert's mother's jewellery, along with the cash that they had stolen from Rupert's parents' home. She smiled smugly to herself, looking out of the window as the coach pulled out of Victoria coach station. The world would become her oyster. Once she arrived in Jamaica, she planned to also go to some other Caribbean islands. She would show her sister Martha that she was a survivor.

Bridie had left Rupert earlier that morning slumped on the bed. She had purchased some cheap narcotics after bartering with a local dealer who had a reputation for mixing the 'white'. While Rupert was incoherent after popping the ecstasy tablet she had given him, she inserted a needle into his vein and then left the flat.

Bridie felt no empathy for Rupert Mendez. He was of no concern to her. He was merely an appendage to her plan to eventually head for the Caribbean. She knew that the police would not get any information from him. The double dose of the mixed heroin fix that she had injected him with ensured his silence. Rupert Mendez's part was played out. Taking out her mobile phone, she scanned the internet for cheap hotels in the Albert Docks. Finding a reasonably priced one that would suit her needs, she made an online booking for a week, which would give her time to make plans for the next part of her journey.

....

Twenty-four hours later, the police attending the death of Rupert Mendez found that the fingerprints on the syringe in his vein also matched the prints that were discovered on the typewriter in the room. They had found paper strewn on the floor with various iterations of typed ransom demands. However, the bird had flown the coop and they required more concrete evidence. A diligent officer took out some dirty women's underwear from a wash basket in the bathroom. The DNA from the items was put into a database. Familial DNA searching had come across a paternal match to the DNA from the underwear taken from the crime scene. The father, Brian Murphy, was a convicted criminal who was serving a seven-year prison sentence in Dublin for a racially motivated assault, breaking a man's jaw and spitting in the face at an officer during a pub brawl. The investigator had discovered that Bridie Murphy's father's home address was in County Wexford. A warrant for her arrest was issued; she would be charged with the murder of Rupert Mendez and the kidnapping of a child.

Bridie was disillusioned on her arrival at Liverpool port. The busy docks held no attraction for her. The fog horns that once conjured fond memories of her excitement on arriving in England now grated on her. Bridie had thought about applying for a position on one of the cruise ships, but that idea soon passed. She wanted to be unencumbered and free to travel.

The second night after her arrival, Bridie entered the Albert One O'Clock bar. She was not a drinker, as alcohol reminded her of her drunken father, but she planned to while away a few hours by people-watching. She headed towards the bar where a few suited men were sitting. She assumed they were office workers who had just finished work. It was approaching 7 pm and the bar was not overly busy. Taking the glass of pure orange juice from the barman, she adjusted the rucksack that she carried everywhere. She took a seat at a table at the rear of the bar. From her vantage point opposite the entrance, Bridie observed the comings and goings. She had no intention of acknowledging the smile that was directed at her by the young man who had a half-full glass of what appeared to be Guinness in front of him. She looked away after she caught his wink. From out of her peripheral vision, she caught movement.

He did not wait to be asked. He sat next to her. "Ye look a wee tad lonely. Are ye on yer own?" He supped from the glass, wiping the froth with the back of his hand. Bridie adjusted her position, facing him. His blue eyes smiled into hers. She fought against her attraction to someone from her home country.

"I am grand!" Bridie hid her pleasure in the attention that he was paying her.

"I am Connie O'Brian from Donegal. Ye are a Dubliner!" he stated, smiling impishly, cocking an eyebrow and resting his forearms on the table. Bridie noted his muscular arms. He pressed on, "I work on the docks unloading container ships and the like." Bridie gave a slight nod without replying. "Hopefully that ye are not taken?" he said, glancing at her bare left hand.

Bridie judged him to be in his mid-twenties, not bad looking nor overly tall. She found his charming and confident manner arresting. "I suppose that ye are going to say that ye are single," she stated flippantly.

"Too many family responsibilities," he countered. "My ma was left with five bairns at a time when she was ailing. The old man dropped her for a younger woman who worked in the boozer where he drank every night after working on the docks. There were mouths to be fed," he said, raising his shoulders. "Being the eldest and the only boy, I stepped up, becoming the man of the house."

Bridie was impressed. Come the end of the evening, Connie had convinced her to meet him the following night in the bar. That was the beginning of their mutual attraction. The following night Connie O'Brian was in Bridie's bed. She had confided in him about her siblings and her goals to travel, but she did not reveal her financial status. Her rucksack went everywhere with her. He had offered to carry it on the way home one night from the bar, but she refused. She did not trust anyone.

Bridie had been seeing Connie each night for a week. Any doubts she may have had about him dissipated. At first, she wasn't sure if he was genuine, but she became drawn to him. Connie O'Brian's plight had touched her. Nevertheless, Bridie felt torn. She wanted a new life overseas and to see the world. However, Connie had told her that he could not break his commitment to his mother and siblings. He did not want to leave them in a lurch. The wage he earned at the docks was spent on his family. She was impressed by the consideration that he had for his family. It added to the attraction that she felt for him. Although she did not reveal where the money she had stashed away had come from, she confided that her windfall would enable them both to begin a new life together. The couple made love and Bridie had fallen asleep, blissfully happy, cradled in Connie's arms.

Bridie slowly opened her eyes on hearing the foghorn warning out in the river Mersey resounding in the room. Sidling from the bed, she wiped her eyes with the back of her hand. She smiled fondly when she saw the shaft of light under the bathroom door. She figured that Connie was getting ready to go to work.

She went to turn the kettle on but noticed that the sandwiches that she had made for his lunch were already gone.

Baffled, she called his name while taking two cups from the table. After dropping a teabag in each cup, Bridie headed to the bathroom. She pressed her ear against the door. Silence. Turning the doorknob and opening the door, she found the bathroom vacant. Her heart began racing as she hurried across the room to the small wardrobe. Her rucksack with the forty-six thousand pounds inside was gone. Bridie's scream blended with the warning of fog out on the river Mersey. Connie O'Brian had hoodwinked her.

Two hours later, Benny Harris passed the phone to Martha, mouthing to her that it was Bridie. Benny sat on the arm of the settee while Martha took the phone. He wanted to hear the conversation. Benny was not a controlling man, but he had come to realise that heavily pregnant Martha was a sucker for being reeled in by her younger sister. He sucked air through his teeth as he heard the high-pitched demands for money coming through the phone. Smiling warmly towards Martha, he gently but firmly eased the phone from her clutch. Benny spoke to Bridie, promising her some financial aid. He asked for Bridie's address.

He had no intention of actually giving her any money. However, Benny Harris knew of someone who would be able to resolve all their problems. Walking outside, closing the terrace doors behind him, he phoned his boss, asking for an urgent meeting. He then returned to Martha who thanked him for helping her sister. Benny went upstairs to their bedroom and snapped a picture on his mobile phone of the framed photo of the three Murphy siblings. On his way out he called out to Martha to rest up and that he would not be long.

Benny Harris did not feel any guilt about what he was doing. Time and again he had tried to help Martha's younger sister. However, it had reached his ears that Bridie was involved in the kidnapping of his boss's son, Niall. Benny had tried his best to keep it from Martha, but he realised that it would only be a matter of time before it was made public that there was a warrant out for Bridie's arrest for kidnapping and murder. His concern was for Martha who was two weeks away from her due date, and up to the present time he had ensured that she was free from stress. Hence, he knew that the thorn in the side of his beautiful, sweet-natured woman would shortly be extricated – permanently.

22

Big Dave Broadbent did not have any qualms regarding his mission, although the contract was unusual in that it involved a female. He had been sent the photograph, then deleted it after memorising the face. He'd been filled in regarding the background of the offence. Big Dave had looked at the address on Google Earth. He judged that if all went according to plan, he could take an early flight from Alicante to John Lennon airport and would be able to board the return flight at 10 pm that same evening. It had been easy to get the medical documentation needed to take the insulin on the aircraft with him.

Bridie rushed to open the door after hearing the sharp rap, she had informed the young guy on the reception desk at the small hotel that she was expecting an important package, and to let her know as soon as it arrived. He had flirted with her, reassuring Bridie that he would see to it personally. There was no time for her to realise that the man who shoved her with such force that she hit her head on the wall, knocking her unconscious, was not the hotel receptionist.

The overdose of insulin caused a seizure, then death. Once Big Dave had confirmed that his job was finalised, he did not look back at the bed where Bridie lay with the needle still inserted in her vein.

Just before midnight that same day, Big Dave Broadbent inserted the key into his front door. He smiled warmly seeing the shaft of light from the ajar bedroom door. He knew that his wife was waiting for him. He had promised her when he left earlier that day that he would be home from his business trip before the clock struck twelve. Dave never went back on his word.

23

A soft, warm breeze played with the palm tree fronds in the grounds of Eamon's villa as Cindy, looking every inch like the blushing bride, appeared in the French Alençon needle lace gown. Marcia and Suzette had pressed her to try it on at the bridal boutique in Barcelona where the three women had spent hours trying on various styles of wedding dresses. When Cindy put it on, the other customers in the bridal shop turned their heads, nodding in approval as she emerged from the changing room.

Cindy declared that she would not pay such an extortionate amount for a dress that would be worn for one day. However, the other two women had other ideas. Marcia and Suzette had to practically wrestle Cindy to allow them to purchase it for her as a wedding gift. She resisted due to the ten-thousand-euro markup. Nevertheless, for once, Cindy the warrior lost the toss.

Lloyd had done Cindy's hair into an updo with Swarovski red birth stones interspersed among the strands. Keiron had given her a facial and created the make-up artistry that he was renowned for. It was their wedding gift to her.

Cindy had wanted Aisling and Aine to be bridesmaids, but Marcia declined because she thought that they were too young and that their attention span was too short. She didn't want Cindy's day to be disrupted if the girls started acting up.

Marcia wore a chartreuse, slash neck, silk, above-the-knee dress. Although Eamon had seen the two hat boxes arrive from the milliners in Rome, it was the first time that was seeing Marcia in her full wedding finery. She looked stunning in the Borsalino black and white, hand-crafted, wide-brim hat, reminding Eamon of when Marcia had worn a similar style emerald-green hat to Jimmy Grant's daughter's wedding, just before their relationship had begun. Eamon's former wife, Eve, had recently died in a car crash. Any heartbreak he may have felt soon dissipated at the discovery of her diary, which revealed every intimate detail of her affair with Jimmy Grant. She became history. Eamon had wiped her from his memory and moved forward. He vowed to play the field and not to become involved in a relationship.

However, Destiny had another plan in mind for him. Marcia drew him. Their mutual magnetism pulled them together and he was unable to extricate himself from constant thoughts of wanting her. He remembered how he had teased her that the emerald-green hat had been a nod to his Irish heritage.

Marcia had been haughty with him at the time. Eamon had been sitting with Aye and her daughter at the wedding ceremony, and Marcia had assumed that he and Aye were an item. Aye and her daughter had arrived in Spain from Thailand on Eamon's insistence since Aye's husband had been murdered in his bed, shot in the back of the head by intruders with a silenced gun, while Aye slept alongside him.

Eamon thought as he observed his wife that the outfit that she wore complimented the emerald and diamond earrings and rings that years ago he had placed on her left hand to seal their union. He was just as captivated by her now as he had been right from the beginning. His two daughters wore custom-made frilly dresses in ivory satin and black patent leather shoes with emerald-green bows that matched the ribbons that secured their top knots. Aisling had previously wanted to wear a hat like her mother's, pulling the ribbon out of her hair and stamping her foot. Aye had tried cajoling her and finally convinced her to leave the ribbon intact. Aine had made no fuss. Aisling could be wilful and demanding at times, however, one stern look from Eamon and she would toe the line.

Niall and Quinn were dressed in long-sleeved white shirts with emerald-green silk ties, coupled with black trousers and handmade black Italian leather shoes, similar to their father's. Both handsome boys looked every inch the image of their father.

Heads swivelled and there were murmurs of admiration as Cindy came into view. The backless, off-the-shoulder, lace dress looked breathtakingly beautiful on her. She carried a bouquet of red roses surrounded by jasmine tendrils. The red roses were requested by Dan. Billy, with his arm linked through Cindy's, looked dapper in a three-piece suit, which, on his tall, lean, muscular frame, gave him the air of a movie star on the red carpet in Cannes.

Cindy walked down the aisle towards Dan. Dan and Eamon stood side by side on the podium with the clergyman. Dan had asked Eamon to be his best man and he asked Billy to give Cindy away as he was his oldest friend. Billy readily agreed. There was not a dry eye from the women as the couple took their vows. Cindy's voice wavered nervously as she repeated the vows – something, no one had ever seen before from the straight-from-the-hip speaking Cindy. They were declared man and wife and the couple kissed. Confetti rained down on the radiant pair as the guests applauded.

The crowd erupted in cheering as Suzette caught the bouquet of red roses that Cindy had thrown over her shoulder, beating two of the pole dancers to it. Suzette beamed, declaring that she would be next to marry.

Later that day, Eamon strolled across the lawns with purpose. Benny Harris had stepped to one side while Martha was being fussed over by a group of women who were ensuring that she was comfortable on the large chair that had been put on the terrace for her. Although Martha was due to give birth at any time, she had insisted that she was fine to attend Cindy and Dan's wedding.

Benny sidestepped, moving further out of earshot of the women upon seeing Eamon approach.

"I cannot tank ye enough. I can imagine what it took!" Eamon did not need to go into detail.

Benny pressed his lips together, and then with a flick of his head said, "Right is right and wrong is wrong in my book, boss." Benny exhaled. "Martha is a gentle soul, and at times easily manipulated. I could not stand by and watch her being used and emotionally drained by someone, sibling or not!" he stated firmly. Eamon nodded. Benny turned to look at Martha. She was fanning herself, legs raised on a stool. "I am taking Martha home in a while. The baby is due shortly and I want her to rest."

Eamon pondered on how Benny could be hard-nosed at times, like himself and the rest of his men who worked for him, but on the other side of the coin, Benny Harris had a softer, more caring side when it came to his woman.

Eamon had been busy not only being Dan's best man, but earlier that morning he had also met up with Big Dave Broadbent at Cova del Barber on the outskirts of Benidorm to pay him. He had not asked Big Dave the details of Bridie's demise. Furthermore, he did not have a guilty conscience. He thought that she had it coming for the torment that she had inflicted on his family. He suddenly felt arms encircling his waist from behind. Before he turned, Marcia's signature fragrance filled his senses. Smiling, he turned to face her, pulling her close to him.

"I went to check on the girls," she said, smiling. "Niall is being entertained by Billy and Quinn is with Mathew, Thomas's son. I noticed when Thomas arrived at the ceremony with his sons that he was without his wife." Marcia said, showing concern. She continued when Eamon did not reply, "I seem to think that they are having a few problems." Marcia felt that Thomas and Isabella's marriage would worsen before it eventually got better, however, she kept her own counsel. Marcia knew that Eamon would not tell her anything about his men or their private lives.

He put his arm around her shoulder, fingers affectionately squeezing. "We all have had our problems. One way or another they get resolved," he said, looking at her, kissing the bridge of her nose. She returned his kiss. She broke away when she saw Dan crossing the lawns towards them. "I am going to mingle. It won't be long before Lloyd will want us to join them in the marquee for some dancing!" Eamon nodded, smiling.

Dan stood next to Eamon, smiling fondly, looking towards Cindy whose raucous laughter rang out in the group of women that surrounded her. Among the guests were staff from the Hawk Wind, pole dancers, bar and cloakroom workers, security men and some of their partners. For the most part, they were friends from the club. Dan did not want a big wedding, being a private man, much like Eamon. "I would like to thank you, boss, for everything that you have done for me and Cindy."

Eamon sucked air through his teeth, tearing his eyes away from Marcia who had been waylaid before she reached the marquee by one of the new security men that Dan had taken on at the club through a recommendation. He judged him to be in his mid-to-late thirties – a handsome guy of Caribbean heritage, with dreadlocks to his wide shoulders. His charismatic smile directed at Marcia irked Eamon. He put him in mind of Samuel, Elliot's brother, who at one time had begun training Marcia in self-defence, albeit at his insistence. When Eamon had observed Marcia's first lesson with the powerfully built Muay Thai expert, he was in no doubt that Samuel was coming on to her. His jealousy, he knew at the time, had not been unfounded. He had put a stop to her training with him. The man had been disrespectful. Samuel had played around with one of the other men's women who was in their circle. The irate husband had gone after the Jamaican with a sawn-off shotgun. Samuel, fortunately, had decided to make a quick exit back to the Caribbean, and, up to this point, had not returned to Spain. What Eamon knew of the new security guy was that he worked out at Elliot's gym where some of his men and Billy trained in Muay Thai.

Eamon turned his attention to Dan, putting his suspicions about the new guy on the back burner for the moment. "Dan, 'tis worth noting what ye have done for me. How could I run my business and this place without ye? Ye and Billy step up without a word that ye family also need ye. Thomas Harper-Watts is from the same mould." He continued, "We are facing a difficult time wit the undercover agent in our midst. Let's hope that Aaron Birchwood, alias, Leyton Borewood, continues to make a play for the new pole dancer, Tanya. Her Bulgarian boyfriend won't be too happy wit him." He briefly looked over towards Marcia. The new security guard was still talking to her. She was smiling. The security guy placed his hand on Marcia's bare arm. Eamon bristled. Nevertheless, he turned to continue to speak to Dan. "Our hands are tied due to the agent being the Law. However, the Bulgarians and Russians have no such reservations." Both men nodded in agreement.

"Speaking of Thomas," Dan indicated towards the terrace where Tanya Green, minus her Bulgarian boyfriend, was deep in conversation with Thomas. "Apparently, the man is struggling with his relationship." Eamon looked to where the couple were laughing together. Dan remarked, "His wife wants to curtail her temper and her constant nagging. Thomas revealed to me and Billy that he bends over backwards to please her, to no avail. However, it looks to me as if the new pole dancer has Thomas in her sights. I don't think it will take much for Thomas to begin to look elsewhere. Who could blame the man!" Eamon pressed his lips together and nodded.

"I am wanted!" Dan stated, raising his hand towards Cindy who called to him from the marquee. Eamon followed the crowd towards the music. Upon entry, the newly married couple were pulled up onto the dance floor by Lloyd and Keiron.

Lloyd, grabbing the microphone, broke in, "Please, ladies and gentlemen," he directed, "Can you clear the area and make way for our special couple, whom I have the pleasure of serenading – my dear friend and work colleague, Cindy and her dark and brooding, handsome husband, Dan."

Cindy, all previous nervousness forgotten, led Dan by the hand to the centre of the dance floor. Background music filtered through the speakers as Lloyd broke into song, belting out the opening lines of Al Green's 'Let's Stay Together'. To everyone's surprise, Dan, not usually known for open displays of affection, unabashedly cupped Cindy's chin in his hand and kissed her. Cindy was stunned as Dan grabbed the microphone and joined Lloyd in singing the second verse, continuing to serenade his new wife when Lloyd bowed out. Dan's baritone echoed around the packed marquee singing words of love, which brought tears of joy to Cindy's eyes.

Eamon stroked his goatee, smiling softly at Marcia as she spotted him and made eye contact while she was speaking to Suzette. She broke away from the conversation and moved through the crowd towards where he was standing at the back of the marquee. Although he smiled, she knew that he would have seen the new security guy who had been speaking to her. Eamon's eyes remained hardened even though his actions softened towards her when the next song began to play. The voice of the Queen of Soul, Aretha Franklin sang, 'I Say a Little Prayer for You', one of Eamon's favourite songs. Slipping his arm around her waist, Eamon guided Marcia to the dance floor, joining the other guests. "Ye learn something every day," he said of Dan's rendition of Al Green's song. "I had no idea he could sing!"

"Will you sing to me?" Marcia asked, moving closer, her mound pressing into his crotch. He gave a small laugh. Marcia continued, "Irishmen are renowned for having lovely singing voices." Marcia put her arms around his neck. His hands moved slowly down the backless dress over her flesh. She sensed that he was annoyed about something, although his actions denied it. "I have often heard you on the monitor humming to the girls when you put them to bed or if they have been fretful."

"Hmm." He smiled. "That's as maybe. Having my children as my audience is a different matter. I have no real skills." He felt his arousal heighten from the proximity of her pelvis and braless nipples hardening on contact with his chest, their bodies igniting passion. He held her look. His dark eyes reflected in hers.

"The new security guy appeared to have held yer attention earlier," he stated.

"He was telling me that his mother is from Haiti and is a firm believer in the afterlife." She did not say that he had introduced himself as Winston. Admitting that they were on first-name terms would have ignited Eamon further. She kept the conversation light as she continued to recount the conversation to Eamon. She explained that he wanted to book a tarot reading and spoke to her at length about various spiritual beliefs. She had told him to telephone the Mystique beauty salon to make an appointment. Marcia had felt uncomfortable with Winston's prolonged conversation, knowing that Eamon would quiz her at some point. She changed the subject. "I have purchased a sexy dress and matching silk cupless bra and ouvert panties, especially for you."

Eamon sucked air through his teeth, nodding. However, his hold on her became firmer, pressing her into his forming erection. "Ye, my wee mystic are nothing but a tease, knowing at this moment that ye have me panting." He cocked his eyebrow. "However, my wanton woman, ye will pay later," Eamon warned, smiling. "The handcuffs are coming out tonight. Then let's see how long it'll be before ye will beg me," he threatened, playfully.

Eamon felt a tap on his shoulder. Scott Lord apologised, "Sorry to interrupt, boss," he said with a hint of alarm. "Benny rang me from the IMED hospital in Valencia. He rushed Martha to the maternity department when her waters broke after pains started up in the car on the way home from here earlier. The man is at his wit's end as Martha and the baby are having difficulties." Scott appeared agitated. "The baby's heartbeat is irregular. As we speak, Martha is undergoing a caesarean section. I need to get to him!" Scott said, concerned. "The man sounded broken!"

"Scott, I will see that Sandy is alright," Marcia offered. Sandy was also pregnant, with her and Scott's second child. Scott made his way over to Sandy to tell her what was happening. Eamon and Marcia followed behind him.

Eamon ran his fingers through his hair. "It takes me back to yer pregnancies. At least Benny did not have to fly over six thousand miles to Asia as I did when ye was struggling with Niall's birth. Although it is no consolation!" he said heavily. "The fear of losing yer loved ones is hard no matter what." Eamon held her look. "I have put ye through so much since we first met," he said wistfully. Marcia slipped her arm through his while they crossed the grounds.

"Benny's fears will be unfounded. Martha will give him a wonderful healthy son!" Marcia predicted, adding. "He will be a big, red-headed baby!" Eamon shook his head. "Eamon, I know that we had to be separated when I was pregnant with Niall, but I would have gone through hell and back if it meant that we could remain together." She countered softly, caressing his forearm.

He stopped, turning to face her. "I know that I don't deserve ye." He held her at arm's length. "I selfishly wanted ye in my life. However, unfortunately for ye, I came with so much baggage." A thin smile formed at the corners of his mouth.

Two hours later, Marcia and Eamon drove Sandy home. Marcia drove as, unlike Eamon, she had not been drinking. Sandy's son Brady and his girlfriend were babysitting and Scott had phoned to say that he was keeping Benny company for a while. Although the baby boy had been born, mother and child were not yet out of the woods.

Marcia was in the bathroom when Eamon, propped up on the bed with a towel wrapped around his waist, reached across to the bedside cabinet to take the call. He saw Scott

Lord's number come up. Eamon had asked him earlier to keep him updated, no matter the time, regarding the situation with Benny and Martha.

"That's grand!" Eamon replied, smiling when Marcia came into the bedroom. Turning onto his side, resting his chin on his hand, he crooked his finger. "Come here till I tell ye, my wee mystic. Martha and the ten-pound, red-headed baby boy are both grand!" He adjusted the towel, to accommodate his growing erection. "Now we can get on wit the show wit no interruption!" Putting his phone on flight mode, he switched to record.

Marcia beamed her delight at the news, continuing to taunt him, slipping off the shoulder straps of the scarlet silk mini dress as she circled the bed in black, five-inch stilettos.

Her red gloss mouth broke into a smile. She tilted her head to one side as she sat on the dressing table stool, her legs akimbo, revealing matching silk panties.

Eamon sat up. "Don't make me get off the bed to get ye. I promise ye that ye will regret it if I do!" he threatened, smiling as he opened the cabinet drawer. Without taking his eyes from hers, he dangled two pairs of handcuffs.

Marcia momentarily stood by the stool while he held her transfixed. "Don't play games wit me. Many have tried. Believe me, I am renowned for teaching those who cross me a lesson." She giggled, sashaying over to him.

"I wanted to give you a good time," she purred while kneeling on the bed. She slowly trailed two fingernails down his inner thigh towards his rock hardness. In one swift movement, his firm grip lifted her gently, pinning her beneath him and holding her small frame between his powerful thighs. He laughed softly when her hand encased his erection. He released her fingers and removed her shoes, dropping them on the floor by the bed.

"As much as I like to see ye in high heels, they will get in the way of what I have in mind." He whipped the dress over her head, leaving the underwear on. The red silk cupless bra enhanced the fullness of her breasts and revealed erect nipples. He held her arms above her head, preventing her manipulation. "My wee hot siren looks every bit the lady of the night. Not that I have any complaints," he threw in. "Ye may have been accurate wit ye prediction about Martha and Benny's baby, but…" he paused for two seconds, "sexy lady, ye will not be able to foresee the punishment that I aim to inflict upon ye before I have my way wit ye. Let me see how long ye can take being taunted, as ye did to me earlier as we were dancing in the marquee. Fortunately for me, Scott Lord interrupted, ending my torture of wanting ye. I don't tink that ye have any idea of what a man endures if he cannot find release!" They both smiled.

He snapped the cuffs on her wrists, securing them with bands to the headboard. He did the same with her ankles. With her legs spread wide, ouvert panties allowed him easy access. She did not resist. She had no intention. Marcia hoped that his teasing would not last too long, as he would want if roles were reversed. Eamon was no game player in or outside of the bedroom. He aimed to win. Looming over her, taking his weight on his arms on either side of her head, he smiled smugly. Hungrily opening her mouth, tongue meeting tongue, she bucked beneath him. She felt his warm breath as his teeth nipped, moving down her body.

She strained against the handcuffs, begging him as his fingertips brushed across her hardened nipples followed by the fluttering tip of his tongue. She felt the hardness of his bell end moving with measured motion between her legs without entering. She called his name, pleading for an age as he continued.

When he finally released her bonds, Eamon covered her, raising her hips as he filled her to aid deeper entry. Hungrily, their bodies, mouths and tongues mingled, igniting the first spark. The heat of their bodies soared, she held him tight as he thrust without force. He would not hurt her, no matter the urgency. Reaching the plateau, feeling the beginning of release, Eamon joined her. Their hearts pounded in unison, vibrating through each other's chests. He remained inside of her, ardour gradually dissipating as they lay in one another's embrace. He remembered to end the recording.

Marcia played with the silver-grey hair sprinkled across his pectoral muscles. "That was beastly to torment me for so long. I only teased you for a while on the dance floor!" She pouted feigning her upset.

Cupping her firm rear with both hands, he said, "That was toying wit ye. I was tempted to use my tongue to pleasure ye. However, selfish as it may be, observing the fullness beneath yer mound, I could not resist mounting ye."

She giggled, reaching for his mouth, softly kissing it, contentment filling her heart.

24

For the third time, Eamon sat in the 12-seater Gulfstream G650 Jet which Eamon had hired on two previous occasions. The first time was for the emergency flight that had flown him to Marcia's side when she went into labour with Niall in Thailand. The second time he used the company's services to find Marcia when she had fled from him to a Chiang Mai wellness retreat. However, this time the trip was for pleasure. The destination, Disney World Paris for a three-day break. He realised that it was an extravagance, but it was one that he could afford

As the entourage moved across the tarmac to board the private jet, Nathaniel, the concierge, stole a look out of the co-pilot's window while to co-pilot went to use the lavatory. "I told you that it was him. Mr Emerald Isle has returned!" he said, feigning swooning. "He appears even more desirable with that silver-fox look," he added, turning in the co-pilot's seat. "If that is possible – the Irish hunk!"

Oliver, the pilot, smiled. He had worked with Nathaniel for ten years. Benjamin, the co-pilot, had worked with him for a mere two years. However, for the most part, they enjoyed Nathaniel's banter. His revelations about his love life with his latest love, Kanya, who was a handsome young pilot, five years his junior, who worked for a rival company. However, sometimes the concierge overshare. Oliver had to ask him to reign it in when he thought there was too much information.

Nathaniel peeped out the window once again, "He has been busy. Even from this distance, I can see two small, dark-haired boys who are his mirror image and two little red-headed girls holding his hands." Nathanial continued his running commentary even though his audience was not really interested. "There is an Asian woman with them, who I assume is the nanny. The hunk's wife has not aged. She still looks like a million dollars. The diamonds and emeralds are flashing on her hands." He gave a dramatic sigh. "Lucky…" he said, leaving it hanging. "Some have all the luck. Not only does she have a handsome stud but a wealthy one!" He pressed his nose closer to the window. "I can judge from here that he dresses to the left. Hmm!" he exclaimed, grinning. "By the looks of it, he is a big boy!"

Benjamin returned and both pilots shook their heads laughing at the concierge's innuendos. He pressed on, "Two hunky minders are accompanying him. Good-looking men. They appear to be somewhat weathered and on the mature side, and they have women accompanying them. Nevertheless, I would not kick any one of them out of my bed! If they were unaccompanied by females, after having a couple of drinks, I would bet that I could get one of them to join me in the mile-high club before we reached gay Paree!" He turned his head and said, "I would lay money on it that my Irish dish is a drug boss. The cost of this return flight runs into thousands!"

"Stop your gossiping and prepare yourself for our passengers," Oliver directed, chastising playfully, smiling. Nathaniel jumped up, allowing the co-pilot his seat. Walking down the steps to greet them, Nathanial directed his Pan Am smile at the three men. No one reciprocated. Nonetheless, Nathaniel smiled to himself. He was attracted to tough bastards such as the three men moving towards the aircraft steps.

Aisling skipped excitedly along the tarmac, holding her father's hand and clutching her floppy hat that threatened to blow away due to the warm gusts. Aisling said, "Daddy, can we see the princess and the castle in Disneyland?" Eamon had shown them pictures of Disney World before they had left.

"To be sure!" He smiled warmly from one girl to the other. Aine, to his left, clutched his right hand and bounced along happily. Aye walked alongside with a hand on Aine's head, keeping her hat from blowing off.

Cindy and Dan had postponed their honeymoon so they could join the O'Donallys on holiday. They did not want to miss out on the trip and were especially excited about the private chartered flight. Jane had her niece Kalita from England staying for a week to help the stable and kennel hand that Jane and Billy employed. Eamon's two Belgian shepherds were under the care of Scott Lord. Jackie Cooper and Aar were helping Scott and Benny run the Hawk Wind club in Eamon's absence. Eamon had shut his villa up. However, Scott Lord and Benny Harris had access to Eamon's home CCTV cameras so they could keep an eye on the place.

Billy's enthusiasm to go on the rides rubbed off on Niall and Quinn. He had shown them the rides on the internet and all three had made a list of the ones they wanted to go on.

The girls had both napped on the flight and were full of energy by the time they checked into the hotel. The family immediately headed to Disney World after settling in at the hotel. Eamon held Aisling and Aine in his arms as they approached the Enchanted Castle. As the girls squealed in delight, Eamon felt a warm trickle on his chest and abdomen. He did not flinch or chastise, as he realised it was excitement that had brought on the accident. For the most part, both girls had been potty trained, but accidents were still not uncommon. Marcia and Aye took the twins to the nearest toilet. Marcia carried spare panties and baby wipes in her tote bag for times such as this, although they were rare.

Niall and Quinn were under the care of the two couples. Eamon knew that he could rest easy knowing that his sons were protected under the care of Billy and Dan, who, with the women, had taken them to queue for the Big Thunder Mountain Railroad. Eamon, with his urine-stained shirt, remained. He did not want to interrupt the girls' pleasure. He queued along with Marcia and the girls for the Dumbo Flying Elephant ride. Both girls clapped in delight when they saw Mickey Mouse, who they hugged. Aisling insisted her father join in. He drew the line at hugging, however, meeting his daughter's demands, he shook Mickey's hand. Snow White came into view, flanked by seven dwarfs. Cinderella had done it for the girls. Their excitement brought about another 'accident' while Eamon held them in his arms as they were getting tired. He smiled as Marcia tried to clean his wet shirt with a baby wipe.

Later on, laden with bags full of toys and accessories, Aye, Marcia and Eamon returned to the hotel to prepare Aisling and Aine for bed.

Billy and Niall were laughing as they spoke to Eamon from their suite of rooms. Billy said that he had pictures of Dan's fearful look on the Thunder Mountain ride, his terror plain for all to see on the photograph of them all, as they travelled through the mountain and then dropped at great speed down a steep incline. Dan took the ribbing about his fear of heights in good humour. Niall, Quinn and Billy were beaming. Cindy was laughing with Jane.

Eamon sat on the large bed while Marcia was in the shower. Aisling and Aine had had a couple more 'accidents' earlier due to their overexcitement when they rode on the water boat cruise. Eamon had wanted the girls to share his and Marcia's bed in the hotel room. He was concerned about their safety, sleeping in single beds by themselves, in case they woke in the night. But Aisling had cried; she wanted the pink bed. Her sister followed suit. Eamon reluctantly gave in. Aye was in the room with the girls in a double bed, and she was a light sleeper, so convinced Eamon that it would be OK. At home in Spain, there were monitors in all the children's bedrooms.

Eamon's thoughts turned to his sons. Niall had laughed easily with Billy throughout the day. Quinn talked gaily and laughed with everyone. He was satisfied that he had done the right thing in taking them all away on holiday. Niall appeared to Eamon to be his normal self. Outwardly, it seemed that the kidnapping ordeal had not affected him. The school psychologist who had spoken to Eamon and Marcia said that the impact of the traumatic experience could reveal itself later when Niall felt ready to speak about it. Both Marcia and Eamon had not replied. They realised that Niall's stoic response was normal to them. Eamon thought that the apple did not fall far from the tree. Eamon kept the trauma of his childhood to himself.

25

Suzette looked radiant as she went to greet Marcia as she parked her car near the steps of Suzette's villa. Her signature black bob skimmed her shoulders and her flawless skin was perfectly made up. Marcia did not need to ask who the designer was of the black knee-length dress she wore. She recognised that it was Loewe. Marcia had previously purchased a Loewe long-sleeve midi dress. Her Bottega Veneta high heels completed the elegant look.

Marcia grinned at her friend as she got out of the car. "Please don't tell me, there is someone new!" She paused for effect, smiling.

Suzette beamed, linking her arm through Marcia's while they made their way up the steps. "Let's sit on the terrace. I have some exciting news about my new young man."

Despite herself, Marcia smiled. She sensed that there could be another drama about to unfold in Suzette's life. There had been many times when she had told Suzette to hold fire on relationships until genuine true love was ready to come into her life. They moved towards the large, ornate garden table.

Suzette gushed, "He is gorgeous! And extremely wealthy, I might add. Tolya Fedorin is Russian, with fair hair.

His accent is to die for. His temple has flecks of grey, giving him a distinguished air. He is an absolute gentleman. He is to absolutely die for!" she repeated. "He has recently arrived in Spain for the opening of his new nightclub. Fortunately, for me, fate intervened and I met him in the nightclub in Calpe when I was out with the boys."

Marcia knew that she was referring to Lloyd and Kieron. She did not ask Suzette about the much younger lover that she had previously been seeing. Knowing her friend, he would now be history. Suzette did not pay heed to any of Marcia's previous warnings that she had given during her tarot readings. She wanted to say something about the reputation that some Russians have for being ruthless but knew that she would not listen.

Marcia felt that Suzette's latest relationship with the Russian would not last. Once again, she kept her own counsel, even though she had a sense of foreboding.

"Tolya has wined and dined me. He spoke to me of his early years of poverty and then how one day at the age of seventeen he had a chance meeting in St Petersburg Square with a beautiful, wealthy and influential woman. She pulled up alongside him in her chauffeur-driven car and invited him in. A while later, after a short conversation with this mysterious benefactor, Tolya was offered employment. He was honest about their relationship. Their friendship with benefits grew!" Suzette laughed. "She was married to a wealthy old man twice her age. She was thirty-five at the time. Although Tolya was also half her age, he said that his height and build gave him the appearance of being far older. However, that is a thing of the past. He is SOOO hot!" she enthused. "You must meet him, Marcia. He has a residence in St Petersburg and Knightsbridge in London." Excitedly, she clapped her hands. "Furthermore, Tolya is going to purchase a property on the Costa Blanca."

Marcia was not interested in meeting the man or hearing about him, but she humoured Suzette by pretending to be interested.

"I did not mention to Tolya that my dearest friend and her husband owned the Hawk Wind adult club," Suzette smiled slightly, "due to rivalry."

Marcia exhaled without replying. She was certain that Eamon would be informed about Suzette's relationship with the Russian club owner. It would not go down well with him. Suzette was not one of Eamon's favourite people.

Suzette reached across and took Marcia's hand. "How are you coping since the nasty business with Niall? I do not doubt that your husband has dealt with it. Dreadful business!" she said, shaking her head.

Marcia smiled wryly. "Eamon has demanded that the school provide escorts for his sons when they go to the lavatory. They are not allowed to go anywhere on their own at the school. The security system in the building is sufficient. It was through no fault of the school. The head had followed procedure and had taken every precaution when vetting school employees, including making checks for criminal offences. The school janitor who kidnapped Niall did not have any previous convictions. He is facing many years behind bars."

Suzette patted her hand, smiling warmly. "I remember you mentioning the ominous feelings that plagued you each time you took the boys to school. It was not the fact that I did not believe you when you voiced your unease. I assumed that it was due to stress."

Marcia sighed softly. "I feel guilty that I stood back without informing Eamon of the feelings of portent that I had before the kidnapping. My son's life was in danger. Niall could have been harmed. It torments me to think that my child had to experience such a terrifying ordeal." Marcia wiped away the tears that began to fall as she spoke.

Suzette jumped up, moving around the table, embracing her, brushing her face and holding her at arm's length. "Marcia, I know how strong you have been from the beginning when Reuben left. You stood strong when you were assaulted previously. There are many people that you have helped throughout the years with your guidance – me included," she stated firmly. She then smiled and said, "I know that there have been times when I did not heed your advice. However, it was you who always came to my aid." Her tone became serious. "Now I am going to help you rid yourself of this guilty burden. You must not carry the blame for Niall's kidnapping. Think of it this way – if the ominous feeling had been pressing you to the extent that you had felt the outcome would have been disastrous, knowing you as I do, you would have informed Eamon."

Suzette waited. Marcia exhaled. "I know!" she reluctantly agreed. "The time of the blood moon brought on the same ominous feeling that I experienced when Reuben disappeared from my life. I also sense that other changes are occurring that Eamon keeps from me. He withholds certain things to prevent me from worrying. Nonetheless, he does not realise that I can read it in his eyes. His lovemaking alters. He does not need to tell me. I can feel his moods when he is troubled. It's as if he is afraid that we will become separated again." She stared out towards the vista. "He also blames himself for bringing me into his world and for exposing the children to danger. He has said as much."

She turned to face Suzette and said, "Although I did not understand at the time why Eamon had the boys sent away to boarding school," Marcia smiled wanly, "I now know that he did it to protect them from situations such as what Niall has encountered. Eamon is a wonderful father. The children have not stopped talking about their experience at Disney World Paris. The girls are still wearing their Cinderella dresses. Aisling and Aine, in their state of excitement, wet themselves while Eamon was carrying them, and he continued around the park, going on the rides with them wearing a urine-soaked shirt, without a single complaint!" Marcia laughed and had Suzette in fits of giggles at her story.

"You and I are going to make a date for some retail therapy. My treat!" Suzette said, raising her hand to Marcia's protests. "I insist. Bring the twins. I need to spoil them." Suzette stood up, straightening her dress, which Marcia knew cost a small fortune. Some things about her friend would never change. Suzette had introduced Marcia to designer clothing and accessories at a time when Marcia lived from one day to the next. Suzette was many things; one of her finer points was her generosity. Marcia also had Suzette to thank for her meeting Eamon. Their friendship bond was never to be broken until their destiny ended.

....

Tanya Green was about to step out of the shower. She switched off the tap upon hearing Mitre's mobile phone ring in the lounge. She moved to the bathroom door. Holding her ear against the wood, she listened to the conversation. Fortunately, Mitre Akov spoke to the caller in English and not his mother tongue. Tanya snatched her phone from the cabinet – she never left her phone out of her sight. She heard him say that the vessel was coming into Calpe port and she began noting down the date and time of the narcotic shipment. Even though she could only hear one side of the conversation, it was all that she required to make her next move. She had told both Mitre and Eamon about the undercover detective in their midst, however, she had different motives for telling each of them. If all went according to plan, the results would be in her favour.

Tanya realised that she needed to up her game. Playing on Mitre's possessiveness, she had shown him the bar mat with the undercover agent's alias and mobile number written on it. She had filled Mitre in on her past and how her mother's flat had been raided, and how she had recognised 'Leyton Borewood' as being the same detective, Aaron Birchwood, who had led the raid. "He was pestering me, pressing for a date!" Tanya declared almost tearfully to Mitre, stating how she felt that she could not refuse his offer because he was a member of the club where she worked.

Mitre railed about the undercover agent, shouting the odds that he would put a stop to Aaron Birchwood.

....

Two days later, two young, male nightclubbers had seen a man slumped in a doorway next to the Irish bar in a pool of blood and called the emergency services. The ambulance medics applied CPR to try to save the man whose life hung in the balance. He had sustained multiple life-threatening stab wounds. No one had any information to give to the Guardia Civil officers in attendance. There were no CCTV cameras in operation. No one could pinpoint the reason for the attack. The officers found the victim's wallet inside of his jacket, giving a clue as to where he lived. However, a search of his apartment above the bar revealed the man's identity and raised questions.

When questioned by the police, Michael appeared mystified. He had known the man as Leyton Borewood. However, among the man's belongings was a photographic ID identifying him as Aaron Birchwood. Later, it was discovered that he was an undercover agent working with London's Special Branch. Comisario Anton Rodriguez was informed and he immediately placed a call to London.

Eamon took the call from Rodriguez in his office. He thanked him for the heads up. He told the comisario that it went without saying that he would reimburse him for the information. However, Eamon knew that he would have to wait it out. Rodriguez promised to keep him in the loop as to the condition of the agent from the UK.

Marcia and Suzette took the twins out shopping with them. They had set off early for Barcelona. The boys were in school. Eamon decided to swim to help release the tension. He had been pondering on who could have been behind the attack on the undercover agent. His thoughts turned to Tanya Green. He knew that she was involved with the Bulgarian who worked for the Russian who was opening a nightclub. He also knew that narcotics, arms dealing and people trafficking was financing the wealthy Russian.

When Tanya had informed him of the identity of the undercover agent, Eamon sensed that she was game-playing, without knowing her aim. Now the penny had dropped. He smirked to himself while he pounded the water, length after length of the pool. Tanya Green had informed her Bulgarian boyfriend about the agent who had been trying to hit on her. She knew that he would retaliate. Clever girl! Eamon thought.

Billy and Dan arrived later at Eamon's villa. They had been to check on the haulage company with the detection dogs. Dan reported that all appeared as it should. Eamon brought the two men up to date regarding the murder attempt on the undercover agent. While he was speaking to them, a call came through. He raised his finger, indicting for silence. Nodding to the caller. He thanked him and ended the call.

Eamon exhaled and sat back in the garden chair, locking his hands behind his head. He grinned at Billy and Dan, who were sitting opposite him at the garden table. "We are off the hook. Sad as it may be, Aaron Birchwood, alias Leyton Borewood, has not made it." Billy and Dan nodded with relief. "It looks to me that the Bulgarian gave us a helping hand without realising it." The three celebrated their newfound sense of freedom by having a beer.

....

Tanya Green had finished massaging Mitre. She had hinted earlier that at some point in the not-too-distant future, she would like to have his child, although, in reality, she had no intention of becoming pregnant by anyone. Mitre was thrilled. He said to her that he was going to take her out the following day to choose an engagement ring. He had mounted her, placing her legs upon his shoulders twice that night before she went to work at the Hawk Wind club, informing Tanya that he was ensuring that his seed was planted, or so he thought.

Earlier that day, on the pretext of going to Benidorm to do some shopping, Tanya had placed a different SIM card in her mobile and made a call. She had given the Guardia Civil officer all the details. He had written down the name of the perpetrator, Mitre Aklov, along with a description and nationality. He also noted the time and date when the narcotics would be arriving at Calpe port on the fishing boat from Andorra. Tanya then cut the SIM card in two with her nail scissors and dropped the pieces down a sewer grating. Tanya had left nothing to chance. She would go with Mitre to purchase the ring, which she did not intend to wear once the deed was finalised. It would mean nothing more to Tanya than collateral.

Mitre had spent twenty thousand euros on Tanya's exquisite diamond ring. She had rewarded him by allowing him to satisfy himself as she knelt on the bed on all fours before him. Tanya knew that it would be the last time that she had to prostitute herself to him. However, she thought that the outcome would be worth it.

Mitre Aklov would not be attending the opening of his Russian boss's new nightclub. Tolya had a more important appointment for his right-hand man to oversee – the shipment of narcotics that was coming into Calpe port where the Bulgarian had men who could aid in moving the illegal cargo through customs without any problem.

Everything appeared to be running like clockwork. Mitre observed the large white van as it approached the port and stopped in a parking bay. Right on schedule, the fishing vessel came into view. Mitre waited unobserved while men he recognised secured the ropes as the boat docked. He rubbed his hands with glee, knowing that the multimillion-euro cargo would enable him to purchase a villa for himself and Tanya and their child. He was certain that he had made her pregnant, taking her from every position, ensuring that his seed had been planted. He smiled to himself as he visualised her earlier on the bed on all fours as he took her from behind, holding her firm, young buttocks and thrusting deep so that his sperm could not escape. He was proud of the fact that she had been a virgin before she met him. It was a rarity, especially for a beautiful young woman. He mused about how he would be a good father before he returned his attention to the job at hand, watching the men unload the shipment.

Mitre's van was loaded with iceboxes full of crab, lobster and sea bass. The weight of the load caused the engine to strain, and the axel groaned, but Mitre was unperturbed, reassured by the Spanish driver in his employ, who said that the vehicle could withstand the load. The Spanish driver stated that he would take the journey to the warehouse slowly.

The van and its contents made their way onto the N-332 on the main coastal road towards the warehouse that Mitre used for storage. The pure heroin from Nicaragua had reached Belgium safely. The switch had gone without a hitch. There was one more thing that Mitre was required to carry out before arriving at the warehouse. Half an hour into the journey, he instructed the driver to pull over on the darkened road as he wanted to take a leak. The driver pulled up alongside the wasteland that bordered the road and got out of the vehicle to join him, which made it easier for Mitre. He delivered a single shot to the back of the skull – the body fell on the wasteland. Mitre zipped his trousers without looking back and jumped into the driver's seat, continuing his journey.

The three scruffy men in the small, black Fiat, kept their distance behind the white van. However, they were keeping their colleagues at the other end informed of the whereabouts of the vehicle up ahead. Although the three officers had also witnessed the murder that took place, they knew that there were more important things that awaited them at the end of the line.

Mitre was home and dry. He smiled to himself upon reaching the warehouse. He parked in front of the warehouse. As he went to open the back doors of the van, a group of men dressed in black slid open the warehouse doors, M16 assault rifles raised, aiming at Mitre Aklov's head with menace. Mitre sank to his knees, raising his arms in the air.

Tanya Green looked at the wall clock in the kitchen at Mitre's apartment. It was 4:28 am. The disquiet she felt permeated the rooms. Mitre had told her that he would call her after his job was complete, but there was only silence. She waited with bated breath. Every hour seemed like an age to her, not knowing if her plan had worked. She phoned Lloyd at the Mystique beauty salon to ask him if he had any spare time for her to book a body wrap and facial. He was fully booked, however, he said for her to come into the salon anyway, as Kieron had a cancellation. She had time to kill before she went to work.

The following day, Tanya purchased a newspaper from a tabac in Benidorm. Her Spanish was passable. She had picked up a little in her short time in Spain. She saw the front page of the newspaper with Mitre Aklov's photograph and she bought a copy. She understood the headlines written in bold print in Spanish *'ATAQUE DE NARCOTICS'*. She read further on regarding the murder charge that Mitre faced. Scanning the front page, she came to understand that an undercover operation had been successful in intercepting the narcotic shipment and that the agents working on the sting had also witnessed Mitre Aklov murder someone. Tanya was aware that the holdall in Mitre's wardrobe contained money – a great deal of it. She had seen him take twenty thousand euros out of it to purchase the diamond engagement ring.

Tanya returned to Mitre Aklov's apartment and locked the door. She spread the newspaper on the table and drew up a chair. She was now faced with a dilemma but would continue as normal for the time being. Her shift at the Hawk Wind did not start until 10 pm that night. She decided to sleep on it.

……………………

As Tanya approached, Billy stepped forward, away from the group of security men who were talking outside of the

Hawk Wind club. "The boss would like to see you in his office before you begin work." Billy smiled, opening the door for her. Tanya returned it.

On hearing the knock at his door Eamon responded. He smiled when Tanya entered and closed the door behind her. His dark eyes projected indifference. "Take a seat, Tanya," he directed, sitting up straight in his chair. "I am not normally someone to advise my staff, nonetheless, I am being considerate, due to yer age and inexperience in delving into what could become dangerous waters." He left the implication hanging. He knew that she was game-playing with the Bulgarian. Eamon paused for a couple of seconds, then continued. "I appreciate that ye previously informed me regarding the undercover agent. Not that I could do anything about the Law taking an interest in someone in the club. Opening the desk drawer, he took out a package and slid it towards her. Tanya's eyes followed, resting on it. "I would like to offer ye sound advice. 'Tis up to ye if ye take it. I would not hang around. If it was discovered that ye were involved with the Bulgarian, who knows what might happen to you." He did not elaborate. He cocked his head and raised an eyebrow.

Tanya took the package, and dropped it into her shoulder bag, rising from the chair. "Thank you," was all she said.

"Good luck to ye," Eamon replied to her retreating back. Tanya did not look back.

Eamon exhaled. As much as he knew that Tanya had tried to play both sides, he sensed that she was somehow involved in her Bulgarian boyfriend's capture. Eamon had given Tanya ten thousand euros. He was willing to pay for her services. After all, Tanya had done him a justice.

Back at Mitre Aklov's apartment, Tanya locked the door. She had butterflies in her stomach as she removed the holdall from the wardrobe and placed it on the table. Upon opening it, Tanya froze. She could not try to hazard a guess as to the amount of money that was there. She went back to get her bag and had a quick look inside the package that Eamon O'Donally had given to her. There were ten bundles. Telephoning a taxi, she returned to her flat to collect the engagement ring and money that she had saved up from the allowance that Mitre Aklov had given her. She placed two dresses and two sets of underwear on top of the money in the holdall before zipping it shut. Then she phoned for a cab to take her to Alicante airport. Tanya said a prayer to her auntie Joanie, who she knew watched over her from heaven, as she had throughout Tanya's life when she was on the earthly plane. She was hoping for some divine intervention to allow her easy passage through customs with the bag of money.

She placed the hand luggage, bag and phone in two trays on the conveyor belt that was moving towards the security worker who was intently studying the items that were being x-rayed. He looked up. The handsome Spaniard's dark-brown eyes lit up with recognition. He had visited the Hawk Wind club on a few occasions when Tanya was dancing. She smiled. He winked, allowing her two trays to go through without inspection. Tanya was home and dry.

26

Eamon was lying on the bed pondering on the opening that night of the new nightclub that the Russian, Fedorin, was backing. The club owner's right-hand man, the Bulgarian, Mitre Aklov, was not going to see daylight for a very long time, if ever. He had a murder charge hanging over his head without any chance of wriggling out of it. Three law enforcement agents had witnessed him shooting the Spanish driver of the van carrying the drug shipment he orchestrated. It was certain that he would be handed a life sentence. Eamon was not concerned about any competition from the Russian's club. Eamon had had a meeting with Comisario Anton Rodriguez, who had informed him that the police had made a deal with the Bulgarian in exchange for information about his boss Tolya Fedorin.

Eamon knew that once the Russian had been charged, the new club would be shut down. The comisario had reassured him that he would not tolerate any undesirable traffickers on his turf. Once the way was clear he would put in a bid. Rodriguez assured Eamon that within six months of the Russian's club being closed down, the paperwork would be finalised and Eamon's name would be on the door.

Eamon smiled, turning onto his side, resting his chin on his hand. The towel that was wrapped around his waist slipped, revealing his delight at seeing his wife when she entered the bedroom from her dressing room. "Ye are courting serious trouble coming onto me dressed like that. If ye want it rough, I'll oblige ye!" he said, laughing.

Marcia smiled. His mood seemed to have lightened since the morning. She sensed that whatever had been perturbing him had been put to rest. "I slipped away to the boutique in Barcelona while Suzette occupied the girls in a restaurant so that I could buy some lingerie." Marcia was dressed in a black silk, above-the-thigh negligee with a matching thong and cupless bra and red five-inch heels. She wore her hair swept back, which accentuated her high cheekbones. "Do you like it?" she asked, moving across the bedroom towards him, stopping just beyond his reach. He lunged, encircling her waist, lifting her and removing her shoes. In seconds she was beneath him, giggling as his erection stabbed for entry.

He slipped his solidness between her legs without inserting."Ye are fortunate that I am a man who prefers to savour sex with my wife. Most men, seeing a woman dressed as ye are, would be over in a few minutes. However, my wee mystic, I must admit that this is becoming painful!"

Marcia smiled as she began fondling his erection. "Or ye can…" Marcia silenced him. Running her fingernails along his top lip, she reached up, tongue seeking his mouth. Involun-tarily, her legs slackened and her hand guided.

"Good choice!" Eamon murmured, covering her. Adjusting her position, she curled her leg over his to take him deep within. "After the first one, stay wit me," he directed, taking her breast in his hand and gently teasing the nipple with his tongue.

She was at his mercy as she felt the fire within raging. She clung onto him, nails raking his back, freefalling into the deep chasm. He continued, holding her, speaking words of love while she stayed with him. Their bodies locked together, their tongues united in a French kiss, igniting joint orgasms.

Marcia, naked, slept curled up alongside him. His arm was numb beneath her. Easing up slowly so as not to wake her, he extricated his arm and gently placed her head on the pillow, covering her with the cotton sheet. Marcia sighed in her sleep, her breathing steady. Sleep evading him, Eamon sidled from the bed. He changed into swimming trunks and threw on a towelling robe. He put his mobile phone in his pocket out of habit.

He left the bedroom door ajar as he tiptoed out. The Belgian shepherds fell in line as he moved across the tiled floor towards the terrace doors. Throwing the robe down on a sunbed, he stretched. Embracing the tendrils of pre-dawn mist that rolled in from Altea Bay. He dove into the cool water, without surfacing until he reached the steps at the far end. He wallowed in the sense of freedom, releasing endorphins with powerful yet unhurried strokes. After he had swum fifty lengths, shafts of daylight began to break through. Dawn was arriving across Costa Blanca. Eamon strode up the steps, the two dogs' almond-shaped eyes, one pair aged, the other young, observed as he dried himself.

He suddenly felt at ease with the world and he pondered retirement. He was in a good financial position now that his businesses were for the most part legitimate. All his dues and taxes had been paid. He thought about the new home in County Wicklow that was in the process of being refurbished. He did not think that Marcia would have any objection. Their life would be at a slower pace. The children would settle into a new routine. His brother Patrick would be living a couple of hours' journey away from him in County Armagh. Patrick's family could stay over. Eamon liked the idea of having his younger sibling within reach.

He would make a decision about the property, weighing up the pros and cons of leaving or remaining in Spain before informing Marcia. He relaxed, hands locked behind his head, sitting at the garden table, long legs stretched out, taking in the vista that had changed his life and fortune.

Breaking his reverie, he sensed her, as did the dogs, although she moved silently. The ankle-length, sky-blue silk kimono embroidered with cherry blossom outlined her nakedness beneath. His hand reached for her, and she took it, smiling, easing onto his lap. Marcia sat astride, arms around Eamon's neck. He fixed her with his dark eyes and asked, "How would ye feel about relocating?"

Marcia looked startled."Where are you thinking about moving to?"

Reaching for his phone, he clicked on the pictures of the house in County Wicklow and handed it to her.

She scanned each photograph of the house undergoing extension work. She perused the plans for the indoor swimming pool and the six stables that were under construction. There were also photographs of the grounds surrounding the property with the Wicklow mountain range as the backdrop. Marcia smiled and exclaimed, "Eamon it is beautiful!" She continued to view the photographs.

"That's grand. 'Tis settled then," he said when she handed him back the phone. "Once the building work is completed in a couple of months, we can take the family and Aye, not forgetting the dogs, to Ireland." He grinned as she smothered his face in kisses. "Let us see how County Wicklow fares wit us. Perhaps we can finally get some semblance of order to our lives."

Eamon was tired of constantly looking over his shoulder. He could purchase the Russian's club and surrounding land once the Fedorin was out of the way. Eamon had enough trusted men around him to help run his businesses in Spain if he decided to make County Wicklow his main residence. However, he did not voice his thoughts as he didn't want to tempt providence.

"Let us return to bed to celebrate," he said, lifting Marcia in his arms and carrying her into the house as the dogs followed, wagging their tails.

"I want this celebration recorded!" Marcia brooked no argument. Eamon turned his phone to silent and pressed the record.

A short while later, after Eamon had transferred the SIM card with the intimate recording to his safe in his office, his phone rang. Recognising the caller as Lucca Barossa, he answered. After hanging up, he sat on the corner of his desk, shaking his head in disbelief, running his fingers through his hair. Eamon could not believe it. Lucca Barossa wanted Marcia to come to him in Miami. He said that he urgently required Marcia's advice on an important matter. Lucca added that his private jet would be at Marcia's disposal. He praised the accuracy of her prediction that he would have two children at a time when he had assumed that he would never be a father because of the risk pregnancy would have on his wife's health. He went on to say that, unfortunately, his wife had died hours after the birth of the second child.

Eamon exhaled, pondering on the high-stakes game of chess that Marcia had played with the Miami boss, Ricardo Barossa. Marcia had won the game and her trophy had been

Eamon's safety. When Eamon had realised that Marcia had withheld the information regarding the threat to Ricardo's life, he had warned her that Lucca was astute and would be able to figure out that she had known but not said anything to prevent the murder of his brother and nephew. Eamon's old fear had come back to haunt him. He reluctantly agreed that Marcia would meet Lucca in Miami in two days. In the world that Eamon had lived in for so long, when people of influence ask a favour there is an unspoken rule that you do not refuse. This was such an occasion.

Acknowledgements

Writing the *Eighth House* series has been a team effort. I'd like to thank the first person to read the untitled manuscripts that were to become *The Eighth House, Karmic Winds* and *Blood Moon,* Jane Whiteley, my sister-in-law, who had a belief in my writing and pressed me forward. She also helped by contributing her expertise of canine behaviour. The title of the first book and series, *The Eighth House,* was put forward by my niece Carly Broad. Clark Denford, Karina Stevens, Deonne Ayres, Nicky Cheetham, Lesley Partridge and Tina Jopling have each helped me in various ways. I am grateful to the City of Portsmouth Libraries for stocking my books. Many thanks also to my children Serena, Stacey and my daughter-in-law Jai, as well as my beautiful granddaughters Coa and Maya. Thanks to my amazing editor, Kerry Boettcher, Gary Thompson for the cover designs and typesetting and Jess Barnard for my author photograph. To all of my readers in the UK, USA and Australia – I thank you all.

If you enjoyed reading the series, please kindly leave an Amazon review.

Dreena Whitely lives in Portsmouth, UK and is the author of *The Eighth House* and *Karmic Winds*. This is the third novel in the *Eighth House* series.

Printed in Great Britain
by Amazon

34887858R00195